CONFESSIONS OF A YOUNG MAN

GEORGE MOORE

Confessions of a Young Man

EDITED BY SUSAN DICK

McGILL-QUEEN'S UNIVERSITY PRESS

MONTREAL AND LONDON 1972

Introduction and notes by Susan Dick
© 1972 McGill-Queen's University Press

The texts of *Confessions of a Young Man,*
by George Moore, are published with
the permission of J. C. Medley and
R. G. Medley, the owners of the copyright
in George Moore.

International Standard Book Number 0-7735-0097-9
Library of Congress Catalog Card No. 70-183725

Legal Deposit 2nd quarter 1972

Design and jacket illustration by Mary Cserepy

Printed in Canada by T. H. Best Printing Co. Ltd.

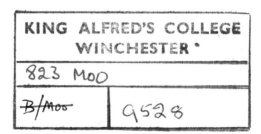

CONTENTS

When George Moore's autobiographical novel, *Confessions of a Young Man*, was suggested to me as a possible topic for a doctoral dissertation, I had never read it. I proceeded to do so. After reading the version published in a paperback edition, I had a look at another, earlier edition. I was already enthusiastic about the book, and I grew even more interested in it as I began to find differences between the texts of these two editions. I unearthed a third version, then a fourth, then a French edition, which was again different from the others. I decided that a proper study of Moore's early novel would have to begin with an examination of the text. This led eventually to the establishment of a variorum edition of rather staggering proportions. It has been pruned for this edition.

The collation of the texts proved to be only one challenge. Moore's autobiographical novel is filled with details which break with fact as often as they conform to it. Feeling at times like one of Yeats's shuffling scholars, I examined as many documents as I could find which would tell me something about Moore's early life. The relationship between fact and fiction in this book is a fascinating one, and in commenting on it I have been especially concerned with *how* Moore used his past in *Confessions*. My findings have been recorded in critical notes to the text.

I am grateful to many people for advice and encouragement in my work. My greatest debt is to Richard Ellmann, whose knowledge and kindness have been a constant support. I am also indebted to Harrison Hayford for advising me on editorial matters and to Jean Hagstrum and

Lawrence Evans for their helpful criticism. I owe special thanks to Edwin Gilcher, Moore's bibliographer, whose generous help saved me from wandering up many blind alleys. In the preparation of the edition for publication, I am especially indebted to George Whalley for sharing with me his editorial knowledge. I also wish to thank Norman MacKenzie, Kerry McSweeney, and Roger McHugh for helping me to identify quotations in the text. And I owe a continuing debt to my parents, who have given both technical aid and moral support throughout.

I am indebted to Northwestern University and to Queen's University for grants-in-aid, and to the Woodrow Wilson Foundation for a Dissertation Year Fellowship. This book has been published with the help of a grant from the Humanities Research Council of Canada, using funds provided by the Canada Council.

I wish to thank J. C. Medley and R. G. Medley, the owners of the copyright in George Moore, for allowing me to publish this edition of *Confessions*. I am also grateful to the following libraries for generously granting me permission to publish material: the National Library of Ireland; the British Museum; the Henry W. and Albert A. Berg Collection of the New York Public Library, Astor, Lenox and Tilden Foundations; and the Bibliothèque Nationale.

S.D.

George Moore named only one prototype for his first autobiography, *Confessions of a Young Man*: "St. Augustine wrote the story of a God-tortured soul; would it not be interesting to write the story of an art-tortured soul?"[1] While St. Augustine addressed God and confessed his sins as a testament to grace, Moore, in a very different mood, addressed the "hypocritical reader" of late nineteenth century England and proclaimed his sins in order to flaunt them as virtues. He reversed the traditional Christian mode of confession and with a candour as ultimately self-aggrandizing as that of Rousseau, and often as splenetic as that of Dostoevsky's Underground Man, demonstrated pride rather than contrition for his sins. Although he challenged his readers to condemn him, that challenge was purely rhetorical; Moore hoped to provoke his reader, not to entreat his sympathy.

Moore's *Confessions* are, as he reminded Jacques-Emile Blanche, who had suggested a drawing of a young woman for the cover, "purely literary."[2] He described the general outline of the book to another friend, Edouard Dujardin: "I am writing a book called 'The Confessions of a Young Man.' A young man who goes to Paris to study painting— I develop his character through the three schools—romantic, naturalist, and symbolist; he returns to London and I continue the development of his character. The idea: to contrast the art of two great cities: Paris and London. There is a chapter entitled 'La Synthèse of the Nouvelle Athènes.'"[3] That contrast was not to prove complimentary to the art

---

1 Preface to *Confessions*, 1889.
2 Jacques-Emile Blanche, *Portraits of a Lifetime*, ed. and trans. Walter Clement (London: Dent & Sons, 1937), p. 292. Blanche's drawing of a very Victorian young lady kneeling on a chair and lighting a lamp was finally used.
3 John Eglinton, ed. and trans., *Letters from George Moore to Ed. Dujardin, 1886–1922* (New York: Crosby-Gaige, 1929), pp. 20–21, 17 May 1887.

of London. Through it, Moore would pose his challenge to the English literary establishment.

As long as critics discuss George Moore, they will discuss *Confessions of a Young Man*. Moore's first autobiography has remained a focal point for studies of both his work and his life. That Moore published, after the first edition of 1888, extensively revised versions of *Confessions* in 1889, 1904, 1917, and 1918 is perhaps testimony enough to its importance to him. As this introduction will attempt to show, readers are drawn to *Confessions* for two reasons: first, it is an index to many of the major artistic movements in France and England in the late nineteenth century and as such is a valuable period piece; second, it is also an index to the ideas and experiences which proved to be seminal in Moore's artistic career. His habit of referring others to "my confessions" has become our habit as well.

The flamboyant hero of *Confessions* was originally named Edwin Dayne. Even before the French edition of 1889 was issued, however, Moore decided that he should use his own name in his confessions. "Sincerity is the soul of confession," he wrote his French editor Edouard Dujardin, "and now I think I was wrong in not employing my own name; I beg of you therefore that you will substitute 'George Moore' for 'Edward Dayne.' "[4]

In a passage later removed from *Confessions*, Dayne recalls his dramatic return to London after spending six and a half years in Paris: "I was as covered with 'fads' as a distinguished foreigner with stars. Naturalism I wore round my neck, Romanticism was pinned over the heart, Symbolism I carried like a toy revolver in my waistcoat pocket, to be used on an emergency" (p. 149). The hero of *Confessions* learned to wear artistic enthusiasm with bravado. Naturalism, symbolism, and romanticism were only several of the movements Moore read and heard about in Paris in the 1870s. He arrived on the scene during an

---

4 Eglinton, *Letters to Dujardin*, p. 25, 12 February 1888. Moore's own confusion over his hero's name (he calls him Edwin, Edward, and Eduard at various points) suggests both the pressure of publication deadlines under which he was writing and his lack of conviction in the use of a pseudonym in the first place. Its use does underscore, however, the fictional element in the original version of *Confessions*.

exciting and fertile period of French intellectual history. Romanticism was still a powerful influence on contemporary writers (indeed, Roger Shattuck marks Hugo's death in 1885 as the end of an era);[5] Parnassian poets such as Théophile Gautier, Catulle Mendès, José-Maria de Hérédia, and François Coppée were reacting against the excesses of romantic poetry and writing clear, precise, cameolike verse; symbolist poets, lead by Mallarmé, were distressed by the loss of mystery and suggestion in Parnassian poetry and were beginning to form their own literary movement; realists of the generation of Balzac and Flaubert were finding their theories narrowed by the naturalists, led by Zola and the brothers Goncourt; Impressionist painters were challenging the sentimental realism of the Academicians and were finding support among the symbolists, realists, and naturalists.[6] While living in this highly charged atmosphere, Moore adopted a new style; it was a blend of the boulevardier, a young man addicted to the pleasures of the fashionable *salons*, and the apprentice artist, a young man dedicated to "aestheticizing" all night in the cafés. In the painting studios and then in the café Nouvelle Athènes, Moore found himself immersed in a way of life which was liberating, intense, and instructive.[7] His acquaintances in Paris during the 1870s—Leconte de Lisle and Catulle Mendès among the Parnassians, Mallarmé among the symbolists, Duranty among the realists, Zola, Goncourt, and Huysmans among the naturalists, and Manet, Degas, and Pissarro among the Impressionists—were all fighting to establish new artistic movements. Moore's description of himself as a veteran armed with the spoils of war aptly captures the mood of the period.

The effect of all this activity on Moore is demonstrated in numerous ways in *Confessions*. His first autobiography, like all of his early works, is highly eclectic. During this period, Moore was adopting ideas, styles, and opinions without concern for the consistency of one with another;

5 Roger Shattuck, *The Banquet Years: The Origins of the Avant Garde in France, 1885 to World War I*, rev. ed. (New York: Random House, Vintage Books, 1968), p. 4.

6 For an excellent account of the many literary movements in France during this period and their relationships with one another, see Jules Huret, *Enquête sur l'évolution littéraire* (Paris: Charpentier, 1891).

7 This café, along with the Café Guerbois, "had nurtured the first artistic movement entirely organized in cafés: impressionism." Shattuck, *Banquet Years*, p. 11.

yet at the same time, he seemed instinctively drawn toward those artistic forms and themes which would in the future prove most germane to himself and his contemporaries: the paganism and aestheticism of Gautier, the decadence and cynicism of Baudelaire, the elitism of the symbolists, the precision and concreteness of Parnassian verse, and the uninhibited choice of subject matter enjoyed by the Impressionists and naturalists. Arthur Symons, W. B. Yeats, and other writers who followed Moore in looking to French literature for invigoration would find more subtle qualities to praise.[8] If Moore was most affected by the daring themes, decadent mood, and uncompromising public stance of the French avant-garde, it was because these qualities were what most distinguished them from the English. The impatience and scepticism Moore displays in *Confessions* toward nuances of experimentation in language and form is only partly satirical exaggeration; it also reflects his eagerness to overthrow the stale literary establishment as quickly as possible.

This emphasis on the unorthodox gives *Confessions* its particularly exuberant and rebellious tone. In its display of intellectual attitudes, although not in its playful tone, it echoes Huysmans' novel *A Rebours* (1884). Moore reread *A Rebours* in 1886 and told Theodore Duret that it was "very good, very good."[9] Huysmans' hero, Des Esseintes, expresses contempt for the bourgeois, love of the artificial and arcane; he admires the poetry of Baudelaire, Verlaine, and Mallarmé and the opera of Wagner. To complete his decadent tastes, he endorses a Schopenhauerian outlook on life.[10] All of these themes have a place in

8 For a fuller discussion of the influence of French symbolism on English writers see Ruth Zabriskie Temple, *The Critic's Alchemy* (New York: Twayne Publishers, 1953) and, by the same author, "The Ivory Tower," in *Edwardians and Late Victorians*, ed. Richard Ellmann (New York: Columbia University Press, 1960).

9 Moore to Theodore Duret, undated, Henry W. and Albert A. Berg Collection, the New York Public Library, Astor, Lenox and Tilden Foundations.

10 The ideas of Schopenhauer and Wagner were very much in the air while Moore was in Paris, and he undoubtedly picked up much of what he knew about them from conversations. Zola's novels (*Joie de Vivre* in particular) probably contributed to his knowledge of Schopenhauer as well. Wagner's theories of the relationship of language to music attracted the interest of the symbolists; Moore's friend Edouard Dujardin edited both the symbolist magazine *La Revue Indépendante*, where *Confessions* appeared, and the *Revue Wagnérienne* during the 1880s. See William F. Blissett, "George Moore and Literary Wagnerism," *Comparative Literature* 13 (Winter 1961):

the intricate fabric of *Confessions* and recreate for English audiences the aura of decadence which was to transform their artistic world in the 1890s.

Thus when Moore returned to London in 1879, he was filled with both revolutionary artistic theories and a naive confidence in his role as chief importer of French aesthetic tastes into England. In reading the section of *Confessions* which deals with this effort (the last five chapters) it is important to keep in mind the mixture of fact and fiction which makes up the book. At this point in the narrative, the margin between the two becomes increasingly blurred. Ostensibly, *Confessions* ends with the young hero struggling to write his first novel—which would date the ending as 1882, for *A Modern Lover* appeared in 1883. But Moore seems to have become less self-conscious about maintaining his fiction as he embarked on his criticism of English literature, and hence books which were published as late as 1887 are discussed in the narrative. Often the satire turns to invective, the fiction to journalism, and the reader will notice that it is this latter part of the book which underwent the most extensive revision in later editions. The tone of the original is highly instructive, however, for it suggests the degree of anxiety and dedication Moore felt for his task. The victories won by French writers from the 1850s onward would now be won for the English.

The hostility of the English reading public of the 1880s toward any liberalizing forces has been well documented.[11] Moore faced the conservative establishment which had attacked the Pre-Raphaelite Brotherhood, Swinburne, Thomas Hardy, and all threats from France before him. Moore places himself on the side of the rebels in *Confessions* by praising Swinburne and Rossetti and by connecting their art with the French avant-garde. He ignores Thomas Hardy's difficulties with the censors and Henry James' gentlemanly feud with Walter Besant, prob-

---

52–71. This article is included in Graham Owens, ed., *George Moore's Mind and Art* (Edinburgh: Oliver & Boyd, 1968).

11 See, e.g., George J. Becker, ed., *Documents of Modern Literary Realism* (Princeton: Princeton University Press, 1963), which contains The National Vigilance Association's indictment of Vizetelly & Co., publishers of Moore and Zola.

ably because he judged them small skirmishes in a war which was to require full-scale assaults.[12]

Confessions was far from being Moore's first gesture of defiance. He had begun his campaign against literary censorship even before he settled in London in 1881. In an article in *Le Voltaire* in 1879 (probably his first publication in a journal),[13] he had described the contemporary English prejudice against Zola's writings and had decried as the cause of that hostility the censorship imposed by the circulating libraries.[14] Upon returning to London, it had been his intention, as he later said, to establish the "aesthetic novel" in England.[15] His first novel marked the beginning of his campaign.

By "aesthetic novel" Moore meant a novel free from moral lessons and reflective of the true spirit of the age it grew out of. The hero of *A Modern Lover*, Lewis Seymour, was an amoral young man whose selfish indolence involved three women in the successive satisfaction of his financial needs. Moore did not present Seymour as a laudable hero: he satirized his effeminate, weak character and ridiculed his pretensions to being an artist. But unlike most contemporary writers, Moore did not evolve a final triumph of good over evil in his plot; although a foolish man, Seymour leads a happy and comfortable life.

Besides creating a hero who was bound to offend his Victorian

12 Henry James' essay "The Art of Fiction," originally published in *Longman's Magazine* in 1884, was a reply to Walter Besant's defence of contemporary sentimental fiction. James preceded Moore in publishing critical articles in England on Zola, but his distaste for the "monstrous uncleanness" in Zola's novels made him less than an ardent champion of naturalism. See *"Nana"* in Becker, *Modern Literary Realism*.

13 Paul Alexis, "Emile Zola à l'étranger, II En Angleterre et en Amérique," *Le Voltaire* (1 November 1879), n.p. Alexis quotes a long letter from Moore, whom he identifies as a *"poète distingué"* (Moore had recently published *Flowers of Passion*).

14 Two circulating libraries, Smith's and Mudie's, had exercised a strong influence over popular literature since the 1840s. English novels were published in three volumes and priced at 31/6. Thus they were both too bulky and too expensive for the average reader to buy. Smith and Mudie bought novels from the publishers and then loaned them to readers, who paid one guinea a year for their subscription. The libraries catered to the majority's taste, which was a preference for sentimental romances. They refused to buy any novel that might offend their readers and disdained especially the French realists and naturalists. Writers were trapped by this system, and Moore was determined to break it.

15 Geraint Goodwin, *Conversations with George Moore* (London: Jonathan Cape, 1937), p. 87.

readers, Moore included in his novel a number of aesthetic theories which ran counter to those accepted by Victorian society. In London, Seymour became acquainted with a group of painters and writers called "The Moderns" who, like their prototypes at the Nouvelle Athènes, disdained the sentimentality of popular art and advocated the methods and subjects of realism. Seymour enjoyed the company of these artists, but did not share their commitment to art: he was willing to paint sentimental pictures for anyone who would pay him to do so.

While sufficiently offensive in its themes, *A Modern Lover* was largely a failure as a novel. Moore's main character was quite obviously derived from the young heroes of several French novels; the novel lacked a coherent plot, and the language was generally verbose and laden with jargon.[16] Some of the individual scenes were vividly drawn, however, and when the *Spectator* praised his book and hailed him as a talented new writer,[17] Moore turned to plans for his second novel with new confidence.

The circulating libraries banned *A Modern Lover*,[18] and Moore, now

16 For discussions of the French models for Moore's first novels, see Mildred Adams, "The Apprenticeship of George Moore" (Ph.D. diss., Columbia University, 1960); Milton Chaikin, "George Moore's Early Fiction," in Owens, *George Moore's Mind and Art*; and Walter Ferguson, *The Influence of Flaubert on George Moore* (Philadelphia: University of Pennsylvania Press, 1934).

17 "The 'naturalism' which Mr. Moore occasionally affects does not come to him by nature. Certain passages of his novel make us aware that he admires and would fain imitate Zola and his odious school; but we venture to predict that he will never succeed in doing this. He has to combat two powerful obstacles to an achievement so much to be regretted; they are the faith of a Christian and the instincts of a gentleman. If M. Zola, or any of the hogs of his sty, could write such an episode in which the keynote to the character of Lewis Seymour is struck, we should have as much hope for them as we have confidence in Mr. Moore's future work;—even they might yet 'purge, and live cleanly.'" Anon. reviewer, *Spectator* 56 (18 August 1883): 1069.

18 Moore described, in an article published on 10 December 1884 in the *Pall Mall Gazette* ("A New Censorship of Literature"), how astounded he was when he learned that Smith, who usually took three times as many copies of a book as his colleague Mudie, had ordered only fifty copies of *A Modern Lover* and had refused to circulate even those. Moore rushed to Smith's and demanded an explanation. Smith, called Mr. X in the article, answered, "Your book was considered immoral. Two ladies from the country wrote to me objecting to that scene where the girl sat to the artist as a model for Venus. After that I naturally refused to circulate the book." Moore pointed out that the reviewer for the *Spectator* had singled out that scene for praise, but Smith would not listen to argument. Moore's article was a lively

directly involved in the issue of censorship, decided to make his next
book an even greater affront to the library system by patterning it
closely after the naturalism of Zola. *A Mummer's Wife* (1884) was a
detailed study of the stages of disintegration of a character. The major
ingredients in his second novel—actors, adultery, and alcoholism—
were all shocking to the average patron of Smith's and Mudie's libraries.
Moore's emulation of Zola's method of exact description of environment and its effect upon character drew the contumely of the critics
who deplored the unwholesomeness of French naturalism. But Moore
achieved his goal, for although the critics attacked his subject, they
would not deny that he wrote well.[19] Some even drew a lesson from
the realistic portrait of Kate Ede's moral disintegration.[20] Nevertheless,
Smith and Mudie again banned his novel. Moore not only put the
libraries in the awkward position of having refused to circulate a novel
praised in some prominent journals, he further undercut their power
by publishing *A Mummer's Wife* in one volume, a move suggested to
him by Zola.[21] Early in 1885, he published a revised one-volume edition

---

denunciation of the library system, and it provoked an article in the *Saturday Review* of 13 December 1884 (pp. 747–48) which supported his position.
Moore had planned his article to coincide with the publication of *A
Mummer's Wife* and was delighted to receive support from another
journalist.

19 William Wallace wrote in the *Academy* (26, no. 60 [29 November 1884]:
354) that *A Mummer's Wife* was the most repulsive story ever written. He
added, however, that Moore showed "unquestionable power" in telling his
heroine's story.

20 "Vice in its pages is loathsome in its hideousness. Mr. Moore has not gone
out of his way to invest with adventitious attractiveness the sins with
which he deals. Roses and raptures are not without a place in his record,
but there are plenty of thorns and torments; and assuredly if art, literary or
pictorial, fulfils its true mission in photographic presentation of the details
of sensuality and sottishness, it is well that such presentation should have
the photographic veracity which allows no item of foulness or ugliness to
escape." The reviewer goes on to denounce Moore and to claim pleasure,
rather than photographic veracity, as the purpose of art. "An English
Disciple of Zola," *Spectator* 57 (17 January 1885): 83–85.

21 Moore wrote to Zola on 22 September 1884, "Mon roman est fini, et je le
crois vingt fois mieux què mon premier effort; mais chose plus importante,
il va être imprimé en un seul volume—ce que vous m'avez consullié de
faire, et a quoi je vous avez repondu que c'était impossible a Londres"
(Bibliothèque Nationale, NAF 24522, no. 361; the library will hereafter be
referred to as BN; Moore's letters are uncorrected).

of *A Modern Lover* which superseded the original three-volume version.[22]

In his third novel, *A Drama in Muslin* (1886), Moore continued in his effort to "shock the sentimental school."[23] Set in Ireland, his book was an indictment of a society which warped its children by forcing them to live by its superficial values. He focused on the annual State Ball held at Dublin Castle and the marriage market there, where young girls vied with one another for husbands. The poverty-stricken Dubliners who stood outside the castle watching the aristocracy arrive for the ball were portrayed with vivid realism. Predictably, the circulating libraries again banned Moore's book.

With the banning of his third novel, Moore decided to try another tactic in his fight against the libraries. Soon after the publication of *A Drama in Muslin*, he wrote a scathing letter to the *Times* in which he first derided the library system and then declared his desertion from the ranks of English writers. After describing the censorship he had suffered he concluded:

> In the face of such opposition it would be useless for me to continue as an English writer. Happily there is no reason why I should; I am nearly as well known in France as in England; I have an admirable translator, as a glance at the series of articles I began last Saturday in the *Figaro* will show; I will therefore no longer expose myself to the risk of insult by having books again refused by Messrs. Mudie and Smith, I will publish my next book in French; and as I notice that librarians here do not object to Daudet's "Sapho," it is hardly to be supposed, unless indeed they would pursue their flying foe across the Straits, that they will take exception to what I write so long as I do not write it in

22 In 1885, Moore also published a pamphlet entitled *Literature at Nurse, or Circulating Morals*, in which he soundly denounced the libraries and the kind of literature they favoured. He again received support from another journalist: on 12 August 1885, "Mudie and Nude-y," an article defending Moore's argument in *Literature at Nurse*, appeared in *The World*.

23 Moore wrote to Zola in 1884, while he was writing *A Mummer's Wife*, "Si j'arrive de planté un coup, comme je le medite, en plein poitrine de l'ecole sentimentale j'aurais de l'espoir de pouvoir faire quelque changements dans la literature de mon pays—d'être enfin en ricocher de Zola en Angleterre" (BN, NAF 24522, no. 401, undated, c. January).

English; and so it comes that I look forward confidently to appearing next year on the book stalls in a yellow cover.[24]

The series of essays he mentions, originally entitled *Lettres sur Irlande*, appeared in *Le Figaro* in July and August of 1886. Although written for a French audience, Moore's essays were, like *A Drama in Muslin*, in large part another indictment of Ireland. His descriptions of the poverty of the peasants and the supercilious unconcern of the landlords echoes Balzac and Zola in its realism. The essays were expanded and published in France as *Terre d'Irlande* in 1886, and as *Parnell and His Island* in England in 1887.

Parnell and His Island anticipates *Confessions* in a number of ways. The style of *Parnell*, for one thing, is very like that of *Confessions*: written in the first person, it shifts from discursive narration to emotive soliloquy ("The novel I am writing will never be finished—never!")[25] to prose-poem evocation of mood ("And then the thing ceases to snore in the moonlight, and a white form passes softly down the length of stair, softly away; and then the large and beautifully soft white form comes back, comes up softly, so softly towards the moonlight and me").[26] Important too is the attitude of the narrator toward the Irish landlord, newly arrived from Paris, whom he accompanies while he collects rents from angry tenants. The landlord is a mirror image of Edwin Dayne, "a young man in a long green coat. His tiny hat, his long hair, his Parisian-cut clothes and his Capoul-like beard give him a very strange and very anomalous air. On the Boulevard he might pass muster, but where he stands he is *un être de féerie*."[27] The narrator satirizes his friend quite mercilessly: "Notwithstanding his cynicism my friend was touched to the heart. Three days afterwards he began a poem on the subject, the chief merit of which lay in the ingenuity of rhyming Lilith with lit."[28]

Moore's ironical attitude toward the poet in *Parnell* is clearly

---

24 *Times* (London), 12 August 1886, p. 10.
25 *Parnell and His Island* (London: Swan Sonnenschein, Lowrey, & Co., 1887), p. 161.
26 *Parnell*, p. 167. The soft white form turns out to be an owl.
27 *Parnell*, p. 52.
28 *Parnell*, p. 76. See chapter 4, critical note 19, for an account of Moore's early poetry, which is not unlike this poet-landlord's.

carried over to the narrative of *Confessions*. Many of Moore's early readers, including his first translator, misread the tone of his book. He was forced to write to Dujardin, "If my translator is a young man you may tell him that the irony of the English disappears somewhat in the French. I achieve I think a lighter and more spirited phrase, and there is always the touch of exaggeration which the French fails to convey. In English I have my tongue in my cheek, in French I am deadly serious. For example—I say that I was 'stricken by the art of Jules Lefebvre,' which he translates 'je fus frappé.' 'Stricken' is a more emphatic word than 'frappé'; he misses, you see, the slight exaggeration. My book is a *satire*."[29]

Finally, besides anticipating *Confessions* in style and tone, *Parnell* shows Moore merging, as he will in *Confessions*, two opposing impulses within one character: the reformer's social criticism goes hand in hand with the aesthete's claim to detachment. The narrator assures us that "the scenes in the pages of this book point to no moral. . . . Unconcerned with this or that interest, indifferent to this or that opinion, my desire was to produce a series of pictures to touch the fancy of the reader as a Japanese ivory or fan, combinations of hue and colour calculated to awake in him fictitious feelings of pity, pitiful curiosity and nostalgia of the unknown."[30]

Parnell and His Island in itself was strong evidence that Moore's defection from English literature would not last long. In March of 1887, he published an article in the English journal *Time*,[31] in which he defended *A Drama in Muslin* and at the same time set the stage for his next novel, already completed, *A Mere Accident*. In his article, he urged the critics to recognize that he had abandoned the methods of naturalism and was now concerned with more complex character studies. He was as interested, he said, in examining the psychology of his characters as he was in recreating the external world in which they lived. To an even greater degree than *A Drama in Muslin*, *A Mere Accident* marked a definite swing away from the naturalism of Zola,

29 Eglinton, *Letters to Dujardin*, p. 27, 11 March 1888.
30 *Parnell*, pp. 233–34.
31 "Defensio pro Scriptis Meis," *Time* 5 (March 1887): 277–84.

toward the interior character studies of Pater and Huysmans.[32] In
A Drama in Muslin the psychology of his characters had been partially
determined by the external forces of environment. In *A Mere Accident*,
the mental and emotional disposition of the main character, John
Norton, is wholly intrinsic; his environment is merely a source of frus-
tration for him.

While he moved away from naturalism in his method of character-
ization, Moore persisted in writing of subjects which would offend
the majority of his English readers. John Norton's celibacy and his
Schopenhauerian distaste for life find an outlet in a perverted version
of Catholicism. Then within this decadent atmosphere, Moore creates
a bold and original situation with which to end his story: Norton's
fiancée Kitty is raped by a tramp and then driven to madness and
suicide by fantastic dreams. Some of the critics praised Moore's fourth
novel because it was a movement away from naturalism;[33] the circulating libraries banned it, and other critics,[34] including Pater,[35] Moore says,
denounced the rape scene as gratuitous.

It should be apparent, then, that each of the novels which preceded
Confessions had a double identity. From the outset of his career, Moore
was a serious writer and his experiments with fictional forms were
genuine attempts to find his voice as a novelist. At the same time, Moore
was never forgetful of his public or of the kind of fiction which would

32 Moore reflects his reading of *Marius the Epicurean* and *A Rebours* in *A
Mere Accident* mainly by his focus on a character who, like Marius and
Des Esseintes, prefers a contemplative life and the pursuit of arcane knowledge to an active, more conventional life. John Norton is writing a history
of Christian Latin, an idea he has taken, he says, from *Marius the Epicurean*.

33 William Wallace wrote that *A Mere Accident* was the best written and
least realistic of Moore's novels. He was encouraged by Moore's portrait of
Kitty (a normal, innocent young girl) to hope that Moore would turn to
healthy characters when he had finished studying "the skin-diseases of
humanity." *Academy* 32, no. 794 (23 July 1887): 51.

34 The reviewer for the *Athenaeum* wrote that the "revolting incident is
introduced without even the excuse of a purpose in the story." *Athenaeum*,
no. 3118 (30 July 1887): 144.

35 Regarding Pater's criticism, Moore wrote, "I shall tell in vain that he said
that he was no proper critic of the story I sent him, and that the recording
of violent acts was not clear to him. He said something very like that, and
he may have added that the object of art is to enable us to forget the crude
and the violent." *Avowals* (London: William Heinemann, 1924), p. 195;
unless otherwise indicated, all references to Moore's works will be made to
the Uniform Edition published by Heinemann, 1924–33.

be most likely to upset the middle class, or villa, conventions. If these early novels were not wholly successful works of art—and Moore soon agreed that they were not—their failure can be blamed on the dual role they were expected to play. The artist who confronts an age inimical to experimentation, one which threatens his development as an artist, can either use his art to fight that age and thus, as Moore did, create works with definite flaws, or he can choose, as the aesthetes of the nineties would, to scorn his age in the belief that art has ultimately the power to alter life. During this period, Moore was convinced that the artist was to a large extent determined by his age. He wrote in *Evelyn Innes*, in a passage reminiscent of the opening of *Confessions*, "We come into the world with nothing in our own right except the capacity for the acquisition of ideas. We cannot invent ideas; we can only gather some of those in circulation since the beginning of the world. We endow them with the colour and form of our time. . . . Genius is merely the power of assimilation; only the fool imagines he invents."[36]

Since the particular colouring and form an artist gives his ideas is affected by the age he lives in, he must make that age as healthy for art as he can. During his long career, Moore was involved in other campaigns besides those mounted in *Confessions*. He championed Ibsenesque drama and Wagnerian opera in the 1890s, and he was a leading figure during the formative years of the Irish Renaissance. All of these various movements demanded from him resilience in the face of public hostility and patience in the slow work of educating audiences to accept or at least suffer new artistic forms. In his later years, when he became the sage of Ebury Street, respected and consulted by both his contemporaries and younger writers, Moore grew increasingly detached from his age. His late novels suggest both in subject and style that their author had withdrawn into the contemplative life. But Moore never really mellowed. He wrote to Nancy Cunard in 1922, "Moreover whosoever follows the fashion loses all individuality—it is necessary to be stiff-necked and obdurate and to treat one's contemporaries with contumely. In the great periods the artist took strength from his environment; he was concentric, but in

36 *Evelyn Innes* (London: T. Fisher Unwin, 1898), p. 178.

periods of decadence like the present, the artist must be eccentric, stand aloof and disdainfully."[37]

Interestingly enough, the first sentence of this late letter succinctly describes the tone and perspective of the latter part of *Confessions*. Moore is hard on contemporary English writers for he sees them as willing victims of villa standards. He must secure a place in the literary establishment without compromising his newly learned commitment to artistic integrity. Henry James, W. D. Howells, George Meredith, Thomas Hardy, and Robert Louis Stevenson among the first-rate novelists, and Richard Blackmore, David Christie Murray, Walter Besant, James Rice, Robert Buchanan, Mary Elizabeth Braddon, "Ouida," Rhoda Broughton, and many others among the second- and third-rate writers are all berated for their capitulations to the puerilities of public taste and for their failures to write novels which reflect definite aesthetic principles. The reader can find in these critiques Moore's own aesthetic adumbrated: he defends character as the central interest in the novel; he calls for rhythm and melody of narration, criteria he has learned from Wagnerian opera; he asks for proportion in the novel, for a balance between a man's character and his actions, thus deriding the contemporary taste for melodrama. Most importantly, he insists that novelists must write well; his praise of the French realists and harsh criticism of the naturalists earlier in *Confessions* was based on this assumption. The three-volume format for novels required writers to spin out their tales beyond their natural limits, and this was another reason for toppling that venerable institution.[38]

Only one contemporary English writer could win Moore's respect— Walter Pater, whose *Marius the Epicurean* Moore read soon after its publication in 1885.[39] The protean chronology of *Confessions* is again betrayed when Moore proclaims Pater his fourth "echo-augury."[40] Shelley, Gautier, Balzac (or Shelley, France, Zola, depending on how one tallies them up) had each awakened Moore's imagination to new

---

37 Nancy Cunard, *G. M.: Memories of George Moore* (London: Rupert Hart-Davis, 1956), p. 137.
38 See Forrest Reid, "Minor Fiction in the Eighties," in *The Eighteen-Eighties*, ed. Walter de la Mare (Cambridge: Cambridge University Press, 1930).
39 Joseph Hone, *The Life of George Moore* (London: Victor Gollancz, 1936), p. 110.
40 See critical note 1, chapter 1.

ranges of artistic experience. Significantly, these echo-auguries begin and end with English writers; Moore enjoyed finding dramatic proof that he was destined to be an English rather than a French writer. Pater's prose convinced Moore that English could be written well, that melody was possible in a language which struck him as disturbingly inelegant compared to French. Pater's hero Marius also had a profound effect on him, for Marius' paganism, his intense inner life, and his quest for sensation and meaning all seemed to mirror his own experiences. Now Gautier's aggressive hedonism was modified by Pater's milder English "lesson in the skilled cultivation of life, of experience, of opportunity."[41] Moore never followed Pater's aestheticism to an extreme as Wilde and his contemporaries would;[42] Pater's influence refined Moore's prose and his critical method (which was impressionistic even before he found Pater), and it confirmed his belief in the right of art to be free from all external moral restraints. But an inner check saved Moore from extending Pater's aesthetic dictum to "burn always with this hard, gemlike flame" into a self-destructive ethic.[43] This inner check, an inherent moral code, is hinted at in *Confessions*, and it functions there as a subtle and amusing counterpoint to the assertive amorality of the hero.

Moore summed up his view of his age in a proposed cover design for *Confessions*. "The design," he wrote in a letter to his editor, "is supposed to represent a bird of prey devouring a heart in midair; the world—a very effete world is below."[44] He wanted desperately to charge the exhausted literary scene with new energy. He would stir

41 Walter Pater, *Marius the Epicurean*, 1 (London: Macmillan & Co., 1885): 33–34.
42 See Harold Bloom, *Yeats* (New York: Oxford University Press, 1970), pp. 23–37, for an excellent discussion of Pater's bequest to the nineties.
43 Walter Pater, *The Renaissance* (London, Macmillan & Co., 1912), p. 236.
44 Letter to a Mr. Wigram, an editor for Swan Sonnenschein, Lowrey, & Co. Moore tried to draw the cover design himself, and for a one-time artist, he had little success. He wrote in the same letter, "I send you a sketch of my own. It would have to be more or less redrawn but I think the engraver could manage that. I cannot go any further with the sketch I never drew a bird from nature in my life; here I have nothing to draw from and I have only one pencil that will not come to a sufficiently fine point to draw with. ... I cannot draw the world because I have no globe here and haven't seen one since the year one" (National Library of Ireland, MS. 3888, no. 18, undated; the library will hereafter be referred to as NLI).

it up by publishing boldly realistic novels, then he would support his campaign with insults and challenges.[45] The war was to prove a long and bitter one, but by 1894, with the publication of *Esther Waters*, Moore had succeeded in setting the English novel free from many of the old restrictions.[46] In 1922, *Ulysses* would still find a publisher only in Paris; but Moore had helped to establish a climate and audience sympathetic to realism, and this audience would eventually be large enough to support the demand for total artistic freedom.

Confessions ushered in a decade which was fast to become infamous.[47] The aestheticism, the taste for decadence, the celebration of French poetry and painting, and the irreverence and contempt expressed for the powerful villa in *Confessions* all became hallmarks of the 1890s. One hears less about Moore's role in this spectacular decade because he was less flamboyant than Wilde, Beardsley, Whistler, and the others. As always, he spent much of his time working on his books. The number of works published after *Confessions* and during the nineties testify to his persistence. He published five novels: *Spring Days* (1888), *Mike Fletcher* (1889), *Vain Fortune* (1891), *Esther Waters* (1894), and *Evelyn*

45 *Confessions*, of course, played a central role in this effort. Moore had baited the critics with his earlier novels and journal polemics, and they were quick to see *Confessions* as another foray in this campaign. The reviews were on the whole favourable, however. Even critics who disapproved of Edwin Dayne's character couldn't deny that *Confessions* was a lively and entertaining book. For example, William Sharp, the reviewer for the *Academy*, wrote, "Mr. George Moore's new book defies adequate review. It raises a hundred points for literary discussion, and deals so trenchantly with difficult problems and is so bold in its personalities that one can simply say—get it and read it. It is a brilliant sketch; much the best thing that Mr. Moore has yet done: the production of a man of wide culture, and containing scarcely a single page void of something suggestive, amusing, daring, or—impertinent. . . . With regard to the audacious personalities, I confess that I find it difficult to formulate any sweeping censure, for it would be hypocritical to deny that Mr. Moore's pungent criticisms of contemporary writers have interested and amused me. There are, however, certain remarks which transgress the bounds of courtesy, and one or two epithets which are as objectionable as they are uncalled for." *Academy* 33, no. 828 (17 March 1888): 184–85.
46 See Introduction by Lionel Stevenson, ed., *Esther Waters* (Boston: Houghton Mifflin Co., Riverside Edition, 1963).
47 Two of the more useful among the many studies of the 1890s are William Gaunt, *The Aesthetic Adventure* (New York: Schocken Books, 1967) and Karl Beckson, ed., *Aesthetes and Decadents of the 1890's* (New York: Random House, Vintage Books, 1966).

Innes (1898); a collection of short stories entitled *Celibates* (1895); two collections of critical essays, *Impressions and Opinions* (1891) and *Modern Painting* (1893); an Ibsenesque drama, *The Strike at Arlingford* (1893), and the first act of *The Fool's Hour*, which appeared in the first issue of *The Yellow Book*;[48] and a preface to the translation of Dostoevsky's *Poor Folk* (1894). Moore knew the aesthetes and published in their journals, but he did not share their way of life. Perhaps he felt, and the conclusion to *Confessions* suggests this, that he had outgrown posturing and must now concentrate all his energies on his art.

By the end of the century, Moore was in Dublin, deeply involved in the Irish Renaissance. Yeats had left the Rhymers' Club and also gone to Ireland, Wilde had left Reading Gaol and would soon die in exile, and Beardsley was dead at twenty-five. The age was over. "Then in 1900 everybody got down off his stilts; henceforth nobody drank absinthe with his black coffee; nobody went mad; nobody committed suicide; nobody joined the Catholic Church . . . Victorianism had been defeated."[49] Moore got down off his stilts a bit sooner than the others; he had been on them longer. *Confessions* and his early novels had played an important part in the defeat of Victorianism. Moore would now turn his attention to quieter themes: the spiritual life and music, Irish, Biblical, and classical themes. But he would never forget the formative years of his career or abandon the book which had chronicled them.

Moore later called *Confessions* the genesis of everything he had written after it.[50] The reader can easily see justification for this claim. Moore contributed to a number of literary genres: autobiography, criticism, the novel and short story, drama, and least significantly, poetry. Each of these is present in some guise in the narrative of *Confessions*. Autobiography most interests us here since *Confessions* was the first but by no means the last of Moore's autobiographical works.

48 With John Oliver Hobbes, "The Fool's Hour: The First Act of a Comedy," *The Yellow Book* 1 (April 1894): 253–72.
49 W. B. Yeats, Introduction to *The Oxford Book of Modern Verse, 1892–1935* (London: Oxford University Press, 1936), p. xi.
50 Preface to *Confessions*, 1904.

In five other autobiographies, plus one unfinished autobiographical fragment, he recorded and refashioned segments of his past life. The first to be written after *Confessions* was *Memoirs of My Dead Life* (1906), which is composed of chapters loosely related to one another by the continuity of the narrator.[51] Speaking in the first person, Moore muses about his past and remembers many of the women in his life, especially the younger ones. The amount of truth in the episodes he recounts is questionable, and his whimsical, sometimes humorous, manner suggests that his narrative is more fiction than fact. He tells, for example, of a young woman who comes from Texas to ask him to sire a child for her. Her noble aim is to give a writer to Texas, and Moore obliges her with a mixture of wonder and aplomb.[52]

Memoirs is an autobiography of a personality, not of facts. Every anecdote adds to the configuration of the narrator's character, and it becomes the real subject of the book. Moore's narrator, although apparently simply the author, is as much a refracted image of Moore as is the hero of *Confessions*. In his earlier autobiography, he is the exuberant prodigal; in *Memoirs*, he is the urbane lover. Both images had firm roots in Moore's personality and both were self-portraits he sought to emulate in his own life. The latter, the urbane lover, was to many of his friends an affectation. His companions were often embarrassed by his outspoken tales, but they were seldom convinced. Moore's love affairs, like his early life in Paris, became staple legends in his repertoire.

His next autobiographical work, *Avowals*, was subtitled, "Being a New Series of Confessions of a Young Man" when it first appeared in *Lippincott's Magazine* in 1904.[53] Published in book form in 1919, *Avowals*, like *Confessions* (and unlike *Memoirs*), is a mixture of literary criticism and autobiographical references. Its form is not that of a novel, but a combination of dialogue, in the manner of Landor's *Imagi-*

---

51 Portions of *Memoirs of My Dead Life* appeared in *The Hawk* as "Notes and Sensations" (5–6 [11, 18 February; 11 March; 8, 22 April; 29 July; 9, 16, 30 September 1890]) and in *Dana* as "Moods and Memories" (1–7 [May–October 1904]).

52 "Euphorion in Texas," added to the 1915 edition.

53 Vol. 72, pp. 347–52, 481–88, 608–16; vol. 73, p. 168. Chapters of *Avowals* also appeared in the *Pall Mall Magazine*, March–July, 1904. The reference to *Confessions* in the subtitle was removed from the book version.

nary Conversations, and monologue, the musing voice heard in *Memoirs*. The emphasis is on critical rather than autobiographical commentary, and when Moore cites his past, it is to support some opinion. His memories seem to be clustered together in constellations rather than preserved in a sequential form, and the freedom with which he ranges over the different segments of his past, connecting reminiscences with no regard for chronological accuracy, creates a timeless narrative. The only point of reference is the narrator, and the exfoliation of his personality dominates, as it does in *Memoirs* and *Confessions*, the mood of the book.

The narrator of *Avowals*, perhaps because his subject is mainly his opinions rather than his actions, seems to be less a created persona and more a clear reflection of the author. The reader feels a similar identity of author and narrator in Moore's next autobiography, *Hail and Farewell*. This long trilogy—*Ave* (1911), *Salve* (1912), *Vale* (1914)—grew out of his memories of his eleven years in Dublin (1900–11) and his participation in the Irish Renaissance. As in *Memoirs* and *Avowals*, the past resurrected in *Hail and Farewell* is made up of constellations or atoms of memories. Based in the present, Moore's mind moves into the past, like Proust's, by focusing on complete and isolated segments of time. While the structure of his memories is similar, his method of remembrance differs from Proust's, for his memories are not triggered by sensation, but spun on a purely mental thread of suggestion. The opening of *Ave* establishes the method of narration used throughout the three books. He begins in the present and talks with Edward Martyn about the revival of the Irish language in Ireland. Leaving Martyn, Moore walks back to his rooms in the Temple, and as he walks, his thoughts roam from the discussion he has just had to the Irish writers who have remained in Ireland, to the idea of nationality in art, to his own self-exile from Ireland, and to a conversation he once had with Dujardin which, as he recounts it, expands his present attraction to and rejection of Ireland. This skillful weaving of past and present, of the general and the particular, is never disgressive, for Moore maintains a firm control over the direction of his thoughts. He creates a sense of timelessness, ranging from the present to the mythic past, while retaining simultaneously a clear sense of the setting of his narrative in a definite time and place.

Hail and Farewell possesses the characteristic mingling of fact and fancy found in *Confessions, Memoirs,* and *Avowals.* Like *Confessions, Hail and Farewell* has a narrative line which is formed by Moore's discovering a pattern in his past. He emphasizes, as he does in *Confessions,* certain actions and opinions and suppresses others. He recalls not only his eleven years in Dublin, but also his early life in Mayo, London, and Paris, and he recounts again, and in greater detail, many of the events found in *Confessions.* In weaving these memories into his narrative, Moore recasts them to suit his present theme, for besides being a chronicle of his part in the Irish Renaissance, *Hail and Farewell* is an autobiography aimed at self-discovery. Throughout his narrative, Moore confesses to flaws in his character and moral lapses in a manner similar to that in Rousseau's *Confessions* or Gide's later *Si le grain ne meurt.* Unlike his *Confessions,* in which candour is joined with bravado, his candid self-revelations are earnest here, and like Rousseau and Gide, he anatomizes his past self to seek in it hints of his present self.

Among the works written after *Hail and Farewell* are two in which Moore again returned to his past for his subject. *A Story-Teller's Holiday* (1918) is a rambling reminiscence which is composed of several stories (some told by Moore and some by "Alec Trusselby," an old fern gatherer), memories of his childhood and Paris in the 1870s, thoughts about Protestantism and Catholicism, and other reflections which occur to him as he returns to Ireland on holiday. His memories of Paris and the Nouvelle Athènes are juxtaposed to memories of Moore Hall. Although he feels an aversion toward his home, he acknowledges that it made his Paris life possible. *A Story-Teller's Holiday* is a celebration of the past rather than a chronicle of it, and like *Memoirs of My Dead Life,* an expression of the emotional texture of Moore's personality.

In contrast to this emphasis on mood, *Conversations in Ebury Street* (1924) is, like *Avowals,* a collection of Moore's opinions on literature. He again mixes dialogue and monologue to present in an informal manner his critical judgments on subjects ranging from Baudelaire to Roger Fry. As *Confessions* was the first to show, Moore's life and his literary opinions were always inextricably joined, and he refers in this book to his early life in Paris when he speaks of Balzac and Zola.

After these two mixtures of reminiscence, fiction, and criticism,

Moore returned in his final work to "pure" autobiography. In *A Com-munication to My Friends*, which he was writing at the time of his death in 1933, he recreated the period of his life which had been the subject of his first autobiography. His reason for writing this book, he explained, was to describe "how literature hailed me."[54] He obviously felt that *Confessions*, which had dramatized the same summons, was an inadequate account of his early career, and he even cited it as "one of the hardships" he encountered in writing this later version.[55] These declarations give *A Communication* the semblance of a factual account, but Moore was actually mingling fiction and fact as he had in all his earlier autobiographies. His memory may very well have been clouded by age (he was eighty) and confused by the earlier interpretations he had given his past, but his obvious desire to tell a good story was also a source of distortion.

Although *A Communication* is unreliable as history, it is an invalu-able reflection of Moore's mature opinions on aspects of his personality. His comment that "a mate and the writing of books are incompatible," for example, while simplifying the question of why he never married, also expresses his lifelong obsession with art.[56]

Few writers have been so assiduous as Moore in the exercise of auto-biography. Many artists have put as much of themselves into their work—Yeats and Joyce are two good examples—but few have chosen to display their past as directly as Moore did. He reflected upon the function of memory at the end of *A Story-Teller's Holiday*: "It is the past that explains everything, I say to myself. It is in our sense of the past that we find our humanity, and there are no moments in our life so dear to us as when we lean over the taffrail and watch the waters we have passed through. The past tells us whence we have come and what we are."[57] One is reminded of Proust's exhaustive search into his past and of his final discovery that time is incarnate and holds the clue to what men are. For Moore the process of revision was very like the process of remembrance. Returning to past works with the hope of

---

54 *A Communication to My Friends*, published with *A Mummer's Wife* in Uniform Edition, p. x.
55 *A Communication*, p. x.
56 *A Communication*, p. xxxvii.
57 *A Story-Teller's Holiday*, p. 263.

bringing them closer to perfection was not unlike returning to memories in order to find their durable significance. In revising *Confessions*, Moore was involved in both worlds, his work and his life. Thus the revised versions instruct us on his changing conceptions of himself both as a writer and as a man.

The text used for this edition of *Confessions of a Young Man* is that of the first edition. Misspelled words and proper names have been silently corrected; the majority of these errors (probably attributable to both Moore and his publisher) were set right in later editions. The quotations have also been silently corrected with the exception of one from Gautier which Moore meant to have the character of a remembered impression (p. 79). That the other quotations were corrected in later editions supports the belief that Moore wanted them to be accurate. The use of both quotation marks and italics to designate the titles of books in the first edition has been retained. Other punctuation has been silently corrected where necessary.

The variorum notes which accompany the text are a selective account of the many revisions Moore made in successive editions. Apart from the many reprints of *Confessions*, there exist nine distinct versions. Seven of these nine differ from one another in numerous substantive and accidental revisions made by Moore. The writing of *Confessions* began in 1887 and did not end until 1923. The versions which span these years are as follows:

1 *Time, A Monthly Magazine,* July through November, 1887 (the first nine of the original twelve chapters)

2 First English edition, Swan Sonnenschein, Lowrey & Co., March 1888

3 *La Revue Indépendante,* March through August, 1888

4 French edition, Nouvelle Librairie Parisienne, Albert Savine, editor, 1889

5 Second English edition, Swan Sonnenschein, Lowrey & Co., 1889 (listed as third English edition on the title page)

6 Third English edition, T. Werner Laurie, 1904

7 American edition, Brentano's, 1917

8 Fourth English edition, William Heinemann, 1918

9 Carra Edition, Boni and Liveright, 1923

The Carra Edition was the text which Moore used in what he considered the canon of his writings, the Uniform Edition published by Heinemann in London between 1924 and 1933. The 1926 edition of *Confessions* published by Heinemann was based on the text of the 1918 edition, as was the Ebury Edition of 1937. *Confessions* was published in the Uniform Edition in 1933. (Edwin Gilcher, *A Bibliography of George Moore* [Dekalb, Ill.: Northern Illinois University Press, 1970], pp. 20–27.) No manuscript of the original version of *Confessions* has been located. Only one manuscript of the revised editions seems to exist. This is a copy of the 1904 English edition on which Moore wrote his revisions for the 1917 American edition (Henry W. and Albert A. Berg Collection, the New York Public Library). A comparison of the revisions made on this copy with the text published in 1917 reveals that of the 223 revisions made in this copy, 196 occur in identical form in the 1917 text. The 27 other revisions underwent further alteration before the final text was published (presumably at the galley or page-proof stage) and in every case, the revision became more extensive. No reference is made to this manuscript in the variorum notes since it contains (with these few exceptions) revisions which were later published.

The revisions given in the textual notes will in every case be the final ones, that is, the 1923 version. Moore habitually revised his revisions in subsequent editions and I have chosen to print the final versions rather than to reproduce the stages of revision. The textual notes will indicate when the revision was first introduced and whether it was then modified in later editions, as is generally the case. The contrast between the style of the original text and the style of the revisions is often sharp, and the reader should keep in mind that Moore also made hundreds of isolated changes in the text which created a suitable context for the larger revisions. Those noted here are, in the main, revisions of fairly long passages which alter details in the text, add new information, clarify, or significantly alter the tone of the narrative. These take the form of additions of new material, revisions within the original text, or removal of passages or phrases from the original.

A brief discussion of the characteristics of each version may help the reader to appreciate the slow process of maturation which followed the creation of *Confessions*.

Between the publication of the first nine chapters of *Confessions* in *Time* and its appearance in book form in March of 1888, Moore made a number of revisions in his text. A comparison of the *Time* version with the first edition reveals variants of several kinds. Many are clearly misprints in the *Time* version, which were not repeated in the text of the book form. Moore's letters to a Mr. Wigram, who was evidently an editor for both *Time* and Swan Sonnenschein, indicate that he was correcting proof sheets for the book while the magazine version was being published. He was angry over the many errors in the *Time* text and demanded that Wigram employ better proofreaders. The reduction of compositorial errors in the book version suggests that his complaints had good effect.

Another type of variant which is not specifically a revision is the inclusion in the book of several long passages which Wigram had censored in the magazine. In his letters, Moore rails against his editor for removing passages from his text, but he concedes that censorship is preferable to silence. The passages were Moore's strident denunciations of Christianity (see pp. 123–26 and critical note). Other variants are, however, clearly changes Moore introduced as improvements in the narrative. The main tendency of these revisions was towards compression: he eliminated redundant passages and focused more sharply on his subject.

Moore's next opportunity to revise *Confessions* came soon after the publication of the first edition. While *Confessions* was appearing in translation in *La Revue Indépendante*, Moore decided to use his own name in the narrative in place of Edwin Dayne. This change was the only one made in this version.

Moore read this translation as it appeared and wrote long letters to Edouard Dujardin, editor of *La Revue Indépendante*, complaining about its tone and suggesting better translations. Dujardin soon agreed to issue a corrected translation in book form, and Moore began to send him changes to be incorporated into it. He retranslated several passages and sent them to Dujardin, but they were not used in the revised translation; he sent the additions to the text to Dujardin in English, and Dujardin translated them. He expanded two paragraphs, and added a few new phrases and two long passages: the account of the death of his father and the chapter entitled "Examen de Minuit" (see pp. 195 and 217). Besides these changes in the text itself, he added a short preface and a dedication to Jacques-Emile Blanche, which was expanded and included in all versions of *Confessions* after 1904.

In 1889, a revised English edition of *Confessions* was also published. Edwin Gilcher, Moore's bibliographer, agrees that the 1889 French edition is probably the earlier of the two. Moore was on hand for the printing of the English edition, Mr. Gilcher writes, "and probably continued his rewriting on the proof sheets up to the very last minute, a practice he engaged in all of his literary life" (letter to me from Edwin Gilcher, 31 October 1966). He wrote a preface for this edition in which he discussed what he then considered to be the most significant characteristics of his book: its compression and its expression of his Schopenhauerian philosophy of life. This edition contained the additions made to the 1889 French edition, as well as three new long revisions (see pp. 198, 201, and 216). All three of these revisions suggest that he wanted to strengthen both narrative and theme in *Confessions*.

The twenty-two other minor revisions made in the 1889 edition were slight and occur mainly in the first third of the book. Moore's style had not yet changed, and he was, for the time being, relatively satisfied with the style of his book.

Edwin Gilcher suggests that Moore published a revised edition of *Confessions* in 1889 in order to discredit the edition which the American publisher Brentano had pirated in the previous year and published as "authorized" (letter of 31 October 1966). A series of letters in the *Athenaeum* (8 December 1888 through 9 February 1889) in which Moore challenges American publishers for their habit of pirating and is answered by George Haven Putnam, the Secretary of the American Publishers Copyright League, documents Moore's outrage at Brentano's act, and this motive undoubtedly did play some part in the preparation of a new edition. It is probable too, however, that he wanted to include in *Confessions* the additions which he had written for the French edition. He thought highly of his book and wanted it before the public in its complete form. In the brief preface to the French edition, Moore states that he considers "la version française comme mon livre plutôt que l'autre."

Between 1889 and 1904, the date of the fourth revised edition of *Confessions*, Moore's prose style changed radically. In his early works, he had been experimenting with styles, and although his prose was often lively and his manner entertaining, he showed little feeling for prose rhythms. Even his reading of Pater seems to have had no influence on his style until after 1900. The novels written between 1888 and 1903 were later either substantially revised or finally excluded from his canon. In their original forms they are, like *Confessions*, stylistically imperfect works, stronger in plot than in language. (For discussions of Moore's revisions of his early novels, see John Denny Fischer's "*Evelyn Innes* and *Sister Teresa*, a Variorum Edition" [Ph.D. diss., University of Illinois, 1959], and Jay Jernigan's "George Moore's 'Retying of Bows': A Critical Study of the Eight Early Novels and Their Revisions" [Ph.D. diss., Kansas State College, 1966].) With *The Untilled Field* (1903) a marked change in his prose became apparent. He now wrote carefully structured rhythmical prose and unfolded his stories with skill and economy.

The revisions in the 1904 edition were extensive. Unlike the 1889 editions, which contained large additions to the text, the 1904 edition had only one addition, three poems which were meant to represent the kind of poetry Moore wrote in London in 1881. The other revisions in the 1904 edition are of several kinds. Many are corrections of proper names and French words which had been misspelled in the original and 1889 editions. Others are stylistic revisions centred on various failures in the original. Moore restructured sentences to make them more varied and melodious, he removed redundancies, he replaced many colourless words with more unusual, vivid ones, and he paid special attention to verb forms, revising them to introduce more energy into the narrative. These habits of revision are demonstrated by the large passages which Moore rewrote; in every case, he was seeking greater precision and increased dramatic effect.

The pattern of revision established in the 1904 edition of *Confessions* was the basis for the more extensive changes made in the next edition, which was published in the United States in 1917. This edition was published by Brentano and superseded the text of the first edition which Brentano had reprinted in 1901, 1906, 1907, 1911, and 1915. The text of the first edition was, however, used for the Modern Library edition, first published in 1917 with an introduction by Floyd Dell; plates of this edition were used for a reprint published circa 1943 by Carlton House, New York (Gilcher, *Bibliography of George Moore*, p. 22). Many of the revisions in the Brentano 1917 edition were radical; passages in which Moore had merely altered a word or two in 1904 now often underwent complete transformations.

Between 1904 and 1917, Moore had perfected the prose style which was first evident in *The Untilled Field* and which became his hallmark after *Hail and Farewell*. Its central characteristic was the long sentence, the melodic line. It is significant that Moore, who lived until 1933, wrote fewer new novels than he revised old ones after 1911. He had formed a style which he wanted to perfect in all his works, and he returned to many of his early novels to redeem them from their immature style. The energy of much of his early writing is muted in his later works, for in the later prose style there are few moments of extravagance. Many of the sentences in the early prose are long, but they are generally constructed by joining several simple sentences, or linking a series of phrases, rather than by skillfully using appositives, subordinate clauses, and other more complex structures. Moore's voice in his later works owes something to the tradition of the Irish sennachie, the storyteller whose melodious, unhurried narration dominates his tale. This later style found its way into *Confessions* through the 1917 and 1918 revisions.

In revising *Confessions* in 1917, Moore often shifted his attention from the sentence and individual words, his general method in 1904, to rewrite entire paragraphs. For example, in the original version he described his hatred of Catholic Ireland and his love of Protestant England in a style and language both vehement and emotional in tone. The originual passage has twenty-three verbs, thirteen of which are forms of "to be." The absence of active verbs contributes to the impressionistic tone of his diatribe. By contrast, the 1917 version of this passage contains twenty-eight verbs, only nine of which are forms of "to be." The structure of the passage in the revision is logical rather than emotional, and Moore's impressions gain greater force since they are explicated rather than merely presented. Many of the revisions made in 1917 demonstrate, as does this one, his desire to infuse a sharper intellectual tone into the originally impulsive narrative. This change in perspective makes *Confessions* in 1917 a subtler, yet still highly effective, book.

The preparation of the 1917 edition of *Confessions* must have planted the seed in Moore's mind for even further revisions of his book, for in 1918 another revised edition was published. As we have seen, the method of revision grew more radical with each edition, beginning with the inclusion of blocks of new material in 1889 and moving to small stylistic revisions in 1904, to larger rewritings in 1917, and finally in 1918, to replacing entire paragraphs with wholly new material. He was preparing a uniform edition of his works during this time, and he clearly wanted *Confessions* to endure in a form which would reflect his mature style.

The stylistic revisions in the 1918 edition followed the pattern of revision established in 1904. Moore again frequently salvaged his original prose by restructuring his sentences. As in the earlier editions, he showed a consistent concern with individual words and was still able, even after five revisions, to find many words which could be improved upon.

Within the context of the 1918 revision, the added passages present no glaring incongruities. In one long addition, for example, Moore replaced his rather dull and perfunctory discussion of several minor English writers with a passage which gives his criticisms a dramatic setting (see p. 212). He describes the Gaiety Bar on the Strand, where he found a nucleus for literary discussion to parallel the café Nouvelle Athènes. The style of this addition is distinctly that of his later prose, but the mood and commentary refer to the general plot line and are an improvement on the journalistic style of the original. This passage is clearly cast as a reminiscence and Moore emphasizes that perspective with the phrase "till at the end of a couple of years." He was originally writing out of his immediate feelings about contemporary literature and indicated no margin of time separating his opinions from the narration of them. It is interesting to note too, that while improving the perspective of his narrative and conforming it more closely to the earlier part of the book, he did not caricature himself as he had done formerly. The young man of the original version would not have been likely to scowl reprovingly at excessive drinking, as he does in the revision, being a student of excess himself.

The absence of burlesque in this passage is indicative of Moore's later attitude toward his hero. Stylistic sophistication has given the narrator a new voice, and although he continues to be outspoken and self-assertive, he is now much less the *enfant terrible*.

The 1918 edition of *Confessions* was the last to be extensively revised. In 1923, when the Carra Edition was in preparation, Moore merely augmented *Confessions* by adding another poem to the poetry section. In 1926, William Heinemann published an edition of *Confessions* which included at the end five essays Moore had chosen from *Impressions and Opinions*. These were the only essays from that collection worth keeping, he explained in a note, and they served as commentary on some of the ideas in *Confessions*. The essays were "An Eighteenth-Century Actress," "Mummer-Worship," "A Visit to Médan," "Le Revers d'un grand homme," and "Epistle to the Cymry."

The span of years between the composition of *Confessions* and Moore's final revision is wide. He was thirty-six when he first wrote and revised it and seventy-four when he last considered it for publication. At each stage of its evolution, the text of *Confessions* has a basic unity which stems partly from the continuity between Moore's early and later selves. Each time he returned to *Confessions*, he saw it as both a portrait and a mirror—an interpretation of his youthful self and a reflection of his present self. The revisions indicate his desire to reduce the margin of fiction separating these two images. As an older and venerated writer, he would identify more candidly with his young hero. This change in attitude did not mean that he would abandon the fiction, which is an integral and formative part of *Confessions*, but rather that he would refine it by improving the narrative style.

One of Moore's favourite anecdotes concerned a painter who had worked for years on his masterpiece; when it was unveiled his companions saw "only confused colour and incoherent form" and a foot barely visible in one corner. Ironically, Moore tells this anecdote, taken from Balzac's tale "Le Chef d'oeuvre inconnu" in the preface to the 1909 edition of *Sister Teresa*, a novel which he revised extensively but did not include in his final canon.

Overwriting can be as destructive as overpainting, and some of the novels were eventually scrapped. Undoubtedly the flexibility of the structure of *Confessions*, the variety of genres within it, allowed Moore to deviate from the style of the original in his revisions without producing clashing incongruities. Much of *Confessions* was never revised, but the reader senses no discordant stylistic contrasts as he reads any of the editions. The form which encapsulates the various genres, the confession, is characterized in Moore's use of it by the constantly fluctuating emotional and historical perspectives of the narrator. His revisions succeed in adding, through both style and content, new dimensions and subtleties to this flux.

SYMBOLS

The following symbols within the text direct the reader to the variorum notes:

⸨ ⸩ Enclosed material was revised or omitted in later editions.

⸎ An addition was made, at this point, in later editions.

Superscript numbers within the text indicate critical notes.

CONFESSIONS OF A YOUNG MAN

A Jacques Blanche

L'âme de l'ancien Egypien s'éveillait en moi quand mourut ma jeunesse, et j'ai eu l'idée de conserver mon passé, son esprit et sa forme, dans l'art.

Alors trempant le pinceau dans ma mémoire, j'ai peint ses joues pour qu'elles prissent l'exacte ressemblance de la vie, et j'ai enveloppé le mort dans les plus fins linceuls. Rhamesès le second n'a pas reçu des soins plus pieux! Que ce livre soit aussi durable que sa pyramide!

Votre nom, cher ami, je voudrais l'inscrire ici comme épitaphe, car vous êtes mon plus jeune et mon plus cher ami; et il se trouve en vous tout ce qui est gracieux et subtil dans ces mornes années qui s'égouttent dans le vase du vingtième siècle.

G. M.

Moore wrote three prefaces to introduce readers to *Confessions*—the first in 1889, the second in 1904, and the third in 1917. The final preface was used in the 1918 and later editions of the book. They have all been reproduced here because they illustrate, in concentrated form, the evolution both of Moore's style and of his attitude toward *Confessions*. Moore's growing affection for the book and for its young hero, and his modest assurances that honesty forbids rewriting one's confessions, help the reader to gain a fuller picture of Moore and to appreciate the special place *Confessions* held for him in his canon.

1889 ENGLISH EDITION

Numa Roumestan, when asked why he talks so unceasingly, first hesitates, and then answers thus naïvely: "I can't think, unless I talk."

What race relation exists between the Gascon and the Irish, I know not; but I confess I often find my brain will not work except in collaboration with my tongue; and when Daudet speaks of his manner of composition in "Trente ans de Paris," he seems to be speaking for me. For when I am composing a novel I must tell my ideas; and as I talk I formulate and develop my scheme of narrative and character. And any listener will do, for I am unaffected by advice. Once, however, I did take advice. My listener was Madame Henry Greville.

"St. Augustine," I said, "wrote the story of a God-tortured soul; would it not be interesting to write the story of an art-tortured soul?"

"I would advise you," she said, "not to use your own name; with a fictitious name, no matter how obviously personal the narrative may be, you could tell the story of your soul more boldly."

I felt I should not, and that my book would lose in sense of reality and power of conviction; but I yielded, and adopted the name of Eduard Dayne.

When I returned to London I offered my book to the editor of a weekly paper. He accepted it, conditioning I was not to write more than thirty or forty thousand words. By condensing till I reached the essence of each idea, by expressing by symbols that which I judged adventitious, extraneous, ephemeral, and circumstantial, I succeeded in squeezing my life within these limits; but when I began to write, my narrative leaped like a rivulet from rock to rock, so narrow was the channel; and I saw it might never flow like a stream, lingering now and then, a quiet pool, beneath pleasant boughs. In such difficulties I wrote about sixty pages; then fortune came to me, and the editor of the weekly journal offered to release me from my engagement, and I took my book to *Time*, a monthly magazine. There the narrative might flow more easily; but I could not break the original lines of my composition. Did I gain or lose by this excessive, I may almost say unnatural, concision? Sometimes I think if I had written all I should have written a book that would have lived; at other times I think it was this concision that gave the book what life it possesses.

Nor have I now attempted to alter the lines on which the book was composed. I have merely enlarged the first chapters with a view of bringing them into harmony with those that were written in easier circumstances. These additions, though they do not amount in all to above sixty pages, seem to me of the utmost importance; for they enabled me to accentuate the philosophy of the book (that of Schopenhauer), that philosophy which alone helps us to live while in the evil of living, that philosophy which alone shows us the real good and leads us from the real evil.

I owe much of my mind to Schopenhauer; but I will not say here that if these confessions induce any one to turn to "The World, as Will and Idea," they will have effected their purpose. My book was written to be read, not to help another book to be read.

G. M.

1904   ENGLISH EDITION (*this preface also appeared in* Dana *in November 1904*)

I

Dear little book, what shall I say about thee? Belated offspring of mine, out of print for twenty years, what shall I say in praise of thee? For twenty years I have only seen thee in French, and in this English text thou comest to me like an old love, at once a surprise and a recollection. Dear little book, I would say nothing about thee if I could help it, but a publisher pleads, and "No" is a churlish word. So for him

I will say that I like thy prattle; that while travelling in a railway carriage on my way to the country of "Esther Waters," I passed my station by, and had to hire a carriage and drive across the downs.

Like a learned Abbé I delighted in the confessions of this young man, a *naïf* young man, a little vicious in his *naïveté*, who says that his soul must have been dipped in Lethe so deeply that he came into the world without remembrance of previous existence. He can find no other explanation for the fact that the world always seems to him more new, more wonderful than it did to anyone he ever met on his faring; every wayside acquaintance seemed old to this amazing young man, and himself seemed to himself the only young thing in the world. Am I imitating the style of these early writings? A man of letters who would parody his early style is no better than the ancient light-o'-love who wears a wig and reddens her cheeks. I must turn to the book to see how far this is true. The first thing I catch sight of is some French, an astonishing dedication written in the form of an epitaph, an epitaph upon myself, for it appears that part of me was dead even when I wrote "Confessions of a Young Man." The youngest have a past, and this epitaph dedication, printed in capital letters, informs me that I have embalmed my past, that I have wrapped the dead in the finest winding-sheet. It would seem I am a little more difficult to please to-day, for I perceived in the railway train a certain coarseness in its tissue, and here and there a tangled thread. I would have wished for more care, for *un peu plus de toilette*. There is something pathetic in the loving regard of the middle-aged man for the young man's coat (I will not say winding-sheet, that is a morbidity from which the middle-aged shrink). I would set his coat collar straighter, I would sweep some specks from it. But can I do aught for this youth, does he need my supervision? He was himself, that was his genius; and I sit at gaze. My melancholy is like her's—the ancient light-o'-love of whom I spoke just now, when she sits by the fire in the dusk, a miniature of her past self in her hand.

II

This edition has not been printed from old plates, no chicanery of that kind: it has been printed from new type, and it was brought about by Walter Pater's evocative letter. (It wasn't, but I like to think that it was.) Off and on, his letter was sought for during many years, hunted for through all sorts of portfolios and bookcases, but never found until it appeared miraculously, just as the proof of my Pater article was being sent back to the printer, the precious letter transpired—shall I say "transpired?"—through a crack in the old bookcase.

BRASENOSE COLLEGE,
Mar. 4.

My dear, audacious Moore,—Many thanks for the "Confessions" which I have read with great interest, and admiration for your originality—your delightful criticisms—your Aristophanic joy, or at least enjoyment, in life—your unfailing liveliness. Of course, there are many things in the book I don't agree with. But then, in the case of so satiric a book, I suppose one is hardly expected to agree or disagree. What I cannot doubt is the literary faculty displayed. "Thou com'st in such a questionable shape!" I feel inclined to say on finishing your book; "shape" morally, I mean; not in reference to style.

You speak of my own work very pleasantly; but my enjoyment has been independent of that. And still I wonder how much you may be losing, both for yourself and for your writings, by what, in spite of its gaiety and good-nature and genuine sense of the beauty of many things, I must still call a cynical, and therefore exclusive, way of looking at the world. You call it only "realistic." Still!

With sincere wishes for the future success of your most entertaining pen.—Very sincerely yours,

WALTER PATER.

Remember, reader, that this letter was written by the last great English writer, by the author of "Imaginary Portraits," the most beautiful of all prose books. I should like to break off and tell of my delight in reading "Imaginary Portraits," but I have told my delight elsewhere; go, seek out what I have said in the pages of the *Pall Mall Magazine* for August 1904, for here I am obliged to tell you of myself. I give you Pater's letter, for I wish you to read this book with reverence; never forget that Pater's admiration has made this book a sacred book. Never forget that.

My special pleasure in these early pages was to find that I thought about Pater twenty years ago as I think about him now, and shall certainly think of him till time everlasting, world without end. I have been accused of changing my likes and dislikes—no one has changed less than I, and this book is proof of my fidelity to my first ideas; the ideas I have followed all my life are in this book—dear crescent moon rising in the south-east above the trees at the end of the village green. It was in that ugly but well-beloved village on the south coast I discovered my love of Protestant England. It was on the downs that the instinct of Protestantism lit up in me.

But when Zola asked me why I preferred Protestantism to Roman Catholicism I could not answer him.

He had promised to write a preface for the French translation of the "Mummer's Wife"; the translation had to be revised, months and months passed away, and forgetting all about the "Mummer's Wife," I expressed my opinion about Zola, which had been changing, a little too fearlessly, and in view of my revolt he was obliged to break his promise to write a Preface, and this must have been a great blow, for he was a man of method, to whom any change of plan was disagreeable and unnerving. He sent a letter, asking me to come to Médan, he would talk to me about the "Confessions." Well do I remember going there with dear Alexis in the May-time, the young corn six inches high in the fields, and my delight in the lush luxuriance of the l'Oise. That dear morning is remembered, and the poor master who reproved me a little sententiously, is dead. He was sorrowful in that dreadful room of his, fixed up with stained glass and morbid antiquities. He lay on a sofa lecturing me till breakfast. Then I thought reproof was over, but after a walk in the garden we went upstairs and he began again, saying he was not angry. "It is the law of nature," he said, "for children to devour their parents. I do not complain." I think he was aware he was playing a part; his sofa was his stage; and he lay there theatrical as Leo XI or Beerbohm Tree, saying that the Roman Church was an artistic church, that its rich externality and ceremonial were pagan. But I think he knew even then, at the back of his mind, that I was right; that is why he pressed me to give reasons for my preference. Zola came to hate Catholicism as much as I, and his hatred was for the same reason as mine; we both learnt that any religion which robs a man of the right of free-will and private judgment degrades the soul, renders it lethargic and timid, takes the edge off the intellect. Zola lived to write "that the Catholic countries are dead, and the clergy are the worms in the corpses." The observation is "quelconque"; I should prefer the more interesting allegation that since the Reformation no born Catholic has written a book of literary value! He would have had to concede that some converts have written well; the convert still retains a little of his ancient freedom, some of the intellectual virility he acquired elsewhere, but the born Catholic is still-born. But however we may disapprove of Catholicism, we can still admire the convert. Cardinal Manning was aware of the advantages of a Protestant bringing up, and he often said that he was glad he had been born a Protestant. His Eminence was, therefore, of opinion that the Catholic faith should be reserved, and exclusively, for converts, and in this he showed his practical sense, for it is easy to imagine a country prosperous in which all the inhabitants should be brought up Protestants or agnostics, and in which conversions to Rome are only permitted after a certain age or in clearly defined circumstances. There would be something beyond mere practical wisdom in such law-giving, an exquisite sense of the pathos of human life and its requirements; scapulars, indulgences and sacraments are needed by the weak and the ageing, sacraments especially. "They make you believe but they stupefy you;" these words are Pascal's, the great light of the Catholic Church.

III

My Protestant sympathies go back very far, further back than these Confessions; I find them in a French sonnet, crude and diffuse in versification, of the kind which finds favour with the very young, a sonnet which I should not publish did it not remind me of two things especially dear to me, my love of France and Protestantism.

> Je t'apporte mon drame, o poète sublime,
> Ainsi qu'un écolier au maître sa leçon:
> Ce livre avec fierté porte comme écusson
> Le sceau qu'en nos esprits ta jeune gloire imprime.
>
> Accepte, tu verras la foi mélée au crime,
> Se souiller dans le sang sacré de la raison,
> Quand surgit, redémpteur du vieux peuple saxon,
> Luther à Wittemberg comme Christ à Solime.
>
> Jamais de la cité le mal entier ne fuit,
> Hèlas! et son autel y fume dans la nuit;
> Mais notre âge a ceci de pareil à l'aurore.
>
> Que c'est un divin cri du chanteur éternal,
> Le tien, qui pour forcer le jour tardif d'éclore
> Déchire avec splendeur le voile épars du ciel.

I find not only my Protestant sympathies in the "Confessions" but a proud agnosticism, and an exalted individualism which in certain passages leads the reader to the sundered rocks about the cave of Zarathoustra. My book was written before I heard that splendid name, before Zarathoustra was written; and the doctrine, though hardly formulated, is in the "Confessions," as Darwin is in Wallace. Here ye shall find me, the germs of all I have written are in the "Confessions," "Esther Waters" and "Modern Painting," my love of France—the country as Pater would say of my instinctive election—and all my prophecies. Manet, Degas, Whistler, Monet, Pissarro, all these have come into their inheritance. Those whom I brushed aside, where are they? Stevenson, so well described as the best-dressed young man that ever walked in the Burlington Arcade, has slipped into nothingness despite the journalists and Mr Sidney Colvin's batch of letters. Poor Colvin, he made a mistake, he should have hopped on to Pater.

Were it not for a silly phrase about George Eliot, who surely was no more than one of those dull clever people, unlit by any ray of genius, I might say with Swinburne I have nothing to regret, nothing to withdraw. Maybe a few flippant remarks about my private friends; but to withdraw them would be unmanly, unintellectual, and no one may re-write his confessions.

A moment ago I wrote I have nothing to regret except a silly phrase about George Eliot. I was mistaken, there is this preface. If one has succeeded in explaining oneself in a book a preface is unnecessary, and if one has failed to explain oneself in the book, it is still more unnecessary to explain oneself in a preface.

GEORGE MOORE

1917 AMERICAN EDITION

If I say that the end of the Nineteenth Century cannot brag of a more original book than "The Confessions of a Young Man," I shall be deemed boastful and arrogant, but if the reader doesn't lay the book aside, he will probably discover me to be a man who would speak truthfully on all occasions, even about his own writings, a subject which lends itself to the exposition of a great deal of hypocrisy and insincerity, vices peculiarly disagreeable to me, and which I would avoid in the preface as I have avoided them in the book. Therefore, I relate that the adjec-

tives that came up in my mind on looking through these Confessions
were "original" and "incomplete." No one will object to my applying
the word "incomplete" to my own book, but the word "original," how
is that to be justified? By a simple statement that the book owes its
originality to the circumstances out of which it came rather than from
any special talent in the writer. Gaiety, liveliness in plenty . . . talent?
I am not sure that the word "talent" is applicable to these Confessions.

At the time of writing them I knew nothing of Jean Jacques Rousseau.
It is barely credible that I could have lived into early manhood without
having heard of him, but "The Confessions of a Young Man" testifies
that I never read him; a page of Jean Jacques would have made the book
I am prefacing an impossibility; another book more complete but less
original might have been written. I wrote without a model; Jean
Jacques, too, wrote without a model, but he wrote at the end of his life,
between sixty and sixty-five. His book is life seen in long mysterious
perspectives, whereas mine is merely the evanescent haze by the edge of
the wood, the enchantment of a May morning. Youth goes forth singing;
the song is often crude and superficial; youth cannot be other than
superficial; but the book babbles spontaneously and truthfully, and this
is why Pater liked it and why it drew from him the letter that I print.

BRASENOSE COLLEGE, Mar. 4.

MY DEAR, AUDACIOUS MOORE.—Many thanks for the "Confessions," which
I have read with great interest and admiration for your originality—your
delightful criticisms—your Aristophanic joy, or at least enjoyment, in life—
your unfailing liveliness. Of course, there are many things in the book I
don't agree with. But then, in the case of so satiric a book, I suppose one
is hardly expected to agree or disagree. What I cannot doubt is the literary
faculty displayed. "Thou com'st in such a questionable shape!" I feel inclined to say on finishing your book; "shape" morally, I mean; not in
reference to style.

You speak of my own work very pleasantly; but my enjoyment has
been independent of that. And still I wonder how much you may be losing, both for yourself and for your writings, by what, in spite of its gaiety
and good-nature and genuine sense of the beauty of many things, I must
still call a cynical, and therefore exclusive, way of looking at the world.
You call it "realistic." Still!

With sincere wishes for the future success of your most entertaining pen,

Very sincerely yours,

WALTER PATER.

A delightful letter, but Pater could not do else than write "almost" delightfully. Delightful is his word, perhaps, more than any other. It reveals him; and I would continue the revelation with other letters if I had managed to preserve them. His invitations to dinner, had I kept them, would have enabled me to reveal him still more plainly, and in the light that it pleases me to place him before the reader as one that held himself forbidden to put pen to paper without getting some of his art on to the paper though the subject matter was merely: "Will you dine with me, Thursday?" We have lost a great artist in Pater, for he could do this without suspicion of that priggishness which begins as soon as the artist lays his mind to the consideration of means rather than of ends: Pater always held the end in view; and his rule of life never to separate himself wholly from his art came out of an instinct; his art was to him what the nest is to the sitting bird; were he to remain away for long, he might find the nest disarrayed or himself might be changed. The sights and sounds of the outer world might have rendered his own original aim less desirable—to raise literature to the condition of music. To do other things and not to have achieved this would have been, in his view, to have done nothing, and to do this, I repeat, he felt that he must never separate himself wholly from his art. He was, therefore, always at composition: comma, semicolon, colon, dash, note of exclamation and interrogation always before his eyes. But Pater was also the most courteous of men and as he would not have us think that he was composing whilst in our midst, he trained his face to wear a formal impassive expression behind which he could pursue his rhythms undisturbed. Pater's mask was the subject of many a debate as we turned out of Earl's Terrace into the High Street, but I doubt if anybody ever avouched the true reason for Pater's reservations of himself. We noticed, however, that he did not care for his disciples to accost him when he was out walking; a rapid sign of recognition was enough, and he hastened away, composing his slowly moving rhythms. We guessed that he was composing but the natural conclusion that his rule of life was never to separate himself wholly from his art escaped us. . . . Now it all comes back to me. I can see Pater at André Raffalowich's dinner table, two very full blown roses on either side of him, composing always. I doubt if he ever ceased composing except when he was asleep.

From talk of Pater I drag myself with almost the same difficulty as I drag myself from talk of Manet, both having such deep roots in my mind; but perforce I must abandon Pater now for the "Confessions of a Young Man." The book is a sort of genesis; the seed of everything I have written since will be found herein. A friend once said to me, "you always had 'Esther Waters' in your mind"; and when I asked him what he meant, he said, "well, she is in the 'Confessions of a Young Man.'" And for some time his meaning eluded me; then I understood that the servant girl, Emma, must have given rise to the story. It is also a book that may be described as a declaration of ideas and tastes, my love of the best things in modern literature and my love of the best things in modern painting, and my whilom weakness for subtle passionate women. The one that writes a letter describing the sale of my furniture in the Rue de la Tour des Dames is an example. She, a ray of erotism, falls across the pages but to disappear a moment afterwards, the book being more concerned with art than with the relaxations of the artist; and I am pleased to find that my tastes are today what they were in the early eighties.

The first eulogies written in England, I might almost say in any language, of Manet, Degas, Whistler, Monet, Pissarro, are in this book of Confessions, and whosoever reads will find himself unable to deny that time has splendidly vindicated all of them.

To the present edition I have added some French poems, but the reader will not think that because I have done this I attach any literary importance to these trifles; I know that any writing done in a foreign language is worthless, but the poems were written in or about the time of the Confessions; they belong to that period. In the sonnet I dedicate "Martin Luther," a drama, to Swinburne, and it is remarkable for a mistake in French that Mallarmé detected at once which no one else has been able to discover, though it has been submitted to many poets. I have also added a third translation from Mallarmé, the original edition containing translations of two prose poems, but there are three; the third was omitted through laziness, I suppose, or it may be it did not please me as much as the first two. It seems to me now singularly beautiful even in the translation, and I think readers will probably thank me for having included it.

A third addition is some verses inspired by Rubens' picture of a second wife, Helen Fromont, and the fourth is a ballade in the manner of Master François Villon, somewhat weak in versification and containing, I think, a fault in prosody, the counting of "louis" as one syllable; it surely should have been counted as two. This mistake in versification has been corrected on the proof and the ballade is now free from false prosody unless it be deemed false prosody to neglect the hemistich in verses of ten syllables; in verses of twelve (the real French line), the hemistich has been abolished as antiquated ever since Banville wrote the famous line, *"Elle filait pensivement la blanche laine,"* and Richepin imitated it, *"Elle tirait nonchalamment les bas de soie."* It is, however, for the subject rather than for the versification that I print this ballade of old time; for I would tell how, at the end of the seventies, we who spent our evenings in the Nouvelle Athènes used to look to the brothel for our literary inspirations. Every age has its favourite subject. Byron and Shelley looked to incest for theirs, and the brothel that had been neglected by poets since Villon wrote his celebrated ballade, *La Grosse Margot*, began to show aloft again, on the lower slopes, perhaps; but still it was on the slopes of Parnassus that Richepin wrote *Les Chansons des Gueux*; Maupassant came later with his *La Maison Tellier*. My old friend, Paul Alexis, contributed something and my ballade is the last example of a literature about which professors of literature like to write, or rather to which they like to allude, never failing to add, "now happily extinct."

THE TEXT

CONFESSIONS OF A YOUNG MAN

M y soul, so far as I understand it, has very kindly taken colour and form from the many various modes of life that self-will and an impetuous temperament have forced me to indulge in. Therefore I may say that I am free from original qualities, defects, tastes, etc. What I have I acquire, or, to speak more exactly, chance bestowed, and still bestows, upon me. I came into the world apparently with a nature like a smooth sheet of wax, bearing no impress, but capable of receiving any; of being moulded into all shapes. Nor am I exaggerating when I say I think that I might equally have been a Pharaoh, an ostler, a pimp, an archbishop, and that in the fulfilment of the duties of each a certain measure of success would have been mine. I have felt the goad of many impulses, I have hunted many a trail; when one scent failed another was taken up, and pursued with the pertinacity of an instinct, rather than the fervour of a reasoned conviction. Sometimes, it is true, there came moments of weariness, of despondency, but they were not enduring: a word spoken, a book read, or yielding to the attraction of environment, I was soon off in another direction, forgetful of past failures. Intricate, indeed, was the labyrinth of my desires; all lights were followed with the same ardour, all cries were eagerly responded to: they came from the right, they came from the left, from every side. But one cry was more persistent, and as the years passed I learned to follow it with increasing vigour, and my strayings grew fewer and the way wider.

I was eleven years old when I first heard and obeyed this cry, or, shall I say, echo-augury?[1]

Scene: A great family coach, drawn by two powerful country horses, lumbers along a narrow Irish road. The ever recurrent signs—long ranges of blue mountains, the streak of bog, the rotting cabin, the flock of plover rising from the desolate water. Inside the coach there are two children. They are smart, with new jackets and neckties; their faces are pale with sleep, and the rolling of the coach makes them feel a little sick. It is seven o'clock in the morning. Opposite the children are their parents, and they are talking of a novel the world is reading. Did Lady Audley murder her husband? Lady Audley! What a beautiful name; and she, who is a slender, pale, fairy-like woman, killed her husband. Such thoughts flash through the boy's mind; his imagination is stirred and quickened, and he begs for an explanation. The coach lumbers along, it arrives at its destination, and Lady Audley is forgotten in the delight of tearing down fruit trees and killing a cat.

But when we returned home I took the first opportunity of stealing the novel in question. I read it eagerly, passionately, vehemently. I read its successor and its successor. I read until I came to a book called "The Doctor's Wife"—a lady who loved Shelley and Byron. There was magic, there was revelation in the name, and Shelley became my soul's divinity. Why did I love Shelley? Why was I not attracted to Byron? I cannot say. Shelley! Oh, that crystal name, and his poetry also crystalline. I must see it, I must know him. Escaping from the schoolroom, I ransacked the library, and at last my ardour was rewarded. The book—a small pocket edition in red boards, no doubt long out of print—opened at the "Sensitive Plant." Was I disappointed? I think I had expected to understand better; but I had no difficulty in assuming that I was satisfied and delighted. And henceforth the little volume never left my pocket, and I read the dazzling stanzas by the shores of a pale green Irish lake, comprehending little, and loving a great deal. Byron, too, was often with me, and these poets were the ripening influence of years otherwise merely nervous and boisterous.

And my poets were taken to school, because it pleased me to read "Queen Mab" and "Cain," amid the priests and ignorance of a hateful Roman Catholic college. And there my poets saved me from intellectual savagery; for I was incapable at that time of learning anything. What determined and incorrigible idleness! I used to gaze fondly on a book, holding my head between my hands, and allow my thoughts to wander far into dreams and thin imaginings. Neither Latin, nor Greek, nor

French, nor History, nor English composition could I learn, unless, indeed, my curiosity or personal interest was excited,—then I made rapid strides in that branch of knowledge to which my attention was directed. A mind hitherto dark seemed suddenly to grow clear, and it remained clear and bright enough so long as passion was in me; but as it died, so the mind clouded, and recoiled to its original obtuseness. Couldn't, with wouldn't, was in my case curiously involved; nor have I in this respect ever been able to correct my natural temperament. I have always remained powerless to do anything unless moved by a powerful desire.[2]

The natural end to such schooldays as mine was expulsion. I was expelled when I was sixteen, for idleness and general worthlessness.[3] I returned to a wild country home, where I found my father engaged in training racehorses. For a nature of such intense vitality as mine, an ambition, an aspiration of some sort was necessary; and I now, as I have often done since, accepted the first ideal to hand. In this instance it was the *stable*. I was given a hunter, I rode to hounds every week, I rode gallops every morning, I read the racing calendar, stud-book, latest betting, and looked forward with enthusiasm to the day when I should be known as a successful steeplechase rider. To ride the winner of the Liverpool seemed to me a final achievement and glory; and had not accident intervened, it is very possible that I might have succeeded in carrying off, if not the meditated honour, something scarcely inferior, such as—alas, *eheu fugaces*! I cannot now recall the name of a race of the necessary value and importance. About this time my father was elected Member of Parliament; our home was broken up, and we went to London.[4] But an ideal set up on its pedestal is not easily displaced, and I persevered in my love, despite the poor promises London life held out for its ultimate attainment; and surreptitiously I continued to nourish it with small bets made in a small tobacconist's. Well do I remember that shop, the oily-faced, sandy-whiskered proprietor, his betting-book, the cheap cigars along the counter, the one-eyed nondescript who leaned his evening away against the counter, and was supposed to know some one who knew Lord ———'s footman, and the great man often spoken of, but rarely seen—he who made "a two-'undred pound book on the Derby"; and the constant coming and going of the cabmen—"Half an ounce of shag, sir." I was then at a military tutor's in the Euston Road; for, in answer to my father's demand as to what occupation I intended to pursue, I had consented to enter the army. In my heart I knew that when it came to the point I should refuse—the idea of military discipline was very repugnant, and the possibility of an anonymous death on a battle-field could not be accepted by so self-conscious a youth, by one so full of his own personality. I said Yes to my father, because the moral courage to say No was lacking, and I put my trust in the future, as well I might, for a fair prospect of idleness lay before me, and the chance of my passing any examination was, indeed, remote.

In London I made the acquaintance of a great blond man, who talked incessantly about beautiful women, and painted them sometimes larger than life, in somnolent attitudes, and luxurious tints.[5] His studio was a welcome contrast to the spitting and betting of the tobacco shop. His pictures—Doré-like improvisations, devoid of skill, and, indeed, of artistic perception, save a certain sentiment for the grand and noble—filled me with wonderment and awe. "How jolly it would be to be a painter," I once said, quite involuntarily. "Why, would you like to be a painter?" he asked abruptly. I laughed, not suspecting that I had the slightest gift, as indeed was the case, but the idea remained in my mind, and soon after I began to make sketches in the streets and theatres. My attempts were not very successful, but they encouraged me to tell my father that I would go to the military tutor no more, and he allowed me to enter the Kensington Museum as an Art student. There, of course, I learned nothing, and, from a merely Art point of view, I had much better have continued my sketches in the streets; but the museum was a beautiful and beneficent influence, and one that applied marvellously well to the besetting danger of the moment; for in the galleries I met young men who spoke of other things than betting and steeplechase riding, who, I remember, it was clear to me then, looked to a higher ideal than mine, breathed a purer atmosphere of thought than I. And then the sweet, white peace of antiquity! The great, calm gaze that is not sadness nor joy, but something that we know not of, which is lost to the world for ever.

"But if you want to be a painter you must go to France—France is the only school of Art." I must again call attention to the phenomenon of echo-augury, that is to say, words heard in an unlooked-for quarter, that, without an appeal to our reason, impel belief. France! The word rang in my ears and gleamed in my eyes. France! All my senses sprang from sleep like a crew when the man on the look-out cries, "Land ahead!" Instantly I knew I should, that I must, go to France, that I would live there, that I would become as a Frenchman. I knew not when nor how, but I knew I should go to France. . . .

⁋ Then my father died, and I suddenly found myself heir to considerable property—some three or four thousands a year; and then I knew that I was free to enjoy life as I pleased; no ⁋ further trammels, no further need of being a soldier, of being anything but myself; eighteen, with life and France before me![6] But the spirit did not move me yet to leave home. I would feel the pulse of life at home before I felt it abroad. I would hire a studio. A studio—tapestries, smoke, models, conversations.[7] But here it is difficult not to convey a false impression. I fain would show my soul in these pages, like a face in a pool of clear water; and although my studio was in truth no more than an amusement, and a means of effectually throwing over all restraint, I did not view it at all in this light. My love of Art was very genuine and deep-rooted; the tobacconist's betting-book was now as nothing, and a certain Botticelli in the National Gallery held me in tether. And when I look back and consider the past, I am forced to admit that I might have grown up in less fortunate circumstances, for even the studio, with its dissipations— and they were many—was not unserviceable; it developed the natural man, who educates himself, who allows his mind to grow and ripen under the sun and wind of modern life, in contradistinction to the University man, who is fed upon the dust of ages, and after a formula which has been composed to suit the requirements of the average human being.

Nor was my reading at this time so limited as might be expected from the foregoing. The study of Shelley's poetry had led me to read pretty nearly all the English lyric poets; Shelley's atheism had led me to read Kant, Spinoza, Godwin, Darwin, and ⁋ Mill; and these, again, in their turn, introduced me to many writers and various literature. I do not think that at this time I cared much for novel reading. ⁋ [8] Scott seemed to me on a par with Burke's speeches; that is to say, too impersonal for my very personal taste. Dickens I knew by heart, and "Bleak House" I thought his greatest achievement. Thackeray left no deep impression on my mind; in no way did he hold my thoughts. He was not picturesque like Dickens, and I was at that time curiously eager for some adequate philosophy of life, and his social satire seemed very small beer indeed. I was really young. I hungered after great truths: "Middlemarch," "Adam Bede," "The Rise and Fall of Rationalism," "The History of Civilisation," were momentous events in my life. But I loved life better than books, and I cultivated with care the acquaintance of a neighbour who had taken the Globe Theatre for the purpose of producing Offenbach's operas.[9] Bouquets, stalls, rings, delighted me. I was not dissipated, but I loved the abnormal. I loved to spend as much on scent and toilette knick-knacks as would keep a poor man's family in affluence for ten months; and I smiled at the fashionable sunlight in the Park, the dusty cavalcades; and I loved to shock my friends by bowing to those whom I should not bow to; above all, the life of the theatres, that life of raw gaslight, whitewashed walls, of light, doggerel verse, slangy polkas and waltzes, interested me beyond legitimate measure, so curious and unreal did it seem. I lived at home, but dined daily at a fashionable restaurant; at half-past eight I was at the theatre. Nodding familiarly to the doorkeeper, I passed up the long passage to the stage. Afterwards supper. Cremorne and the Argyle Rooms were my favourite haunts. My mother suffered, and expected ruin, for I took no trouble to conceal anything; I boasted of dissipations. But there was no need for fear; I was naturally endowed with a very clear sense indeed of self-preservation; I neither betted nor drank, nor contracted debts, nor a secret marriage; from a worldly point of view, I was a model young man indeed; and when I returned home about four in the morning, I watched the pale moon setting, and repeating some verses of Shelley, I thought how I should go to Paris when I was of age, and study painting.

At last the day came, and with several trunks and boxes full of clothes, books, and pictures, I started, accompanied by an English valet, for Paris and Art.[1]

We all know the great grey and melancholy Gare du Nord, at half-past six in the morning; and the miserable carriages, and the tall, haggard city. Pale, sloppy, yellow houses; an oppressive absence of colour; a peculiar bleakness in the streets. The *ménagère* hurries down the asphalte to market; a dreadful *garçon de café*, with a napkin tied round his throat, moves about some chairs, so decrepit and so solitary that it seems impossible to imagine a human being sitting there. Where are the Boulevards? where are the Champs Elysées? I asked myself; and feeling bound to apologise for the appearance of the city, I explained to my valet that we were passing through some by-streets, and returned to the study of a French vocabulary. Nevertheless, when the time came to formulate a demand for rooms, hot water, and a fire, I broke down, and the proprietress of the hotel, who spoke English, had to be sent for.

My plans, so far as I had any, were to enter the beaux arts— Cabanel's studio for preference; for I had then an intense and profound admiration for that painter's work. I did not think much of the application I was told I should have to make at the Embassy; my thoughts were fixed on the master, and my one desire was to see him. To see him was easy, to speak to him was another matter, and I had to wait three weeks, until I could hold a conversation in French. How I achieved this feat I cannot say. I never opened a book, I know, nor is it agreeable to think what my language must have been like—like nothing ever heard under God's sky before, probably. It was, however, sufficient to waste a good hour of the painter's time. I told him of my artistic sympathies, what pictures I had seen of his in London, and how much pleased I was with those then in his studio. He went through the ordeal without flinching. He said he would be glad to have me as a pupil. . . .

But life in the beaux arts is rough, coarse, and rowdy. The ❡ model sits only three times a week; the other days we worked from the plaster cast; and to be there by seven o'clock in the morning required so painful an effort of will, that I glanced in terror down the dim and grey perspective of early risings that awaited me; then, demoralised by the lassitude of Sunday, I told my valet on Monday morning to leave the room, that I would return to the beaux arts no more. I felt humiliated at my own weakness, for much hope had been centred in that academy; and I knew no other. Day after day I walked up and down the Boulevards, studying the photographs of the *salon* pictures, ❡ and ❡ was stricken by the art of Jules Lefebvre. True it is that I saw it was wanting in that tender grace which I am forced to admit even now, saturated though I now am with the aesthetics of different schools, is inherent in Cabanel's work; but at the time I am writing of, my nature was too young and mobile to resist the conventional attractiveness of nude figures, indolent attitudes, long hair, slender hips and hands, and I accepted Jules Lefebvre wholly and unconditionally. He hesitated, however, when I asked to be taken as a private pupil, but he wrote out the address of a studio where he gave instruction every Tuesday morning.[2] This was even more to my taste, for I had an instinctive liking for Frenchmen, and was anxious to see as much of them as possible.

The studio was perched high up in the Passage des Panoramas. There I found M. Julien, a typical meridional—the large stomach, the dark eyes, crafty and watchful; the seductively mendacious manner, the sensual mind. We made friends at once—he consciously making use of me, I unconsciously making use of him. To him my forty francs, a month's subscription, were a godsend, nor were my invitations to dinner and to the theatre to be disdained. I was curious, odd, quaint. To be sure, it was a little tiresome to have to put up with a talkative person, whose knowledge of the French language had been acquired in three months, but the dinners were good. No doubt Julien reasoned so; I did not reason at all. I felt this crafty, clever man of the world was necessary to me. I had never met such a man before, and all my curiosity was awake. He spoke of art and literature, of the world and the flesh; he told me of the books he had read, he narrated thrilling incidents in his own life; and the moral reflections with which he sprinkled his conversation I thought very striking. Like every young man of twenty, I was on the look-out for something to set up that would do duty for an ideal. The world was to me, at this time, what a toy shop had been fifteen years before: everything was spick and span, and every illusion was set out straight and smart in new paint and gilding. But Julien kept me at a distance, and the rare occasions when he favoured me with his society only served to prepare my mind for the friendship which awaited me, and which was destined to absorb some years of my life.

In the studio there were some eighteen or twenty young men, and among these there were some four or five from whom I could learn; and there were also some eight or nine young English girls. We sat round in a circle, and drew from the model. And this reversal of all the world's opinions and prejudices was to me singularly delightful; I loved the sense of unreality that the exceptionalness of our life in this studio conveyed. Besides, the women themselves were young and interesting, and were, therefore, one of the charms of the place, giving, as they did, that sense of sex which is so subtle a mental pleasure, and which is, in its outward aspect, so interesting to the eye—the gowns, the hair lifted, showing the neck; the earrings, the sleeves open at the elbow. Though all this was very dear to me I did not fall in love: but he who escapes a woman's dominion generally comes under the sway of some friend who ever uses a strange attractiveness, and fosters a sort of dependency that is not healthful or valid: and although I look back with undiminished delight on the friendship I contracted about this time—a friendship which permeated and added to my life—I am nevertheless forced to recognise that, however suitable it may have been in my special case, in the majority of instances it would have proved but a shipwrecking reef, on which a young man's life would have gone to pieces. What saved me was the intensity of my passion for Art, and a moral revolt against any action that I thought could or would definitely compromise me in that direction. I was willing to stray a little from my path, but never further than a single step, which I could retrace when I pleased.

One day I raised my eyes, and saw there was a new-comer in the studio; and, to my surprise, for he was fashionably dressed, and my experience had not led me to believe in the marriage of genius and well-cut cloth, he was painting very well indeed. His shoulders were beautiful and broad; a long neck, a tiny head, a narrow, thin face, and large eyes, full of intelligence and fascination. And although he could not have been working more than an hour, he had already sketched in his figure, and with all the surroundings—screens, lamps, stoves, etc. I was deeply interested. I asked the young lady next me if she knew who he was. She could give me no information. But at four o'clock there was a general exodus from the studio, and we adjourned to a neighbouring *café* to drink beer. The way led through a narrow passage, and as we stooped under an archway, the young man (Marshall was his name) spoke to me in English.[3] Yes, we had met before; we had exchanged a few words in So-and-So's studio—the great blond man, whose Doré-like improvisations had awakened aspiration in me.

The usual reflections on the chances of life were of course made, and then followed the inevitable "Will you dine with me to-night?" Marshall thought the following day would suit him better, but I was very pressing. He offered to meet me at my hotel; or would I come with him to his rooms, and he would show me some pictures—some trifles he had brought up from the country? Nothing would please me better. We got into a cab. Then every moment revealed new qualities, new superiorities, in my new-found friend. Not only was he tall, strong, handsome, and beautifully dressed, infinitely better dressed than I, but he could talk French like a native. It was only natural that he should, for he was born and had lived in Brussels all his life, but the accident of birth rather stimulated than calmed my erubescent admiration. He spoke of, and he was clearly on familiar terms with, the fashionable restaurants and actresses; he stopped at a hairdresser's to have his hair curled. All this was very exciting, and a little bewildering. I was on the tiptoe of expectation to see his apartments; and, not to be utterly outdone, I alluded to my valet.

His apartments were not so grand as I expected; but when he explained that he had just spent ten thousand pounds in two years, and was now living on six or seven hundred francs a month, which his mother would allow him until he had painted and had sold a certain series of pictures, which he contemplated beginning at once, my admiration increased to wonder, and I examined with awe the great fireplace which had been constructed at his orders, and admired the iron pot which hung by a chain above an artificial bivouac fire. This detail will suggest the rest of the studio—the Turkey carpet, the brass harem lamps, the Japanese screen, the pieces of drapery, the oak chairs covered with red Utrecht velvet, the oak wardrobe that had been picked up somewhere,—a ridiculous bargain, and the inevitable bed with spiral columns. There were vases filled with foreign grasses, and palms stood in the corners of the rooms. Marshall pulled out a few pictures; but he paid very little heed to my compliments; and, sitting down at the piano, with a great deal of splashing and dashing about the keys, he rattled off a waltz.

"What waltz is that?" I asked.

"Oh, nothing; something I composed the other evening. I had a fit of the blues, and didn't go out. What do you think of it?"

"I think it beautiful; did you really compose that the other evening?"

At this moment a knock was heard at the door, and a beautiful English girl entered. Marshall introduced me. With looks that see nothing, and words that mean nothing, an amorous woman receives the man she finds with her sweetheart. But it subsequently transpired that Alice had an appointment, that she was dining out. She would, however, call in the morning, and give him a sitting for the portrait he was painting of her.

I had hitherto worked very regularly and attentively at the studio, but now Marshall's society was an attraction I could not resist. For the sake of his talent, which I religiously believed in, I regretted he was so idle; but his dissipation was winning, and his delight was thorough, and his gay, dashing manner made me feel happy, and his experience opened to me new avenues of enjoyment and knowledge of life. On my arrival in Paris I had visited, in the company of my taciturn valet, the Mabille and the Valentino, and I had dined at the Maison d'Or by myself; but now I was taken to strange students' *cafés*, where dinners were paid for in pictures; to a mysterious place, where a *table d'hôte* was held under a tent in a back garden; and afterwards we went in great crowds to *Bullier*, the *Château Rouge*, or the *Elysée Montmartre*. ⁋ The clangour of the band, the unreal greenness of the foliage, the thronging of the dancers, and the chattering of women, whose Christian names we only knew. And then the returning in open carriages rolling through the white dust beneath the immense heavy dome of the summer night, when the dusty darkness of the street is chequered by a passing glimpse of light skirt or flying feather, and the moon looms like a magic lantern out of the sky. ⁋

Now we seemed to live in fiacres and restaurants, and the afternoons were filled with febrile impressions. Marshall had a friend in this street, and another in that. It was only necessary for him to cry "Stop" to the coachman, and to run up two or three flights of stairs. . . .

"*Madame* ———, *est-elle chez elle?*"

"*Oui, Monsieur; si Monsieur veut se donner la peine d'entrer.*" And we were shown into a handsomely furnished apartment. A lady would enter hurriedly, and an animated discussion was begun. I did not know French sufficiently well to follow the conversation, but I remember it always commenced *mon cher ami*, and was plentifully sprinkled with the phrase *vous avez tort*. The ladies themselves had only just returned from Constantinople or Japan, and they were generally involved in mysterious lawsuits, or were busily engaged in prosecuting claims for several millions of francs against different foreign governments.

And just as I had watched the chorus girls and mummers, three years ago, at the Globe Theatre, now, excited by a nervous curiosity, I watched this world of Parisian adventures and lights o' love. And this craving for observation of manners, this instinct for the rapid notation of gestures and words that epitomise a state of feeling, of attitudes that mirror forth the soul, declared itself a main passion; and it grew and strengthened, to the detriment of the other Art still so dear to me. With the patience of a cat before a mouse-hole, I watched and listened, picking one characteristic phrase out of hours of vain chatter, interested and amused by an angry or loving glance. Like the midges that fret the surface of a shadowy stream, these men and women seemed to me; and though I laughed, danced, and made merry with them, I was not of them. But with Marshall it was different: they were my amusement, they were his necessary pleasure. And I knew of this distinction that made twain our lives; and I reflected deeply upon it. Why could I not live without an ever-present and acute consciousness of life? Why could I not love, forgetful of the harsh ticking of the clock in the perfumed silence of the chamber?[4]

And so my friend became to me a study, a subject for dissection. The general attitude of his mind and its various turns, all the apparent contradictions, and how they could be explained, classified, and reduced to one primary law, were to me a constant source of thought. Our confidences knew no reserve. I say our confidences, because to obtain confidences it is often necessary to confide. All we saw, heard, read, or felt was the subject of mutual confidences: the transitory emotion that a flush of colour and a bit of perspective awakens, the blue tints that the sunsetting lends to a white dress, or the eternal verities, death and love. But, although I tested every fibre of thought and analysed every motive, I was very sincere in my friendship, and very loyal in my admiration. Nor did my admiration wane when I discovered that Marshall was shallow in his appreciations, superficial in his judgments, that his talents did not pierce below the surface; *il avait si grand air;* there was fascination in his very bearing, in his large, soft, colourful eyes, and a go and dash in his dissipations that carried you away.

To any one observing us at this time it would have seemed that I was but a hanger-on, and a feeble imitator of Marshall. I took him to my tailor's, and he advised me on the cut of my coats; he showed me how to arrange my rooms, and I strove to copy his manner of speech and his general bearing; and yet I knew very well indeed that mine was a rarer and more original nature. I was willing to learn, that was all. There was much that Marshall could teach me, and I used him without shame, without stint. I used him as I have used all those with whom I have been brought into close contact. Search my memory as I will, I cannot recall a case of man or woman who ever occupied any considerable part of my thoughts and did not contribute largely towards my moral or physical welfare. In other words, and in very colloquial language, I never had useless friends hanging about me. From this crude statement of a signal fact, the thoughtless reader will at once judge me rapacious, egotistical, false, fawning, mendacious. Well, I may be all this and more, but not because all who have known me have rendered me eminent services. I can say that no one ever formed relationships in life with less design than myself. Never have I given a thought to the advantage that might accrue from being on terms of friendship with this man and avoiding that one. "Then how do you explain," cries the angry reader, "that you have never had a friend whom you did not make a profit out of? You must have had very few friends." On the contrary, I have had many friends, and of all sorts and kinds—men and women: and, I repeat, none took part in my life who did not contribute something towards my well-being. It must, of course, be understood that I make no distinction between mental and material help; and in my case the one has ever been adjuvant to the other. "Pooh, pooh!" again exclaims the reader; "I for one will not believe that chance has only sent across your way the people who were required to assist you." Chance! dear reader, is there such a thing as chance? Do you believe in chance? Do you attach any precise meaning to the word? Do you employ it at haphazard, allowing it to mean what it may? Chance! What a field for psychical investigation is at once opened up; how we may tear to shreds our past lives in search of—what? Of the Chance that made us. I think, reader, I can throw some light on the general question, by replying to your taunt: Chance, or the conditions of life under which we live, sent, of course thousands of creatures across my way who were powerless to benefit me; but then an instinct of which I knew nothing, of which I was not even conscious, withdrew me from them, and I was attracted to others. Have you not seen a horse suddenly leave a corner of a field to seek pasturage further away?

Never could I interest myself in a book if it were not the exact diet my mind required at the time, or in the very immediate future. The mind asked, received, and digested. So much was assimilated, so much expelled; then, after a season, similar demands were made, the same processes were repeated out of sight, below consciousness, as is the case in a well-ordered stomach. Shelley, who fired my youth with passion, and purified and upbore it for so long, is now to me as nothing: not a dead or faded thing, but a thing out of which I personally have drawn all the sustenance I may draw from him; and, therefore, it (that part which I did not absorb) concerns me no more. And the same with Gautier. Mdlle. de Maupin, that godhead of flowing line, that desire not "of the moth for the star," but for such perfection of hanging arm and leaned thigh as leaves passion breathless and fain of tears, is now, if I take up the book and read, weary and ragged as a spider's web, that has hung the winter through in the dusty, forgotten corner of a forgotten room. My old rapture and my youth's delight I can regain only when I think of that part of Gautier which is now incarnate in me.

As I picked up books, so I picked up my friends. I read friends and books with the same passion, with the same avidity; and as I discarded my books when I had assimilated as much of them as my system required, so I discarded my friends when they ceased to be of use to me. I use the word "use" in its fullest, not in its limited and twenty-shilling sense. This reduction of the intellect to the blind unconsciousness of the lower organs will strike some as a violation of man's best beliefs, and as saying very little for the particular intellect that can be so reduced. But I am not sure these people are right. I am inclined to think that as you ascend the scale of thought to the great minds, these unaccountable impulses, mysterious resolutions, sudden, but certain knowings, falling whence, or how it is impossible to say, but falling somehow into the brain, instead of growing rarer, become more and more frequent; indeed, I think that if the really great man were to confess to the working of his mind, we should see him constantly besieged by inspirations . . . inspirations! Ah! how human thought only turns in a circle, and how, when we think we are on the verge of a new thought, we slip into the enunciation of some time-worn truth. But I say again, let general principles be waived; it will suffice for the interest of these pages if it be understood that brain instincts have always been, and still are, the initial and the determining powers of my being.

*   *   *   *   *

But the studio, where I had been working for the last three or four months so diligently, became wearisome to me, and for two reasons. First, because it deprived me of many hours of Marshall's company. Secondly—and the second reason was the graver—because I was beginning to regard the delineation of a nymph, or youth bathing, etc., as a very narrow channel to carry off the strong, full tide of a man's thought. For now thoughts of love and death, and the hopelessness of life, were in active fermentation within me and sought for utterance with a strange unintermittingness of appeal. I yearned merely to give direct expression to my pain. Life was then in its springtide; every thought was new to me, and it would have seemed a pity to disguise even the simplest emotion in any garment when it was so beautiful in its Eden-like nakedness. The creatures whom I met in the ways and by ways of Parisian life, whose gestures and attitudes I devoured with my eyes, and whose souls I hungered to know, awoke in me a tense irresponsible curiosity, but that was all,—I despised, I hated them, thought them contemptible, and to select them as subjects of artistic treatment, could not then, might never, have occurred to me, had the suggestion to do so not come direct to me from the outside.

At the time I am writing I lived in an old-fashioned hotel on the Boulevard, which an enterprising Belgian had lately bought and was endeavouring to modernise; an old-fashioned hotel, that still clung to its ancient character in the presence of half a dozen old people, who, for antediluvian reasons, continue to dine on certain well-specified days at the *table d'hôte*. Fifteen years have passed away, and these old people, no doubt, have joined their ancestors; but I can see them still sitting in that *salle à manger*; the *buffets en vieux chêne*; the opulent candelabra *en style d'empire*; the waiter lighting the gas in the pale Parisian evening. That white-haired man, that tall, thin, hatchet-faced American, has dined at this *table d'hôte* for the last thirty years —he is still talkative, vain, foolish, and authoritative. The clean, neatly-dressed old gentleman who sits by him, looking so much like a French gentleman, has spent a great part of his life in Spain. With that piece of news, and its subsequent developments, your acquaintance with him begins and ends; the eyes, the fan, the mantilla, how it began, how it was broken off, and how it began again. Opposite sits another French gentleman, with beard and bristly hair. He spent twenty years of his life in India, and he talks of his son who has been out there for the last ten, and who has just returned home. There is the Italian comtesse of sixty summers, who dresses like a girl of sixteen and smokes a cigar after dinner—if there are not too many strangers in the room. She terms a stranger any one whom she has not seen at least once before. The little fat, neckless man, with the great bald head, fringed below the ears with hair, is M. Duval.[5] He is a dramatic author—the author of a hundred and sixty plays. He does not intrude himself on your notice, but when you speak to him on literary matters he fixes a pair of tiny, sloe-like eyes on you, and talks affably of his collaborateurs.

I was soon deeply interested in M. Duval, and I invited him to come to the *café* after dinner. I paid for his coffee and liqueurs, I offered him a choice cigar. He did not smoke; I did. It was, of course, inevitable that I should find out that he had not had a play produced for the last twenty years, but then the aureole of the hundred and sixty was about his poor bald head. I thought of the chances of life, he alluded to the war; and so this unpleasantness was passed over, and we entered on more genial subjects of conversation. He had written plays with everybody; his list of collaborateurs was longer than any list of lady patronesses for an English county ball; there was no literary kitchen in which he had not helped to dish up. I was at once amazed and delighted. Had M. Duval written his hundred and sixty plays in the seclusion of his own rooms, I should have been less surprised; it was the mystery of the *séances* of collaboration, the rendezvous, the discussion, the illustrious company, that overwhelmed me in a rapture of wonder and respectful admiration. Then came the anecdotes. They were of all sorts. Here are a few specimens: He, Duval, had written a one-act piece with Dumas *père*; it had been refused at the Français, and then it had been about, here, there, and everywhere; finally the *Variétés* had asked for some alterations, and *c'etait une affaire entendue.* "I made the alterations one afternoon, and wrote to Dumas, and what do you think,—by return of post I had a letter from him saying he could not consent to the production of a one-act piece, signed by him, at the *Variétés*, because his son was then giving a five-act piece at the Gymnase." Then came a string of indecent witticisms by Suzanne Lagier and Dejazet. They were as old as the world, but they were new to me, and I was amused and astonished. These *bon-mots* were followed by an account of how Gautier wrote his Sunday feuilleton, and how he and Balzac had once nearly come to blows. They had agreed to collaborate. Balzac was to contribute the scenario, Gautier the dialogue. One morning Balzac came with the scenario of the first act. "Here it is, Gautier! I suppose you can let me have it back finished by to-morrow afternoon?" And the old gentleman would chirp along in this fashion till midnight. I would then accompany him to his room in the

Quartier Montmartre—rooms high up on the fifth floor—where, between two pictures, supposed to be by Angelica Kauffmann, M. Duval had written unactable plays for the last twenty years, and where he would continue to write unactable plays until God called him to a world, perhaps, of eternal cantatas, but where, by all accounts, *l'exposition de la pièce selon la formule de M. Scribe* is still unknown.

How I used to enjoy these conversations! I remember how I used to stand on the pavement after having bid the old gentleman good-night, regretting I had not demanded some further explanation regarding *le mouvement Romantique*, or *la façon de M. Scribe de ménager la situation*.

Why not write a comedy? So the thought came. I had never written anything save a few ill-spelt letters; but no matter. To find a plot, that was the first thing to do. Take Marshall for hero and Alice for heroine, surround them with the old gentlemen who dined at the *table d'hôte*, flavour with the Italian countess who smoked cigars when there were not too many strangers present. After three weeks of industrious stirring, the ingredients did begin to simmer into something resembling a plot. Put it upon paper. Ah! there was my difficulty. I remembered suddenly that I had read "Cain," "Manfred," "The Cenci," as poems, without ever thinking of how the dialogue looked upon paper; besides, they were in blank verse. I hadn't a notion how prose dialogue would look upon paper. Shakespeare I had never opened; no instinctive want had urged me to read him. He had remained, therefore, unread, unlooked at. Should I buy a copy? No; the name repelled me—as all popular names repelled me. In preference I went to the Gymnase, and listened attentively to a comedy by M. Dumas *fils*. But strain my imagination as I would, I could not see the spoken words in their written form. Oh, for a look at the prompter's copy, the corner of which I could see when I leaned forward! At last I discovered in Galignani's library a copy of Leigh Hunt's edition of the old dramatists, and after a month's study of Congreve, Wycherley, Vanbrugh, and Farquhar, I completed a comedy in three acts, which I entitled "Worldliness." It was, of course, very bad; but, if my memory serves me well, I do not think it was nearly so bad as might be imagined.[6]

No sooner was the last scene written than I started at once for London, confident I should find no difficulty in getting my play produced.

¶ **I**s it necessary to say that I did not find a manager to produce my play? A printer was more attainable, and the correction of proofs amused me for a while. I wrote another play;[1] and when the hieing after theatrical managers began to lose its attractiveness my thoughts reverted to France, which always haunted me; and which now possessed me as if with the sweet and magnetic influence of home.[2]

How important my absence from Paris seemed to me; and how Paris rushed into my eyes!—Paris—public ball-rooms, *cafés*, the models in the studio and the young girls painting, and Marshall, Alice, and Julien. Marshall!—my thoughts pointed at him through the intervening streets and the endless procession of people coming and going. ¶

"M. Marshall, is he at home?" "M. Marshall left here some months ago." "Do you know his address?" "I'll ask my husband." "Do you know M. Marshall's address!" "Yes, he's gone to live in the Rue de Douai." "What number?" "I think it is fifty-four." "Thanks." "Coachman, wake up; drive me to the Rue de Douai."

But Marshall was not to be found at the Rue de Douai; and he had left no address. There was nothing for it but to go to the studio; I should be able to obtain news of him there,—perhaps find him. But when I pulled aside the curtain, the accustomed piece of slim nakedness did not greet my eyes; only the blue apron of an old woman enveloped in a cloud of dust. "The gentlemen are not here to-day, the studio is closed; I am sweeping up." "Oh, and where is M. Julien?" "I cannot say, sir: perhaps at the *café*, or perhaps he is gone to the country." This was not very encouraging, and now, my enthusiasm thoroughly damped, I strolled along *le Passage*, looking at the fans, the bangles and the litter of cheap trinkets that each window was filled with. On the left at the corner of the Boulevard was our *café*. As I came forward the waiter moved one of the tin tables, and then I saw the fat Provençal. But just as if he had seen me yesterday he said, *"Tiens! c'est vous; une demi-tasse? oui . . . garçon, une demi-tasse."* Presently the conversation turned on Marshall; they had not seen much of him lately. *"Il parait qu'il est plus amoureux que jamais,"* Julien replied sardonically.

I found my friend in large furnished apartments on the ground floor in the Rue Duphot. The walls were stretched with blue silk, there were large mirrors and great gilt cornices. Passing into the bedroom I found the young god wallowing in the finest of fine linen—in a great Louis XV. bed, and there were cupids above him. "Holloa! what, you back again, Dayne? we thought we weren't going to see you again."

"It's nearly one o'clock: get up. What's the news?"

"To-day is the opening of the exposition of the Impressionists.[3] We'll have a bit of breakfast round the corner, at Durant's, and we'll go on there. I hear that Bedlam is nothing to it; there is a canvas there twenty feet square and in three tints: pale yellow for the sunlight, brown for the shadows, and all the rest is sky-blue. There is, I am told, a lady walking in the foreground with a ring-tailed monkey, and the tail is said to be three yards long."

And so we went to jeer a group of enthusiasts that willingly forfeit all delights of the world in the hope of realising a new aestheticism; we went insolent with patent leather shoes and bright kid gloves and armed with all the jargon of the school. *"Cette jambe ne porte pas;" "la nature ne se fait pas comme ça;" "on dessine par les masses; combien de têtes?" "Sept et demi." "Si j'avais un morceau de craie je mettrais celle-là dans un bocal, c'est un foetus,"* etc.; in a word, all that the journals of culture are pleased to term an artistic education. And then the boisterous laughter, exaggerated in the hope of giving as much pain as possible.

The history of Impressionist art is simple. In the beginning of this century the tradition of French art—the tradition of Boucher, Fragonard, and Watteau—had been completely lost; having produced genius, their art died. Ingres is the sublime flower of the classic art which succeeded the art of the palace and the boudoir: further than Ingres it was impossible to go, and his art died. Then the Turners and Constables came to France, and they begot Troyon, and Troyon begot Millet, Courbet, Corot, and Rousseau, and these in turn begot Degas, Pissarro, Madame Morisot, and Guillaumin. Degas is a pupil of Ingres, but he applies the marvellous acuteness of drawing he learned from his master to delineating the humblest aspects of modern life. Degas draws not by the masses, but by the character;—his subjects are shop-girls, ballet-girls, and washerwomen, but the qualities that endow them with im-mortality are precisely those which eternalise the virgins and saints of Leonardo da Vinci in the minds of men. You see the fat, vulgar woman in the long cloak trying on a hat in front of the pier-glass. So marvellously well are the lines of her face observed and rendered that you can tell exactly what her position in life is; you know what the furniture of her rooms is like; you know what she would say to you if she were to speak. She is as typical of the nineteenth century as Fragonard's ladies are of the Court of Louis XV. To the right you see a picture of two shop-girls with bonnets in their hands. So accurately are the habitual movements of the heads and the hands observed that you at once realise the years of bonnet-showing and servile words that these women have lived through. We have seen Degas do this before— it is a welcome repetition of a familiar note, but it is not until we turn to the set of nude figures that we find the great artist revealing any new phase of his talent. The first, in an attitude which suggests the kneeling Venus, washes her thighs in a tin bath. The second, a back view, full of the malformations of forty years, of children, of hard work, stands gripping her flanks with both hands. The naked woman has become impossible in modern art; it required Degas' genius to infuse new life into the worn-out theme. Cynicism was the great means of eloquence of the middle ages, and with cynicism Degas has rendered the nude again an artistic possibility. What Mr. Horsley or the British matron would say it is difficult to guess. Perhaps the hideousness de-picted by M. Degas would frighten them more than the sensuality which they condemn in Sir Frederick Leighton. But, be this as it may, it is certain that the great, fat, short-legged creature, who in her humble and touching ugliness passes a chemise over her lumpy shoulders, is a triumph of art. Ugliness is trivial, the monstrous is terrible; Velasquez knew this when he painted his dwarfs.

Pissarro exhibited a group of girls gathering apples in a garden—sad greys and violets beautifully harmonised. The figures seem to move as in a dream: we are on the thither side of life, in a world of quiet colour and happy aspirations. Those apples will never fall from the branches, those baskets that the stooping girls are filling will never be filled: that garden is the garden of the peace that life has not for giving, but which the painter has set in an eternal dream of violet and grey.

Madame Morisot exhibited a series of delicate fancies. Here are two young girls; the sweet atmosphere folds them as with a veil; they are all summer; their dreams are limitless, their days are fading, and their ideas follow the flight of the white butterflies through the standard roses. Take note, too, of the stand of fans; what delicious fancies are there—willows, balconies, gardens, and terraces.

Then, contrasting with these distant tendernesses, there was the vigorous painting of Guillaumin. There life is rendered in violent and colourful brutality. The ladies fishing in the park, with the violet of the skies and the green of the trees descending upon them, is a *chef d'oeuvre*. Nature seems to be closing about them like a tomb; and that hillside,—sunset flooding the skies with yellow and the earth with blue shadow,—is another piece of painting that will one day find a place in one of the public galleries; and the same can be said of the portrait of the woman on a background of chintz flowers.

We could but utter coarse gibes and exclaim, "What could have induced him to paint such things? surely he must have seen that it was absurd. I wonder if the Impressionists are in earnest or if it is only *une blague qu'on nous fait?*" Then we stood and screamed at Monet, that most exquisite painter of blonde light. We stood before the "Turkeys," and seriously we wondered if "it was serious work,"— that *chef d'oeuvre!* the high grass that the turkeys are gobbling is flooded with sunlight so swift and intense that for a moment the illusion is complete. "Just look at the house! why, the turkeys couldn't walk in at the door. The perspective is all wrong." Then followed other remarks of an educational kind; and when we came to those piercingly personal visions of railway stations by the same painter,—those rapid sensations of steel and vapour,—our laughter knew no bounds. "I say, Marshall, just look at this wheel; he dipped his brush into cadmium yellow and whisked it round, that's all." Nor did we understand any more Renoir's rich sensualities of tone; nor did the mastery with which he achieves an absence of shadow appeal to us. You see colour and light in his pictures as you do in nature, and the child's criticism of a portrait—"Why is one side of the face black?" is answered. There was a half length nude figure of a girl. How the round fresh breasts palpitate in the light! such a glorious glow of whiteness was attained never before. But we saw nothing except that the eyes were out of drawing.

For art was not for us then as it is now,—a mere emotion, right or wrong only in proportion to its intensity; we believed then in the grammar of art, perspective, anatomy, and *la jambe qui porte*; and we found all this in Julien's studio.[4]

A year passed; a year of art and dissipation—one part art, two parts dissipation. We mounted and descended at pleasure the rounds of society's ladder. One evening we would spend at Constant's, Rue de la Gaieté, in the company of thieves and housebreakers; on the following evening we were dining with a duchess or a princess in the Champs Elysées. And we prided ourselves vastly on our versatility in using with equal facility the language of the "fence's" parlour, and that of the literary salon; on being able to appear as much at home in one as in the other. Delighted at our prowess, we often whispered, "The princess, I swear, would not believe her eyes if she saw us now;" and then in terrible slang we shouted a benediction on some "crib" that was going to be broken into that evening. And we thought there was something very thrilling in leaving the Rue de la Gaieté, returning home to dress, and presenting our spotless selves to the *élite*.[5] And we succeeded very well, as indeed all young men do who waltz perfectly and avoid making love to the wrong woman.

But the excitement of climbing up and down the social ladder did not stave off our craving for art; and there came about this time a very decisive event in our lives. Marshall's last and really *grande passion* had come to a violent termination, and monetary difficulties forced him to turn his thoughts to painting as a means of livelihood. ¶ This decided me. I asked him to come and live with me, and to be as near our studio as possible, I took an *appartement* in the Passage des Panoramas. It was not pleasant that your window should open, not to the sky, but to an unclean prospect of glass roofing; nor was it agreeable to get up at seven in the morning; and ten hours of work daily are trying to the resolution even of the best intentioned. But we had sworn to forego all pleasures for the sake of art—table d'hôtes in the Rue Maubeuge, French and foreign duchesses in the Champs Elysées, thieves in the Rue de la Gaieté.[6]

I was entering therefore on a duel with Marshall for supremacy in an art for which, as has already been said, I possessed no qualifications. It will readily be understood how a mind like mine, so keenly alive to all impulses, and so unsupported by any moral convictions, would suffer in so keen a contest waged under such unequal and cruel conditions. It was in truth a year of great passion and great despair. Defeat is bitter when it comes swiftly and conclusively, but when defeat falls by inches like the fatal pendulum in the pit, the agony is a little out of reach of words to define. It was even so. I remember the first day of my martyrdom. The clocks were striking eight; we chose our places, got into position. After the first hour, I compared my drawing with Marshall's. He had, it is true, caught the movement of the figure better than I, but the character and the quality of his work was miserable. That of mine was not. I have said I possessed no artistic facility, but I did not say faculty; my drawing was never common; it was individual in feeling; it was refined. I possessed all the rarer qualities, but not that primary power without which all is valueless;—I mean the talent of the boy who can knock off a clever caricature of his schoolmaster or make a *lifelike* sketch of his favourite horse on the barn door with a piece of chalk.

The following week Marshall made a great deal of progress; I thought the model did not suit me, and hoped for better luck next time. That time never came, and at the end of the first month I was left toiling hopelessly in the distance. Marshall's mind, though shallow, was bright, and he understood with strange ease all that was told him, and was able to put into immediate practice the methods of work inculcated by the professors. In fact, he showed himself singularly capable of education; little could be drawn out, but a great deal could be put in (using the word in its modern, not in its original sense). He showed himself intensely anxious to learn and to accept all that was said: the ideas and feelings of others ran into him like water into a bottle whose neck is suddenly stooped below the surface of the stream. He was an ideal pupil. It was Marshall here, it was Marshall there, and soon the studio was little but an agitation in praise of him, and his work, and anxious speculation arose as to the medals he would obtain. I continued the struggle for nine months. I was in the studio at eight in the morning; I measured my drawing; I plumbed it throughout; I sketched in, having regard to *la jambe qui porte*; I modelled *par les masses*. During breakfast I considered how I should work during the afternoon; at night I lay awake thinking of what I might do to attain a better result. But my efforts availed me nothing; it was like one who, falling, stretches his arms for help and grasps the yielding air. How terrible are the langours and yearnings of impotence! how wearing! what an aching void they leave in the heart! And all this I suffered until the burden of unachieved desire grew intolerable.

I laid down my charcoal and said, "I will never draw or paint again." That vow I have kept.

Surrender brought relief, but my life seemed at an end. I looked upon a blank space of years desolate as a grey and sailless sea. "What shall I do?" I asked myself, and my heart was weary and hopeless. Literature? my heart did not answer the question at once. I was too broken and overcome by the shock of failure; failure precise and stern, admitting of no equivocation. I strove to read: but it was impossible to sit at home almost within earshot of the studio, and with all the memories of defeat still ringing their knells in my heart. Marshall's success clamoured loudly from without; every day, almost every hour of the day, I heard of the medals which he would carry off; of what Lefebvre thought of his drawing this week, of Boulanger's opinion of his talent. I do not wish to excuse my conduct, but I cannot help saying that Marshall showed me neither consideration nor pity; he did not even seem to understand that I was suffering, that my nerves had been terribly shaken, and he flaunted his superiority relentlessly in my face —his good looks, his talents, his popularity. I did not know then how little these studio successes really meant.

Vanity? no, it was not his vanity that maddened me; to me vanity is rarely displeasing, sometimes it is singularly attractive; but by a certain insistence and aggressiveness in the details of life he allowed me to feel that I was only a means for the moment, a serviceable thing enough, but one that would be very soon discarded and passed over. This was intolerable. I broke up my establishment. By so doing I involved my friend in grave and cruel difficulties; by this action I imperilled his future prospects. It was a dastardly action; but his presence had grown unbearable; yes, unbearable in the fullest acceptation of the word, and in ridding myself of him I felt as if a world of misery were being lifted from me.

A fter three months spent in a sweet seaside resort, where unoccupied men and ladies whose husbands are abroad happily congregate, I returned to Paris refreshed.[1]

Marshall and I were no longer on speaking terms, but I saw him daily, in a new overcoat, of a cut admirably adapted to his figure, sweeping past the fans and the jet ornaments of the Passage des Panoramas. The coat interested me, and I remembered that if I had not broken with him I should have been able to ask him some essential questions concerning it. Of such trifles as this the sincerest friendships are made; he was as necessary to me as I to him, and after some demur on his part a reconciliation was effected.

Then I took an *appartement* in one of the old houses in Rue de la Tour des Dames, for the windows there overlooked a bit of tangled garden with a few dilapidated statues.[2] It was Marshall of course who undertook the task of furnishing, and he lavished on the rooms the fancies of an imagination that suggested the collaboration of a courtesan of high degree and a fifth-rate artist. Nevertheless, our salon was a pretty resort —English cretonne of a very happy design—vine leaves, dark green and golden, broken up by many fluttering jays. The walls were stretched with this colourful cloth, and the arm-chairs and the couches were to match. The drawing-room was in cardinal red, hung from the middle of the ceiling and looped up to give the appearance of a tent; a faun, in terra cotta, laughed in the red gloom, and there were Turkish couches and lamps. In another room you faced an altar, a Buddhist temple, a statue of the Apollo, and a bust of Shelley. The bedrooms were made unconventual with cushioned seats and rich canopies; and in picturesque corners there were censers, great church candlesticks, and palms; then think of the smell of burning incense and wax and you will have imagined the sentiment of our apartment in Rue de la Tour des Dames. I bought a Persian cat, and a python that made a monthly meal off guinea pigs; Marshall, who did not care for pets, filled his rooms with flowers—he used to sleep beneath a tree of gardenias in full bloom. We were so, Henry Marshall and Edwin Dayne, when we went to live in 76, Rue de la Tour des Dames, we hoped for the rest of our lives. He was to paint, I was to write.

Before leaving for the seaside I had bought some volumes of Hugo and De Musset; but in pleasant, sunny Boulogne poetry went flat, and it was not until I got into my new rooms that I began to read seriously. Books are like individuals; you know at once if they are going to create a sense within the sense, to fever, to madden you in blood and brain, or if they will merely leave you indifferent, or irritable, having unpleasantly disturbed sweet intimate musings as might a draught from an open window. Many are the reasons for love, but I confess I only love woman or book, when it is as a voice of conscience, never heard before, heard suddenly, a voice I am at once endearingly intimate with. This announces feminine depravities in my affections. I am feminine, morbid, perverse. But above all perverse, almost everything perverse interests, fascinates me. Wordsworth is the only simple-minded man I ever loved, if that great austere mind, chill even as the Cumberland year, can be called simple. But Hugo is not perverse, nor even personal. Reading him was like being in church with a strident-voiced preacher shouting from out of a terribly sonorous pulpit. "Les Orientales . . ." An East of painted card-board, tin daggers, and a military band playing the Turkish patrol in the Palais Royal . . . The verse is grand, noble, tremendous; I liked it, I admired it, but it did not—I repeat the phrase—awake a voice of conscience within me; and even the structure of the verse was too much in the style of public buildings to please me. Of "Les Feuilles d'Automne" and "Les Chants du Crépuscule" I remember nothing. Ten lines, fifty lines of "La Légende des Siècles," and I always think that it is the greatest poetry I have ever read, but after a few pages I invariably put the book down and forget it. Having composed more verses than any man that ever lived, Hugo can only be taken in the smallest doses; if you repeat any passage to a friend across a café table, you are both appalled by the splendour of the imagery, by the thunder of the syllables.

> "Quel dieu, quel moissonneur de l'éternel été
> Avait en s'en allant négligemment jeté
> Cette faucille d'or dans les champs des étoiles."[3]

But if I read an entire poem I never escape that sensation of the ennui which is inherent in the gaud and the glitter of the Italian or Spanish improvisatore. There never was anything French about Hugo's genius. Hugo was a cross between an Italian improvisatore and a metaphysical German student. Take another verse—

> "Le clair de lune bleu qui baigne l'horizon."[4]

Without a "like" or an "as," by a mere statement of fact, the picture, nay more, the impression, is produced. I confess I have a weakness for the poem which this line concludes—"La fête chez Thérèse;" but admirable as it is with its picture of mediæval life, there is in it, like in all Hugo's work, a sense of fabrication that dries up emotion in my heart. He shouts and raves over poor humanity, while he is gathering coppers for himself; he goes in for an all-round patronage of the Almighty in a last stanza; but of the two immortalities he evidently considers his own the most durable; he does not, however, become really intolerable until he gets on the subject of little children; he sings their innocence in great bombast, but he is watching them; the poetry over, the crowd dispersed, he will appear a veritable Mr. Hyde.

The first time I read of *une bouche d'ombre* I was astonished, nor the second nor third repetition produced a change in my mood of mind; but sooner or later it was impossible to avoid conviction, that of the two "the rosy fingers of the dawn,"[5] although some three thousand years older was younger, truer, and more beautiful. Homer's similes can never grow old; *une bouche d'ombre* was old the first time it was said. It is the birthplace and the grave of Hugo's genius.

Of Alfred de Musset I had heard a great deal. Marshall and the Marquise were in the habit of reading him in moments of relaxation, they had marked their favourite passages, so he came to me highly recommended. Nevertheless, I made but little progress in his poetry. His modernisms were out of tune with the present strain of my aspirations, and I did not find the unexpected word and the eccentricities of expression which were, and are still, so dear to me. I am not a purist; an error of diction is very pardonable if it does not err on the side of the commonplace; the commonplace, the natural, is constitutionally abhorrent to me; and I have never been able to read with any very thorough sense of pleasure even the opening lines of "Rolla," that splendid lyrical outburst. What I remember of it now are those two odious *chevilles—marchait et respirait*, and *Astarte fille de l'onde amère;*[6] nor does the fact that *amère* rhymes with *mère* condone the offence, although it proves that even Musset felt that perhaps the richness of the rhyme might render tolerable the intolerable. And it is to my credit that the Spanish love songs moved me not at all; and it was not until I read that magnificently grotesque poem "La Ballade à la Lune," that I could be induced to bend the knee and acknowledge Musset a poet.

I still read and spoke of Shelley with a rapture of joy,—he was still my soul. But this craft, fashioned of mother o' pearl, with starlight at the helm and moonbeams for sails, suddenly ran on a reef and went down, not out of sight, but out of the agitation of actual life. The reef was Gautier; I read "Mdlle. de Maupin." The reaction was as violent as it was sudden. I was weary of spiritual passion, and this great exaltation of the body above the soul at once conquered and led me captive; this plain scorn of a world as exemplified in lacerated saints and a crucified Redeemer opened up to me illimitable prospects of fresh beliefs, and therefore new joys in things and new revolts against all that had come to form part and parcel of the commonalty of mankind. Till now I had not even remotely suspected that a deification of flesh and fleshly desire was possible, Shelley's teaching had been, while accepting the body, to dream of the soul as a star, and so preserve our ideal; but now suddenly I saw, with delightful clearness and with intoxicating conviction, that by looking without shame and accepting with love the flesh, I might raise it to as high a place and within as divine a light as even the soul had been set in. The ages were as an aureole, and I stood as if enchanted before the noble nakedness of the elder gods: not the infamous nudity that sex has preserved in this modern world, but the clean pagan nude, —a love of life and beauty, the broad fair breast of a boy, the long flanks, the head thrown back; the bold fearless gaze of Venus is lovelier than the lowered glance of the Virgin, and I cried with my master that the blood that flowed upon Mount Calvary *"ne m'a jamais baigné dans ses flots."*[7]

I will not turn to the book to find the exact words of this sublime vindication, for ten years I have not read the Word that has become so inexpressibly a part of me; and shall I not refrain as Mdlle. de Maupin refrained, knowing well that the face of love may not be twice seen? Great was my conversion. None more than I had cherished mystery and dream: my life until now had been but a mist which revealed as each cloud wreathed and went out, the red of some strange flower or some tall peak, blue and snowy and fairylike in lonely moonlight; and now so great was my conversion that the more brutal the outrage offered to my ancient ideal, the rarer and keener was my delight. I read almost without fear: "My dreams were of naked youths riding white horses through mountain passes, there were no clouds in my dreams, or if there were any, they were clouds that had been cut out as if in cardboard with a pair of scissors."[8]

I had shaken off all belief in Christianity early in life, and had suffered much. Shelley had replaced faith by reason, but I still suffered: but here was a new creed which proclaimed the divinity of the body, and for a long time the reconstruction of all my theories of life on a purely pagan basis occupied my whole attention. The exquisite outlines of the marvellous castle, the romantic woods, the horses moving, the lovers leaning to each other's faces enchanted me; and then the indescribably beautiful description of the performance of *As You Like It*, and the supreme relief and perfect assuagement it brings to Rodolph, who then sees Mdlle. de Maupin for the first time in woman's attire. If she were dangerously beautiful as a man, that beauty is forgotten in the rapture and praise of her unmatchable woman's loveliness.

But if "Mdlle. de Maupin" was the highest peak, it was not the entire mountain. The range was long, and each summit offered to the eye a new and delightful prospect. There were the numerous tales,—tales as perfect as the world has ever seen; "La Morte Amoureuse," "Jettatura," "Une Nuit de Cléopâtre," etc., and then the very diamonds of the crown, "Les Emaux et Camées," "La Symphonie en Blanc Majeure," in which the adjective *blanc* and *blanche* is repeated with miraculous felicity in each stanza. And then "Contralto,"—

> "Mais seulement il se transpose
> Et passant de la forme au son,
> Trouve dans la métamorphose
> La jeune fille et le garçon."⁹

Transpose,—a word never before used except in musical application, and now for the first time applied to material form, and with a beauty-giving touch that Phidias might be proud of. I know not how I quote; such is my best memory of the stanza, and here, that is more important than the stanza itself. And that other stanza, "The Châtelaine and the Page;" and that other, "The Doves;" and that other, "Romeo and Juliet," and the exquisite cadence of the line ending "*balcon.*" Novelists have often shown how a love passion brings misery, despair, death, and ruin upon a life, but I know of no story of the good or evil influence awakened by the chance reading of a book, the chain of consequences so far-reaching, so intensely dramatic. Never shall I open these books again, but were I to live for a thousand years, their power in my soul would remain unshaken. I am what they made me. Belief in humanity, pity for the poor, hatred of injustice, all that Shelley gave may never have been very deep or earnest; but I did love, I did believe. Gautier destroyed these illusions. He taught me that our boasted progress is but a pitfall into which the race is falling, and I learned that the correction of form is the highest ideal, and I accepted the plain, simple conscience of the pagan world as the perfect solution of the problem that had vexed me so long; I cried, "ave" to it all: lust, cruelty, slavery, and I would have held down my thumbs in the Colosseum that a hundred gladiators might die and wash me free of my Christian soul with their blood.

The study of Baudelaire aggravated the course of the disease. No longer is it the grand barbaric face of Gautier; now it is the clean shaven face of the mock priest, the slow, cold eyes and the sharp, cunning sneer of the cynical libertine who will be tempted that he may better know the worthlessness of temptation. "Les Fleurs du Mal!" beautiful flowers, beautiful in sublime decay. What great record is yours, and were Hell a reality how many souls would we find wreathed with your poisonous blossoms. The village maiden goes to her Faust; the children of the nineteenth century go to you, O Baudelaire, and having tasted of your deadly delight all hope of repentance is vain. Flowers, beautiful in your sublime decay, I press you to my lips; these northern solitudes, far from the rank Parisian garden where I gathered you, are full of you, even as the sea-shell of the sea, and the sun that sets on this wild moorland evokes the magical verse:—

> "Un soir fait de rose et de bleu mystique
> Nous échangerons un éclair unique
> Comme un long sanglot tout chargé d'adieux."[10]

For months I fed on the mad and morbid literature that the enthusiasm of 1830 called into existence. The gloomy and sterile little pictures of "Gaspard de la Nuit," or the elaborate criminality, "Les Contes Immoraux," laboriously invented lifeless things with creaky joints, pitiful lay figures that fall to dust as soon as the book is closed, and in the dust only the figures of the terrible ferryman and the unfortunate Dora remain. "Madame Potiphar" cost me forty francs, and I never read more than a few pages.

Like a pike after minnows, I pursued the works of Les Jeunes France along the quays and through every *passage* in Paris. The money spent was considerable, the waste of time enormous. One man's solitary work (he died very young, but he is known to have excelled all in length of his hair and the redness of his waistcoats) resisted my efforts to capture it. At last I caught sight of the precious volume in a shop on the Quai Voltaire. Trembling I asked the price. The man looked at me earnestly and answered, "A hundred and fifty francs." No doubt it was a great deal of money, but I paid it and rushed home to read. Many that had gone before had proved disappointing, and I was obliged to admit had contributed little towards my intellectual advancement; but this—this that I had heard about so long—not a queer phrase, not an outrage of any sort of kind, not even a new blasphemy, nothing, that is to say, nothing but a hundred and fifty francs. Having thus rudely, and very pikelike, knocked my nose against the bottom—this book was, most assuredly, the bottom of the literature of 1830—I came up to the surface and began to look around my contemporaries for something to read.

I have remarked before on the instinctiveness of my likes and dislikes, on my susceptibility to the sound of and even to the appearance of a name upon paper. I was repelled by Leconte de Lisle from the first, and it was only by a very deliberate outrage to my feelings that I bought and read "Les Poèmes Antiques," and "Les Poèmes Barbares;" I was deceived in nothing, all I had anticipated I found—long, desolate boredom. Leconte de Lisle produces on me the effect of a walk through the new Law Courts, with a steady but not violent draught sweeping from end to end. Oh, the vile old professor of rhetoric! and when I saw him the last time I was in Paris, his head—a declaration of righteousness, a cross between a Cæsar by Gerome, and an archbishop of a provincial town, set all my natural antipathy instantly on edge. Hugo is often pompous, shallow, empty, unreal, but he is at least an artist, and when he thinks of the artist and forgets the prophet, as in "Les Chansons des Rues et des Bois," his juggling with the verse is magnificent, superb.

> "Comme un geai sur l'arbre
>   Le roi se tient fier;
>   Son coeur est de marbre,
>   Son ventre est de chair.
>
> "On a pour sa nuque
>   Et son front vermeil
>   Fait une perruque
>   Avec le soleil.
>
> "Il règne, il végète
>   Effrayant zéro;
>   Sur qui se projette
>   L'ombre du bourreau.
>
> "Son trône est une tombe,
>   Et sur le pavé
>   Quelque chose en tombe
>   Qu'on n'a point lavé."[11]

But how to get the first line of the last stanza into five syllables I cannot think. If ever I meet with the volume again I will look it out and see how that *rude dompteur de syllables* managed it. But stay, *son trône est la tombe*; that makes the verse, and the generalisation would be in the "line" of Hugo. Hugo—how impossible it is to speak of French literature without referring to him. Let these, however, be the concluding words: he thought that by saying everything, and saying everything twenty times over, he would for ever render impossible the advent of another great poet. ⸙[But a work of art is valuable, and pleasurable in proportion to its rarity; one beautiful book of verses is better than twenty books of beautiful verses. This is an absolute and incontestable truth; a child can burlesque this truth—one verse is better than the whole poem; a word is better than the line; a letter is better than the word; but the truth is not thereby affected. Hugo never had the good fortune to write a bad book, nor even a single bad line, so not having time to read all, the future will read none. What immortality would be gained by the destruction of one half of his magnificent works; what oblivion is secured by the publication of these posthumous volumes.]⸙

To return to the Leconte de Lisle. See his "Discours de Réception." Is it possible to imagine anything more absurdly arid? Rhetoric of this sort, *"des vers d'or sur une écume d'airain,"* and such sententious platitudes (speaking of the realists), *"Les épidémies de cette nature passent, et le génie demeure."*

Theodore de Banville. At first I thought him cold, tinged with the rhetorical ice of the Leconte de Lisle. He had no new creed to proclaim nor old creed to denounce, the inherent miseries of human life did not seem to touch him, and of the languors and ardours of animal or spiritual passion there are none. What is there? a pure, clear song, an instinctive, incurable and lark-like love of the song. The lily is white, and the rose is red, such knowledge of, such observation of nature is enough for the poet, and he sings and he trills, there is silver magic in every note, and the song as it ascends rings, and all the air quivers with the everwidening circle of the echoes, sighing and dying out of the ear until the last faintness is reached, and the glad rhymes clash and dash forth again on their aërial way. Banville is not the poet, he is the bard. The great questions that agitate the mind of man have not troubled him, life, death, and love he only perceives as stalks whereon he may weave his glittering web of living words. Whatever his moods may be, he is lyrical. His wit flies out on clear-cut, swallow-like wings as when he said, in speaking of Paul Alexis' book "Le Besoin d'aimer," *"Vous avez trouvez un titre assez laid pour faire reculer les divines étoiles."* I know not what instrument to compare with his verse. I suppose I should say a flute; but it seems to me more like a marvellously toned piano. His hands pass over the keys, and he produces Chopin-like music.

It is now well known that French verse is not seventy years old. If it was Hugo who invented French rhyme it was Banville who broke up the couplet. Hugo had perhaps ventured to place the pause between the adjective and its noun, but it was not until Banville wrote the line, "*Elle filait pensivement la blanche laine,*" that the cæsura received its final *coup de grâce.* This verse has been probably more imitated than any other verse in the French language. *Pensivement* was replaced by some similar four-syllable adverb, *Elle tirait nonchalamment les bas de soie, etc.* It was the beginning of the end.

I read the French poets of the modern school—Coppée, Mendès, Léon Dierx, Verlaine, José Maria de Hérédia, Mallarmé, Richepin, Villiers de l'Isle Adam. Coppée, as may be imagined, I only was capable of appreciating in his first manner, when he wrote those exquisite but purely artistic sonnets "La Tulipe" and "Le Lys." In the latter a room decorated with daggers, armour, jewellery and china is beautifully described, and it is only in the last line that the lily which animates and gives life to the whole is introduced. But the exquisite poetic perceptivity Coppée showed in his modern poems, the certainty with which he raised the commonest subject, investing it with sufficient dignity for his purpose, escaped me wholly, and I could not but turn with horror from such poems as "La Nourrice" and "Le Petit Epicier." How anyone could bring himself to acknowledge the vulgar details of our vulgar age I could not understand. The fiery glory of José Maria de Hérédia, on the contrary, filled me with enthusiasm—ruins and sand, shadow and silhouette of palms and pillars, negroes, crimson, swords, silence, and arabesques. As great copper pans go the clangour of the rhymes.

> "Entre le ciel qui brûle et la mer qui moutonne,
> Au somnolent soleil d'un midi monotone,
> Tu songes, O guerrière, aux vieux conquistadors;
> Et dans l'énervement des nuits chaudes et calmes,
> Berçant ta gloire éteinte, O cité, tu t'endors
> Sous les palmiers, au long frémissement des palmes."[12]

Catulle Mendès, a perfect realisation of his name, of his pale hair, of his fragile face illuminated with the idealism of a depraved woman. He takes you by the arm, by the hand, he leans towards you, his words are caresses, his fervour is delightful, and listening to him is as sweet as drinking a fair perfumed white wine. All he says is false—the book he has just read, the play he is writing, the woman who loves him, . . . he buys a packet of bonbons in the streets and eats them, and it is false. An exquisite artist; physically and spiritually he is art; he is the muse herself, or rather, he is one of the minions of the muse. Passing from flower to flower he goes, his whole nature pulsing with butterfly voluptuousness. He has written poems as good as Hugo, as good as Leconte de Lisle, as good as Banville, as good as Baudelaire, as good as Gautier, as good as Coppée; he never wrote an ugly line in his life, but he never wrote a line that some one of his brilliant contemporaries might not have written. He has produced good work of all kinds "et voilà tout." Every generation, every country, has its Catulle Mendès. Robert Buchanan is ours, only in the adaptation Scotch gruel has been substituted for perfumed white wine. No more delightful talker than Mendès, no more accomplished *littérateur*, no more fluent and translucid critic. I remember the great moonlights of the *Place Pigalle*, when, on leaving the café, he would take me by the arm, and expound Hugo's or Zola's last book, thinking as he spoke of the Greek sophists. There were for contrast Mallarmé's Tuesday evenings, a few friends sitting round the hearth, the lamp on the table. I have met none whose conversation was more fruitful, but with the exception of his early verses I cannot say I ever frankly enjoyed his poetry. When I knew him he had published the celebrated "L'Après-midi d'un Faune:" the first poem written in accordance with the theory of symbolism. But when it was given to me (this marvellous brochure furnished with strange illustrations and wonderful tassels), I thought it absurdly obscure. Since then, however, it has been rendered by force of contrast with the brain-curdling enigmas the author has since published a marvel of lucidity; and were I to read it now I should appreciate its many beauties. It bears the same relation to the author's later work as *Rienzi* to *The Valkyries*. But what is symbolism? Vulgarly speaking, saying the opposite to what you mean. For example, you want to say that music which is the new art, is replacing the old art, which is poetry. First symbol: a house in which there is a funeral, the pall extends over the furniture. The house is poetry, poetry is dead. Second symbol: "*notre vieux grimoire*," *grimoire* is the parchment, parchment is used for writing, therefore, *grimoire* is the symbol for literature, "*d'où s'exaltent les milliers*," thousands of what? of letters of course.[13] We have heard a great deal in England of Browning obscurity. The "Red Cotton Nightcap Country" is child's play compared to a sonnet by a determined symbolist such as Mallarmé, or better still his disciple Ghil who has added to the difficulties of symbolism those of poetic instrumentation. For according to M. Ghil and his organ *Les Ecrits pour l'Art*, it would appear that the syllables of the French language evoke in us the sensations of different colours; consequently the timbre of the different instruments. The vowel *u* corresponds to the colour yellow, and therefore to the sound of flutes.

Arthur Rimbaud was, it is true, first in the field with these pleasant and genial theories; but M. Ghil informs us that Rimbaud was mistaken in many things, particularly in coupling the sound of the vowel *u* with the colour green instead of with the colour yellow. M. Ghil has corrected this very stupid blunder and many others; and his instrumentation in his last volume, "Le Geste Ingénu," may be considered as complete and definitive.[14] The work is dedicated to Mallarmé, "Père et seigneur des ors, des pierreries, et des poisons," and other works are to follow:—the six tomes of "Légendes des Rêves et de Sang," the innumerable tomes of "La Glose," and the single tome of "La Loi."

And that man Gustave Kahn, who takes the French language as a violin, and lets the bow of his emotion run at wild will upon it producing strange acute strains, unpremeditated harmonies comparable to nothing that I know of but some Hungarian rhapsody; verses of seventeen syllables interwoven with verses of eight, and even nine, masculine rhymes, seeking strange union with feminine rhymes in the middle of the line—a music sweet, subtil, and epicene; the half-note, the inflexion, but not the full tone—as "*se fondre, o souvenir, des lys âcres délices.*"[15]

> Se penchant vers les dahlias,
> Des paons cabrient des rosaces lunaires
> L'assoupissement des branches vénère
> Son pâle visage aux mourants dahlias.
>
> Elle écoute au loin les brèves musiques
> Nuit claire aux ramures d'accords,
> Et la lassitude a bercé son corps
> Au rythme odorant des pures musiques.
>
> Les paons ont dressé la rampe ocellée
> Pour la descente de ses yeux vers le tapis
> De choses et de sens
> Qui va vers l'horizon, parure vermiculée
> De son corps alangui
> En l'âme se tapit
> Le flou désir molli de récits et d'encens.

I laughed at these verbal eccentricities, but they were not without their effect, and that effect was a demoralising one; for in me they aggravated the fever of the unknown, and whetted my appetite for the strange, abnormal and unhealthy in art. Hence all pallidities of thought and desire were eagerly welcomed, and Verlaine became my poet. Never shall I forget the first enchantment of "Les Fêtes Galantes." Here all is twilight.

The royal magnificences of the sunset have passed, the solemn beatitude of the night is at hand but not yet here; the ways are veiled with shadow, and lit with dresses, white, that the hour has touched with blue, yellow, green, mauve, and undecided purple; the voices? strange contraltos; the forms? not those of men or women, but mystic, hybrid creatures, with hands nervous and pale, and eyes charged with eager and fitful light . . . *"un soir équivoque d'automne,"* . . . *"les belles pendent rêveuses à nos bras"* . . . and they whisper *"les mots spéciaux et tout bas."*[16]

Gautier sang to his antique lyre praise of the flesh and contempt of the soul; Baudelaire on a mediæval organ chaunted his unbelief in goodness and truth and his hatred of life. But Verlaine advances one step further: hate is to him as commonplace as love, unfaith as vulgar as faith. The world is merely a doll to be attired to-day in a modern ball dress, to-morrow in aureoles and stars. The Virgin is a pretty thing, worth a poem, but it would be quite too silly to talk about belief or unbelief; Christ in wood or plaster we have heard too much of, but Christ in painted glass amid crosiers and Latin terminations, is an amusing subject for poetry. And strangely enough, a withdrawing from all commerce with virtue and vice is, it would seem, a licentiousness more curiously subtle and penetrating than any other; and the licentiousness of the verse is equal to that of the emotion; every natural instinct of the language is violated, and the simple music native in French metre is replaced by falsetto notes sharp and intense. The charm is that of an odour of iris exhaled by some ideal tissues, or of a missal in a gold case, a precious relic of the pomp and ritual of an archbishop of Persepolis.

> Parsifal a vaincu les filles, leur gentil
> Babil et la luxure amusante et sa pente
> Vers la chair de ce garçon vierge que cela tente
> D'aimer les seins légers et ce gentil babil.

Il a vaincu la femme belle au coeur subtil
Etalant ses bras frais et sa gorge excitante;
Il a vaincu l'enfer, et rentre sous sa tente
Avec un lourd trophée à son bras puéril.

Avec la lance qui perça le flanc suprême
Il a guéri le roi, le voici roi lui-même,
Et prêtre du très-saint trésor essentiel;

En robe d'or il adore, gloire et symbole,
Le vase pur où resplendit le sang réel,
Et, o ces voix d'enfants chantant dans la coupole.[17]

I know of no more perfect thing than this sonnet. The hiatus in the last line was at first a little trying, but I have learned to love it; not in Baudelaire nor even in Poe is there more beautiful poetry to be found. Poe, unread and ill-understood in America and England, here, thou art an integral part of our artistic life.

The Island o' Fay, Silence, Elionore,[18] were the familiar spirits of an apartment beautiful with tapestry and palms; Swinburne and Rossetti were the English poets I read there; and in a golden bondage, I, a unit in the generation they have enslaved, clanked my fetters and trailed my golden chain. I had begun a set of stories in many various metres, to be called "Roses of Midnight."[19] One of the characteristics of the volume was that daylight was banished from its pages. In the sensual lamplight of yellow boudoirs, or the wild moonlight of centenarian forests, my fantastic loves lived out their lives, died with the dawn which was supposed to be an awakening to consciousness of reality.

A last hour of vivid blue and gold glare; but now the twilight sheds softly upon the darting jays, and only the little oval frames catch the fleeting beams. I go to the miniatures. Amid the parliamentary faces, all strictly garrotted with many-folded handkerchiefs, there is a metal frame enchased with rubies and a few emeralds. And this *chef d'œuvre* of antique workmanship surrounds a sharp, shrewdish, modern face, withal pretty. Fair she is and thin.

She is a woman of thirty,—no,—she is the woman of thirty. Balzac has written some admirable pages on this subject; my memory of them is vague and uncertain, although durable, as all memories of him must be. But that marvellous story, or rather study, has been blunted in my knowledge of this tiny face with the fine masses of hair drawn up from the neck and arranged elaborately on the crown. There is no fear of plagiary; he cannot have said all; he cannot have said what I want to say.[1]

Looking at this face so mundane, so intellectually mundane, I see why a young man of refined mind—a bachelor who spends at least a pound a day on his pleasures, and in whose library are found some few volumes of modern poetry—seeks his ideal in a woman of thirty.

It is clear that, by the very essence of her being, the young girl may evoke no ideal but that of home; and home is in his eyes the antithesis of freedom, desire, aspiration. He longs for mystery, deep and endless, and he is tempted with a foolish little illusion—white dresses, water colour drawings, and popular music. He dreams of Pleasure, and he is offered Duty; for do not think that that sylph-like waist does not suggest to him a yard of apron string, cries of children, and that most odious word, "Papa." A young man of refined mind can look through the glass of the years.

He has sat in the stalls, opera-glass in hand; he has met women of thirty at balls, and has sat with them beneath shadowy curtains; he knows that the world is full of beautiful women, all waiting to be loved and amused, the circles of his immediate years are filled with feminine faces, they cluster like flowers on this side and that, and they fade into garden-like spaces of colour. How many may love him? The loveliest may one day smile upon his knee! and shall he renounce all for that little creature who has just finished singing, and is handing round cups of tea? Every bachelor contemplating marriage says, "I shall have to give up all for one, one."

The young girl is often pretty but her prettiness is vague and uncertain, it inspires a sort of pitying admiration, but it suggests nothing; the very essence of the young girl's being is that she should have nothing to suggest, therefore the beauty of the young face fails to touch the imagination. No past lies hidden in those translucid eyes, no story of hate, disappointment, or sin. Nor is there in nine hundred and ninety-nine cases in a thousand any doubt that the hand, that spends at least a pound a day in restaurants and cabs, will succeed in gathering the muslin flower if he so wills it, and by doing so he will delight every one. Where, then, is the struggle? where, then, is the triumph? Therefore, I say that if a young man's heart is not set on children, and tiresome dinner parties, the young girl presents to him no possible ideal. But the woman of thirty presents from the outset all that is necessary to ensnare the heart of a young man. I see her sitting in her beautiful drawing-room, all composed by, and all belonging to her. Her chair is placed beneath an evergreen plant, and the long leaves lean out as if to touch her neck. The great white and red roses of the *d'aubusson* carpet are spread enigmatically about her feline feet; a grand piano leans its melodious mouth to her; and there she sits when her visitors have left her, playing Beethoven's sonatas in the dreamy firelight. The spring-tide shows but a bloom of unvarying freshness; August has languished and loved in the strength of the sun. She is stately, she is tall. What sins, what disappointments, what aspirations lie in those grey eyes, mysteriously still, and mysteriously revealed. These a young man longs to know of, they are his life. He imagines himself sitting by her, when the others have gone, holding her hand, calling on her name; sometimes she moves away and plays the moonlight sonata. Letting her hands droop upon the keys she talks sadly, maybe affectionately; she speaks of the tedium of life, of its disenchantments. He knows well what she means, he has suffered as she has; but could he tell her, could she understand, that in his love reality would dissolve into a dream, all limitations would open into boundless infinity.

The husband he rarely sees. Sometimes a latch-key is heard about half-past six. The man is thick, strong, common; his jaws are heavy; his eyes are expressionless; there is about him the loud swagger of the *caserne*; and he suggests the inevitable question, Why did she marry him?—a question that every young man of refined mind asks a thousand t'mes by day and ten thousand times by night, asks till he is five-and-thirty, and sees that his generation has passed into middle age.

Why did she marry him? Not the sea, nor the sky, nor the great mysterious midnight, when he opens his casement and gazes into starry space will give him answer; riddle that no Œdipus will ever come to unravel; this sphinx will never throw herself from the rock into the clangour of the sea-gulls and waves; she will never divulge her secret; and if she is the woman and not a woman of thirty, she has forgotten.

The young man shakes hands with the husband; he strives not to look embarrassed, and he talks of indifferent things—of how well he (the husband) is looking, of his amusements, his projects; and then he (the young man of refined mind) tastes of that keen and highly-seasoned delight—happiness in crime. He knows not the details of her home life; the husband is merely a dark cloud that fills one side of the picture, sometimes obliterating the sunlight; a shadowy shape that in certain moments solidifies and assumes the likeness of a rock-sculptured, imminent monster; but the shadow and the shape and the threat are magnetic, and in a sense of danger the fascination is sealed. . . .

See the young man of refined mind in a ball room! He is leaning against the woodwork in a distant doorway, he scarcely knows what to do with himself; and he is now striving to interest himself in the conversation of a group of men twice his age. I will not say he is shunned; but neither the matrons nor the young girls make any advances towards him. The young girls looking so sweet—in the oneness of their fresh hair, flowers, dresses, and glances—are being introduced, are getting up to dance, and the hostess is looking round for partners. She sees the young man in the doorway; but she hesitates and goes to some one else; and if you asked her why, she could not tell you why she avoided him. Presently the woman of thirty enters. She is in white satin and diamonds. She looks for him,—a circular glance,—and calm with possession she passes to a seat. She dances the eighth, twelfth, and fifteenth waltz with him.

Will he induce her to visit his rooms? Will they be like ⁋ mine— strange debauches of colour and Turkish lamps, Marshall's taste, ⁋ an old cabinet, a faded pastel which embalms the memory of a pastoral century, my taste; or will it be a library,—two leather library chairs, a large escritoire, etc.? Be this as it may, whether the apartments be the ruthless extravagance of artistic impulse, or the subdued taste of the student, she, the woman of thirty, shall be there by night and day: her statue is there, and even when she is sleeping safe in her husband's arms with fevered brow, he, the young man of refined mind, alone and lonely shall kneel and adore her.

And should she *not* visit his rooms? If the complex and various accidents of existence should have ruled out her life virtuously; if the many inflections of sentiment have decided against this last consummation, then she will wax to the complete, the unfathomable temptress—the Lilith of old—she will never set him free, and in the end will be found about his heart "one single golden hair." She shall haunt his wife's face and words (should he seek to rid himself of her by marriage), a bitter sweet, a half-welcome enchantment; she shall consume and destroy the strength and spirit of his life, leaving it desolation, a barren landscape, burnt and faintly scented with the sea. Fame and wealth shall slip like sand from him. She may be set aside for the cadence of a rhyme, for the flowing line of a limb, but when the passion of art has raged itself out, she shall return to blight the peace of the worker.

A terrible malady is she, a malady the ancients knew of and called nympholepsy—a beautiful name evocative and symbolic of its ideal aspect, "the breasts of the nymphs in the brake."[2] And the disease is not extinct in these modern days, nor will it ever be so long as men shall yearn for the unattainable; and the prosy bachelors who trail their ill-fated lives from their chambers to their clubs know of, and they call their malady—the woman of thirty.

A Japanese dressing gown, the ideality of whose tissue delights me, some fresh honey and milk set by this couch hung with royal fringes; and having partaken of this odorous refreshment, I call to Jack my great python that is crawling about after a two months' fast. I tie up a guineapig to the *tabouret*, pure Louis XV., the little beast struggles and squeaks, the snake, his black, bead-like eyes are fixed, how superb are the oscillations . . . now he strikes, and slowly and with what exquisite gourmandise he lubricates and swallows.

Marshall is at the organ in the hall, he is playing a Gregorian chant, that beautiful hymn, the "Vexilla Regis," by Saint Fortunatus, the great poet of the Middle Ages. And, having turned over the leaves of "Les Fêtes Gallantes," I sit down to write.

My original intention was to write some thirty or forty stories varying from thirty to three hundred lines in length. The nature of these stories is easy to imagine: there was the youth who wandered by night into a witches' sabbath, and was disputed for by the witches, young and old. There was the light o' love who went into the desert to tempt the holy man; but he died as he yielded, and the arms stiffening by some miracle to iron-like rigidity, she was unable to free herself, and died of starvation, as her bondage loosened in decay. And I had increased my difficulties by adopting as part of my task the introduction of all sorts of elaborate, and in many cases extravagantly composed metres, and I had begun to feel that I was working in sand, I could make no progress, the house I was raising crumbled and fell away on every side. These stories had one merit: they were all, so far as I can remember, perfectly constructed. For the art of telling a story clearly and dramatically, *selon les procédés de M. Scribe*, I had thoroughly learnt from old M. Duval, the author of a hundred and sixty plays, written in collaboration with more than a hundred of the best writers of his day, including the master himself, Gautier. I frequently met M. Duval at breakfast at a neighbouring *café*, and our conversation turned on *l'exposition de la pièce, préparer la situation, nous aurons des larmes*, etc. One day, as I sat waiting for him, I took up the *Voltaire*. It contained an article by M. Zola.[1] *Naturalisme, la vérité, la science*, were repeated some half-a-dozen times. Hardly able to believe my eyes, I read that you should write, with as little imagination as possible, that plot in a novel or in a play was illiterate and puerile, and that the art of M. Scribe was an art of strings and wires, etc. I rose up from breakfast, ordered my coffee, and stirred the sugar, a little dizzy, like one who has received a violent blow on the head.

Echo-augury! Words heard in an unexpected quarter, but applying marvellously well to the besetting difficulty of the moment. The reader who has followed me so far will remember the instant effect the word "Shelley" had upon me in childhood, and how it called into existence a train of feeling that illuminated the vicissitudes and passions of many years, until it was finally assimilated and became part of my being; the reader will also remember how the mere mention, at a certain moment, of the word "France" awoke a vital impulse, even a sense of final ordination, and how the irrevocable message was obeyed, and how it led to the creation of a mental existence.

And now for a third time I experienced the pain and joy of a sudden and inward light. Naturalism, truth, the new art, above all the phrase, "the new art," impressed me as with a sudden sense of light. I was dazzled, and I vaguely understood that my "Roses of Midnight" were sterile eccentricities, dead flowers that could not be galvanised into any semblance of life, passionless in all their passion.

I had read a few chapters of the "Assommoir," as it appeared in *La République des Lettres*; I had cried, "ridiculous, abominable," only because it is characteristic of me to instantly form an opinion and assume at once a violent attitude. But now I bought up the back numbers of the *Voltaire*, and I looked forward to the weekly exposition of the new faith with febrile eagerness. The great zeal with which the new master continued his propaganda, and the marvellous way in which subjects the most diverse, passing events, political, social, religious, were caught up and turned into arguments for, or proof of the truth of naturalism astonished me wholly. The idea of a new art based upon science, in opposition to the art of the old world that was based on imagination, an art that should explain all things and embrace modern life in its entirety, in its endless ramifications, be, as it were, a new creed in a new civilisation, filled me with wonder, and I stood dumb before the vastness of the conception, and the towering height of the ambition. In my fevered fancy I saw a new race of writers that would arise, and with the aid of the novel would continue to a more glorious and legitimate conclusion the work that the prophets had begun; and at each development of the theory of the new art and its universal applicability, my wonder increased and my admiration choked me. If any one should be tempted to turn to the books themselves to seek an explanation of this wild ecstacy, they would find nothing—as well drink the dregs of yesterday's champagne. One is lying before me now, and as I glance through the pages listlessly I say, "Only the simple crude statements of a man of powerful mind, but singularly narrow vision."

Still, although eager and anxious for the fray, I did not see how I was to participate in it. I was not a novelist, not yet a dramatic author, and the possibility of a naturalistic poet seemed to me not a little doubtful. I had clearly understood that the lyrical quality was to be for ever banished; there were to be no harps and lutes in our heaven, only drums; and the preservation of all the essentials of poetry, by the simple enumeration of the utensils to be found in a back kitchen, did, I could not help thinking (here it becomes necessary to whisper), sound not unlike rigmarole. I waited for the master to speak. He had declared that the Republic would fall if it did not become instantly naturalistic; he would not, he could not pass over in silence so important a branch of literature as poetry, no matter how contemptible he might think it. If he could find nothing to praise, he must at least condemn. At last the expected article came. It was all that could be desired by one in my fever of mind. Hugo's claims had been previously disproven, but now Banville and Gautier were declared to be warmed up dishes of the ancient world; Baudelaire was a naturalist, but he had been spoilt by the romantic influence of his generation. *Cependant* there were indications of the naturalistic movement even in poetry. I trembled with excitement, I could not read fast enough. Coppée had striven to simplify language; he had versified the street cries, *Achetez la France, le Soir, le Rappel*; he had sought to give utterance to humble sentiments as in "Le Petit Epicier de Montrouge," the little grocer *qui cassait le sucre avec mélancolie*; Richepin had boldly and frankly adopted the language of the people in all its superb crudity. All this was, however, preparatory and tentative. We are waiting for our poet, he who will sing to us fearlessly of the rude industry of dustmen and the comestible glories of the market-places. The subjects are to hand, the formula alone is wanting.

The prospect was a dazzling one; I tried to calm myself. Had I the stuff in me to win and to wear these bays, this stupendous laurel crown? —bays, laurel crown, a distinct *souvenir* of Parnassus, but there is no modern equivalent, I must strive to invent a new one, in the meantime let me think. True it is that Swinburne was before me with the "Romantiques." The hymn to Proserpine and Dolores are wonderful lyrical versions of Mdlle. de Maupin. In form the Leper is old English, the colouring is Baudelaire, but the rude industry of the dustmen and the comestible glories of the market-place shall be mine. A bas "*Les Roses de Minuit*"!

I felt the "naturalisation" of the "Roses of Midnight" would prove a difficult task. I soon found it an impossible one, and I laid the poems aside and commenced a volume redolent of the delights of Bougival and Ville d'Avray. This book was to be entitled "Poems of 'Flesh and Blood.' "

"*Elle mit son plus beau chapeau, son chapeau bleu*" . . . and then? Why, then picking up her skirt she threads her way through the crowded streets, reads the advertisements on the walls, hails the omnibus, inquires at the *concierge*'s loge, murmurs as she goes upstairs, "*Que c'est haut le cinqième*," and then? Why, the door opens, and she cries, "*Je t'aime*."

But it was the idea of the new æstheticism—the new art corresponding to modern, as ancient art corresponded to ancient life—that captivated me, that led me away, and not a substantial knowledge of the work done by the naturalists. I had read the "Assommoir," and had been much impressed by its pyramid size, strength, height, and decorative grandeur, and also by the immense harmonic development of the idea; and the fugal treatment of the different scenes had seemed to me astonishingly new—the washhouse, for example: the fight motive is indicated, then follows the development of side issues, then comes the fight motive explained; it is broken off short, it flutters through a web of progressive detail, the fight motive is again taken up, and now it is worked out in all its fulness; it is worked up to *crescendo*, another side issue is introduced, and again the theme is given forth. And I marvelled greatly at the lordly, river-like roll of the narrative, sometimes widening out into lakes and shallowing meres, but never stagnating in fen or marshlands. The language, too, which I did not then recognise as the weak point, being little more than a boiling down of Chateaubriand and Flaubert, spiced with Goncourt, delighted me with its novelty, its richness, its force. Nor did I then even roughly suspect that the very qualities which set my admiration in a blaze wilder than wildfire, being precisely those that had won the victory for the romantic school forty years before, were very antagonistic to those claimed for the new art; I was deceived, as was all my generation, by a certain externality, an outer skin, a nearness, *un approchement*; in a word, by a substitution of Paris for the distant and exotic backgrounds so beloved of the romantic school. I did not know then, as I do now, that art is eternal, that it is only the artist that changes, and that the two great divisions —the only possible divisions—are: those who have talent, and those who have no talent. But I do not regret my errors, my follies; it is not well to know at once of the limitations of life and things. I should be less than nothing had it not been for my enthusiasms; they were the saving clause in my life.[2]

But although I am apt to love too dearly the art of my day, and at the cost of that of other days, I did not fall into the fatal mistake of placing the realistic writers of 1877 side by side with and on the same plane of intellectual vision as the great Balzac; I felt that that vast immemorial mind rose above them all, like a mountain above the highest tower.

And, strange to say, it was Gautier that introduced me to Balzac; for mention is made in the wonderful preface to "Les Fleurs du Mal" of Seraphita: Seraphita, Seraphitus; which is it?—woman or man? Should Wilfred or Mona be the possessor? A new Mdlle. de Maupin, with royal lily and aureole, cloudcapped mountains, great gulfs of sea-water flowing up and reflecting as in a mirror the steep cliff's side; the straight white feet are set thereon, the obscuring weft of flesh is torn, and the pure, strange soul continues its mystical exhortations. Then the radiant vision, a white glory, the last outburst and manifestation, the trumpets of the apocalypse, the colour of heaven; the closing of the stupendous allegory when Seraphita lies dead in the rays of the first sun of the nineteenth century.

I, therefore, had begun, as it were, to read Balzac backwards; instead of beginning with the plain, simple, earthly tragedy of the Père Goriot, I first knelt in a beautiful but distant coigne of the great world of his genius—Seraphita. Certain *nuances* of soul are characteristic of certain latitudes, and what subtle instinct led him to Norway in quest of this fervent soul? The instincts of genius are unfathomable; but he who has known the white northern women with their spiritual eyes, will aver that instinct led him aright. I have known one, one whom I used to call Seraphita; Coppée knew her too, and that exquisite volume, "L'Exilé," so Seraphita-like in the keen blond passion of its verse, was written to her, and each poem was sent to her as it was written. Where is she now, that flower of northern snow, once seen for a season in Paris? Has she returned to her native northern solitudes, great gulfs of sea water, mountain rock, and pine?

Balzac's genius is in his titles as heaven is in its stars: "Melmoth Reconcilé," "Jésus-Christ en Flandres," "Le Revers d'un Grand Homme," "La Cousine Bette." I read somewhere not very long ago, that Balzac was the greatest thinker that had appeared in France since Pascal. Of Pascal's claim to be a great thinker I confess I cannot judge. No man is greater than the age he lives in, and, therefore, to talk to us, the legitimate children of the nineteenth century, of logical proofs of the existence of God strikes us in just the same light as the logical proof of the existence of Jupiter Ammon. "Les Pensées" could appear to me only as infinitely childish; the form is no doubt superb, but tiresome and sterile to one of such modern and exotic taste as myself. Still, I accept thankfully, in its sense of two hundred years, the compliment paid to Balzac; but I would add that personally he seems to me to have shown greater wings of mind than any artist that ever lived. I am aware that this last statement will make many cry "fool" and hiss "Shakespeare!" But I am not putting forward these criticisms axiomatically, but only as the expressions of an individual taste, and interesting so far as they reveal to the reader the different developments and the progress of my mind. It might prove a little tiresome, but it would no doubt "look well," in the sense that going to church "looks well," if I were to write in here ten pages of praise of our national bard. I must, however, resist the temptation to "look well;" a confession is interesting in proportion to the amount of truth it contains, and I will, therefore, state frankly I never derived any profit whatsoever, and very little pleasure from the reading of the great plays. The beauty of the verse! Yes; he who loved Shelley so well as I could not fail to hear the melody of—

> "Music to hear, why hearest thou music sadly
> Sweets with sweets war not, joy delights in joy.[3]

Is not such music as this enough? Of course but I am a sensualist in literature. I may see perfectly well that this or that book is a work of genius, but if it doesn't "fetch me," it doesn't concern me, and I forget its very existence. What leaves me cold to-day will madden me to-morrow. With me literature is a question of sense, intellectual sense if you will, but sense all the same, and ruled by the same caprices—those of the flesh? Now we enter on very subtle distinctions. No doubt that there is the brain-judgment and the sense-judgment of a work of art. And it will be noticed that these two forces of discrimination exist sometimes almost independently of each other, in rare and radiant instances confounded and blended in one immense and unique love. Who has not been, unless perhaps some dusty old pedant, thrilled and driven to pleasure by the action of a book that penetrates to and speaks to you of your most present and most intimate emotions. This is of course pure sensualism; but to take a less marked stage. Why should Marlowe enchant me? why should he delight and awake enthusiasm in me, while Shakespeare leaves me cold? The mind that can understand one can understand the other, but there are affinities in literature corresponding to, and very analogous to, sexual affinities—the same unreasoned attractions, the same pleasures, the same lassitudes. Those we have loved most we are most indifferent to. Shelley, Gautier, Zola, Flaubert, Goncourt! how I have loved you all; and now I could not, would not, read you again. How womanly, how capricious;

but even a capricious woman is constant, if not faithful to her *amant de cœur*. And so with me; of those I have loved deeply there is but one that still may thrill me with the old passion, with the first ecstacy—it is Balzac. Upon that rock I built my church, and his great and valid talent saved me often from destruction, saved me from the shoaling waters of new æstheticisms, the putrid mud of naturalism, and the faint and sickly surf of the symbolists. Thinking of him, I could not forget that it is the spirit and not the flesh that is eternal; that, as it was thought that in the first instance gave man speech, so to the end it shall still be thought that shall make speech beautiful and remember-able. The grandeur and sublimity of Balzac's thoughts seem to me to rise to the loftiest heights, and his range is limitless; there is no passion he has not touched, and what is more marvellous, he has given to each in art a place equivalent to the place it occupies in nature; his intense and penetrating sympathy for human life and all that concerns it enabled him to surround the humblest subjects with awe and crown them with the light of tragedy. There are some, particularly those who are capable of understanding neither and can read but one, who will object to any comparison being drawn between the Dramatist and the Novelist; but I confess that I—if the inherent superiority of verse over prose, which I admit unhesitatingly, be waived—that I fail, utterly fail to see in what Shakespeare is greater than Balzac. The range of the poet's thought is of necessity not so wide, and his concessions must needs be greater than the novelist's. On these points we will cry quits, and come at once to the vital question—the creation. Is Lucien inferior to Hamlet? Is Eugénie Grandet inferior to Desdemona? Is her father inferior to Shylock? Is Macbeth inferior to Vautrin? Can it be said that the apothecary in the "Cousine Bette," or the Baron Hulot, or the Cousine Bette herself is inferior to anything the brain of man has ever conceived? And it must not be forgotten that Shakespeare has had three hundred years and the advantage of stage representation to im-press his characters on the sluggish mind of the world; and as mental impressions are governed by the same laws of gravitation as atoms, our realisation of Falstaff must of necessity be more vivid than any character in contemporary literature, although it were equally great. And so far as epigram and aphorism are concerned, and here I speak with absolute sincerity and conviction, the work of the novelist seems to me richer than that of the dramatist. Who shall forget those terrible words of the poor life-weary orphan in the boarding-house? Speaking of Vautrin she says, "His look frightens me as if he put his hand on my dress;"[4] and another epigram from the same book, "Woman's virtue is man's greatest invention." Find me anything in La Rochefoucauld that goes more incisively to the truth of things. One more; here I can give the exact words: *"La gloire est le soleil des morts."*[5] It would be easy to compile a book of sayings from Balzac that would make all "Maximes" and "Pensées," even those of La Rochefoucauld or Joubert, seem trivial and shallow.

Balzac was the great moral influence of my life, and my reading culminated in the "Comédie Humaine." I no doubt fluttered through some scores of other books, of prose and verse, sipping a little honey, but he alone left any important or lasting impression upon my mind. The rest was like walnuts and wine, an agreeable after-taste.[6]

But notwithstanding all this reading I can lay no claim to scholarship of any kind; for save life I could never learn anything correctly. I am a student only of ball rooms, bar rooms, streets, and alcoves. I have read very little; but all I read I can turn to account, and all I read I remember. To read freely, extensively, has always been my ambition, and my utter inability to study has always been to me a subject of grave inquietude,—study as contrasted with a general and haphazard gathering of ideas taken in flight. But in me the impulse is so original to frequent the haunts of men that it is irresistible, conversation is the breath of my nostrils, I watch the movement of life, and my ideas spring from it uncalled-for, as buds from branches. Contact with the world is in me the generating force; without it what invention I have is thin and sterile, and it grows thinner rapidly, until it dies away utterly, as it did in the composition of my unfortunate "Roses of Midnight."

Men and women, oh the strength of the living faces! conversation, oh the magic of it! It is a fabulous river of gold where the precious metal is washed up without stint for all to take, to take as much as he can carry. Two old ladies discussing the peerage? Much may be learned, it is gold; poets and wits, then it is fountains whose spray solidifies into jewels, and every herb and plant is begemmed with the sparkle of the diamond and the glow of the ruby.

I did not go to either Oxford or Cambridge, but I went to the
"Nouvelle Athènes." What is the "Nouvelle Athènes"? He who would
know anything of my life must know something of the academy of
the fine arts. Not the official stupidity you read of in the daily papers,
but the real French academy, the *café*. The "Nouvelles Athènes" is a
café on the Place Pigalle. Ah! the morning idlenesses and the long evenings when life was but a summer illusion, the grey moonlights on the
Place where we used to stand on the pavements, the shutters clanging
up behind us, loath to separate, thinking of what we had left said,
and how much better we might have enforced our arguments. Dead and
scattered are all those who used to assemble there, and those years and
our home, for it was our home, live only in a few pictures and a few
pages of prose. The same old story, the vanquished only are victorious;
and though unacknowledged, though unknown, the influence of the
"Nouvelle Athènes" is inveterate in the artistic thought of the nineteenth century.

How magnetic, intense, and vivid are these memories of youth. With
what strange, almost unnatural clearness do I see and hear,—see the
white face of that *café*, the white nose of that block of houses, stretch-
ing up to the Place, between two streets. I can see down the incline of
those two streets, and I know what shops are there; I can hear the
glass-door of the *café* grate on the sand as I open it. I can recall the
smell of every hour. In the morning that of eggs frizzling in butter, the
pungent cigarette, coffee and bad cognac; at five o'clock the fragrant
odour of absinthe; and soon after the steaming soup ascends from the
kitchen; and as the evening advances, the mingled smells of cigarettes,
coffee, and weak beer. A partition, rising a few feet or more over the
hats, separates the glass front from the main body of the *café*. The
usual marble tables are there, and it is there we sat and æstheticised
till two o'clock in the morning. But who is that man? he whose prominent eyes flash with excitement. That is Villiers de l'Isle-Adam. The last
or the supposed last of the great family. He is telling that girl a story—
that fair girl with heavy eyelids, stupid and sensual. She is, however,
genuinely astonished and interested, and he is striving to play upon
her ignorance. Listen to him. "Spain—the night is fragrant with the sea
and the perfume of the orange trees, you know—a midnight of stars
and dreams. Now and then the silence is broken by the sentries chal-

lenging—that is all. But not in Spanish but in French are the challenges given; the town is in the hands of the French; it is under martial law. But now an officer passes down a certain garden, a Spaniard disguised as a French officer; from the balcony the family—one of the most noble and oldest families Spain can boast of, a thousand years, long before the conquest of the Moors—watches him. Well then"—Villiers sweeps with a white feminine hand the long hair that is falling over his face—he has half forgotten, he is a little mixed in the opening of the story, and he is striving in English to "scamp," in French to *escamoter*. "The family are watching, death if he is caught, if he fails to kill the French sentry. The cry of a bird, some vague sound attracts the sentry, he turns; all is lost. The Spaniard is seized. Martial law, Spanish conspiracy must be put down. The French general is a man of iron." (Villiers laughs, a short hesitating laugh that is characteristic of him, and continues in his abrupt, uncertain way), "man of iron; not only he declares that the spy must be beheaded, but also the entire family—a man of iron that, ha, ha; and then, no you cannot, it is impossible for you to understand the enormity of the calamity—a thousand years before the conquest by the Moors, a Spaniard alone could—there is no one here, ha, ha, I was forgetting—the utter extinction of a great family of the name, the oldest and noblest of all families in Spain, it is not easy to understand that, no, not easy here in the 'Nouvelle Athènes'—ha, ha, one must belong to a great family to understand, ha, ha.

"The father beseeches, he begs that one member may be spared to continue the name—the youngest son—that is all; if he could be saved, the rest what matter; death is nothing to a Spaniard; the family, the name, a thousand years of name is everything. The general is, you know, a 'man of iron.' 'Yes, one member of your family shall be respited, but on one condition.' To the agonised family conditions are as nothing. But they don't know the man of iron is determined to make a terrible example, and they cry, 'Any conditions.' 'He who is respited must serve as executioner to the others.' Great is the doom; you understand; but after all the name must be saved. Then in the family council the father goes to his youngest son and says, 'I have been a good father to you, my son; I have always been a kind father, have I not? answer me; I have never refused you anything. Now you will not fail us, you will prove yourself worthy of the great name you bear. Remember your great ancestor who defeated the Moors, remember.' " (Villiers strives to get in a little local colour, but his knowledge of Spanish names and history is limited, and he in a certain sense fails.) "Then the mother comes to her son and says, 'My son, I have been a good mother, I have always loved you; say you will not desert us in this hour of our great need.' Then the little sister comes, and the whole family kneels down and appeals to the horror-stricken boy. . . .

" 'He will not prove himself unworthy of our name,' cries the father. 'Now, my son, courage, take the axe firmly, do what I ask you, courage, strike straight.' The father's head falls into the sawdust, the blood all over the white beard; then comes the elder brother, and then another brother; and then, oh, the little sister was almost more than he could bear, and the mother had to whisper, 'Remember your promise to your father, to your dead father,' The mother laid her head on the block, but he could not strike. 'Be not the first coward of our name, strike; remember your promise to us all,' and her head was struck off."

"And the son," the girl asks, "what became of him?"

"He never was seen, save at night, walking, a solitary man, beneath the walls of his castle in Granada."

"And whom did he marry?"

"He never married."

Then after a long silence some one said,—

"Whose story is that?"

"Balzac's."[7]

At that moment the glass door of the *café* grated upon the sanded floor, and Manet entered. Although by birth and by art essentially Parisian, there was something in his appearance and manner of speaking that often suggested an Englishman. Perhaps it was his dress—his clean-cut clothes and figure. That figure! those square shoulders that swaggered as he went across a room and the thin waist; and that face, the beard and nose, satyr-like shall I say? No, for I would evoke an idea of beauty of line united to that of intellectual expression—frank words, frank passion in his convictions, loyal and simple phrases, clear as well-water, sometimes a little hard, sometimes, as they flowed away, bitter, but at the fountain head sweet and full of light.[8] He sits next to Degas, that round-shouldered man in suit of pepper and salt. There is nothing very trenchantly French about him either, except the large necktie; his eyes are small and his words are sharp, ironical, cynical. These two men are the leaders of the impressionist school. Their friendship has been jarred by inevitable rivalry. "Degas was painting 'Semiramis' when I was painting 'Modern Paris,'" says Manet. "Manet is in despair because he cannot paint atrocious pictures like Durant, and be fêted and decorated; he is an artist, not by inclination, but by force. He is as a galley slave chained to the oar," says Degas. Different too are their methods of work. Manet paints his whole picture from nature, trusting his instinct to lead him aright through the devious labyrinth of selection. Nor does his instinct ever fail him, there is a vision in his eyes which he calls nature, and which he paints unconsciously as he digests his food, thinking and declaring vehemently that the artist should not seek a synthesis, but should paint merely what he sees. This extraordinary oneness of nature and artistic vision does not exist in Degas, and even his portraits are composed from drawings and notes.[9] About midnight Catulle Mendès will drop in, when he has corrected his proofs. He will come with his fine paradoxes and his strained eloquence. He will lean towards you, he will take you by the arm, and his presence is a nervous pleasure. And when the *café* is closed, when the last bock has been drunk, we shall walk about the great moonlight of the Place Pigalle, and through the dark shadows of the streets, talking of the last book published, he hanging on to my arm, speaking in that high febrile voice of his, every phrase luminous, aerial, even as the soaring moon and the fitful clouds. Duranty, an unknown Stendhal, will come in for an hour or so; he will talk little and go away quietly; he knows, and his whole manner shows that he knows that he is a defeated man; and if you ask him why he does not write another novel, he will say, "What's the good, it would not be read; no one read the others, and I mightn't do even as well if I tried again."[10] Paul Alexis, Léon Dierx, Pissarro, Cabaner, are also frequently seen in the "Nouvelle Athènes."

Cabaner! the world knows not the names of those who scorn the world: somewhere in one of the great populous churchyards of Paris there is a forgotten grave, and there lies Cabaner. Cabaner! since the beginning there have been, till the end of time there shall be Cabaners; and they shall live miserably and they shall die miserable, and shall be forgotten; and there shall never arise a novelist great enough to make live in art that eternal spirit of devotion, disinterestedness, and aspiration, which in each generation incarnates itself in one heroic soul. Better than those who stepped to opulence and fame upon thee fallen thou wert; better, loftier-minded, purer; thy destiny was to fall that others might rise upon thee, thou wert one of the noble legion of the conquered; let praise be given to the conquered, for the brunt of victory lies with the conquered. Child of the pavement, of strange sonnets and stranger music, I remember thee; I remember the silk shirts, the four sous of Italian cheese, the roll of bread, and the glass of milk;—the streets were thy dining-room. And the five-mile walk daily to the suburban music hall where five francs were earned by playing the accompaniments of comic songs. And the wonderful room on the fifth floor, which was furnished when that celebrated heritage of two thousand francs was paid. I remember the fountain that was bought for a wardrobe, and the American organ with all the instruments of the orchestra, and the plaster casts under which the homeless ones that were never denied a refuge and a crust by thee slept. I remember all, and the buying of the life-size "Venus de Milo." Something extra-ordinary would be done with it, I knew, but the result exceeded my wildest expectation. The head must needs be struck off, so that the rapture of thy admiration should be secure from all jarring reminis-cence of the streets.

Then the wonderful story of the tenor, the pork butcher, who was heard giving out such a volume of sound that the sausages were set in motion above him; he was fed, clothed, and educated on the five francs a day earned in the music hall in the Avenue de la Motte Piquet; and when he made his *début* at the Théâtre Lyrique, thou wert in the last stage of consumption and too ill to go to hear thy pupil's success. He was immediately engaged by Mapleson and taken to America.

I remember thy face, Cabaner; I can see it now—that long sallow face ending in a brown beard, and the hollow eyes, the meagre arms covered with a silk shirt, contrasting strangely with the rest of the dress. In all thy privation and poverty, thou didst never forego thy silk shirt. I remember the paradoxes and the aphorisms, if not the exact words, the glamour and the sentiment of a humour that was all thy own. Never didst thou laugh; no, not even when in discussing how silence might be rendered in music, thou didst say, with thy extra-ordinary Pyrenean accent, *"Pour rendre le silence en music il me faudrait trois orchestres militaires."* And when I did show thee some poor verses of mine, French verses, for at this time I hated and had partly forgotten my native language—

"My dear Dayne, you always write about love, the subject is nause-ating."

"So it is, so it is; but after all Baudelaire wrote about love and lovers; his best poem. . . ."

"C'est vrai, mais il s'agissait d'une charogne et cela relève beaucoup la chose."

I remember, too, a few stray snatches of thy extraordinary music, "music that might be considered by Wagner as a little too advanced, but which Liszt would not fail to understand;" also thy settings of sonnets where the *melody* was continued uninterruptedly from the first line to the last; and that still more marvellous feat, thy setting, likewise with unbroken melody, of Villon's ballade "Les Dames du Temps Jadis;" and that Out-Cabanering of Cabaner, the putting to music of Cros's "Hareng Saur."

And why didst thou remain ever poor and unknown? Because of something too much, or something too little? Because of something too much! so I think, at least; thy heart was too full of too pure an ideal, too far removed from all possible contagion with the base crowd.

But, Cabaner, thou didst not labour in vain; thy destiny, though obscure, was a valiant and fruitful one; and, as in life, thou didst live for others so now in death thou dost live in others. Thou wert in an hour of wonder and strange splendour when the last tints and loveli-nesses of romance lingered in the deepening west; when out of the clear east rose with a mighty effulgence of colour and lawless light Realism; when showing aloft in the dead pallor of the zenith, like a white flag fluttering faintly, Symbolists and Decadents appeared. Never before was there so sudden a flux and conflux of artistic desire, such aspiration in the soul of man, such rage of passion, such fainting fever, such cerebral erethism. The roar and dust of the daily battle of the Realists was continued under the flush of the sunset, the arms of the Romantics glittered, the pale spiritual Symbolists watched and waited, none knowing yet of their presence. In such an hour of artistic convulsion and renewal of thought thou wert, and thou wert a magnificent rallying point for all comers; it was thou who didst theorise our confused aspirations, and by thy holy example didst save us from all base commercialism, from all hateful prostitution; thou wert ever our high priest, and from thy high altar turned to us the white host, the ideal, the true and living God of all men.

Cabaner, I see you now entering the "Nouvelle Athènes;" you are a little tired after your long weary walk, but you lament not and you never cry out against the public that will accept neither your music nor your poetry. But though you are tired and footsore, you are ready to æstheticise till the *café* closes; for you the homeless ones are waiting: there they are, some three or four, and you will take them to your strange room, furnished with the American organ, the fountain, and the decapitated Venus, and you give them a crust each and cover them with what clothes you have; and, when clothes are lacking, with plaster casts, and though you will take but a glass of milk yourself, you will find a few sous to give them *lager* to cool their thirsty throats. So you have ever lived—a blameless life is yours, no base thought has ever entered there, not even a woman's love; art and friends, that is all.

Reader, do you know of anything more angelic? If you do you are more fortunate than I have been.[11]

CHAPTER SEVEN

THE SYNTHESIS OF THE NOUVELLE ATHÈNES

Two dominant notes in my character—an original hatred of my native country, and a brutal loathing of the religion I was brought up in. All the aspects of my native country are violently disagreeable to me, and I cannot think of the place I was born in without a sensation akin to nausea. These feelings are inherent and inveterate in me. I am instinctively averse to my own countrymen; they are at once remote and repulsive; but with Frenchmen I am conscious of a sense of nearness; I am one with them in their ideas and aspirations, and when I am with them, I am alive with a keen and penetrating sense of intimacy. Shall I explain this by atavism? Was there a French man or woman in my family some half dozen generations ago? I have not inquired. The English I love, and with a love that is foolish—mad, limitless; I love them better than the French, but I am not so near to them. ¶ Dear, sweet Protestant England, the red tiles of the farmhouse, the elms, the great hedgerows, and all the rich fields adorned with spreading trees, and the weald and the wold, the very words are passionately beautiful . . . southern England, not the north—there is something Celtic in the north,—southern England, with its quiet, steadfast faces;—a smock frock is to me one of the most delightful things in the world; it is so absolutely English. The villages clustered round the greens, the spires of the churches pointing between the elm trees. . . . This is congenial to me; and this is Protestantism. England is Protestantism, Protestantism is England. Protestantism is strong, clean, and westernly, Catholicism is eunuch-like, dirty, and Oriental. . . . Yes, Oriental; there is something even Chinese about it. What made

England great was Protestantism, and when she ceases to be Protestant she will fall. . . . Look at the nations that have clung to Catholicism, starving moonlighters and starving brigands. The Protestant flag floats on every ocean breeze, the Catholic banner hangs limp in the incense silence of the Vatican. Let us be Protestant, and revere Cromwell. ⟩ [1]

———

Garçon, un bock! I write to please myself, just as I order my dinner; if my books sell I cannot help it—it is an accident.

But you live by writing.

Yes, but life is only an accident—art is eternal.

———

What I reproach Zola with is that he has no style; there is nothing you won't find in Zola from Chateaubriand to the reporting in the *Figaro*.

He seeks immortality in an exact description of a linendraper's shop; if the shop conferred immortality it should be upon the linendraper who created the shop, and not on the novelist who described it.

And his last novel "l'Œuvre," how terribly spun out, and for a franc a line in the "Gil Blas." Not a single new or even exact observation. And that terrible phrase repeated over and over again—"La Conquête de Paris." What does it mean? I never knew any one who thought of conquering Paris;—no one ever spoke of conquering Paris except, perhaps, two or three provincials. [2]

———

You must have rules in poetry, if it is only for the pleasure of breaking them, just as you must have women dressed, if it is only for the pleasure of imagining them as Venuses.

———

Fancy, a banquet was given to Julien by his pupils! He made a speech in favour of Lefebvre, and hoped that every one there would vote for Lefebvre. Julien was very eloquent. He spoke of *Le grand art, le nu*, and Lefebvre's unswerving fidelity to *le nu* . . . elegance, refinement, an echo of ancient Greece: and then,—what do you think? when he had exhausted all the reasons why the medal of honour should be accorded to Lefebvre, he said, "I ask you to remember, gentlemen, that he has a wife and eight children." Is it not monstrous?

———

But it is you who are monstrous, you who expect to fashion the whole world in conformity with your æstheticisms . . . a vain dream, and if realised it would result in an impossible world. A wife and children are the basis of existence, and it is folly to cry out because an appeal to such interests as these meets with response . . . it will be so till the end of time.

And these great interests that are to continue to the end of time began two years ago, when your pictures were not praised in the *Figaro* as much as you thought they should be.

Marriage—what an abomination! Love—yes, but not marriage. Love cannot exist in marriage, because love is an ideal; that is to say, something not quite understood—transparencies, colour, light, a sense of the unreal. But a wife—you know all about her—who her father was, who her mother was, what she thinks of you and her opinion of the neighbours over the way. Where, then, is the dream, the *au delà*? There is none. I say in marriage an *au delà* is impossible. . . . the endless duet of the marble and the water, the enervation of burning odours, the baptismal whiteness of women, light, ideal tissues, eyes strangely dark with kohl, names that evoke palm trees and ruins, Spanish moonlight or maybe Persepolis. The monosyllable which epitomises the ennui and the prose of our lives is heard not, thought not there—only the nightingale-harmony of an eternal yes. Freedom limitless; the Mahometan stands on the verge of the abyss, and the spaces of perfume and colour extend and invite him with the whisper of a sweet unending yes. The unknown, the unreal. . . . Thus love is possible, there is a delusion, an *au delà*.

Good heavens! and the world still believes in education, in teaching people the "grammar of art." Education is fatal to any one with a spark of artistic feeling. Education should be confined to clerks, and even them it drives to drink. Will the world learn that we never learn anything that we did not know before? The artists, the poet, painter, musician, and novelist go straight to the food they want, guided by an unerring and ineffable instinct; to teach them is to destroy the nerve of the artistic instinct, it is fatal. But above all in painting . . . "correct drawing," "solid painting." Is it impossible to teach people, to force it into their heads that there is no such thing as correct drawing, and that if drawing were correct it would be wrong? Solid painting; good heavens! Do they suppose that there is one sort of painting that is better than all others, and that there is a recipe for making it as for making chocolate! Art is not mathematics, it is individuality. It does not matter how badly you paint, so long as you don't paint badly like other people. Education destroys individuality. That great studio of Julien's is a sphinx, and all the poor folk that go there for artistic education are devoured. After two years they all paint and draw alike, every one; that vile execution,—they call it execution,— *la pâte, la peinture au premier coup.* I was over in England last year, and I saw some portraits by a man called Richmond. They were horrible, but I liked them because they weren't like painting. Stott and Sargent are clever fellows enough; I like Stott the best. If they had remained at home and hadn't been taught, they might have developed a personal art, but the trail of the serpent is over all they do—that vile French painting, *le morceau,* etc. Stott is getting over it by degrees. He exhibited a nymph this year. I know what he meant; it was an interesting intention. I liked his little landscapes better . . . simplified into nothing, into a couple of primitive tints, wonderful clearness, light. But I doubt if he will find a public to understand all that.

Democratic art! Art is the direct antithesis to democracy. . . . Athens! a few thousand citizens who owned many thousand slaves, call that democracy! No! what I am speaking of is modern democracy—the mass. The mass can only appreciate simple and *naïve* emotions, puerile prettiness, above all conventionalities. See the Americans that come over here; what do they admire? Is it Degas or Manet they admire? No, Bouguereau and Lefebvre. What was most admired at the International Exhibition?—The Dirty Boy. And if the medal of honour had been decided by a *plébiscite,* the dirty boy would have had an overwhelming majority. What is the literature of the people? The idiotic stories of the *Petit Journal.* Don't talk of Shakespeare, Molière, and the masters; they are accepted on the authority of the centuries. If the people could understand *Hamlet,* the people would not read the *Petit Journal;* if the people could understand Michel Angelo, they would not look at our Bouguereau or your Bouguereau, Sir F. Leighton. For the last hundred years we have been going rapidly towards democracy, and what is the result? The destruction of the handicrafts. That there are still good pictures painted and good poems written proves nothing, there will always be found men to sacrifice their lives for a picture or a poem. But the decorative arts which are executed in collaboration, and depend for support on the general taste of a large number, have ceased to exist. Explain that if you can. I'll give you five thousand, ten thousand francs to buy a beautiful clock that is not a copy and is not ancient, and you can't do it. Such a thing does not exist. Look here; I was going up the staircase of the Louvre the other day. They were puttting up a mosaic; it was horrible; every one knows it is horrible. Well, I asked who had given the order for this mosaic, and I could not find out; no one knew. An order is passed from bureau to bureau, and no one is responsible; and it will be always so in a republic, and the more republican you are the worse it will be.

The world is dying of machinery; that is the great disease, that is the plague that will sweep away and destroy civilisation; man will have to rise against it sooner or later. . . . Capital, unpaid labour, wage-slaves, and all the rest—stuff. . . . Look at these plates; they were painted by machinery; they are abominable. Look at them. In old times plates were painted by the hand, and the supply was necessarily limited to the demand, and a china in which there was always something more or less pretty, was turned out; but now thousands, millions of plates are made more than we want, and there is a commercial crisis; the thing is inevitable. I say the great and the reasonable revolution will be when mankind rises in revolt, and smashes the machinery and restores the handicrafts.[3]

Goncourt is not an artist, notwithstanding all his affections and outcries; he is not an artist. *Il me fait l'effet* of an old woman shrieking after immortality and striving to beat down some fragment of it with a broom. Once it was a duet, now it is a solo. They wrote novels, history, plays, they collected *bric-à-brac*—they wrote about their *bric-à-brac*; they painted in water-colours, they etched—they wrote about their water-colours and etchings; they have made a will settling that the *bric-à-brac* is to be sold at their death, and the proceeds applied to founding a prize for the best essay or novel, I forget which it is. They wrote about the prize they are going to found; they kept a diary, they wrote down everything they heard, felt, or saw, *radotage de vieille femme*; nothing must escape, not the slightest word; it might be that very word that might confer on them immortality; everything they heard, or said, must be of value, of inestimable value. A real artist does not trouble himself about immortality, about everything he hears, feels, and says; he treats ideas and sensations as so much clay wherewith to create.

And then the famous collaboration; how it was talked about, written about, prayed about; and when Jules died, what a subject for talk for articles; it all went into pot. Hugo's vanity was Titanic, Goncourt's is puerile.[4]

And Daudet?

Oh, Daudet, *c'est de la bouillabaisse.*

Whistler, of all artists, is the least impressionist; the idea people have of his being an impressionist only proves once again the absolute inability of the public to understand the merits or the demerits of artistic work. Whistler's art is absolutely classical; he thinks of nature, but he does not see nature; he is guided by his mind, and not by his eyes; and the best of it is he says so. Oh, he knows it well enough! Any one who knows him must have heard him say, "Painting is absolutely scientific; it is an exact science." And his work is in accord with his theory; he risks nothing, all is brought down, arranged, balanced, and made one,— a well-determined mental conception. I admire his work; I am merely showing how he is misunderstood, even by those who think they understand. Does he ever seek a pose that is characteristic of the model, a pose that the model repeats oftener than any other?—Never. He advances the foot, puts the hand on the hip, etc., with a view to rendering his *idea*. Take his portrait of Duret. Did he ever see Duret in dress clothes? Probably not. Did he ever see Duret with a lady's opera cloak?— I am sure he never did. Is Duret in the habit of going to the theatre with ladies? No; he is a *littérateur* who is always in men's society, rarely in ladies'. But these facts mattered nothing to Whistler as they matter to Degas, or to Manet. Whistler took Duret out of his environment, dressed him up, thought out a scheme—in a word, painted his idea without concerning himself in the least with the model. Mark you, I deny that I am urging any fault or flaw; I am merely contending that Whistler's art is not modern art, but classic art—yes, and severely classical, far more classical than Titian's or Velasquez;—from an opposite pole as classical as Ingres. No Greek dramatist ever sought the synthesis of things more uncompromisingly than Whistler. And he is right. Art is not nature. Art is nature digested. Art is a sublime excrement. Zola and Goncourt cannot, or will not understand that the artistic stomach must be allowed to do its work in its own mysterious fashion. If a man is really an artist he will remember what is necessary, forget what is useless; but if he takes notes he will interrupt his artistic digestion, and the result will be a lot of little touches, inchoate and wanting in the elegant rhythm of the synthesis.

I am sick of synthetical art; we want observation direct and un-reasoned. What I reproach Millet with is that it is always the same thing, the same peasant, the same *sabot*, the same sentiment. You must admit that it is somewhat stereotyped.

What does that matter; what is more stereotyped than Japanese art? But that does not prevent it from being always beautiful.

People talk of Manet's originality; that is just what I can't see. What he has got, and what you can't take away from him, is a magnificent execution. A piece of still life by Manet is the most wonderful thing in the world; vividness of colour, breadth, simplicity, and directness of touch—marvellous!

French translation is the only translation; in England you still continue to translate poetry into poetry, instead of into prose. We used to do the same, but we have long ago renounced such follies. Either of two things—if the translator is a good poet, he substitutes his verse for that of the original;—I don't want his verse, I want the original;— if he is a bad poet, he gives us bad verse, which is intolerable. Where the original poet put an effect of cæsura, the translator puts an effect of rhyme; where the original poet puts an effect of rhyme, the translator puts an effect of cæsura. Take Longfellow's "Dante." Does it give as

good an idea of the original as our prose translation? Is it as interesting reading? Take Bayard Taylor's translation of "Goethe." Is it readable? Not to any one with an ear for verse. Will any one say that
Taylor's would be read if the original did not exist. The fragment translated by Shelley is beautiful, but then it is Shelley. Look at Swinburne's
translation of Villon. They are beautiful poems by Swinburne, that is
all; he makes Villon speak of a "splendid kissing mouth." Villon could
not have done this unless he had read Swinburne. "Heine," translated
by James Thomson, is not different from Thomson's original poems;
"Heine," translated by Sir Theodore Martin, is doggerel.

But in English blank verse you can translate quite as literally as you
could into prose?

I doubt it, but even so, the rhythm of the blank line would carry your
mind away from that of the original.

But if you don't know the original?

The rhythm of the original can be suggested in prose judiciously used;
even if it isn't, your mind is at least free, whereas the English rhythm
must destroy the sensation of something foreign. There is no translation except a word-for-word translation. Baudelaire's translation of
Poe, and Hugo's translation of Shakespeare, are marvellous in this
respect; a pun or joke that is untranslatable is explained in a note.

But that is the way young ladies translate—word for word!

No; 'tis just what they don't do; they think they are translating word
for word, but they aren't. All the proper names, no matter how un-
pronounceable, must be rigidly adhered to; you must never transpose
versts into kilometres, or roubles into francs;—I don't know what a
verst is or what a rouble is, but when I see the words I am in Russia.
Every proverb must be rendered literally, even if it doesn't make very
good sense; if it doesn't make sense at all, it must be explained in a note.
For example, there is a proverb in German: "*Quand le cheval est sellé
il faut le monter;*" in French there there is a proverb: "*Quand le vin*

est tiré il faut le boire." Well, a translator who would translate *quand le cheval*, etc., by *quand le vin*, etc., is an ass, and does not know his business. In translation, only a strictly classical language should be used; no word of slang, or even word of modern origin should be employed; the translator's aim should be never to dissipate the illusion of an exotic. If I were translating the "Assommoir" into English, I should strive after a strong, flexible, but colourless language, some-thing—what shall I say?—a sort of a modern Addison.

What, don't you know the story about Mendès?—when *Chose* wanted to marry his sister? *Chose's* mother, it appears, went to live with a priest. The poor fellow was dreadfully cut up; he was broken-hearted; and he went to Mendès, his heart swollen with grief, determined to make a clean breast of it, let the worst come to the worst. After a great deal of beating about the bush, and apologising, he got it out. You know Mendès, you can see him smiling a little; and looking at *Chose* with that white cameo face of his he said, *"Avec quel meilleur homme voulez-vous que votre mère se fit? vous n'avez donc, jeune homme, aucun sentiment religieux."*

Victor Hugo, he is a painter on porcelain; his verse is mere decoration, long tendrils and flowers; and the same thing over and over again.

How to be happy!—not to read Baudelaire and Verlaine, not to enter the *Nouvelle Athènes*, unless perhaps to play dominoes like the *bourgeois* over there, not to do anything that would awake a too intense con-sciousness of life,—to live in a sleepy country side, to have a garden to work in, to have a wife and children, to chatter quietly every evening over the details of existence. We must have the azaleas out to-morrow and thoroughly cleansed, they are devoured by insects; the tame rook has flown away; mother lost her prayer-book coming from church, she thinks it was stolen. A good, honest, well-to-do peasant, who knows nothing of politics, must be very nearly happy; and to think there are people who would educate, who would draw these people out of the calm satisfaction of their instincts, and give them passions! The philan-thropist is the Nero of modern times.

CHAPTER EIGHT

EXTRACT FROM A LETTER[1]

Why did you not send a letter? We have all been writing to you for the last six months, but no answer—none. Had you written one word I would have saved all. The poor concierge was in despair; she said the *propriétaire* would wait if you had only said when you were coming back, or if you only had let us know what you wished to be done. Three quarters rent was due, and no news could be obtained of you, so an auction had to be called. It nearly broke my heart to see those horrid men tramping over the delicate carpets, their coarse faces set against the sweet colour of that beautiful English cretonne. . . . And all the while the pastel by Manet, the great hat set like an aureole about the face—'the eyes deep set in crimson shadow,' 'the fan widespread across the bosom' (you see I am quoting your own words),[2] looking down, the mistress of that little paradise of tapestry. She seemed to resent the intrusion. I looked once or twice half expecting those eyes 'deep set in crimson shadow' to fill with tears. But nothing altered her great dignity; she seemed to see all, but as a Buddha she remained impenetrable. . . .

"I was there the night before the sale. I looked through the books, taking notes of those I intended to buy—those which we used to read together when the snow lay high about the legs of the poor faun in *terre cuite*, that laughed amid the frosty *boulingrins*. I found a large packet of letters which I instantly destroyed. You should not be so careless; I wonder how it is that men are always careless about their letters.

"The sale was announced for one o'clock. I wore a thick veil, for I did not wish to be recognised; the concierge of course knew me, but she can be depended upon. The poor old woman was in tears, so sorry was she to see all your pretty things sold up. You left owing her a hundred francs, but I have paid her; and talking of you we waited till the auctioneer arrived. Everything had been pulled down; the tapestry from the walls, the picture, the two vases I gave you were on the table waiting the stroke of the hammer. And then the men, all the *marchands de meubles* in the *quartier*, came upstairs, spitting and talking coarsely—their foul voices went through me. They stamped, spat, pulled the things about, nothing escaped them. One of them held up the Japanese dressing-gown and made some horrible jokes; and the auctioneer, who was a humorist, answered, 'If there are any ladies' men present, we shall have some spirited bidding.' The pastel I bought, and I shall keep it and try to find some excuse to satisfy my husband, but I send you the miniature, and I hope you will not let it be sold again. There were many other things I should have liked to have bought but I did not dare—the organ that you used to play hymns on and I waltzes on, the Turkish lamp which we could never agree about . . . but when I saw the satin shoes which I gave you to carry the night of that adorable ball, and which you would not give back, but nailed up on the wall on either side of your bed and put matches in, I was seized with an almost invincible desire to steal them. I don't know why, *un caprice de femme*. No one but you would have ever thought of converting satin shoes into match boxes. I wore them at that delicious ball; we danced all night together, and you had an explanation with my husband (I was a little afraid for a moment, but it came out all right), and we went and sat on the balcony in the soft warm moonlight; we watched the glitter of epaulets and gas, the satin of the bodices, the whiteness of passing shoulders; we dreamed the massy darknesses of the park, the fairy light along the lawny spaces, the heavy perfume of the flowers, the pink of the camellias; and you quoted something: '*les camélias du balcon ressemblent à des désirs mourants.*' It was horrid of you: but you always had a knack of rubbing one up the wrong way. Then do you not remember how we danced in one room, while the servants set the other out with little tables? That supper was fascinating! I suppose it was these pleasant remembrances which made me wish for the shoes, but I could not summon up courage enough to buy them, and the horrid people were comparing me with the pastel; I suppose I did look a little mysterious with a double veil bound across my face. The shoes went with a lot of other things—and oh, to whom?[3]

"So now that pretty little retreat in the *Rue de la Tour des Dames* is ended for ever for you and me. We shall not see the faun in *terre cuite* again; I was thinking of going to see him the other day, but the street is so steep; my coachman advised me to spare the horse's hind legs. I believe it is the steepest street in Paris. And your luncheon parties, how I did enjoy them, and how Fay did enjoy them too; and what I risked, shortsighted as I am, picking my way from the tramcar down to that out-of-the-way little street! Men never appreciate the risks women run for them. But to leave my letters lying about I cannot forgive that. When I told Fay she said, 'What can you expect? I warned you against flirting with boys.' I never did before—never.

"Paris is now just as it was when you used to sit on the balcony and I read you Browning. You never liked his poetry, and I cannot understand why. I have found a new poem which I am sure would convert you; you should be here. There are lilacs in the room and the *Mont Valérien* is beautiful upon a great lemon sky, and the long avenue is merging into violet vapour.

"We have already begun to think of where we shall go to this year. Last year we went to P——, an enchanting place, quite rustic, but within easy distance of a casino. I had vowed not to dance, for I had been out every night during the season, but the temptation proved irresistible, and I gave way. There were two young men here, one the Count of B——, the other the Marquis of G——, one of the best families in France, a distant cousin of my husband. He has written a book which every one says is one of the most amusing things that has appeared for years, *c'est surtout très Parisien*. He paid me great attentions, and made my husband wildly jealous. I used to go out and sit with him amid the rocks, and it was perhaps very lucky for me that he went away. We may return there this year; if so, I wish you would come and spend a month; there is an excellent hotel where you would be very comfortable. We have decided nothing as yet. The Duchesse de—— is giving a costume ball; they say it is going to be a most wonderful affair. I don't know what money is not going to be spent upon the cotillion. I have just got home a fascinating toilette. I am going as a

Pierrotte; you know, a short skirt and a little cap. The Marquise gave a ball some few days ago. I danced the cotillion with L——, who, as you know, dances divinely; *il m'a fait la cour*, but it is of course no use, you know that.

"The other night we went to see the *Maître-de-Forges*, a fascinating play, and I am reading the book; I don't know which I like the best. I think the play, but the book is very good too. Now that is what I call a novel; and I am a judge, for I have read all novels. But I must not talk literature, or you will say something stupid. I wish you would not make foolish remarks about men that *tout-Paris* considers the cleverest. It does not matter so much with me, I know you, but then people laugh at you behind your back, and that is not nice for me. The *marquise* was here the other day, and she said she almost wished you would not come on her 'days,' so extraordinary were the remarks you made. And by the way, the *marquise* has written a book. I have not seen it, but I hear that it is really too *décolleté*. She is *une femme d'esprit*, but the way she affiché's herself is too much for any one. She never goes any-where now without *le petit* D——. It is a great pity.

"And now, my dear friend, write me a nice letter, and tell me when you are coming back to Paris. I am sure you cannot amuse yourself in that hateful London; the nicest thing about you was that you were really *très Parisien*. Come back and take a nice apartment on the Champs Elysées. You might come back for the Duchesse's ball. I will get an invitation for you, and will keep the cotillion for you. The idea of running away as you did, and never telling any one where you were going to. I always said you were a little cracked. And letting all your things be sold! If you had only told me! I should like so much to have had that Turkish lamp. Yours ———"

How like her that letter is,—egotistical, vain, foolish; no, not foolish—narrow, limited, but not foolish; worldly, oh, how worldly! and yet not repulsively so, for there always was in her a certain intensity of feel-ing that saved her from the commonplace, and gave her an inexpres-sible charm. Yes, she is a woman who can feel, and she has lived her life and felt it very acutely, very sincerely—sincerely? . . . like a moth caught in a gauze curtain! Well, would that preclude sincerity? Sin-cerity seems to convey an idea of depth, and she was not very deep, that

is quite certain. I never could understand her;—a little brain that span
rapidly and hummed a pretty humming tune. But no, there was something more in her than that. She often said things that I thought clever,
things that I did not forget, things that I should like to put into books.
But it was not brain power; it was only intensity of feeling—nervous
feeling. I don't know . . . perhaps. . . . She has lived her life . . . yes,
within certain limits she has lived her life. None of us do more than
that. True. I remember the first time I saw her. Sharp, little, and merry
—a changeable little sprite. I thought she had ugly hands; so she has,
and yet I forgot all about her hands before I had known her a month.
It is now seven years ago. How time passes! I was very young then.
What battles we have had, what quarrels! Still we had good times
together. She never lost sight of me, but no intrusion; far too clever
for that. I never got the better of her but once . . . once I did, *enfin!* She
soon made up for lost ground. I wonder what the charm was. I did not
think her pretty, I did not think her clever; that I know. . . . I never
knew if she cared for me, never. There were moments when. . . .
Curious, febrile, subtle little creature, oh, infinitely subtle, subtle in
everything, in her sensations subtle; I suppose that was her charm,
subtleness. I never knew if she cared for me, I never knew if she hated
her husband,—one never knew her,—I never knew how she would
receive me. The last time I saw her . . . that stupid American would
take her downstairs, no getting rid of him, and I was hiding behind
one of the pillars in the Rue de Rivoli, my hand on the cab door. However, she could not blame me that time—and all the stories she used
to invent of my indiscretions; I believe she used to get them up for the
sake of the excitement. She was awfully silly in some ways, once you
got her into a certain line; that marriage, that title, and she used to
think of it night and day. I shall never forget when she went into
mourning for the Count de Chambord. And her tastes, oh, how bourgeois they were! That salon; the flagrantly modern clock, brass work,
eight hundred francs on the Boulevard St. Germain, the cabinets, brass
work, the rich brown carpet, and the furniture set all round the room
geometrically, the great gilt mirror, the ancestral portrait, the arms and
crest everywhere, and the stuffy bourgeois sense of comfort; a little
grotesque no doubt;—the mechanical admiration for all that is about
her, for the general atmosphere; the *Figaro*, that is to say Albert Wolff,

l'homme le plus spirituel de Paris, c'est-à-dire, dans le monde, the success of Georges Ohnet and the talent of Gustave Doré. But with all this vulgarity of taste certain appreciations, certain ebullitions of sentiment, within the radius of sentiment certain elevations and depravities,—depravities in the legitimate sense of the word, that is to say, a revolt against the commonplace. . . .

Ha, ha, ha! how I have been dreaming! I wish I had not been awoke from my reverie, it was pleasant.

The letter just read indicates, if it does not clearly tell, the changes that have taken place in my life; and it is only necessary to say that one morning, a few months ago, when my servant brought me some summer honey and a glass of milk to my bedside, she handed me an unpleasant letter. My agent's handwriting, even when I knew the envelope contained a cheque, has never quite failed to produce a sensation of repugnance in me;—so hateful is any sort of account, that I avoid as much as possible even knowing how I stand at my banker's. Therefore the odour of honey and milk, so evocative of fresh flowers and fields, was spoilt that morning for me; and it was some time before I slipped on that beautiful Japanese dressing-gown, which I shall never see again, and read the odious epistle.

That some wretched farmers and miners should refuse to starve, that I may not be deprived of my *demi-tasse* at *Tortoni's*; that I may not be forced to leave this beautiful retreat, my cat and my python—monstrous. And these wretched creatures will find moral support in England; they will find pity![4]

Pity, that most vile of all vile virtues, has never been known to me. The great pagan world I love knew it not. Now the world proposes to interrupt the terrible austere laws of nature which ordain that the weak shall be trampled upon, shall be ground into death and dust, that the strong shall be really strong,—that the strong shall be glorious, sublime. A little bourgeois comfort, a little bourgeois sense of right, cry the moderns.

Hither the world has been drifting since the coming of the pale socialist of Galilee; and this is why I hate Him, and deny His divinity. His divinity is falling, it is evanescent in sight of the goal He dreamed; again He is denied by His disciples. Poor fallen God! I, who hold nought else pitiful, pity Thee, Thy bleeding face and hands and feet, Thy hanging body; Thou at least art picturesque, and in a way beautiful in the midst of the sombre mediocrity, towards which Thou hast drifted for two thousand years, a flag; and in which Thou shalt find Thy doom as I mine, I, who will not adore Thee and cannot curse Thee now. For verily Thy life and Thy fate has been greater, stranger and more Divine than any man's has been. The chosen people, the garden, the betrayal, the crucifixion, and the beautiful story, not of Mary, but of Magdalen. The God descending to the harlot! Even the great pagan world of marble and pomp and lust and cruelty, that my soul goes out to and hails as the grandest, has not so sublime a contrast to show us as this.

Come to me, ye who are weak. The Word went forth, the terrible disastrous Word, and before it fell the ancient gods, and the vices that they represent, and which I revere, are outcast now in the world of men; the Word went forth, and the world interpreted the Word, blindly, ignorantly, savagely, for two thousand years, but nevertheless nearing every day the end—the end that Thou in Thy divine intelligence foresaw, that finds its voice to-day (enormous though the antithesis may be, I will say it) in the *Pall Mall Gazette*. What fate has been like Thine? Betrayed by Judas in the garden, denied by Peter before the cock crew, crucified between thieves, and mourned for by a harlot, and then sent bound and bare, nothing changed, nothing altered, in Thy ignominious plight, forthward in the world's van the glory and symbol of a man's new idea—Pity. Thy day is closing in, but the heavens are now wider aflame with Thy light than ever before— Thy light, which I, a pagan, standing on the last verge of the old world, declare to be darkness, the coming night of pity and justice which is imminent, which is the twentieth century. The bearers have relinquished Thy cross, they leave Thee in the hour of Thy universal triumph, Thy crown of thorns is falling, Thy face is buffeted with blows, and not even a reed is placed in Thy hand for sceptre; only I and mine are by Thee, we who shall perish with Thee, in the ruin Thou hast created.

Injustice we worship; all that lifts us out of the miseries of life is the sublime fruit of injustice. Every immortal deed was an act of fearful injustice; the world of grandeur, of triumph, of courage, of lofty aspiration, was built up on injustice. Man would not be man but for injustice. Hail, therefore, to the thrice glorious virtue injustice! What care I that some millions of wretched Israelites died under Pharaoh's lash or Egypt's sun? It was well that they died that I might have the pyramids to look on, or to fill a musing hour with wonderment. Is there one amongst us who would exchange them for the lives of the ignominious slaves that died? What care I that the virtue of some sixteen-year-old maiden was the price paid for Ingres' *La Source?* That the model died of drink and disease in the hospital, is nothing when compared with the essential that I should have *La Source*, that exquisite dream of innocence, to think of till my soul is sick with delight of the painter's holy vision. Nay more, the knowledge that a wrong was done —that millions of Israelites died in torments, that a girl, or a thousand girls, died in the hospital for that one virginal thing, is an added pleasure which I could not afford to spare. Oh, for the silence of marble courts, for the shadow of great pillars, for gold, for reticulated canopies of lilies; to see the great gladiators pass, to hear them cry the famous "Ave Cæsar," to hold the thumb down, to see the blood flow, to fill the languid hours with the agonies of poisoned slaves! Oh, for excess, for crime! I would give many lives to save one sonnet by Baudelaire; for the hymn, "*A la très-chère, à la très-belle, qui remplit mon cœur de clarté*," let the first-born in every house in Europe be slain; and in all sincerity I profess my readiness to decapitate all the Japanese in Japan and elsewhere, to save from destruction one drawing by Hokusai. Again I say that all we deem sublime in the world's history are acts of injustice; and it is certain that if mankind does not relinquish at once, and for ever, its vain, mad, and fatal dream of justice, the world will lapse into barbarism. England was great and glorious, because England was unjust, and England's greatest son was the personification of injustice—Cromwell.

But the old world of heroes is over now. The skies above us are dark with sentimentalism, the sand beneath us is shoaling fast, we are running with streaming canvas upon ruin; all ideals have gone; nothing remains to us for worship but the Mass, the blind, inchoate, insatiate Mass; fog and fen land before us, we shall founder in putrefying mud, creatures of the ooze and rushes about us—we, the great ship that has floated up from the antique world. Oh, for the antique world, its plain passion, its plain joys in the sea, where the Triton blew a plaintive blast, and the forest where the whiteness of the nymph was seen escaping! We are weary of pity, we are weary of being good; we are weary of tears and effusion, and our refuge—the British Museum—is the wide sea shore and the wind of the ocean. There, there is real joy in the flesh; our statues are naked, but we are ashamed, and our nakedness is indecency: a fair, frank soul is mirrored in those fauns and nymphs; and how strangely enigmatic is the soul of the antique world, the bare, barbarous soul of beauty and of might![5]

But neither Apollo nor Buddha could help or save me. One in his exquisite balance of body, a skylark-like song of eternal beauty, stood lightly advancing; the other sat sombrously contemplating, calm as a beautiful evening. I looked for sorrow in the eyes of the pastel— the beautiful pastel that seemed to fill with a real presence the rich autumnal leaves where the jays darted and screamed. The twisted columns of the bed rose, burdened with great weight of fringes and curtains, the python devoured a guinea pig, the last I gave him; the great white cat came to me. I said all this must go, must henceforth be to me an abandoned dream, a something, not more real than a summer meditation. So be it, and, as was characteristic of me, I broke with Paris suddenly, without warning anyone. I knew in my heart of hearts that I should never return, but no word was spoken, and I continued a pleasant delusion with myself; I told my *concierge* that I would return in a month, and I left all to be sold, brutally sold by auction, as the letter I read in the last chapter charmingly and touchingly describes.

Not even to Marshall did I confide my foreboding that Paris would pass out of my life, that it would henceforth be with me a beautiful memory, but never more a practical delight. He and I were no longer living together; we had parted a second time, but this time without bitterness of any kind; he had learnt to feel that I wanted to live alone, and had moved away into the Latin quarter, whither I made occasional expeditions. I accompanied him once to the old haunts, but various terms of penal servitude had scattered our friends, and I could not interest myself in the new. Nor did Marshall himself interest me as he had once done. To my eager taste, he had grown just a little trite. My affection for him was as deep and sincere as ever; were I to meet him now I would grasp his hand and hail him with firm, loyal friendship; but I had made friends in the Nouvelle Athènes who interested me passionately, and my thoughts were absorbed by and set on new ideals, which Marshall had failed to find sympathy for, or even to understand. I had introduced him to Degas and Manet, but he had spoken of Jules Lefebvre and Bouguereau, and generally shown himself incapable of any higher education; he could not enter where I had entered, and this was alienation. We could no longer even talk of the same people; when I spoke of a certain *marquise*, he answered with an indifferent "Do you really think so?" and proceeded to drag me away from my glitter of satin to the dinginess of print dresses. It was more than alienation, it was almost separation; but he was still my friend, he was the man, and he always will be, to whom my youth, with all its aspirations, was most closely united. So I turned to say good-bye to him and to my past life. Rap—rap—rap!

"Who's there?"

"I—Dayne."

"I've got a model."

"Never mind your model. Open the door. How are you? what are you painting?"

"This; what do you think of it?"

"It is prettily composed. I think it will come out all right. I am going to England; come to say good-bye."

"Going to England! What will you do in England?"

"I have to go about money matters; very tiresome. I had really begun to forget there was such a place."

"But you are not going to stay there?"

"Oh, no!"

"You will be just in time to see the Academy."

The conversation turned on art, and we æstheticised for an hour. At last Marshall said, "I am really sorry, old chap, but I must send you away; there's that model."

The girl sat waiting, her pale hair hanging down her back, a very picture of discontent.

"Send her away."

"I asked her to come out to dinner."

"D——n her. . . . Well, never mind, I must spend this last evening with you; you shall both dine with me. *Je quitte Paris demain matin, peut-être pour longtemps; je voudrais passer ma dernière soirée avec mon ami; alors si vous voulez bien me permettre, mademoiselle, je vous invite tous les deux à diner; nous passerons la soirée ensemble si cela vous est agréable?*"

"*Je veux bien, monsieur.*"

Poor Marie! Marshall and I were absorbed in each other and art. It was always so. We dined in a gargote, and afterwards we went to a students' ball; and it seems like yesterday. I can see the moon sailing through a clear sky, and on the pavement's edge Marshall's beautiful, slim, manly figure, and Marie's exquisite gracefulness. She was Lefebvre's Chloe; so every one sees her now. Her end was a tragic one. She invited her friend to dinner, and with the few pence that remained she bought some boxes of matches, boiled them, and drank the water. No one knew why; some said it was love.

I went to London in an exuberant necktie, a tiny hat; I wore large trousers and a Capoul beard; and I looked, I believe, as unlike an Englishman as a drawing by Grévin. In the smoking-room of Morley's Hotel I met my agent, an immense nose, and a wisp of hair drawn over a bald skull. He explained, after some hesitation, that I owed him a few thousands, and that the accounts were in his portmanteau. I suggested taking them to a solicitor to have them examined. The solicitor advised me strongly to contest them. I did not take the advice, but raised some money instead, and so the matter ended so far as the immediate future was concerned.[1] The years the most impressionable, from twenty to thirty, when the senses and the mind are widest awake, I, the most impressionable of human beings, had spent in France, not among English residents, but among that which is the quintessence of the nation; I, not an indifferent spectator, but an enthusiast, striving heart and soul to identify himself with his environment, to shake himself free from race and language and to recreate himself as it were in the womb of a new nationality, assuming its ideals, its morals, and its modes of thought, and I had succeeded strangely well, and when I returned home England was a new country to me; I had, as it were, forgotten everything. Every aspect of street and suburban garden was new to me; of the manner of life of Londoners I knew nothing. This sounds incredible, but it is so; I saw, but I could realise nothing. I went into a drawing-room, but everything seemed far away—a dream, a presentment, nothing more; I was in touch with nothing; of the thoughts and feelings of those I met I could understand nothing, nor could I sympathise with them: an Englishman was at that time as much out of my mental reach as an Esquimau would be now. Women were nearer to me than men, and I will take this opportunity to note my observation, for I am not aware that any one else has observed that the difference between the two races is found in the men, not in the women. French and English women are psychologically very similar; the standpoint from which they see life is the same, the same thoughts interest and amuse them; but the attitude of a Frenchman's mind is absolutely opposed to that of an Englishman; they stand on either side of a vast abyss, two animals different in colour, form, and temperament;—two ideas destined to remain irrevocably separate and distinct.

I have heard of writing and speaking two languages equally well: this was impossible to me, and I am convinced that if I had remained two more years in France I should never have been able to identify my thoughts with the language I am now writing in, and I should have written it as an alien. As it was I only just escaped this detestable fate. And it was in the last two years, when I began to write French verse and occasional *chroniques* in the papers, that the great damage was done. I remember very well indeed one day, while arranging an act of a play I was writing with a friend, finding suddenly to my surprise that I could think more easily and rapidly in French than in English; but with all this I did not learn French. I chattered, and I felt intensely at home in it; yes, I could write a sonnet or a ballade almost without a slip, but my prose required a good deal of alteration, ¶ for a greater command of language is required to write in prose than in verse. I found this in French and also in English. For when I returned from Paris, my English terribly corrupt with French ideas and forms of thought, I could write acceptable English verse, but even ordinary newspaper prose was beyond my reach, and an attempt I made to write a novel drifted into a miserable failure; but the following poems opened to me the doors of a first-class London newspaper,[2] and I was at once entrusted with some important critical work: ¶

THE SWEETNESS OF THE PAST[3]

As sailors watch from their prison
For the faint grey line of the coasts,
I look to the past re-arisen,
And joys come over in hosts
Like the white sea birds from their roosts.

I love not the indelicate present,
The future's unknown to our quest,
To-day is the life of the peasant,
But the past is a haven of rest—
The things of the past are the best.

The rose of the past is better
Than the rose we ravish to-day,
'Tis holier, purer, and fitter
To place on the shrine where we pray
For the secret thoughts we obey.

There are there no deceptions or changes,
And there all is lovely and still;
No grief nor fate that estranges,
Nor hope that no life can fulfil,
But ethereal shelter from ill.

The coarser delights of the hour
Tempt, and debauch, and deprave,
And we joy in a poisonous flower,
Knowing that nothing can save
Our flesh from the fate of the grave.

But sooner or later returning
In grief to the well-loved nest,
Our souls filled with infinite yearning,
We cry, in the past there is rest,
There is peace, its joys are the best.

NOSTALGIA

Fair were the dreamful days of old,
When in the summer's sleepy shade,
Beneath the beeches on the wold,
The shepherds lay and gently played
Music to maidens, who, afraid,
Drew all together rapturously,
Their white soft hands like white leaves laid,
In the old dear days of Arcady.

Men were not then as they are now
Haunted and terrified by creeds,

They sought not then, nor cared to know
The end that as a magnet leads,
Nor told with austere fingers beads,
Nor reasoned with their grief and glee,
But rioted in pleasant meads
In the old dear days of Arcady.

The future may be wrong or right,
The present is distinctly wrong,
For life and love have lost delight,
And bitter even is our song;
And year by year grey doubt grows strong,
And death is all that seems to dree.
Wherefore with weary hearts we long
For the old dear days of Arcady.

ENVOI

Glories and triumphs ne'er shall cease,
But men may sound the heavens and sea,
One thing is lost for aye—the peace
Of the old dear days of Arcady.

And so it was that I came to settle down in a Strand lodging-house, determined to devote myself to literature, and to accept the hardships of a literary life.[4] I had been playing long enough, and now I was resolved to see what I could do in the world of work. I was anxious for proof, peremptory proof, of my capacity or incapacity. A book! No. I required an immediate answer, and journalism alone could give me that. So I reasoned in the Strand lodging-house. And what led me to that house? Chance, or a friend's recommendation? I forget. It was uncomfortable, hideous, and not very clean: but curious, as all things are curious when examined closely. Let me tell you about my rooms. The sitting-room was a good deal longer than it was wide; it was panelled with deal, and the deal was painted a light brown; behind it there was a large bedroom: the floor was covered with a ragged carpet, and a big bed stood in the middle of the floor. But next to the sitting-room was a small bedroom which was let for ten shillings a week; and the partition wall was so thin that I could hear every movement the occupant made. This proximity was intolerable, and eventually I decided on adding ten shillings to my rent, and I became the possessor of the entire flat. In the room above me lived a pretty young woman, an actress at the Savoy Theatre. She had a piano, and she used to play and sing in the mornings, and in the afternoon, friends—girls from the theatre—used to come and see her; and Emma, the maid-of-all-work, used to take them up their tea; and, oh! the chattering and the laughter. Poor Miss L——; she had only two pounds a week to live on, but she was always in high spirits except when she could not pay the hire of her piano; and I am sure that she now looks back with pleasure and thinks of those days as very happy ones.

She was a tall girl, a thin figure, and she had large brown eyes; she liked young men, and she hoped that Mr. Gilbert would give her a line or two in his next opera. Often have I come out on the landing to meet her; we used to sit on those stairs talking, long after midnight, of what?—of our landlady, of the theatre, of the most suitable ways of enjoying ourselves in life. One night she told me she was married; it was a solemn moment. I asked in a sympathetic voice why she was not living with her husband. She told me, but the reason of the separation I have forgotten in the many similar reasons for separation and part-ings which have since been confided to me. The landlady bitterly resented our intimacy, and I believe Miss L—— was charged indirectly for her conversations with me in the bill. On the first floor there was a large sitting-room and bedroom, solitary rooms that were nearly always unlet. The landlady's parlour was on the ground floor, her bed-room was next to it, and further on was the entrance to the kitchen stairs, whence ascended Mrs. S——'s brood of children, and Emma, the awful servant, with tea things, many various smells, that of ham and eggs predominating.

Emma, I remember you—you are not to be forgotten—up at five o'clock every morning, scouring, washing, cooking, dressing those in-famous children; seventeen hours at least out of the twenty-four at the beck and call of landlady, lodgers, and quarrelling children; seven-teen hours at least out of the twenty-four drudging in that horrible kitchen, running up stairs with coals and breakfasts and cans of hot water; down on your knees before a grate, pulling out the cinders with those hands—can I call them hands? The lodgers sometimes threw you a kind word, but never one that recognised that you were akin to us, only the pity that might be extended to a dog. And I used to ask you all sorts of cruel questions, I was curious to know the depth of ani-malism you had sunk to, or rather out of which you had never been raised. And you generally answered innocently and naïvely enough. But sometimes my words were too crude, and they struck through the thick hide into the quick, into the human, and you winced a little; but this was rarely, for you were very nearly, oh, very nearly an animal: your temperament and intelligence was just that of a dog that has picked up a master, not a real master, but a makeshift master who may turn it out at any moment. Dickens would sentimentalise or laugh over you; I do neither. I merely recognise you as one of the facts of civilisation. You looked—well, to be candid,—you looked neither young nor old; hard work had obliterated the delicate markings of the years, and left you in round numbers something over thirty. Your hair was reddish brown, and your face wore that plain honest look that is so essentially English. The rest of you was a mass of stuffy clothes, and when you rushed up stairs I saw something that did not look like legs; a horrible rush that was of yours, a sort of cart-horse like bound. I have spoken angrily to you; I have heard others speak angrily to you, but never did that sweet face of yours, for it was a sweet face—that sweet, natural goodness that is so sublime—lose its expression of perfect and unfailing kindness. Words convey little sense of the real horrors of the reality. Life in your case meant this: to be born in a slum, and to leave it to work seventeen hours a day in a lodging-house; to be a Londoner, but to know only the slum in which you were born and the few shops in the Strand at which the landlady dealt. To know nothing of London meant in your case not to know that it was not England; England and London! you could not distinguish between them. Was England an island or a mountain? you had no notion. I remember when you heard that Miss L—— was going to America, you asked me, and the question was sublime: "Is she going to travel all night?" You had heard people speak of travelling all night, and that was all you knew of travel or any place that was not the Strand. I asked you if you went to church, and you said "No, it makes my eyes bad." I said, "But you don't read; you can't read." "No, but I have to look at the book." I asked you if you had heard of God; you hadn't; but when I pressed you on the point you suspected I was laughing at you, and you would not answer, and when I tried you again on the subject I could see that the landlady had been telling you what to say. But you had not understood, and your conscious ignorance, grown conscious within the last couple of days, was even more pitiful than your unconscious ignorance when you answered that you couldn't go to church because it made your eyes bad. It is a strange thing to know nothing; for instance, to live in London and to have no notion of the House of Commons, nor indeed of the Queen, except perhaps that she is a rich lady; the police—yes, you knew what a policeman was because you used to be sent to fetch one to make an organ-man or a Christy minstrel move on. To know of nothing but a dark kitchen, grates, eggs and bacon, dirty children; to work seventeen hours a day and to get cheated out of your wages; to answer, when asked, why you did not get your wages or leave if you weren't paid, that you "didn't know how Mrs. S—— would get on without me."

This woman owed you forty pounds, I think, so I calculated it from what you told me; and yet you did not like to leave her because you did not know how she would get on without you. Sublime stupidity! At this point your intelligence stopped. I remember you once spoke of a half-holiday; I questioned you, and I found your idea of a half-holiday was to take the children for a walk and buy them some sweets. I told my brother of this and he said—Emma out for a half-holiday! why, you might as well give a mule a holiday. The phrase was brutal, but it was admirably descriptive of you. Yes, you are a mule, there is no sense in you; you are a beast of burden, a drudge too horrible for anything but work; and I suppose, all things considered, that the fat landlady with a dozen children did well to work you seventeen hours a day, and cheat you of your miserable wages. You had no friends; you could not have a friend unless it were some forlorn cat or dog; but you once spoke to me of your brother, who worked in a potato store, and I was astonished, and I wondered if he were as awful as you. Poor Emma! I shall never forget your kind heart and your unfailing good humour; you were born beautifully good as a rose is born with perfect perfume; you were as unconscious of your goodness as the rose of its perfume. And you were taken by this fat landlady as 'Arry takes a rose and sticks it in his tobacco-reeking coat; and you will be thrown away, shut out of doors when health fails you, or when, overcome by base usage, you take to drink. There is no hope for you; even if you were treated better and paid your wages there would be no hope. That forty pounds even, if they were given to you, would bring you no good fortune. They would bring the idle loafer, who scorns you now as something too low for even his kisses, hanging about your heels and whispering in your ears. And his whispering would drive you mad, for your kind heart longs for kind words; and then when he had spent your money and cast you off in despair, the gin shop and the river would do the rest. Providence is very wise after all, and your best destiny is your present one. We cannot add a pain, nor can we take away a pain; we may alter, but we cannot subtract nor even alleviate. But what truisms are these; who believes in philanthropy nowadays?[5]

*   *   *   *   *

"Come in."

"Oh, it is you, Emma!"

"Are you going to dine at home to-day, sir?"

"What can I have?"

"Well, yer can 'ave a chop or a steak."

"Anything else?"

"Yes, yer can 'ave a steak, or a chop, or ————"

"Oh yes, I know; well then, I'll have a chop. And now tell me, Emma, how is your young man? I hear you have got one, you went out with him the other night."

"Who told yer that?"

"Ah, never mind; I hear everything."

"I know, from Miss L——."

"Well, tell me, how did you meet him, who introduced him?"

"I met 'im as I was a-coming from the public 'ouse with the beer for missus' dinner."

"And what did he say?"

"He asked me if I was engaged; I said no. And he come round down the lane that evening."

"And he took you out?"

"Yes."

"And where did you go?"

"We went for a walk on the Embankment."

"And when is he coming for you again?"

"He said he was coming last evening, but he didn't."

"Why didn't he?"

"I dunno; I suppose because I haven't time to go out with him. So it was Miss L—— that told you; well, you do 'ave chats on the stairs. I suppose you likes talking to 'er."

"I like talking to everybody, Emma; I like talking to you."

"Yes, but not as you talks to 'er; I 'ears you jes do 'ave fine times. She said this morning that she had not seen you for this last two nights—that you had forgotten 'er, and I was to tell yer."

"Very well, I'll come out to-night and speak to her."

"And missus is so wild about it, and she daren't say nothing 'cause she thinks yer might go."

*   *   *   *   *

A young man in a house full of women must be almost supernaturally unpleasant if he does not occupy a great deal of their attention. Certain at least it is that I was the point of interest in that house; and I found there that the practice of virtue is not so disagreeable as many young men think it. The fat landlady hovered round my doors, and I obtained perfectly fresh eggs by merely keeping her at her distance; the pretty actress, with whom I used to sympathise with on the stairs at midnight, loved me better, and our intimacy was more strange and subtle, because it was pure, and it was not quite unpleasant to know that the awful servant dreamed of me as she might of a star, or something equally unattainable; but the landlady's daughter, a nasty girl of fifteen, annoyed me with her ogling, which was a little revolting, but the rest was, and I speak quite candidly, not wholly unpleasant. It was not aristocratic, it is true, but, I repeat, it was not unpleasant, nor do I believe that any young man, however refined, would have found it unpleasant.

¶ But if I was offered a choice between a chop and steak in the evening, in the morning I had to decide between eggs and bacon and bacon and eggs. A knocking at the door, "Nine o'clock, sir; 'ot water sir; what will you have for breakfast?" "What can I have?" "Anything you like, sir. You can have bacon and eggs, or ——" "Anything else?"—Pause.—"Well, sir, you can have eggs and bacon, or ——" "Well, I'll have eggs and bacon."

The streets seemed to me like rat holes, dark and wandering as chance directed, with just an occasional rift of sky, seen as if through an occasional crevice, so different from the boulevards widening out into bright space with fountains and clouds of green foliage. The modes of life were so essentially opposed. I am thinking now of intellectual rather than physical comforts. I could put up with even lodging-house food, but I found it difficult to forego the glitter and artistic enthusiasm of the café. The tavern, I had heard of the tavern.

Some seventy years ago the Club superseded the Tavern, and since then all literary intercourse has ceased in London. Literary clubs have been founded, and their leather arm-chairs have begotten Mr. Gosse; but the tavern gave the world Villon and Marlowe. Nor is this to be wondered at. What is wanted is enthusiasm and devil-may-careism; and the very aspect of a tavern is a snort of defiance at the hearth, the leather arm-chairs are so many salaams to it. I ask, Did any one ever see a gay club room? Can any one imagine such a thing? You can't have a club room without mahogany tables, you can't have mahogany tables without magazines—*Longman's*, with a serial by Rider Haggard, the *Nineteenth Century*, with an article, "The Rehabilitation of the Pimp in Modern Society," by W. E. Gladstone—a dulness that's a purge to good spirits, an aperient to enthusiasm; in a word, a dulness that's worth a thousand a year. You can't have a club without a waiter in red plush and silver salver in his hand; then you can't bring a lady to a club, and you have to get into a corner to talk about them. Therefore I say a club is dull.

As the hearth and home grew all-powerful it became impossible for the husband to tell his wife that he was going to the tavern; everyone can go to the tavern, and no place in England where everyone can go is considered respectable. This is the genesis of the Club—out of the Housewife by Respectability. Nowadays every one is respectable—jockeys, betting-men, actors, and even actresses. Mrs. Kendal takes her children to visit a duchess, and has naughty chorus girls to tea, and tells them of the joy of respectability. There is only one class left that is not respectable, and that will succumb before long; how the transformation will be effected I can't say, but I know an editor or two who would be glad of an article on the subject.

Respectability!—a suburban villa, a piano in the drawing-room, and going home to dinner. Such things are no doubt very excellent, but they do not promote intensity of feeling, fervour of mind; and as art is in itself an outcry against the animality of human existence, it would be

well that the life of the artist should be a practical protest against the
so-called decencies of life; and he can best protest by frequenting a
tavern and cutting his club. In the past the artist has always been an
outcast; it is only latterly he has become domesticated, and judging by
results, it is clear that if Bohemianism is not a necessity it is at least an
adjuvant. For if long locks and general dissoluteness were not an aid and
a way to pure thought, why have they been so long his characteristics?
If lovers were not necessary for the development of poet, novelist, and
actress, why have they always had lovers—Sappho, George Eliot,
George Sand, Rachel, Sara? Mrs. Kendal nurses children all day and
strives to play Rosalind at night. What infatuation, what ridiculous
endeavour! To realise the beautiful woodland passion and the idea of
the transformation, a woman must have sinned, for only through sin
may we learn the charm of innocence. To play Rosalind a woman must
have had more than one lover, and if she has been made to wait in the
rain and has been beaten she will have done a great deal to qualify
herself for the part. The ecstatic Sara makes no pretence to virtue, she
introduces her son to an English duchess, and throws over a nation for
the love of Richepin, she can, therefore, say as none other—

> "Ce n'est plus qu'une ardeur dans mes veines cachée,
>   C'est Venus tout entière à sa proie attachée."[6]

Swinburne, when he dodged about London, a lively young dog, wrote
"Poems and Ballads," and "Chastelard," since he has gone to live at
Putney, he has contributed to the *Nineteenth Century*, and published an
interesting little volume entitled, "A Century of Rondels," in which he
continues his plaint about his mother the sea.[7]

Respectability is sweeping the picturesque out of life; national cos-
tumes are disappearing. The kilt is going or gone in the highlands, and
the smock in the southlands, even the Japanese are becoming Christian
and respectable; in another quarter of a century silk hats and pianos
will be found in every house in Yeddo. Too true that universal unifor-
mity is the future of the world; and when Mr. Morris speaks of the
democratic art to be when the world is socialistic, I ask, whence will
the unfortunates draw their inspiration? To-day our plight is pitiable
enough—the duke, the jockey-boy, and the artist are exactly alike; they
are dressed by the same tailor, they dine at the same clubs, they swear

the same oaths, they speak equally bad English, they love the same women. Such a state of things is dreary enough, but what unimaginable dreariness there will be when there are neither rich nor poor, when all have been educated, when self-education has ceased. A terrible world to dream of, worse, far worse, in darkness and hopelessness than Dante's lowest circle of hell. The spectres of famine, of the plague, of war, etc., are mild and gracious symbols compared with that menacing figure, Universal Education, with which we are threatened, which has already eunuched the genius of the last five-and-twenty years of the nineteenth century, and produced a limitless abortion in that of future time. Education, I tremble before thy dreaded name. The cruelties of Nero, of Caligula, what were they?—a few crunched limbs in the amphitheatre; but thine, O Education, are the yearning of souls sick of life, of maddening discontent, of all the fearsome and fathomless sufferings of the mind. When Goethe said "More light," he said the wickedest and most infamous words that human lips ever spoke. In old days, when a people became too highly civilised the barbarians came down from the north and regenerated that nation with darkness; but now there are no more barbarians, and sooner or later I am convinced that we shall have to end the evil by summary edicts—the obstruction no doubt will be severe, the equivalents of Gladstone and Morley will stop at nothing to defeat the Bill; but it will nevertheless be carried by patriotic Conservative and Unionist majorities, and it will be written in the Statute Book that not more than one child in a hundred shall be taught to read, and no more than one in ten thousand shall learn the piano.

Such will be the end of Respectability, but the end is still far distant. We are now in a period of decadence growing steadily more and more acute. The old gods are falling about us, there is little left to raise our hearts and minds to, and amid the wreck and ruin of things only a snobbery is left to us, thank heaven, deeply graven in the English heart; the snob is now the ark that floats triumphant over the democratic wave; the faith of the old world reposes in his breast, and he shall proclaim it when the waters have subsided.

In the meanwhile Respectability, having destroyed the Tavern, and created the Club, continues to exercise a meretricious and enervating influence on literature. All audacity of thought and expression has been stamped out, and the conventionalities are rigorously respected. It has been said a thousand times that an art is only a reflection of a certain age; quite so, only certain ages are more interesting than others, and consequently produce better art, just as certain seasons produce better crops. We heard in the Nouvelle Athènes how the Democratic movement, in other words, Respectability, in other words, Education, has extinguished the handicrafts; it was admitted that in the more individual arts—painting and poetry—men would be always found to sacrifice their lives for a picture or a poem: but no man is, after all, so immeasurably superior to the age he lives in as to be able to resist it wholly; he must draw sustenance from some quarter, and the contemplation of the past will not suffice. Then the pressure on him from without is as water upon the diver; and sooner or later he grows fatigued and comes to the surface to breathe; he is as a flying-fish pursued by sharks below and cruel birds above; and he neither dives as deeply nor flies as high as his freer and stronger ancestry. A daring spirit in the nineteenth century would have been but a timid nursery soul indeed in the sixteenth. We want tumult and war to give us forgetfulness, sublime moments of peace to enjoy a kiss in; but we are expected to be home to dinner at seven, and to say and do nothing that might shock the neighbours. Respectability has wound itself about society, a sort of octopus, and nowhere are you quite free from one of its horrible suckers. The power of the villa residence is supreme: art, science, politics, religion, it has transformed to suit its requirements. The villa goes to the Academy, the villa goes to the theatre, and therefore the art of to-day is mildly realistic; not the great realism of idea, but the puny reality of materialism; not the deep poetry of a Peter de Hogue, but the meanness of a Frith—not the winged realism of Balzac, but the degrading naturalism of a coloured photograph.

To my mind there is no sadder spectacle of artistic debauchery than a London theatre; the overfed inhabitants of the villa in the stalls hoping for gross excitement to assist them through their hesitating digestions; an ignorant mob in the pit and gallery forgetting the miseries of life in imbecile stories reeking of the sentimentality of the back stairs. Were other ages as coarse and as common as ours? It is difficult to imagine Elizabethan audiences as not more intelligent than those that applaud Mr. Pettitt's plays. Impossible that an audience that could sit out Edward II. could find any pleasure in such sinks of literary infamies as *In the*

Ranks and *Harbour Lights*. Artistic atrophy is benumbing us, we are losing our finer feeling for beauty, the rose is going back to the briar. I will not speak of the fine old crusted stories, ever the same, on which every drama is based, nor yet of the musty characters with which they are peopled—the miser in the old castle counting his gold by night, the dishevelled woman whom he keeps for ambiguous reasons confined in a cellar. Let all this be waived. We must not quarrel with the ingredients. The miser and the old castle are as true, and not one jot more true, than the million events which go to make up the phenomena of human existence. Not at these things considered separately do I take umbrage, but at the miserable use that is made of them, the vulgarity of the complications evolved from them, and the poverty of beauty in the dialogue.

Not the thing itself, but the idea of the thing evokes the idea. Schopenhauer was right; we do not want the thing, but the idea of the thing. The thing itself is worthless; and the moral writers who embellish it with pious ornamentation are just as reprehensible as Zola, who embellishes it with erotic arabesques. You want the idea drawn out of obscuring matter, this can best be done by the symbol. The symbol, or the thing itself, that is the great artistic question.[8] In earlier ages it was the symbol; a name, a plume, sufficed to evoke the idea; now we evoke nothing, for we give everything; the imagination of the spectator is no longer called into play. In Shakespeare's days to create wealth in a theatre it was only necessary to write upon a board, "A magnificent apartment in a palace." This was no doubt primitive and not a little barbarous, but it was better by far than by dint of anxious archæology to construct the Doge's palace upon the stage. By one rich pillar, by some projecting balustrade taken in conjunction with a moored gondola, we should strive to evoke the soul of the city of Veronese: by the magical and unequalled selection of a subtle and unexpected feature of a thought or aspect of a landscape, and not by the up-piling of extraneous detail, are all great poetic effects achieved.

> "By the tideless dolorous midland sea,
>   In a land of sand and ruin, and gold."[9]

And, better example still,

> "Dieu que le son du cor est triste au fond des bois,"[10]

that impeccable, that only line of real poetry Alfred de Vigny ever wrote; and being a great poet Shakespeare consciously or unconsciously observed more faithfully than any other poet these principles of art; and, as is characteristic of the present day, nowhere do we find these principles so grossly violated as in the representation of his plays. I had painful proof of this some few nights after my arrival in London. I had never seen Shakespeare acted, and I went to the Lyceum and there I saw that exquisite love-song—for *Romeo and Juliet* is no more than a love song in dialogue—tricked out in silks and carpets and illuminated building, a vulgar bawd suited to the gross passion of an ignorant public. I hated all that with the hatred of a passionate heart, and I longed for a simple stage, a few simple indications, and the simple recitation of that story of the sacrifice of the two white souls for the reconciliation of two great families. My hatred did not reach to the age of the man who played the boy-lover, but to the offensiveness with which he thrust his individuality upon me, longing to realize the poet's divine imagination: and the woman, too, I wished with my whole soul away, subtle and strange though she was, and I yearned for her part to be played by a youth as in old time: a youth cunningly disguised, would be a symbol; and my mind would be free to imagine the divine Juliet of the poet, whereas I could but dream of the bright eyes and delicate mien and motion of the woman who had thrust herself between me and it.

But not with symbol and subtle suggestion has the villa to do, but with such stolid, intellectual fare as corresponds to its material wants. The villa has not time to think, the villa is the working bee. The tavern is the drone. It has no boys to put to school, no neighbours to study, and is therefore a little more refined, or, should I say? depraved, in its taste. The villa in one form or other has always existed, and always will exist so long as our present social system holds together. It is the basis of life, and more important than the tavern. Agreed: but that does not say that the tavern was not an excellent corrective influence to the villa, and that its disappearance has not had a vulgarising effect on artistic work of all kinds, and the club has been proved impotent to replace it, the club being no more than the correlative of the villa. Let the reader trace villa through each modern feature. I will pass on at once to the circulating library, at once the symbol and glory of villaism.

The subject is not unfamiliar to me; I come to it like the son to his father, like the bird to its nest. (Singularly inappropriate comparison, but I am in such excellent humour to-day; humour is everything. It is said that the tiger will sometimes play with the lamb! Let us play.) We have the villa well in our mind. The father who goes to the city in the morning, the grown-up girls waiting to be married, the big drawing-room where they play waltz music, and talk of dancing parties. But waltzes will not entirely suffice, nor even tennis; the girls must read. Mother cannot keep a censor (it is as much as she can do to keep a cook, housemaid, and page-boy), besides the expense would be enormous, even if nothing but shilling and two-shilling novels were purchased. Out of such circumstances the circulating library was hatched.

The villa made known its want, and art fell on its knees. Pressure was put on the publishers, and books were published at 31s. 6d.; the dirty, outside public was got rid of, and the villa paid its yearly subscription, and had nice large handsome books that none but the *élite* could obtain, and with them a sense of being put on a footing of equality with my Lady This and Lady That, and certainty that nothing would come into the hands of dear Kate and Mary and Maggie that they might not read, and all for two guineas a year. English fiction became pure, and the garlic and assafœtida with which Byron, Fielding, and Ben Jonson so liberally seasoned their works, and in spite of which, as critics say, they were geniuses, have disappeared from our literature.[11] English fiction became pure, dirty stories were to be heard no more, were no longer procurable. But at this point human nature intervened; poor human nature! when you pinch it in in one place it bulges out in another, after the fashion of a lady's figure. Human nature has from the earliest time shown a liking for dirty stories; dirty stories have formed a substantial part of every literature (I employ the words "dirty stories" in the circulating library sense); therefore a taste for dirty stories may be said to be inherent in the human animal. Call it a disease if you will—an incurable disease—which, if it is driven inwards, will break out in an unexpected quarter in a new form and with redoubled virulence. This is exactly what has happened. Actuated by the most laudable motives, Mudie cut off our rations of dirty stories, and for forty years we were apparently the most moral people on the face of the earth. It was confidently asserted that an English woman of sixty would not read what would bring the blush of shame to the cheeks of a maiden of any other nation. But humiliation and sorrow were awaiting Mudie. True it is that we still continued to subscribe to his library, true it is that we still continued to go to church, true it is that we turned our faces away when *Mdlle. de Maupin* or the *Assommoir* was spoken of; to all appearance we were as good and chaste as even Mudie might wish us; and no doubt he looked back upon his forty years of effort with pride; no doubt he beat his manly breast and said, "I have scorched the evil one out of the villa; the head of the serpent is crushed for evermore;" but lo, suddenly, with all the horror of an earthquake, the slumbrous law courts awoke, and the burning cinders of fornication and the blinding and suffocating smoke of adultery were poured upon and hung over the land. Through the mighty columns of our newspapers the terrible lava rolled unceasing, and in the black stream the villa, with all its beautiful illusions, tumbled and disappeared.[12]

An awful and terrifying proof of the futility of human effort, that there is neither bad work nor good work to do, nothing but to await the coming of the Nirvana.

I have written much against the circulating library, and I have read a feeble defence or two; but I have not seen the argument that might be legitimately put forward in its favour. It seems to me this: the circulating library is conservatism, art is always conservative; the circulating library lifts the writer out of the precariousness and noise of the wild street of popular fancy into a quiet place where passion is more restrained and there is more reflection. The young and unknown writer is placed at once in a place of comparative security, and he is not forced to employ vile and degrading methods of attracting attention; the known writer, having a certain market for his work, is enabled to think more of it and less of the immediate acclamation of the crowd; but all these possible advantages are destroyed and rendered *nil* by the veracious censorship exercised by the librarian.

*   *   *   *   *

There is one thing in England that is free, that is spontaneous, that reminds me of the blitheness and nationalness of the Continent;—but there is nothing French about it, it is wholly and essentially English, and in its communal enjoyment and its spontaneity it is a survival of Elizabethan England—I mean the music-hall; the French music-hall

seems to me silly, effete, sophisticated, and lacking, not in the popularity, but in the vulgarity of an English hall—I will not say the Pavilion,
which is too cosmopolitan, dreary French comics are heard there—for
preference let us say the Royal. I shall not easily forget my first evening
there, when I saw for the time a living house—the dissolute para-
graphists, the elegant mashers (mark the imaginativeness of the slang)
the stolid, good-humoured costers, the cheerful lights o' love, the extraordinary comics. What delightful unison of enjoyment, what una-
nimity of soul, what communality of wit; all knew each other, all
enjoyed each other's presence; in a word, there was life. Then there
were no cascades of real water, nor London docks, nor offensively rich
furniture, with hotel lifts down which some one will certainly be
thrown, but one scene representing a street; a man comes on—not, mind
you, in a real smock-frock, but in something that suggests one—and
sings of how he came up to London, and was "cleaned out" by thieves.
Simple, you will say; yes, but better than a *fricassée* of *Faust*, garnished
with hags, imps, and blue flame; better, far better than a drawing-room
set at the St. James's, with an exhibition of passion by Mrs. and Mr.
Kendal; better, a million times better than the obscene popularity of
Wilson Barrett—an elderly man posturing in a low-necked dress to
some poor trull in the gallery; nor is there in the hall any affectation of
language, nor that worn-out rhetoric which reminds you of a broken-
winded barrel-organ playing *a che la morte*, bad enough in prose, but
when set up in blank verse awful and shocking in its more than natural
deformity—but bright quips and cracks fresh from the back-yard of
the slum where the linen is drying, or the "pub" where the unfortunate
wife has just received a black eye that will last her a week. That in-
imitable artist, Bessie Bellwood, whose native wit is so curiously accentuated that it is sublimated, that it is no longer repellent vulgarity but
art, choice and rare—see, here she comes with "What cheer, Rea; Rea's
on the job." The sketch is slight, but is welcome and refreshing after the
eternal drawing-room and Mrs. Kendal's cumbrous domesticity; it is
curious, quaint, perverted, and are not these the *aions* and the attributes
of art? Now see that perfect comedian, Arthur Roberts, superior to
Irving because he is working with living material; how trim and saucy
he is! and how he evokes the soul, the brandy-and-soda soul, of the
young men, delightful and elegant in black and white, who are so

vociferously cheering him, "Will you stand me a cab-fare, ducky, I am feeling so awfully queer?" The soul, the spirit, the entity of Piccadilly Circus is in the words, and the scene the comedian's eyes—each look is full of suggestion; it is irritating, it is magnetic, it is symbolic, it is art.

Not art, but a sign, a presentiment of an art, that may grow from the present seeds, that may rise into some stately and unpremeditated efflorescence, as the rhapsodist rose to Sophocles, as the miracle play rose through Peele and Nash to Marlowe, hence to the wondrous summer of Shakespeare, to die later on in the mist and yellow and brown of the autumn of Crowes and Davenants. I have seen music-hall sketches, comic interludes that in their unexpectedness and naïve naturalness remind me of the comic passages in Marlowe's *Faustus*, I waited (I admit in vain) for some beautiful phantom to appear, and to hear an enthusiastic worshipper cry out in his agony:—

> "Was this the face that launched a thousand ships
> And burnt the topless towers of Ilium?
> Sweet Helen, make me immortal with a kiss.
> Her lips suck forth my soul; see where it flies!
> Come, Helen, come; give me my soul again.
> Here will I dwell, for heaven is in these lips,
> And all is dross that is not Helena."

And then the astonishing change of key:—

> "I will be Paris, and for love of thee,
> Instead of Troy shall Wittenberg be sacked," etc.

The hall is at least a protest against the wearisome stories concerning wills, misers in old castles, lost heirs, and the woeful solutions of such things—she who has been kept in the castle cellar for twenty years restored to the delights of hair-pins and a mauve dress, the *ingénue* to the protecting arm, etc. The music-hall is a protest against Mrs. Kendal's marital tendernesses and the abortive platitudes of Messrs. Pettitt and Sims; the music-hall is a protest against Sardou and the immense drawing-room sets, rich hangings, velvet sofas, etc., so different from the movement of the English comedy with its constant change of scene. The music-hall is a protest against the villa, the circulating library, the club, and for this the "'all" is inexpressibly dear to me.

But in the interests of those illiterate institutions called theatres it is not permissible for several characters to narrate events in which there is a sequel, by means of dialogue, in a music-hall. If this vexatious restriction were removed it is possible, if it is not certain, that while some halls remained faithful to comic songs and jugglers others would gradually learn to cater for more intellectual and subtle audiences, and that out of obscurity and disorder new dramatic forms, coloured and permeated by the thought and feeling of to-day, might be definitely evolved. It is our only chance of again possessing a dramatic literature. ⌇

⁊ It is said that young men of genius come to London with great poems and dramas in their pockets and find every door closed against them. Chatterton's death perpetuated this legend. But when I, Edward Dayne, came to London in search of literary adventure, I found a ready welcome. Possibly I should not have been accorded any welcome had I been anything but an ordinary person. Let this be waived. I was as covered with "fads" as a distinguished foreigner with stars. Naturalism I wore round my neck, Romanticism was pinned over the heart, Symbolism I carried like a toy revolver in my waistcoat pocket, to be used on an emergency. I do not judge whether I was charlatan or genius, I merely state that I found all—actors, managers, editors, publishers, docile and ready to listen to me. The world may be wicked, cruel, and stupid, but it is patient; on this point I will not be gainsaid, it is patient; I know what I am talking about; I maintain that the world is patient. If it were not, what would have happened? I should have been murdered by the editors of (I will suppress names), torn in pieces by the sub-editors, and devoured by the office boys. There was no wild theory which I did not assail them with, there was no strange plan for the instant extermination of the Philistine, which I did not press upon them, and (here I must whisper), with a fair amount of success, not complete success I am glad to say—that would have meant for the editors a change from their arm-chairs to the benches of the Union and the plank beds of Holloway. ⁊ The actress when she returned home from the theatre, suggested I had an enemy, a vindictive enemy, who dogged my steps; but her stage experience led her astray. I had no enemy except

myself; or to put it scientifically, no enemy except the logical consequences of my past life and education, and these caused me a great and
real inconvenience. French wit was in my brain, French sentiment was
in my heart; of the English soul I knew nothing, and I could not remember old sympathies, it was like seeking forgotten words, and if I were
writing a short story, I had to return in thought to Montmartre or the
Champs Elysées for my characters. That I should have forgotten so
much in ten years seems incredible, and it will be deemed impossible
by many, but that is because few are aware of how little they know of
the details of life, even of their own, and are incapable of appreciating
the influence of their past upon their present. The visible world is visible
only to a few, the moral world is a closed book to nearly all. I was full
of France, and France had to be got rid of, or pushed out of sight before
I could understand England; ¶ I was like a snake striving to slough its
skin.

Handicapped as I was with dangerous ideas, and an impossible style,
defeat was inevitable. My English was rotten with French idiom; it was
like an ill-built wall overpowered by huge masses of ivy; the weak
foundations had given way beneath the weight of the parasite; and the
ideas I sought to give expression to were green, sour, and immature as
apples in August.

Therefore ¶ before long the leading journal that had printed two
poems and some seven or eight critical articles, ceased to send me books
for review, and I fell back upon obscure society papers.[1] Fortunately it
was not incumbent on me to live by my pen;[2] so I talked, and watched,
and waited till I grew akin to those around me, and my thoughts
blended with, and took root in my environment. I wrote a play or two,
I translated a French opera, which had a run of six nights, I dramatized
a novel, I wrote short stories, and I read a good deal of contemporary
fiction.[3]

The first book that came under my hand was "A Portrait of a Lady,"
by Henry James. Each scene is developed with complete foresight and
certainty of touch. What Mr. James wants to do he does. I will admit
that an artist may be great and limited; by one word he may light up an
abyss of soul; but there must be this one magical and unique word.
Shakespeare gives us the word, Balzac, sometimes, after pages of vain
striving, gives us the word, Tourgueneff gives it with miraculous cer-

tainty; but Henry James, no; a hundred times he flutters about it; his whole book is one long flutter near to the one magical and unique word, but the word is not spoken; and for want of the word his characters are never resolved out of the haze of nebulæ. You are on a bowing acquaintance with them; they pass you in the street, they stop and speak to you, you know how they are dressed, you watch the colour of their eyes. When I think of "A Portrait of a Lady," with its marvellous crowd of well-dressed people, it comes back to me precisely as an accurate memory of a fashionable soirée—the staircase with its ascending figures, the hostess smiling, the host at a little distance with his back turned; some one calls him. He turns; I can see his white kid gloves; the air is as sugar with the odour of the gardenias; there is brilliant light here; there is shadow in the further rooms; the women's feet pass to and fro beneath the stiff skirts; I call for my hat and coat; I light a cigar; I stroll up Piccadilly . . . a very pleasant evening; I have seen a good many people I knew; I have observed an attitude, and an earnestness of manner that proved that a heart was beating.

Mr. James might say, "If I have done this, I have done a great deal," and I would answer, "No doubt you are a man of great talent, great cultivation and not at all of the common herd; I place you in the very front rank, not only of novelists but of men of letters."

I have read nothing of Henry James's that did not suggest the manner of a scholar; but why should a scholar limit himself to empty and endless sentimentalities? I will not taunt him with any of the old taunts —why does he not write complicated stories? Why does he not complete his stories? Let all this be waived. I will ask him only why he always avoids decisive action? Why does a woman never say "I will"? Why does a woman never leave the house with her lover? Why does a man never kill a man? Why does a man never kill himself? Why is nothing ever accomplished? In real life murder, adultery, and suicide are of common occurrence; but Mr. James's people live in a calm, sad, and very polite twilight of volition. Suicide or adultery has happened before the story begins, suicide or adultery happens some years hence, when the characters have left the stage, but bang in front of the reader nothing happens. The suppression or maintenance of story in a novel is a matter of personal taste; some prefer character-drawing to adventures, some adventures to character-drawing; that you cannot have both at once I take to be a self-evident proposition; so when Mr. Lang says, "I like adventures," I say, "Oh, do you?" as I might to a man who says "I like sherry," and no doubt when I say I like character-drawing, Mr. Lang says, "Oh, do you?" as he might to a man who says, "I like port." But Mr. James and I are agreed on essentials, we ⁋ prefer character-drawing to adventures. One, two, or even three determining actions are not antagonistic to character-drawing, the practice of Balzac, and Flaubert, and Thackeray prove that. Is Mr. James of the same mind as the poet Verlaine—

> "La nuance, pas la couleur,
> Seulement la nuance,
>
> .   .   .   .
>
> Tout le reste est littérature." ⁋ 4

In connection with Henry James I had often heard the name of W. D. Howells. I bought some three or four of his novels. I found them pretty, very pretty, but nothing more,—a sort of Ashby Sterry done into very neat prose. He is vulgar, as Henry James is refined; he is more domestic; girls with white dresses and virginal looks, languid mammas, mild witticisms, here, there, and everywhere; a couple of young men, one a little cynical, the other a little over-shadowed by his love, a strong, bearded man of fifty in the background; in a word, a Tom Robertson comedy faintly spiced with American. Henry James went to France and read Tourgueneff. W. D. Howells stayed at home and read Henry James. Henry James's mind is of a higher cast and temper; I have no doubt at one time of his life Henry James said, I will write the moral history of America, as Tourgueneff wrote the moral history of Russia— he borrowed at first hand, understanding what he was borrowing. W. D. Howells borrowed at second hand, and without understanding what he was borrowing. Altogether Mr. James's instincts are more scholarly. Although his reserve irritates me, and I often regret his concessions to the prudery of the age,—no, not of the age but of librarians,—I cannot but feel that his concessions, for I suppose I must call them concessions, are to a certain extent self-imposed, regretfully, perhaps . . . somewhat in this fashion—"True, that I live in an age not very favourable to artistic production, but the art of an age is the spirit of that age; if I violate the prejudices of the age I shall miss its spirit, and an art that is not redolent of the spirit of its age is an artificial flower, perfumeless, or perfumed with the scent of flowers that bloomed three hundred years ago." ¶ Plausible, ingenious, quite in the spirit of Mr. James's mind; I can almost hear him reason so; nor does the argument displease me, for it is conceived in a scholarly spirit.[5] Now my conception of W. D. Howells is quite different—I see him ¶ the happy father of a numerous family; the sun is shining, the girls and boys are playing on the lawn, they come trooping in to a high tea, and there is dancing in the evening.

My fat landlady lent me a novel by George Meredith,—"Tragic ¶ Comedians"; I was glad to receive it, for my admiration of his poetry, with which I was slightly acquainted, was very genuine indeed. "Love in a Valley" is a beautiful poem, and the "Nuptials of Attila," I read it in the *New Quarterly Review* years ago, is very present in my mind, and it is a pleasure to recall its chanting rhythm, and lordly and sombre refrain—"Make the bed for Attila." I expected, therefore, one of my old passionate delights from his novels. I was disappointed, painfully disappointed. But before I say more concerning Mr. Meredith, I will admit at once frankly and fearlessly, that I am not a competent critic, because emotionally I do not understand him, and all except an emotional understanding is worthless in art. I do not make this admission because I am intimidated by the weight and height of the critical authority with which I am overshadowed, but from a certain sense, of which I am as distinctly conscious, viz., that the author is, how shall I put it? the French would say "quelqu'un," that expresses what I would say in English. I remember, too, that although a man may be able to understand anything, that there must be some modes of thoughts and attitudes of mind which we are so naturally antagonistic to, so entirely out of sympathy with, that we are in no true sense critics of them. Such are the thoughts that come to me when I read Mr. George Meredith. I try to console myself with such reflections, and then I break forth, and crying passionately:—jerks, wire, splintered wood. In ¶ Balzac, which I know by heart, in Shakespeare, which I have just begun to love, I find words deeply impregnated with the savour of life; but in George Meredith there is nothing but crackjaw sentences, empty and unpleasant in the mouth as sterile nuts. I could select hundreds of phrases which Mr. Meredith would probably call epigrams, ¶ and I would defy anyone to say they were wise, graceful or witty. I do not

know any book more tedious than "Tragic Comedians," more preten-
tious, more blatant; it struts and screams, stupid in all its gaud and
absurdity as a cockatoo. More than fifty pages I could not read.

How, I asked myself, could the man who wrote the "Nuptials of
Attila" write this? but my soul returned no answer, and I listened as
one in a hollow mountain side. My opinion of George Meredith never
ceases to puzzle me. He is of the north, I am of the south. Carlyle, Mr.
Robert Browning, and George Meredith are the three essentially northern writers; in them there is nothing of Latin sensuality and subtlety.

I took up "Rhoda Fleming." I found some exquisite bits of description
in it, but I heartily wished them in verse, they were motives for poems;
and there was some wit. I remember a passage very racy indeed, of
middle-class England. Antony, I think is the man's name, he describes
how he is interrupted at his tea; a paragraph of seven or ten lines with
"I am having my tea, I am at my tea," running through it for refrain.
Then a description of a lodging-house dinner: "a block of bread on a
lonely plate, and potatoes that looked as if they had committed suicide
in their own steam." A little ponderous and stilted, but undoubtedly
witty. I read on until I came to a young man who fell from his horse, or
had been thrown from his horse, I never knew which, nor did I feel
enough interest in the matter to make research; the young man was put
to bed by his mother, and once in bed he began to talk! . . . four, five, six,
ten pages of talk, and such talk! I can offer no opinion why Mr.
George Meredith committed them to paper; it is not narrative, it is not
witty, nor is it sentimental, nor is it profound. I read it once; my mind
astonished at receiving no sensation cried out like a child at a milkless
breast. I read the pages again . . . did I understand? Yes, I understood
every sentence, but they conveyed no idea, they awoke no emotion in
me; it was like sand, arid and uncomfortable. The story is surprisingly
commonplace—the people in it are as lacking in subtlety as those of a
Drury Lane melodrama.

"Diana of the Crossways" I liked better, and had I had absolutely
nothing to do I might have read it to the end. I remember a scene with a
rustic—a rustic who could eat hog a solid hour—that amused me. I
remember the sloppy road in the Weald, and the vague outlines of the
South Downs seen in starlight and mist. But to come to the great question, the test by which Time will judge us all—the creation of a human

being, of a live thing that we have met with in life before, and meet for the first time in print, and who abides with us ever after. Into what shadow has not Diana floated? Where are the magical glimpses of the soul? Do you remember in "Pères et Enfants," when Tourgueneff is unveiling the woman's, shall I say, affection, for Bazaroff, or the interest she feels in him? and exposing at the same time the reasons why she will never marry him. . . . I wish I had the book by me, I have not seen it for ten years.

After striving through many pages to put Lucien, whom you would have loved, whom I would have loved, that divine representation of all that is young and desirable in man, before the reader, Balzac puts these words in his mouth in reply to an impatient question by Vautrin, who asks him what he wants, what he is sighing for, *"D'être célèbre et d'être aimé,"*[6]—these are soul-waking words, these are Shakespeare words.

Where in "Diana of the Crossways" do we find soul-evoking words like these? With tiresome repetition we are told that she is beautiful, divine; but I see her not at all, I don't know if she is dark, tall, or fair; with tiresome reiteration we are told that she is brilliant, that her conversation is like a display of fireworks, that the company is dazzled and overcome; but when she speaks the utterances are grotesque, and I say that if any one spoke to me in real life as she does in the novel, I should not doubt for an instant that I was in the company of a lunatic. The epigrams are never good, they never come within measurable distance of La Rochefoucauld, Balzac, or even Goncourt. The admirers of Mr. Meredith constantly deplore their existence, admitting that they destroy all illusion of life. "When we have translated half of Mr. Meredith's utterances into possible human speech, then we can enjoy him," says the *Pall Mall Gazette*. We take our pleasures differently; mine are spontaneous, and I know nothing about translating the rank smell of a nettle into the fragrance of a rose, and then enjoying it.

Mr. Meredith's conception of life is crooked, ill-balanced, and out of tune. What remains?—a certain lustiness. You have seen a big man with square shoulders and a small head, pushing about in a crowd, he shouts and works his arms, he seems to be doing a great deal, in reality he is doing nothing; so Mr. Meredith appears to me, and yet I can only think of him as an artist; his habit is not slatternly, like those of such literary hodmen as Mr. David Christie Murray, Mr. Besant, Mr. Buchanan.

There is no trace of the crowd about him. I do not question his right of place, I am out of sympathy with him, that is all; and I regret that it should be so, for he is one whose love of art is pure and untainted with commercialism, and if I may praise it for nought else, I can praise it for this.

I have noticed that if I buy a book because I am advised, or because I think I ought, my reading is sure to prove sterile. *Il faut que cela vient de moi*, as a woman once said to me, speaking of her caprices; a quotation, a chance word heard in an unexpected ᶘ quarter. Mr. Hardy and Mr. Blackmore I read because I had heard that they were distinguished novelists; neither touched me, I might just as well have bought a daily paper; neither like nor dislike, a shrug of the shoulders—that is all. Hardy seems to me to bear about the same relation to George Eliot as Jules Breton does to Millet—a vulgarisation never offensive, and executed with ability. The story of an art is always the same, . . . a succession of abortive but ever strengthening efforts, a moment of supreme concentration, a succession of efforts weakening the final extinction. George Eliot gathered up all previous attempts, and created the English peasant; and following her peasants there came an endless crowd from Devon, Yorkshire, and the Midland Counties, and, as they came, they faded into the palest shadows until at last they appeared in red stockings, high heels and were lost in the chorus of opera. Mr. Hardy was the first step down. His work is what dramatic critics would call good, honest, straightforward work. It is unillumined by a ray of genius, it is slow and somewhat sodden. It reminds me of an excellent family coach —one of the old sort hung on C springs—a fat coachman on the box and a footman whose livery was made for his predecessor. In criticising Mr. Meredith I was out of sympathy with my author, ill at ease, angry, puzzled; but with Mr. Hardy I am on quite different terms, I am as familiar with him as with the old pair of trousers I put on when I sit down to write; I know all about his aims, his methods; I know what has been done in that line, and what can be done.

I have heard that Mr. Hardy is country bred, but I should not have discovered this from his writings. They read to me more like a report, yes, a report,—a conscientious, well-done report, executed by a thoroughly efficient writer sent down by one of the daily papers. Nowhere do I find selection, everything is reported, dialogues and descriptions.

Take for instance the long evening talk between the farm people when Oak is seeking employment.[7] It is not the absolute and literal transcript from nature after the manner of Henri Monier; for that it is a little too diluted with Mr. Hardy's brains, the edges are a little sharpened and pointed, I can see where the author has been at work filing; on the other hand, it is not synthesized—the magical word which reveals the past, and through which we divine the future—is not seized and set triumphantly as it is in "Silas Marner." The descriptions do not flow out of and form part of the narrative, but are wedged in, and often awkwardly. We are invited to assist at a sheep-shearing scene, or at a harvest supper, because these scenes are not to be found in the works of George Eliot, because the reader is supposed to be interested in such things, because Mr. Hardy is anxious to show how jolly country he is.

Collegians, when they attempt character-drawing, create monstrosities, but a practised writer should be able to create men and women capable of moving through a certain series of situations without shocking in any violent way the most generally applicable principles of common sense. I say that a practised writer should be able to do this; that they sometimes do not is a matter which I will not now go into, suffice it for my purpose if I admit that Mr. Hardy can do this. In farmer Oak there is nothing to object to; the conception is logical, the execution is trustworthy; he has legs, arms, and a heart; but the vital spark that should make him of our flesh and of our soul is wanting, it is dead water that the sunlight never touches. The heroine is still more dim, she is stuffy, she is like tow; the rich farmer is a figure out of any melodrama, Sergeant Troy nearly quickens to life; now and then the clouds are liquescent, but a real ray of light never falls.

The story-tellers are no doubt right when they insist on the difficulty of telling a story. A sequence of events—it does not matter how simple or how complicated—working up to a logical close, or, shall I say, a close in which there is a sense of rhythm and inevitableness is always indicative of genius. Shakespeare affords some magnificent examples, likewise Balzac, likewise George Eliot, likewise Tourgueneff; the "Œdipus" is, of course, the crowning and final achievement in the music of sequence and the massy harmonies of fate. But in contemporary English fiction I marvel, and I am repeatedly struck by the inability of writers, even of the first-class, to make an organic whole of their stories. Here, I say, the course is clear, the way is obvious, but no sooner do we enter on the last chapters than the story begins to show incipient shiftiness, and soon it doubles back and turns, growing with every turn weaker like a hare before the hounds. From a certain directness of construction, from the simple means by which Oak's ruin is accomplished in the opening chapters, I did not expect that the story would run hare-hearted in its close, but the moment Troy told his wife that he never cared for her, I suspected something was wrong; when he went down to bathe and was carried out by the current I knew the game was up, and was prepared for anything, even for the final shooting by the rich farmer, and the marriage with Oak, a conclusion which of course does not come within the range of literary criticism.

"Lorna Doone"[8] struck me as childishly garrulous, stupidly prolix, swollen with comments not interesting in themselves and leading to nothing. Mr. Hardy ⟨ possesses the power of being able to shape events; he can mould them to a certain form; that he cannot breathe into them the spirit of life I have already said, but "Lorna Doone" reminds me of a third-rate Italian opera, *La Fille du Régiment*, or *Ernani*; it is corrupt with all the vices of the school, and it does not contain a single passage of real fervour or force to make us forget the inherent defects of the art of which it is a poor specimen. Wagner made the discovery, not a very wonderful one after all when we think, that an opera had much better be melody from end to end. The realistic school following on Wagner's footsteps discovered that a novel had much better be all narrative—an uninterrupted flow of narrative. Description is narrative, analysis of character is narrative, dialogue is narrative; the form is ceaselessly changing, but the melody of narration is never interrupted. ⟩

But the reading of "Lorna Doone" calls to my mind, and very vividly, an original artistic principle of which English romance writers are either strangely ignorant or neglectful, viz., that the sublimation of the *dramatis personæ* and the deeds in which they are involved must correspond, and their relationship should remain unimpaired. Turner's "Carthage" is nature transposed and wonderfully modified. Some of the passages of light and shade there—those of the balustrade—are fugues, and there his art is allied to Bach in sonority and beautiful combination. Turner knew that a branch hung across the sun looked at separately was black, but he painted it light to maintain the equipoise of atmosphere. In the novel the characters are the voice, the deeds are the orchestra. But the English novelist takes 'Arry and 'Arriet, and without question allows them to achieve deeds; nor does he hesitate to pass them into the realms of the supernatural. Such violation of the first principles of narration is never to be met with in the elder writers. Achilles stands as tall as ॄ Troy, Merlin is as old and as wise as the world. Rhythm and poetical expression are essential attributes of dramatic genius, but the original sign of race and mission is an instinctive modulation of man with the deeds he attempts or achieves. The man and the deed must be cognate and equal, and the melodic balance and blending are what first separate Homer and Hugo from the fabricators of singular adventures. In Scott leather jerkins, swords, horses, mountains, and castles harmonise completely and fully with food, fighting, words, and vision of life; the chords are simple as Handel's, but they are as perfect. Lytton's work, although as vulgar as Verdi's is, in much the same fashion, sustained by a natural sense of formal harmony; but all that follows is decadent, ॄ —an admixture of romance and realism, the exaggerations of Hugo and the homeliness of Trollope; a litter of ancient elements in a state of decomposition.

The spiritual analysis of Balzac equals the triumphant imagination of Shakespeare, and by different roads they reach the same height of tragic awe, but when improbability, which in these days does duty for imagination, is mixed with the familiar aspects of life, the result is inchoate and rhythmless folly, I mean the regular and inevitable alternation and combination of pa and ma, and dear Annie who lives at Clapham, with the Mountains of the Moon, and the secret of eternal life; this violation of the first principles of art—that is to say, of the rhythm of feeling and proportion, is not possible in France. I ask the reader to recall what was said on the subject of the Club, Tavern, and Villa. We have a surplus population of more than two million women, the tradition that chastity is woman's only virtue still survives, the Tavern and its adjunct Bohemianism have been suppressed, and the Villa is omnipotent and omnipresent; tennis-playing, church on Sundays, and suburban hops engender a craving for excitement for the far away, for the unknown; but the Villa with its tennis-playing, church on Sundays, and suburban hops will not surrender its own existence, it must take a part in the heroic deeds that happen in the Mountains of the Moon; it will have heroism in its own pint pot. Achilles and Merlin must be replaced by Uncle Jim and an undergraduate; and so the Villa is the author of "Rider Haggard," "Hugh Conway," "Robert Buchanan," and the author of "The House on the Marsh."

¶ I read two books by Mr. Christie Murray, "Joseph's Coat" and "Rainbow Gold," and one by Messrs. Besant and Rice,—"The Seamy Side." It is difficult to criticise such work, there is absolutely nothing to say but that it is as suited to the mental needs of the Villa as the baker's loaves and the butcher's rounds of beef are to the physical. I do not think that any such literature is found in any other country. In France some three or four men produce works of art, the rest of the fiction of the country is unknown to men of letters. But "Rainbow Gold," I take the best of the three, is not bad as a second-rate French novel is bad; it is excellent as all that is straightforward is excellent; and it is surprising to find that work can be so good, and at the same time so devoid of artistic charm. That such a thing should be is one of the miracles of the Villa.

I have heard that Mr. Besant is an artist in the "Chaplain of the Fleet" and other novels, but this is not possible. The artist shows what he is going to do the moment he puts pen to paper, or brush to canvas; he improves on his first attempts, that is all; and I found "The Seamy Side" so very common, that I cannot believe for a moment that its author or authors could write a line that would interest me.

Mr. Robert Buchanan is a type of artist that every age produces unfailingly: Catulle Mendès is his counterpart in France,—but the pallid Portuguese Jew with his Christ-like face, and his fascinating fervour is more interesting than the spectacled Scotchman. Both began with volumes of excellent but characterless verse, and loud outcries about the dignity of art, and both have—well . . . Mr. Robert Buchanan has collaborated with Gus Harris, and written the programme poetry for the Vaudeville Theatre; he has written a novel, the less said about which the better—he has attacked men whose shoe-strings he is not fit to tie, and having failed to injure them, he retracted all he said, and launched forth into slimy benedictions. He took Fielding's masterpiece, degraded it, and debased it; he wrote to the papers that Fielding was a genius in spite of his coarseness, thereby inferring that he was a much greater genius since he had sojourned in this Scotch house of literary ill-fame. Clarville, the author of "Madame Angot," transformed Madame Marneff into a virtuous woman; but he did not write to the papers to say that Balzac owed him a debt of gratitude on that account.

The star of Miss Braddon has finally set in the obscure regions of servantgalism; Ouida and Rhoda Broughton continue to rewrite the books they wrote ten years ago; Mrs. Lynn Linton I have not read. The "Story of an African Farm" was pressed upon me. I found it sincere and youthful, disjointed but well-written; descriptions of sand-hills and ostriches sandwiched with doubts concerning a future state, and convictions regarding the moral and physical superiority of women: but of art nothing; that is to say, art as I understand it,—rhythmical sequence of events described with rhythmical sequence of phrase.

I read the "Story of Elizabeth" by Miss Thackeray. It came upon me with all the fresh and fair naturalness of a garden full of lilacs and blue sky, and I thought of Hardy, Blackmore, Murray, and Besant as of great warehouses where everything might be had, and even if the article required were not in stock it could be supplied in a few days at latest. The exquisite little descriptions, full of air, colour, lightness, grace; the French life seen with such sweet English eyes; the sweet little descriptions all so gently evocative. "What a tranquil little kitchen it was, with a glimpse of the courtyard outside, and the cocks and hens, and the poplar trees waving in the sunshine, and the old woman sitting in her white cap busy at her homely work." Into many wearisome pages these simple lines have since been expanded, without affecting the beauty of the original. "Will Dampier turned his broad back and looked out of the window. There was a moment's silence. They could hear the tinkling of bells, the whistling of the sea, the voices of the men calling to each other in the port, the sunshine streamed in; Elly was standing in it, and seemed gilt with a golden background. She ought to have held a palm in her hand, poor little martyr!" There is sweet wisdom in this book, wisdom that is eternal, being simple; and near may not come the ugliness of positivism, nor the horror of pessimism, nor the profound greyness of Hegelism, but merely the genial love and reverence of a beautiful-minded woman.

Such charms as these necessitate certain defects, I should say limitations. Vital creation of character is not possible to Miss Thackeray, but ℞ I do not rail against beautiful water-colour indications of balconies, vases, gardens, fields, and harvesters because they have not the fervid glow and passionate force of Titian's Ariadne; Miss Thackeray cannot give us a Maggie Tulliver, and all the many profound modulations of that Beethoven-like countryside: the pine wood and the cripple; this aunt's linen presses, and that one's economies; the boy going forth to conquer the world, the girl remaining at home to conquer herself; the mighty river holding the fate of all, playing and dallying with it for a while, and bearing it on at last to final and magnificent extinction. ¶ That sense of the inevitable which had the Greek dramatists wholly, which had George Eliot sufficiently, that rhythmical progression of events, rhythm and inevitableness (two words for one and the same thing) is not there. Elly's golden head, the back-ground of austere French Protestants, is sketched with a flowing water-colour brush, I do not know if it is true, but true or false in reality, it is true in art. But the jarring dissonance of her marriage is inadmissible; it cannot be led up to by chords no matter how ingenious, the passage, the attempts from one key to the other, is impossible; the true end is the ruin, by death or lingering life, of Elly and the remorse of the mother.

One of the few writers of fiction who seems to me to possess an ear for the music of events is Miss Margaret Veley.[9] Her first novel, "For Percival," although diffuse, although it occasionally flowed into by-channels and lingered in stagnating pools, was informed and held together, even at ends the most twisted and broken, by the sense of rhythmic progression which is so dear to me, and which was afterwards so splendidly developed in "Damocles." Pale, painted with grey and opaline tints of morning passes the grand figure of Rachel Conway, ℞ a victim chosen for her beauty, and crowned with flowers of sacrifice. She has not forgotten the face of the maniac, and it comes back to her in its awful lines and lights when she finds herself rich and loved by the man whom she loves. The catastrophe is a double one. Now she knows she is accursed, and that her duty is to trample out her love. Unborn generations cry to her. ¶ The wrath and the lamentation of the chorus of the Greek singer, the intoning voices of the next-of-kin, the pathetic responses of voices far in the depths of ante-natal night, these the modern novelist, playing on an inferior instrument, may suggest, but cannot give; but here the suggestion is so perfect that we cease to yearn for the real music, as, reading from a score, we are satisfied with the flute and bassoons that play so faultlessly in soundless dots.

There is neither hesitation nor doubt. ᚋ Rachel Conway puts her dreams away, she will henceforth walk in a sad and shady path; her interests are centred in the child of the man she loves, and as she looks for a last time on the cloud of trees, glorious and waving green in the sunset that encircles her home, her sorrow swells once again to passion, and, we know, for the last time.

⁋ The mechanical construction of M. Scribe I had learnt from M. Duval; the naturalistic school had taught me to scorn tricks, and to rely on the action of the sentiments rather than on extraneous aid for the bringing about of a *dénouement*; and I thought of all this as I read "Disenchantment" by Miss Mabel Robinson,[10] and it occurred to me that my knowledge would prove valuable when my turn came to write a novel, for the *mise en place*, the setting forth of this story, seemed to me so loose, that much of its strength had dribbled away before it had rightly begun. But the figure of the Irish politician I accept without reserve. It seems to me grand and mighty in its sorrowfulness. The tall, dark-eyed, beautiful Celt, attainted in blood and brain by generations of famine and drink, alternating with the fervid sensuousness of the girl, her Saxon sense of right alternating with the Celt's hereditary sense of revenge, his dreamy patriotism, his facile platitudes, his acceptance of literature as a sort of bread basket, his knowledge that he is not great nor strong, and can do nothing in the world but love his country; and as he passes his thirtieth year the waxing strong of the disease, nervous disease complex and torturous; to him drink is at once life and death; an article is bread, and to calm him and collect what remains of weak, scattered thought, he must drink. The woman cannot understand that caste and race separate them; and the damp air of spent desire, and the grey and falling leaves of her illusions fill her life's sky. Nor is there any hope for her until the husband unties the awful knot by suicide. ᚋ

I will state frankly that Mr. R. L. Stevenson never wrote a line that failed to delight me; but he never wrote a book. You arrive at a strangely just estimate of a writer's worth by the mere question: "What is he the author of?" for every writer whose work is destined to live is the author of one book that outshines the other, and, in popular imagination, epitomises his talent and position. ¶ What is Shakespeare the author of? What is Milton the author of? What is Fielding the author of? What is Byron the author of? What is Carlyle the author of? What is Thackeray the author of? What is Zola the author of? What is Mr. Swinburne the author of? Mr. Stevenson is the author of shall I say, "Treasure Island," or what? ¶

I think of Mr. Stevenson as a consumptive youth weaving garlands of sad flowers with pale, weak hands, or leaning to a large plate-glass window, and scratching thereon exquisite profiles with a diamond pencil.

I do not care to speak of great ideas, for I am unable to see how an idea can exist, at all events can be great out of language; an allusion to Mr. Stevenson's verbal expression will perhaps make my meaning clear. His periods are fresh and bright, rhythmical in sound, and perfect realizations of their sense; in reading you often think that never before was such definiteness united to such poetry of expression; every page and every sentence rings of its individuality. Mr. Stevenson's style is over smart, well-dressed, shall I say, like a young man walking in the Burlington Arcade? Yes, I will say so, but, I will add, the most gentlemanly young man that ever walked in the Burlington. Mr. Stevenson is competent to understand any thought that might be presented to him, but if he were to use it, it would instantly become neat, sharp, ornamental, light, and graceful; and it would lose all its original richness and harmony. It is not Mr. Stevenson's brain that prevents him from being a thinker, but his style.

Another thing that strikes me in thinking of Stevenson (I pass over his direct indebtedness to Edgar Poe, and his constant appropriation of his methods), is the unsuitableness of the special characteristics of his talent to the age he lives in. He wastes in his limitations, and his talent is vented in prettiness of style. In speaking of Mr. Henry James, I said that, although he had conceded much to the foolish, false, and hypocritical taste of the time, the concessions he made had in little or nothing impaired his talent. The very opposite seems to me the case with Mr. Stevenson. For if any man living in this end of the century needed freedom of expression for the distinct development of his genius, that man is R. L. Stevenson. He who runs may read, and he with any knowledge of literature will, before I have written the words, have imagined Mr. Stevenson writing in the age of Elizabeth or Anne.[11]

Turn your platitudes prettily, but write no word that could offend the chaste mind of the young girl who has spent her morning reading the Colin Campbell divorce case; so says the age we live in. The penny paper that may be bought everywhere, that is allowed to lie on every table, prints seven or eight columns of filth, for no reason except that the public likes to read filth; the poet and novelist must emasculate and destroy their work because. . . . Who shall come forward and make answer? Oh, vile, filthy, and hypocritical century, I at least scorn you.

But this is not a course of literature but the story of the artistic development of me, Edward Dayne; so I will tarry no longer with mere criticism, but go direct to the book to which I owe the last temple in my soul—"Marius the Epicurean." Well I remember when I read the opening lines, and how they came upon me sweetly as the flowing breath of a bright spring. I knew that I was awakened a fourth time, that a fourth vision of life was to be given to me.[12] Shelley had revealed to me the unimagined skies where the spirit sings of light and grace; Gautier had shown me how extravagantly beautiful is the visible world and how divine is the rage of the flesh; and with Balzac I had descended circle by circle into the nether world of the soul, and watched its afflictions. Then there were minor awakenings. Zola had enchanted me with decoration and inebriated me with theory; Flaubert had astonished with the wonderful delicacy and subtlety of his workmanship; Goncourt's brilliant adjectival effects had captivated me for a time, but all these impulses were crumbling into dust, these aspirations were etiolated, sickly as faces grown old in gaslight.

I had not thought of the simple and unaffected joy of the heart of natural things; the colour of the open air, the many forms of the country, the birds flying,—that one making for the sea; the abandoned boat, the dwarf roses and the wild lavender; nor had I thought of the beauty of mildness in life, and how by a certain avoidance of the wilfully passionate, and the surely ugly, we may secure an aspect of temporal life which is abiding and soul-sufficing. A new dawn was in my brain, fresh and fair, full of wide temples and studious hours, and the lurking fragrance of incense; that such a vision of life was possible I had no suspicion, and it came upon me almost with the same strength, almost as intensely, as that divine song of the flesh,—"Mademoiselle de Maupin."

Certainly, in my mind, these books will be always intimately associated; and when a few adventitious points of difference be forgotten, it is interesting to note how firm is the alliance, and how cognate and co-equal the sympathies on which it is based; the same glad worship of the visible world, and the same incurable belief that the beauty of material things is sufficient for all the needs of life. Mr. Pater can join hands with Gautier in saying—*je trouve la terre aussi belle que le ciel, et je pense que la correction de la forme est la vertu.* And I too join issue; I too love the great pagan world, its bloodshed, its slaves, its injustice, its loathing of all that is feeble.

But "Marius the Epicurean" was more to me than a mere emotional influence, precious and rare though that may be, for this book was the first in English prose I had come across that procured for me any genuine pleasure in the language itself, in the combination of words for silver or gold chime, and unconventional cadence, and for all those lurking half-meanings, and that evanescent suggestion, like the odour of dead roses, that words retain to the last of other times and elder usage. Until I read "Marius" the English language (English prose) was to me what French must be to the majority of English readers. I read for the sense and that was all; the language itself seemed to me coarse and plain, and awoke in me neither æsthetic emotion nor even interest. "Marius" was the stepping-stone that carried me across the channel into the genius of my own tongue. The translation was not too abrupt; I found a constant and careful invocation of meaning that was a little aside of the common comprehension, and also a sweet depravity of ear for unexpected falls of phrase, and of eye for the less observed depths of colours, which although new was a sort of sequel to the education I had chosen, and a continuance of it in foreign, but not wholly unfamiliar medium, and having saturated myself with Pater, the passage to De Quincey was easy. He, too, was a Latin in manner and in temper of mind; but he was truly English, and through him I passed to the study of the Elizabethan dramatists, the real literature of my race, and washed myself clean.

CHAPTER ELEVEN

THOUGHTS IN A STRAND LODGING[1]

Awful Emma has undressed and put the last child away—
stowed the last child away in some mysterious and unapproachable
corner that none knows but she; the fat landlady has ceased to loiter
about my door, has ceased to pester me with offers of brandy and water,
tea and toast, the inducements that occur to her landlady's mind; the
actress from the Savoy has ceased to walk up and down the street with
the young man who accompanied her home from the theatre; she has
ceased to linger on the doorstep talking to him, her key has grated in
the lock, she has come upstairs, we have had our usual midnight conversation on the landing, she has told me her latest hopes of obtaining
a part, and of the husband whom she was obliged to leave; we have
bid each other good-night, she has gone up the creaky staircase. I have
returned to my room, littered with MS. and queer publications; the
night is hot and heavy, but now a wind is blowing from the river. I am
listless and lonely. . . . I open a book, the first book that comes to
hand . . . it is *Le Journal des Goncourts*, p. 358, the end of a chapter:—

"*It is really curious that it should be the four men the most free from
all taint of handicraft and all base commercialism, the four pens the
most entirely devoted to art, that were arraigned before the public
prosecutor: Baudelaire, Flaubert, and ourselves.*"

❡ Yes it is indeed curious, and I will not spoil the piquancy of the
moral by a comment. No comment would help those to see who have
eyes to see, no comment would give sight to the hopelessly blind. ❡
Goncourt's statement is eloquent and suggestive enough; I leave it a
naked simple truth; but I would put by its side another naked simple

truth. This: If in England the public prosecutor does not seek to override literature, the means of tyranny are not wanting, whether they be the tittle-tattle of the nursery or the lady's drawing-room, or the shameless combinations entered into by librarians. . . . In England as in France those who loved literature the most purely, who were the least mercenary in their love, were marked out for persecution, and all three were driven into exile. Byron, Shelley, ⁋ and George Moore; ⁋ [2] and Swinburne, he, too, who loved literature for its own sake, was forced, amid cries of indignation and horror, to withdraw his book from the reach of a public that was rooting then amid the garbage of the Yelverton divorce case. I think of these facts and think of Baudelaire's prose poem, that poem in which he tells how a dog will run away howling if you hold to him a bottle of choice scent, but if you offer him some putrid morsel picked out of some gutter hole, he will sniff round it joyfully, and will seek to lick your hand for gratitude. Baudelaire compared that dog to the public. Baudelaire was wrong: that dog was a ————. 🐾

When I read Balzac's stories of Vautrin and Lucien de Rubempré, I often think of Hadrian and the Antinous. I wonder if Balzac did dream of transposing the Roman Emperor and his favourite into modern life. It is the kind of thing that Balzac would think of. No critic has ever noticed this.

Sometimes, at night, when all is still, and I look out on that desolate river, I think I shall go mad with grief, with wild regret for my beautiful *appartement* in *Rue de la Tour des Dames*. How different is the present to the past! I hate with my whole soul this London lodging, and all that concerns it—Emma, and eggs and bacon, the fat lascivious landlady and her lascivious daughter; I am sick of the sentimental actress who lives upstairs, I swear I will never go out to talk to her on the landing again. Then there is failure—I can do nothing, nothing; my novel I know is worthless; my life is a weak leaf, it will flutter out of sight presently. I am sick of everything; I wish I were back in Paris; I am sick of reading; I have nothing to read. Flaubert bores me. What nonsense has been talked about him! Impersonal! Nonsense, he is the most personal writer I know. That odious pessimism! How sick I am of it, it never ceases, it is lugged in *à tout propos*, and the little lyrical phrase with which he winds up every paragraph, how boring it is. Happily, I have "A Rebours" to read, that prodigious book, that beautiful mosaic.[3] Huysmans is quite right, ideas are well enough until you are twenty, afterwards only words are bearable . . . a new idea, what can be more insipid—fit for members of parliament. . . . Shall I go to bed? No. . . . I wish I had a volume of Verlaine, or something of Mallarmé's to read—Mallarmé for preference. I remember Huysmans speaks of Mallarmé in "A Rebours." In hours like these a page of Huysmans is as a dose of opium, a glass of some exquisite and powerful liqueur.

"The decadence of a literature irreparably attacked in its organism, weakened by the age of ideas, overworn by the excess of syntax, sensible only of the curiosity which fevers sick people, but nevertheless hastening to explain everything in its decline, desirous of repairing all the omissions of its youth, to bequeath all the most subtle souvenirs of its suffering on its deathbed, is incarnate in Mallarmé in most consummate and absolute fashion. . . .

"The poem in prose is the form, above all others, they prefer; handled by an alchemist of genius, it should contain in a state of meat the entire strength of the novel, the long analysis and the superfluous description of which it suppresses . . . the adjective placed in such an ingenious and definite way, that it could not be legally dispossessed of its place, would open up such perspectives, that the reader would dream for whole weeks together on its meaning at once precise and multiple, affirm the present, reconstruct the past, divine the future of the souls of the characters revealed by the light of the unique epithet. The novel thus understood, thus condensed into one or two pages, would be a communion of thought between a magical writer and an ideal reader, a spiritual collaboration by consent between ten superior persons scattered through the universe, a delectation offered to the most refined, and accessible only to them."[4]

Huysmans goes to my soul like a gold ornament of Byzantine workmanship; there is in his style the yearning charm of arches, a sense of ritual, the passion of the mural, of the window. Ah! in this hour of weariness for one of Mallarmé's prose poems! Stay, I remember I have some numbers of *La Vogue*. One of the numbers contains, I know,

"Forgotten Pages;" I will translate word for word, preserving the very rhythm, one or two of these miniature marvels of diction:—

FORGOTTEN PAGES[5]

"Since Maria left me to go to another star—which? Orion, Altair, or thou, green Venus? I have always cherished solitude. What long days I have passed alone with my cat. By alone, I mean without a material being, and my cat is a mystical companion—a spirit. I can, therefore, say that I have passed whole days alone with my cat, and, alone with one of the last authors of the Latin decadence; for since that white creature is no more, strangely and singularly I have loved all that the word *fall* expresses. In such wise that my favourite season of the year is the last weary days of summer, which immediately precede autumn, and the hour I choose to walk in is when the sun rests before disappearing, with rays of yellow copper on the grey walls and red copper on the tiles. In the same way the literature that my soul demands—a sad voluptuousness—is the dying poetry of the last moments of Rome, but before it has breathed at all the rejuvenating approach of the barbarians, or has begun to stammer the infantile Latin of the first Christian poetry.

"I was reading, therefore, one of those dear poems (whose paint has more charm for me than the blush of youth), had plunged one hand into the fur of the pure animal, when a barrel organ sang languidly and melancholy beneath my window. It played in the great alley of poplars, whose leaves appear to me yellow, even in the spring-tide, since Maria passed there with the tall candles for the last time. The instrument is the saddest, yes, truly; the piano scintillates, the violin opens the torn soul to the light, but the barrel organ, in the twilight of remembrance, made me dream despairingly. Now it murmurs an air joyously vulgar which awakens joy in the heart of the suburbs, an air old-fashioned and commonplace. Why do its flourishes go to my soul, and make me weep like a romantic ballad? I listen, imbibing it slowly, and I do not throw a penny out of the window for fear of moving from my place, and seeing that the instrument is not singing itself.

II

"The old Saxony clock, which is slow, and which strikes thirteen amid its flowers and gods, to whom did it belong? Thinkest that it came from Saxony by the mail coaches of old time?

"(Singular shadows hang about the worn-out panes.)

"And thy Venetian mirror, deep as a cold fountain in its banks of gilt work; what is reflected there? Ah! I am sure that more than one woman bathed there in her beauty's sin; and, perhaps, if I looked long enough, I should see a naked phantom.

"Wicked one, thou often sayest wicked things.

"(I see the spiders' webs above the lofty windows.)

"Our wardrobe is very old; see how the fire reddens its sad panels! the weary curtains are as old, and the tapestry on the arm-chairs stripped of paint, and the old engravings, and all these old things. Does it not seem to thee that even these blue birds are discoloured by time?

"(Dream not of the spiders' webs that tremble above the lofty windows.)

"Thou lovest all that, and that is why I live by thee. When one of my poems appeared, didst thou not desire, my sister, whose looks are full of yesterdays, the words, the grace of faded things? New objects displease thee; thee also do they frighten with their loud boldness, and thou feelest as if thou shouldest use them—a difficult thing indeed to do, for thou hast no taste for action.

"Come, close thy old German almanack that thou readest with attention, though it appeared more than a hundred years ago, and the Kings it announces are all dead, and, lying on this antique carpet, my head leaned upon thy charitable knees, on the pale robe, oh! calm child, I will speak with thee for hours; there are no fields, and the streets are empty, I will speak to thee of our furniture.

"Thou art abstracted?

"(The spiders' webs are shivering above the lofty windows.)"

To argue about these forgotten pages would be futile. We, the "ten superior persons scattered through the universe" think these prose poems the concrete essence, the osmazome of literature, the essential oil of art,[6] others, those in the stalls, will judge them to be the aberrations of a refined mind, distorted with hatred of the commonplace; the pit will immediately declare them to be nonsense, and will return with satisfaction to the last leading article in the daily paper.

"J'ai fait mes adieux à ma mère et je viens pour vous faire les miens" and other absurdities by Ponson du Terrail amused us many a year in France, and in later days similar bad grammar by Georges Ohnet has not been lost upon us, but neither Ponson du Terrail nor Georges Ohnet sought literary suffrage, such a thing could not be in France, but in England, Rider Haggard, whose literary atrocities are more atrocious than his accounts of slaughter, receives the attention of leading journals and writes about the revival of Romance. As it is as difficult to write the worst as the best conceivable sentence, I take this one and place it for its greater glory in my less remarkable prose:—

"As we gazed on the beauties thus revealed by Good, a spirit of emulation filled our breasts, and we set to work to get ourselves up as well as we could."

A return to romance! a return to the animal, say I.

One thing that cannot be denied to the realists: a constant and intense desire to write well, to write artistically. When I think of what they have done in the matter of the use of words, of the myriad verbal effects they have discovered, of the thousand forms of composition they have created, how they have remodelled and refashioned the language in their untiring striving for intensity of expression for the very osmazome of art, I am lost in ultimate wonder and admiration. What Hugo did for French verse, Flaubert, Goncourt, Zola, and Huysmans have done for French prose. No more literary school than the realists has ever existed, and I do not except even the Elizabethans. And for this our failures are more interesting than the vulgar successes of our opponents; for when we fall into the sterile and distorted, it is through our noble and incurable hatred of the commonplace, of all that is popular.

The healthy school is played out in England; all that could be said has been said; the successors of Dickens, Thackeray, and George Eliot have no ideal, and consequently no language; what can be more pudding than the language of Mr. Hardy, and he is typical of a dozen

other writers, Mr. Besant, Mr. Murray, Mr. Crawford? The reason of
this heaviness of thought and expression is that the avenues are closed,
no new subject matter is introduced, the language of English fiction
has therefore run stagnant. But if the realists should catch favour in
England the English tongue may be saved from dissolution, for with
the new subjects they would introduce, new forms of language would
arise.

———

❦ I wonder why murder is considered less immoral than fornication
in literature?

———

I feel that it is almost impossible for the same ear to seize music so
widely differing as Milton's blank verse and Hugo's alexandrines, and
it seems to me especially strange that critics varying in degree from
Matthew Arnold to the obscure paragraphist, never seem even remotely
to suspect, when they passionately declare that English blank verse is
a more perfect and complete poetic instrument than French alexandrines, that the imperfections which they aver are inherent in the
latter exist only in their British ears, impervious to a thousand subtleties. Mr. Matthew Arnold does not hesitate to say that the regular
rhyming of the lines is monotonous. To my ear every line is different;
there is as much variation in Charles V.'s soliloquy as in Hamlet's; but
be this as it may, it is not unworthy of the inmates of Hanwell for
critics to inveigh against *la rime pleine*, that which is instinctive in the
language as accent in ours, that which is the very genius of the language.

But the principle has been exaggerated, deformed, caricatured until
some of the most modern verse is little more than a series of puns—
in art as in life the charm lies in the unexpected, and it is annoying to
know that the only thought of *every* poet is to couple *les murs* with
des fruits trop mûrs, and that no break in the absolute richness of
sound is to be hoped for. Gustave Kahn whose beautiful volume "Les
Palais Nomades" I have read with the keenest delight, was the first to
recognise that an unfailing use of *la rime pleine* might become cloying
and satiating, and that, by avoiding it sometimes and markedly and
maliciously choosing in preference a simple assonance, new and subtle
music might be produced. ❦ 7

"Les Palais Nomades" is a really beautiful book, and it is free from all the faults that make an absolute and supreme enjoyment of great poetry an impossibility. For it is in the first place free from those pests and parasites of artistic work—ideas. Of all literary qualities the creation of ideas is the most fugitive. Think of the fate of an author who puts forward a new idea to-morrow in a book, in a play, in a poem. The new idea is seized upon, it becomes common property, it is dragged through newspaper articles, magazine articles, through books, it is repeated in clubs, drawing-rooms; it is bandied about the corners of streets; in a week it is wearisome, in a month it is an abomination. Who has not felt a sickening feeling come over him when he hears such phrases as "To be or not to be, that is the question"? Shakespeare was really great when he wrote "Music to hear, why hearest thou music sadly?" not when he wrote, "The apparel oft proclaims the man." Could he be freed from his ideas what a poet we should have! Therefore, let those who have taken firsts at Oxford devote their intolerable leisure to preparing an edition from which everything resembling an idea shall be firmly excluded. We might then shut up our Marlowes and our Beaumonts and resume our reading of the bard, and these witless beings would confer happiness on many, and crown themselves with truly immortal bays. See the fellows! their fingers catch at scanty wisps of hair, the lamps are burning, the long pens are poised, and idea after idea is hurled out of existence.

Gustave Kahn took counsel of the past, and he has successfully avoided everything that even a hostile critic might be tempted to term an idea; for this I am grateful to him. Nor is his volume a collection of miscellaneous verses bound together. He has chosen a certain sequence of emotions; the circumstances out of which these emotions have sprung are given in a short prose note. "Les Palais Nomades" is therefore a novel in essence; description and analysis are eliminated, and only the moments when life grows lyrical with suffering are recorded; recorded in many varying metres conforming only to the play of the emotion, for, unlike many who, having once discovered a tune, apply it promiscuously to every subject they treat, Kahn adapts his melody to the emotion he is giving expression to, with the same propriety and grace as Nature distributes perfume to her flowers. For an example of magical transition of tone I turn to *Intermède*.

"Chère apparence viens aux couchants illuminés
Veux-tu mieux des matins albes et calmes
Les soirs et les matins ont des calmes rosâtres
Les eaux ont des manteaux de cristal irisé
Et des rythmes de calmes palmes
Et l'air évoque de calmes musique de pâtres.

Viens sous des tendelets aux fleuves souriants
Aux lilas pâlis des nuits d'Orient
Aux glauques étendues à falbalas d'argent
A l'oasis des baisers urgents
Seulement vit le voile aux seuls Orients.

Quel que soit le spectacle et quelle que soit la rame
Et quelle que soit la voix qui s'affame et brame,
L'oublié du lointain des jours chatouille et serre,
Le lotos de l'oubli s'est fané dans mes serres,
Cependant tu m'aimais à jamais?
Adieu pour jamais."[8]

The repetitions of Edgar Poe seem hard and mechanical after this, so exquisite and evanescent is the rhythm, and the intonations come as sweetly and suddenly as a gust of perfume; it is as the vibration of a fairy orchestra, flute and violin disappearing in a silver mist; but the clouds break, and all the enchantment of a spring garden appears in a shaft of sudden sunlight.

"L'éphémère idole, au frisson du printemps,
Sentant des renouveaux éclore,
Le guêpe de satins si lointains et d'antan:
Roses exilés des flores!

"Le jardin rima ses branches de lilas;
Aux murs, des roses trémières;
La terre étala, pour fêter les las,
Des divans vert lumière;

"Des rires ailés peuplèrent le jardin;
Souriants des caresses brèves,
Des oiseaux joyeux, jaunes, incarnadins
Vibrèrent aux ciels de rêve."

But to the devil with literature, I am sick of it; who the deuce cares if Gustave Kahn writes well or badly.[9] Yesterday I met a chappie whose views of life coincide with mine. "A ripping good dinner," he says; "get a skinful of champagne inside you, go to bed when it is light, and get up when you are rested." This seems to me as concise as it is admirable; indeed there is little to add to it . . . a note or two concerning women might come in, but I don't know, "a skinful of champagne" implies everything.

Each century has its special ideal, the ideal of the nineteenth is a young man. The ⁅seventeenth⁆ century is only woman—see the tapestries, the delightful goddesses who have discarded their hoops and heels to appear in still more delightful nakedness, the noble woods, the tall castles, with the hunters looking round; no servile archæology chills the fancy, it is but a delightful whim; and this treatment of antiquity is the highest proof of the genius of the ⁅seventeenth⁆ century. See the Fragonards—the ladies in high-peaked bodices, their little ankles show-ing amid the snow of the petticoats. Up they go; you can almost hear their light false voices into the summer of the leaves, where Loves are garlanded even as of roses. Masks and arrows are everywhere, all the machinery of light and gracious days. In the Watteaus the note is more pensive; there is satin and sunset, plausive gestures and reluctance—false reluctance; the guitar is tinkling, and exquisite are the notes in the languid evening; and there is the Pierrot, that marvellous white animal, sensual and witty and glad, the soul of the century—ankles and epi-grams everywhere, for love was not then sentimental, it was false and a little cruel; see the furniture and the polished floor, and the tapestries with whose delicate tints and decorations the high hair blends, the footstool and the heel and the calf of the leg that is withdrawn, showing in the shadows of the lace; look at the satin of the bodices, the fan out-spread, the wigs so adorably false, the knee-breeches, the buckles on the shoes, how false; adorable little comedy, adorably mendacious; and how sweet it is to feast on these sweet lies, it is a divine delight to us, wearied with the hideous sincerity of newspapers. Then it was the man who knelt at the woman's feet, it was the man who pleaded and the woman who acceded; but in our century the place of the man is changed, it is he who holds the fan, it is he who is besought; and if one were to dream of continuing the tradition of Watteau and Fragonard in the nineteenth century, he would have to take note of and meditate deeply and profoundly on this, as he sought to formulate and synthesize the erotic spirit of our age.

The position of a young man in the nineteenth century is the most enviable that has ever fallen to the lot of any human creature. He is the rare bird, and is fêted, flattered, adored. The sweetest words are addressed to him, the most loving looks are poured upon him. The young man can do no wrong. Every house is open to him, and the best of everything is laid before him; girls dispute the right to serve him; they come to him with cake and wine, they sit circlewise and listen to him, and when one is fortunate to get him alone she will hang round his neck, she will propose to him, and will take his refusal kindly and without resentment. They will not let him stoop to tie up his shoe lace, but will rush and simultaneously claim the right to attend on him. To represent in a novel a girl proposing marriage to a man would be deemed unnatural, but nothing is more common; there are few young men who have not received at least a dozen offers, nay, more; it is characteristic, it has become instinctive for girls to choose, and they prefer men not to make love to them; and every young man who knows his business avoids making advances, knowing well that it will only put the girl off.

In a society so constituted, what a delightful opening there is for a young man. He would have to waltz perfectly, play tennis fairly, the latest novel would suffice for literary attainments; billiards, shooting, and hunting, would not come in amiss, for he must not be considered a useless being by men; not that women are much influenced by the opinion of men in their choice of favourites, but the reflex action of the heart, although not so marked as that of the stomach, exists and must be kept in view, besides a man who would succeed with women, must succeed with men; the real Lovelace is loved by all. Like gravitation, love draws all things. Our young man would have to be five feet eleven, or six feet, broad shoulders, light brown hair, deep eyes, soft and suggestive, broad shoulders, a thin neck, long delicate hands, a high instep. His nose should be straight, his face oval and small, he must be clean about the hips, and his movements must be naturally caressing. He comes into the ball-room, his shoulders well back, he stretches his hand to the hostess, he looks at her earnestly (it is characteristic of him to think of the hostess first, he is in her house, the house is well-furnished, and is suggestive of excellent meats and wines). He can read through the slim woman whose black hair, a-glitter with diamonds, contrasts with her white satin; an old man is talking to her, she dances with him, and she refused a young man a moment before. This is a bad sign; our Lovelace knows it; there is a stout woman of thirty-five, who is looking at him, red satin bodice, doubtful taste. He looks away; a little blonde woman fixes her eyes on him, she looks as innocent as a child; instinctively our Lovelace turns to his host. "Who is that little blonde woman over there, the right hand corner?" he asks. "Ah, that is Lady ———." "Will you introduce me?" "Certainly." Lovelace has made up his mind. Then there is a young oldish girl, richly dressed; "I hear her people have a nice house in a hunting country, I will dance with her, and take the mother into supper, and, if I can get a moment, will have a pleasant talk with the father in the evening."

In manner Lovelace is facile and easy; he never says no, it is always yes, ask him what you will; but he only does what he has made up his mind it is his advantage to do. Apparently he is an embodiment of all that is unselfish, for he knows that after he has helped himself, it is advisable to help some one else, and thereby make a friend who, on a future occasion, will be useful to him. Put a violinist into a room filled with violins, and he will try every one. Lovelace will put each woman aside so quietly that she is often only half aware that she has been put aside. Her life is broken; she is content that it should be broken. The real genius for love lies not in getting into, but getting out of love.

———

I have noticed that there are times when every second woman likes you. Is love, then, a magnetism which we sometimes possess and exercise unconsciously, and sometimes do not possess?[10]

Ａnd now, hypocritical reader, I will answer the questions which have been agitating you this long while, which you have asked at every stage of this long narrative of a sinful life.[1] Shake not your head, lift not your finger, exquisitely hypocritical reader; you can deceive me in nothing. I know the baseness and unworthiness of your soul as I know the baseness and unworthiness of my own. This is a magical *tête-à-tête*, such a one as will never happen in your life again; therefore I say let us put off all customary disguise, let us be frank: you have been angrily asking, exquisitely hypocritical reader, why you have been *forced* to read this record of sinful life; in your exquisite hypocrisy, you have said over and over again what good purpose can it serve for a man to tell us of his unworthiness unless, indeed, it is to show us how he may rise, as if on stepping stones of his dead self, to higher things, etc. You sighed, O hypocritical friend, and you threw the magazine on the wicker table, where such things lie, and you murmured something about leaving the world a little better than you found it, and you went down to dinner and lost consciousness of the world in the animal enjoyment of your stomach. I hold out my hand to you, I embrace you, you are my brother, and I say, undeceive yourself, you will leave the world no better than you found it. The pig that is being slaughtered as I write this line will leave the world better than it found it, but you will leave only a putrid carcase fit for nothing but the grave. Look back upon your life, examine it, probe it, weigh it, philosophise on it, and then say, if you dare, that it has not been a very futile and foolish affair. Soldier, robber, priest, Atheist, courtesan, virgin, I care not what you are, if you have not brought children into the world to suffer your life has been as vain and as harmless as mine has been. I hold out my hand to you, we are brothers; but in my heart of hearts I think myself a cut above you, because I do not believe in leaving the world better than I found it; and you, exquisitely hypocritical reader, think that you are a cut above me because you say you would leave the world better than you found it. The one eternal and immutable delight of life is to think, for one reason or another, that we are better than our neighbours. This is why I wrote this book, and this is why it is affording you so much pleasure, O exquisitely hypocritical reader, my friend, my brother, because it helps you to the belief that you are not so bad after all. Now to resume.

The knell of my thirtieth year has sounded, in three or four years my youth will be as a faint haze on the sea, an illusive recollection; so now while standing on the last verge of the hill, I will look back on the valley I lingered in. Do I regret? I neither repent nor do I regret; and a fool and a weakling I should be if I did. I know the worth and the rarity of more than ⧉ fifteen ⧉ years of systematic enjoyment. Nature provided me with as perfect a digestive apparatus, mental and physical, as she ever turned out of her workshop; my stomach and brain are set in the most perfect equipoise possible to conceive, and up and down they went and still go with measured movement, absorbing and assimilating all that is poured into them without friction or stoppage. This book is a record of my mental digestions; but it would take another series of confessions to tell of the dinners I have eaten, the champagne I have drunk! and the suppers! seven dozen of oysters, pâté-de-foie-gras, heaps of truffles, salad, and then a walk home in the early morning, a few philosophical reflections suggested by the appearance of a belated street-sweeper, then sleep, quiet and gentle sleep.

I have had the rarest and most delightful friends. Ah, how I have loved my friends; the rarest wits of my generation were my boon companions; everything conspired to enable me to gratify my body and my brain; and do you think this would have been so if I had been a good man? If you do you are a fool, good intentions and bald greed go to the wall, but subtle selfishness with a dash of unscrupulousness pulls more plums out of life's pie than the seven deadly virtues. ⧉ If you are a good man you want a bad one to convert; if you are a bad man you want a bad one to go out on the spree with. And you, my dear, my exquisite reader, place your hand upon your heart, tell the truth, remember this is a magical *tête-à-tête* which will happen never again in your life, admit that you feel just a little interested in my wickedness, admit that if you ever thought you would like to know me that it is because I know a good deal that you probably don't; admit that your mouth waters when you think of rich and various pleasures that fell to my share in happy, delightful Paris; admit that if this book had been an account of the pious books I had read, the churches I had been to, and the good works I had done, that you would not have bought it or borrowed it. Hypocritical reader, think, had you had courage, health, and money to lead a fast life, would you not have done so? You don't know, no more do I; I have done so, and I regret nothing except that some infernal farmers and miners will not pay me what they owe me and enable me to continue the life that was once mine, and of which I was so bright an ornament. How I hate this atrocious Strand lodging-house, how I long for my apartment in *Rue de la Tour des Dames*, with all its charming adjuncts, palms and pastels, my cat, my python, my friends, blond hair and dark.

It was not long before I wearied of journalism; the daily article soon grows monotonous, even when you know it will be printed, and this I did not know; my prose was very faulty, and my ideas were unsettled, I could not go to the tap and draw them off, the liquor was still fermenting; and partly because my articles were not very easily disposed of, and partly because I was weary of writing on different subjects, I turned my attention to short stories. I wrote a dozen with a view to preparing myself for a long novel. Some were printed in weekly newspapers, others were returned to me from the magazines. But there was a publisher in the neighbourhood of the Strand, who used to frequent a certain bar.[2] I saw the chance, and I seized it. This worthy man conducted his business as he dressed himself, sloppily; a dear kind soul, quite witless and quite *h*-less. From long habit he would make a feeble attempt to drive a bargain, but he generally let himself in: he was, in a word, a literary stepping-stone. Hundreds had made use of him. If a fashionable author asked two hundred pounds for a book out of which he would be certain to make three, it was ten to one that he would allow the chance to drift away from him; but after having refused a dozen times the work of a Strand loafer whom he was in the habit of "treating," he would say, "Send it in, my boy, send it in, I'll see what can be done with it." There was a long counter, and the way to be published by Mr. B. was to straddle on the counter and play with a black cat. There was an Irishman behind this counter who, for three pounds a week, edited the magazine, read the MS., looked after the printer and binder, kept the accounts when he had a spare moment, and entertained the visitors.³ I did not trouble Messrs. Macmillan and Messrs. Longman with polite requests to look at my MS., but straddled on the counter, played with the cat, joked with the Irishman, was treated by Mr. B., and in the natural order of things my stories went into the magazine, and were paid for. Strange were the ways of this office; Shakespeare might have sent in prose and poetry, but he would have gone into the wastepaper basket had he not previously straddled. For those who were in the swim this was a matter of congratulation; straddling, we would cry, "We want no blooming outsiders coming along interfering with our magazine. And you, Smith, you devil, you had a twenty-page story in last month and cut me out. O'Flanagan, do you mind if I send you in a couple of poems as well as my regular stuff, that will make it all square?" "I'll try to manage it; here's the governor." And looking exactly like the unfortunate Mr. Sedley, Mr. B. used to slouch along, and he would fall into his leather armchair, the one in which he wrote the cheques. The last time I saw that chair it was standing in the street, alas! in the hands of the brokers.

But conservative though we were in matters concerning "copy," though all means were taken to protect ourselves against interlopers, one who had not passed the preliminary stage of straddling would occasionally slip through our defences. I remember one especially. It was a hot summer's day, we were all on the counter, our legs swinging, when an enormous young man entered.⁴ He must have been six feet three in height. He was shown into Mr. B.'s room, he asked him to read a MS., and he fled, looking very frightened. "Wastepaper basket, wastepaper basket," we shouted when Mr. B. handed us the roll of paper. "What an odd-looking fish he is!" said O'Flanagan; "I wonder what his MS. is like." We remonstrated in vain, O'Flanagan took the MS. home to read, and returned next morning convinced that he had discovered an embryo Dickens. The young man was asked to call, his book was accepted, and we adjourned to the bar.

A few weeks afterwards this young man took rooms in the house next to me on the ground floor. He was terribly inflated with his success, and was clearly determined to take London by storm. He had been to Oxford, and to Heidelberg, he drank beer and smoked long pipes, he talked of nothing else. Soon, very soon, I grew conscious that he thought me a simpleton; he pooh-poohed my belief in Naturalism and declined to discuss the symbolist question. He curled his long legs upon the rickety sofa and spoke of the British public as the "B. P.," and of the magazine as the "mag." There were generally tea-things and jam-pots on the table. In a little while he brought a little creature about five feet three to live with him, and when the little creature and the long creature went out together, it was like Don Quixote and Sancho Panza setting forth in quest of adventures in the land of Strand. The little creature indulged in none of the loud, rasping affectation of humour that was so maddening in the long creature; the little creature was dry, hard, and sterile, and when he did join in the conversation it was like an empty nut between the teeth—dusty and bitter. He was supposed to be going in for the law, but the part of him to which he drew our attention was his knowledge of the Elizabethan dramatists. He kept a pocket-book, in which he held an account of his reading. Holding the pocket-book between finger and thumb, he would say, "Last year I read ten plays by Nash, twelve by Peele, six by Greene, fifteen by Beaumont and Fletcher, and eleven anonymous plays,—fifty-four in all." ⁋ He neither praised nor blamed, he neither extolled nor criticised; he told you what he had read, and left you to draw your own conclusions.

What the little creature thought of the long creature I never discovered, but with every new hour I became freshly sensible that they held me in still decreasing estimation. This, I remember, was wildly irritating to me. I knew myself infinitely superior to them; I knew the long creature's novel was worthless; I knew that I had fifty books in me immeasurably better than it, and savagely and sullenly I desired to trample upon them, to rub their noses in their feebleness; but oh, it was I who was feeble! and full of visions of a wider world I raged up and down the cold walls of impassable mental limitations. Above me there was a barred window, and, but for my manacles, I would have sprung at it and torn it with my teeth. Then passion was so strong in me that I could scarce refrain from jumping off the counter, stamping my feet, and slapping my friends in the face, so tepid were their enthusiasms, so thin did their understanding appear to me. The Straddlers seemed inclined for a moment to take the long creature very seriously, and in the office which I had marked down for my own I saw him installed as a genius.

Fortunately for my life and my sanity, my interests were, about this time, attracted into other ways—ways that led into London life, and were suitable for me to tread. In a restaurant where low-necked dresses and evening clothes crushed with loud exclamations, where there was ever an odour of cigarette and brandy and soda, I was introduced to a Jew of whom I had heard much, a man who had newspapers and race horses.[5] The bright witty glances of his brown eyes at once prejudiced me in his favour, and it was not long before I knew that I had found another friend. His house was what was wanted, for it was so trenchant in character, so different to all I knew of, that I was forced to accept it, without likening it to any French memory and thereby weakening the impression. It was a house of champagne, late hours, and evening clothes, of literature and art, of passionate discussions. So this house was not so alien to me as all else I had seen in London; and perhaps the cosmopolitanism of this charming Jew, his Hellenism, in fact, was a sort of plank whereon I might pass and enter again into English life. I found in Curzon Street another "Nouvelle Athènes," a Bohemianism of titles that went back to the Conquest, a Bohemianism of the ten sovereigns always jingling in the trousers pocket, of scrupulous cleanliness, of hansom cabs, of ladies' pet names; of triumphant champagne, of debts, gaslight, supper-parties, morning light, coaching; a fabulous Bohemianism; a Bohemianism of eternal hardupishness and eternal squandering of money,—money that rose at no discoverable well-head and flowed into a sea of boudoirs and restaurants, a sort of whirlpool of sovereigns in which we were caught, and sent eddying through music halls, bright shoulders, tresses of hair, and slang; and I joined in the adorable game of Bohemianism that was played round and about Piccadilly Circus, with Curzon Street for a magnificent rallying point.

After dinner a general "clear" was made in the direction of halls and theatres, a few friends would drop in about twelve, and continue their drinking till three or four; but Saturday night was gala night—at half-past eleven the lords drove up in their hansoms, then a genius or two would arrive, and supper and singing went merrily until the chimney sweeps began to go by, and we took chairs and bottles into the street and entered into discussion with the policeman. Twelve hours later we struggled out of our beds, and to the sound of church bells we commenced writing. The paper appeared on Tuesday. Our host sat in a small room off the dining-room from which he occasionally emerged to stimulate our lagging pens.

But I could not learn to see life paragraphically. I longed to give a personal shape to something, and personal shape could not be achieved in a paragraph nor in an article. True it is that I longed for art, but I longed also for fame, or was it notoriety? Both. I longed for fame, fame, brutal and glaring, fame that leads to notoriety. Out with you, liars that you are, tell the truth, say you would sell the souls you don't believe in, or do believe in, for notoriety. I have known you attend funerals for the sake of seeing your miserable names in the paper. You, hypocritical reader, who are now turning up your eyes and murmuring "horrid young man"—examine your weakly heart, and see what divides us; I am not ashamed of my appetites, I proclaim them, what is more I gratify them; you're silent, you refrain, and you dress up natural sins in hideous garments of shame, you would sell your wretched soul for what I would not give the parings of my finger-nails for—paragraphs in a society paper. I am ashamed of nothing I have done, especially my sins, and I boldly confess that I then desired notoriety. I walked along the streets mad; I turned upon myself like a tiger. "Am I going to fail again as I have failed before?" I asked myself. "Will my novel prove as abortive as my paintings, my poetry, my journalism?" I looked back upon my life,—mediocrity was branded about my life. "Would it be the same to the end?" I asked myself a thousand times by day, and a thousand times by night. We all want notoriety, our desire for notoriety is hideous if you will, but it is less hideous when it is proclaimed from a brazen tongue than when it hides its head in the cant of human humanitarianism. Humanity be hanged! Self, and after self a friend; the rest may go to the devil; and be sure that when any man is more stupidly vain and outrageously egotistic than his fellows, he will hide his hideousness in humanitarianism. Victor Hugo was hideous with self, and the innermost stench of the humanitarianism he vented about him is unbearable to any stomach, not excepting even Mr. Swinburne's, who occasionally holds his nose with one hand while he waves the censer with the other. Humanity be hanged! Men of inferior genius, Victor Hugo and Mr. Gladstone, take refuge in it. Humanity is a pigsty, where liars, hypocrites, and the obscene in spirit congregate; it has been so since the great Jew conceived it, and it will be so till the end. Far better the blithe modern pagan in his white tie and evening clothes, and his facile philosophy. He says, "I don't care how the poor live; my only regret is that they live at all;" and he gives the beggar a shilling.

We all want notoriety; our desires on this point, as upon others, are not noble, but the human is very despicable vermin and only tolerable when it tends to the brute, and away from the evangelical. I will tell you an anecdote which is in itself an admirable illustration of my craving for notoriety; and my anecdote will serve a double purpose,— it will bring me some of the notoriety of which I am so desirous, for you, dear, exquisitely hypocritical reader, will at once cry, "Shame! Could a man be so wicked as to attempt to force on a duel, so that he might make himself known through the medium of a legal murder?" You will tell your friends of this horribly unprincipled young man, and they will, of course, instantly want to know more about him.[6]

It was a gala night in Curzon Street, the lords were driving up in hansoms; shouts and oaths; some seated on the roofs with their legs swinging inside; the comics had arrived from the halls; there were ladies, many ladies; choruses were going merrily in the drawing-room; one man was attempting to kick the chandelier, another stood on his head on the sofa. There was a beautiful young lord there, that sort of figure that no woman can resist. There was a delightful chappie who seemed inclined to empty the mustard-pot down my neck; him I could keep in order, but the beautiful lord I saw was attempting to make a butt of me. With his impertinences I did not for a moment intend to put up; I did not know him, he was not then, as he is now, if he will allow me to say so, a friend. About three or half-past the ladies retired, and the festivities continued with unabated vigour. We had passed through various stages, not of intoxication, no one was drunk, but of jubilation; we had been jocose and rowdy, we had told stories of all kinds. The young lord and I did not "pull well together," but nothing decidedly unpleasant occurred until someone proposed to drink to the downfall of Gladstone. The beautiful lord got on his legs and began a speech. Politically it was sound enough, but much of it was plainly intended to turn me into ridicule. I answered sharply, working gradually up crescendo, until at last, to bring matters to a head, I said,

"I don't agree with you; the Land Act of '81 was a necessity."

"Anyone who thinks so must be a fool."

"Very possibly, but I don't allow people to address such language to me, and you must be aware that to call anyone a fool, sitting with you at table in the house of a friend, is the act of a cad."

There was a lull, then a moment after he said,

"I only meant politically."

"And I only meant socially."

He advanced a step or two and struck me across the face with his finger tips; I took up a champagne bottle, and struck him across the head and shoulders. Different parties of revellers kept us apart, and we walked up and down on either side of the table swearing at each other. Although I was very wrath, I had had a certain consciousness from the first that if I played my cards well I might come very well out of the quarrel; and as I walked down the street I determined to make every effort to force on a meeting. If the quarrel had been with one of the music hall singers I should have backed out of it, but I had everything to gain by pressing it. I grasped the situation at once. All the Liberal press would be on my side, the Conservative press would have nothing to say against me, no woman in it and a duel with a lord in it would be carrion for the society papers. ¶ But the danger? To the fear of death I do not think I was ever susceptible. I should have been afraid of a row with a music hall singer, because I should have had much to lose by rowing with him, but as matters stood I had too much to gain to consider the possibilities of danger. Besides there was no need to consider. I knew very well there was no reality in it. I had broken sixteen plates consecutively at the order to fire dozens of times; and yet it was three to one against my shooting a man at twenty paces; so it was ten thousand to one against a man, who had probably only fired off a revolver half-a-dozen times in a back yard, hitting me. In the gallery you are firing at white on black, on the ground you are firing at black upon a neutral tint, a very different matter. In the gallery there is nothing to disturb you;

there is not a man opposite you with a pistol in his hand. In the gallery you are calm and collected, you have risen at your ordinary hour, you are returning from a stroll through the sunlight; on the ground your nerves are altered by unusual rising, by cold air, by long expectation. It was three to one against my killing him, it was a hundred to one against his killing me. So I calculated the chances, so much as I took the trouble to calculate the chances, but in truth I thought very little of them; when I want to do anything I do not fear anything, and I sincerely wanted to shoot this young man. ¶ I did not go to bed at once, but sat in the armchair thinking. Presently a cab came rattling up to the door, and one of the revellers came upstairs. He told me that everything had been arranged; I told him that I was not in the habit of allowing others to arrange my affairs for me, and went to bed. ¶ One thing, and only one thing puzzled me, who was I to ask to be my second? My old friends were scattered, they had disappeared; and among my new acquaintances I could not think of one that would do. None of the Straddlers would do, that was certain; I wanted some one that could be depended upon, and whose social position was above question. ¶ Among my old friends I could think of some half-dozen that would suit me perfectly, but where were they? Ten years' absence scatters friends as October scatters swallows. ¶ At last my thoughts fixed themselves on one man. I took a hansom and drove to his house. I found him packing up, preparing to go abroad. This was not fortunate. I took a seat on the edge of the dining-room table, and told him I wanted him to act for me in an affair of honour. I told him the story in outline. ¶ "I suppose," he said, "it was about one or two in the morning?"

"Later than that," I said; "it was about seven."

"My dear fellow, he struck you, and not very hard, I should imagine; you hit him with a champagne bottle, and now you want to have him out. ¶ I don't mind acting as intermediary, and settling the affair for you; he will no doubt regret he struck you, and you will regret you struck him; but really I cannot act for you, that is to say, if you are determined to force on a meeting. Just think; supposing you were to shoot him, a man who has really done you no wrong."

"My dear ———, ¶ I did not come here to listen to moral reflections; if you don't like to act for me, say so."

I telegraphed to Warwickshire to an old friend:—"Can I count on you to act for me in an affair of honour?" Two or three hours after the reply came. "Come down here and stay with me for a few days, we'll talk it over." I ground my teeth; what was to be done? I must wire to Marshall and ask him to come over; English people evidently will have nothing to do with serious duelling. "Of all importance. Come over at once and act for me in an affair of honour. Bring the count with you; leave him at Boulogne; he knows the colonel of the ———." The next day I received the following: "Am burying my father; so soon as he is underground will come." Was there ever such luck? . . . He won't be here before the end of the week. These things demand the utmost promptitude. Three or four days afterwards dreadful Emma told me a gentleman was upstairs taking a bath. "Holloa, Marshall, how are you? Had a good crossing? Awful good of you to come. . . . The poor old gentleman went off quite suddenly, I suppose?"

"Yes; found dead in his bed. He must have known he was dying, for he lay quite straight as the dead lie, his hands by his side . . . wonderful presence of mind."

"He left no money?"

"Not a penny; but I could manage it all right. Since my success at the Salon, I have been able to sell my things. I am only beginning to find out now what a success that picture was. *Je t'assure, je fais l'école*". . .

"*Tu crois ça . . . on fait l'école après vingt ans de travail.*"

"*Mon ami, je t'assure, j'ai un public qui me suit.*"

"*Mon ami, veux-tu que je te dis ce que tu a fait; tu a fait encore une vulgarization, une jolie vulgarization, je veux bien, de la note inventée par Millet; tu a ajouté la note claire inventée par Manet, enfin tu suis avec talent le mouvement moderne, voilà tout.*"

"*Parlons d'autre chose: sur la question d'art on ne s'entend jamais.*"
When we were excited Marshall and I always dropped into French.

"And now tell me," he said, "about this duel."

I could not bring myself to admit, even to Marshall, that I was willing to shoot a man for the sake of the notoriety it would bring me, not because I feared in him any revolt of conscience, but because I dreaded his sneers; he was known to all Paris, I was an obscure something, living in an obscure lodging in London. Had Marshall suspected the truth he would have said pityingly, "My dear Dayne, how can you be so foolish? why will you not be contented to live?" etc. . . . Such homilies would have been maddening; he was successful, I was not; I knew there was not much in him, *un feu de paille*, no more, but what would I not have done and given for that *feu de paille*? So I was obliged to conceal my real motives for desiring a duel, and I spoke strenuously of the gravity of the insult and the necessity of retribution. But Marshall was obdurate. "Insult?" he said. "He hit you with his hand, you hit him with the champagne bottle; you can't have him out after that, there is nothing to avenge, you wiped out the insult yourself; if you had not struck him with the champagne bottle the case would be different."

We went out to dine, we went to the theatre, and after the theatre we went home and æstheticised till three in the morning. I spoke no more of the duel, I was sick of it; luck, I saw, was against me, and I let Marshall have his way. He showed his usual tact, a letter was drawn up in which my friend withdrew the blow of his hand, I withdrew the blow of the bottle, and the letter was signed by Marshall and two other gentlemen. ℞ 7

Hypocritical reader, you draw your purity garments round you, you say, "How very base;" but I say unto you remember how often you have longed, if you are a soldier in her Majesty's army, for war,—war that would bring every form of sorrow to a million fellow-creatures, and you longed for all this to happen, because it might bring your name into the *Gazette*. Hypocritical reader, think not too hardly of me; hypocritical reader, think what you like of me, your hypocrisy will alter nothing; in telling you of my vices I am only telling you of your own; hypocritical reader, in showing you my soul I am showing you your own; hypocritical reader, exquisitely hypocritical reader, you are my brother, I salute you.

Day passed over day: I lived in that horrible lodging; I continued to labour at my novel; it seemed an impossible task—defeat glared at me from every corner of that frouzy room. My English was so bad, so thin, —stupid colloquialisms out of joint with French idiom. I learnt unusual words and stuck them up here and there; they did not mend the style. Self-reliance had been lost in past failures; I was weighed down on every side, but I struggled to bring the book somehow to a close. Nothing mattered to me, but this one thing. To put an end to the landlady's cheating, and to bind myself to remain at home, I entered into an arrangement with her that she was to supply me with board and lodgings for three pounds a week, and henceforth resisting all Curzon Street temptations, I trudged home through November fogs, to eat a chop in a frouzy lodging-house. I studied the horrible servant as one might an insect under a microscope. "What an admirable book she would make, but what will the end be? if I only knew the end!" I had more and more difficulty in keeping the fat landlady at arm's length, and the nasty child was well beaten one day for lingering about my door. I saw poor Miss L. nightly, on the stairs of this infamous house, and I never wearied of talking to her of her hopes and ambitions, of the young man she admired. She used to ask me about my novel.

Poor Miss L.! Where is she? I do not know, but I shall not forget the time when I used to listen for her footstep on the midnight stairs. Often I was too despondent, when my troubles lay too heavily and darkly upon me, I let her go up to her garret without a word. Despondent days and nights when I cried, Shall I never pass from this lodging? shall I never be a light in that London, long, low, misshapen, that dark monumental stream flowing through the lean bridges; and what if I were a light in this umber-coloured mass,—shadows falling, barges moored midway in a monumental stream? Happiness abides only in the natural affections—in a home and a sweet wife. Would she whom I saw to-night marry me? How sweet she was in her simple naturalness, the joys she has known have been slight and pure, not violent and complex as mine. Ah, she is not for me, I am not fit for her, I am too sullied for her lips. . . . Were I to win her could I be dutiful, true? . . .

"Young men, young men whom I love, dear ones who have rejoiced with me, not the least of our pleasures is the virtuous woman; after excesses there is reaction, all things are good in nature, and they are foolish young men who think that sin alone should be sought for. The feast is over for me, I have eaten and drunk; I yield my place, do you eat and drink as I have; do you be young as I was. I have written it! The word is not worth erasure, if it is not true to-day it will be in two years hence; farewell! I yield my place, do you be young as I was, do you love youth as I did; remember you are the most interesting beings under heaven, for you all sacrifices will be made, you will be fêted and adored upon the condition of remaining young men. The feast is over for me, I yield my place, but I will not make this leavetaking more sorrowful than it is already by afflicting you with advice and instruction how to obtain what I have obtained. I have spoken bitterly against education, I will not strive to educate you, you will educate yourselves. Dear ones, dear ones, the world is your pleasure, you can use it at your will. Dear ones, I see you all about me still, I yield my place; but one more glass I will drink with you; and while drinking I would say my last word—were it possible I would be remembered by you as a young man: but I know too well that the young never realise that the old were not born old. Farewell."

I shivered; the cold air of morning blew in my face, I closed the window, and sitting at the table, haggard and overworn, I continued my novel.

THE END

The dates indicate the year or years in which the revision appeared. The letters *F* and *E* refer to the French and English editions of *Confessions,* which were both published in 1889.

Page 53
¶ Then ... no ⟧ 1889 F and E; slightly rev. 1904, 1917, 1918.

So my youth ran into manhood, finding its way from rock to rock like a rivulet, gathering strength at each leap. One day my father was suddenly called to Ireland. A few days after a telegram came, and my mother read that we were required at his bedside. We journeyed over land and sea; and on a bleak country road, one winter's evening, a man approached us, and I heard him say that all was over, that my father was dead. I loved my father; and yet my soul said, "I am glad." The thought came unbidden, undesired, and I turned aside, shocked at the sight it afforded of my soul.

O my father, I, who love and reverence nothing else, love and reverence thee; thou art the one pure image in my mind, the one true affection that life has not broken or soiled; I remember thy voice and thy kind, happy ways. All I have of worldly goods and native wit I received from thee—and was it I who was glad? No, it was not I; I had no concern in the thought that then fell upon me unbidden and undesired; my individual voice can give you but praise and loving words; and the voice that said "I am glad" was not my voice, but that of the will to live which we inherit from elemental dust through countless generations. Terrible and imperative is the voice of the will to live: let him who is innocent cast the first stone.

Terrible is the day when each sees his soul naked, stripped of all veil; that dear soul which he cannot change or discard, and which is so irreparably his.

My father's death freed me, and I sprang like a loosened bough up to the light. His death gave me power to create myself—that is to say, to create a complete and absolute self out of the partial self which was all that the restraint of home had permitted; this future self, this ideal George Moore, beckoned me, lured like a ghost; and as I followed the funeral the question, Would I sacrifice this ghostly self, if by so doing I should bring my father back? presented itself without intermission, and I shrank horrified at the answer which I could not crush out of mind.

Now my life was like a garden in the emotive torpor of spring; now my life was like a flower conscious of the light. Money was placed in my hands, and I divined all it represented. Before me the crystal lake, the distant mountains, the swaying woods, said but one word, and that word was—self; not the self that was then mine, but the self on whose creation I was enthusiastically determined. But I felt like a murderer when I turned to leave the place which I had so suddenly, and I could not but think unjustly, become possessed of. As I probe this poignant psychological moment, I find that, although I perfectly well realized that all pleasures were then in my reach—women, elegant dress, theatres, and supper-rooms—I hardly thought at all of them, but much more of certain drawings from the plaster cast. I would be an artist. More than ever I was determined to be an artist, and my brain was made of this desire as I journeyed as fast as railway and steamboat could take me to London. No

Page 53
⟨ Mill; . . . reading. ⟩ 1889 F and E, 1904, 1917; slightly rev. 1918.

Mill. So it will be understood that Shelley not only gave me my first soul, but led all its first flights. But I do not think that if Shelley had been no more than a poet, notwithstanding my very genuine love of verse, he would have gained such influence in my youthful sympathies; but Shelley dreamed in metaphysics—very thin dreaming if you will; but just such thin dreaming as I could follow. Was there or was there not a God? And for many years I could not dismiss as parcel of the world's folly this question, and sought a solution, inclining towards atheism, for it was natural in me to oppose the routine of daily thought. I think it was in my early teens, soon after my expulsion from Oscott for refusing to confess, that I resolved to tell my mother that I believed no longer in a God. She was leaning against the chimney-piece in the drawing-room; but although a religious woman, my mother did not seem in the least frightened, she only said, "I am very sorry, George, it is so," and I was deeply shocked at her indifference.

Finding music and atheism in poetry, I cared little for novels.

Page 55
¶ enter . . . rowdy. The ▸ 1917; slightly rev. 1918.

study painting in Cabanel's studio. A satyr breaking through some branches carrying a woman in his arms had inspired an endless admiration, and his picture of Dante sitting on a bench under a wall reading to a frightened audience, increased my desire to identify myself with his vision; to feel the thrill of the girl's shoulder, as no doubt he had when she shrank back into her lover's protection, frightened by the poet's relation of what he had seen in hell. But to go to Cabanel before I could speak French were useless, and at the end of three weeks my patience was exhausted; and three weeks are a short time to master a sufficient number of French phrases to explain my mission.

The man that received me with unaffected courtesy was of medium height, with square and rather high shoulders, and his square-cut beard and a certain nobility of countenance, like that of a lion, are among my remembrances of the great painter who listened in March, 1873, with patience to my praise of *The Florentine Poet*. He gave attentive ear to my jargon, and discovering in it a very genuine admiration of his beautiful decoration for the Louvre hanging on the end wall of his studio, he looked at my drawings, and tried to make plain that he could not take me as a private pupil, having no studio except the one we stood in. It seemed to me that a distant corner would suit me very well, but feeling that I should be in the way of his models and his patrons, I was about to retire apologetically. He stopped me, however, and once more I applied myself to the task of understanding the instruction he seemed bent upon giving: he was one of the professors of the Beaux Arts, and the best thing for me to do would be to make application at the Embassy; no doubt my Ambassador would be able to obtain for me the right of entrance without examination. "He thinks that my drawings are not good enough to get me through," I said to myself as I hastened away in a cab to tell my story to Lord Lyons, an elegant old gentleman, who promised to intercede on my behalf with Le Ministre des Beaux Arts. A few days later an official letter was handed to me, and the morning after I introduced myself to many turbulent fellows whose aspects and manners soon convinced me that I would not be able to endure the life of the Beaux Arts, and that the facilities the schools afforded were not those that I sought for.

The

Page 56

¶ and ◗ 1889 E; slightly rev. 1904; extensively rev. 1917; slightly rev. 1918.

trying to find a painter to whom I might address myself with confidence. I had never forgotten my father showing me, one day when he was shaving, three photographs from pictures. They were by an artist called Sevres. My father liked the slenderer figure, but I liked the corpulent— the Venus standing at the corner of a wood, pouring wine into a goblet, while Cupid, from behind her satin-enveloped knees, drew his bow and shot the doves that flew from glistening poplar-trees. The beauty of this woman, and what her beauty must be in the life of the painter, had inspired many a reverie, and I had concluded—this conclusion being of all others most sympathetic to me—that she was his very beautiful mistress, that they lived in a picturesque happiness in the midst of a shady garden full of birds and tall flowers. She had haunted my imagination in white muslin with wide sleeves open to the elbow, scattering grain from a silver plate to the proud pigeons that strutted about her slippered feet and fluttered to her dove-like hand; and these dreams of her had accompanied me in my rides over the plains of Mayo, and in London I conceived a project of becoming Sevres's pupil and being loved by her!

What coming and going, what inquiries, what difficulties, arose! At last I was advised to go to the Exposition aux Champs Elysées and seek his address in the catalogue; and while the concierge copied out the address for me, I chased his tame magpie that hopped about one of the angles of the great building, for I was a childish boy of one-and-twenty who knew nothing, and to whom the world was astonishingly new. I have often thought that before my soul was given to me it had been plunged deep in Lethe, and as an almost virgin man I stood in front of

Enghien—a suburb not far from Paris, the pretty French country seeming to me like a fairy-book. There were tall green poplars, and a little lake reflected the foliage and the stems of sapling oak and pine, just as in the pictures. The driver pointed with his whip, and I saw a high garden wall shadowed with young trees, and a loose iron gate, and passing through the gate I walked up the gravelled path, looking around for the beautiful mistress who I felt should feed pigeons from a silver plate, asking myself if Monsieur Sevres would invite me to breakfast. A maid-servant opened the door. She showed me into the studio, and before I had time to make examination of the few sketches on the walls Monsieur Sevres came in, a tall, reedy-looking man, who did not wear the appearance of genius like Cabanel. But as the object of my visit was his mistress as much as himself, I prolonged the conversation as far as my knowledge of the French language allowed me. His pictures were all in the Salon, he said, but he drew forth a few sketches, and told me, as Cabanel had done, that he had no room for a pupil in his house. Whereupon I proposed to him that I should take a house in Enghien. "Were there houses to let?" He said there were many, and that if I took one he would have much pleasure in walking over and instructing me. But being by no means sure that Monsieur Sevres had a mistress, I avoided a direct answer, saying that I would write and let him know as soon as I had found a house; and answering that he hoped that I would find one that suited me, he conducted me down the green garden. "I've seen these trees before in your pictures," I said, scanning every nook, hoping that I should see her reading, and that she would raise her eyes as I passed.

It seems to me that I did catch sight of a white dress behind a trellis, but the dress that I saw or imagined may have been worn by his daughter or by his wife. However this may be, Sevres's mistress, if he had one, was not discovered by me that day nor any other day. I never saw him again. He had proven somewhat of a disappointment, and the woman, I reflected, who had sat for the pictures that had stirred my childish imaginations in Mayo may have been painted long ago. "The woman is perhaps an old woman now," I said to myself as the train entered Paris. "But even so, I shall have to learn painting from somebody"; and next day I returned to Enghien with my taciturn valet, who showed no enthusiasm on the subject of Enghien, and was at no pains to disguise from me the fact he was but little disposed to settle in this French suburb.

We were both very much alone in Paris. In the evenings I allowed him to smoke his clay in my room, and in an astounding brogue he counselled me to return to my mother. But I would not listen, and one day on the Boulevards I

Page 60
⁋ The . . . sky. ⁊ 1917, 1918.

It often seemed to me that Marshall was not conscious of the fantastic greenness of the foliage under the gaslights, or of the unreality of the life we were leading in the company of women, known only to us by their Christian names. He took it all for granted, whereas I lived it in my imagination, exalted by the clangour of the band, the thronging of the dancers, and most of all by the returning home in open carriages through the close, warm night, the darkness chequered by an ostrich-feather hanging over the hood of the carriage in front of us, an edge of skirt passing beyond the foot-board. "She is in his arms," I said. "Does she love him?" I asked, and watched the moon and compared it to a magic-lantern hanging out of the sky.

Page 66
⁋ verse . . . produced. ⁊ 1917; slightly rev. 1918.

verse, and prose dialogue would look quite different. As no instinctive want had urged me to read Shakespeare, he remained unread, and I did not turn to him now because of the excessive popularity of his name, but went instead to the Gymnase, and gave an attentive hearing to the play, which, however, did not enable me to see the dialogue upon paper. A corner of the prompter's copy was visible from the stall I sat in; a peep into it would reveal the secret of play-writing to me, but to seek out the prompter's acquaintance would mean a long delay, and being in a hurry, I betook myself to Galignani's library in quest of a book that would assist me, and after a month's study of Congreve, Wycherley, Vanburgh, and Farquhar, Marshall's attempt to marry his mistress to one of his friends was related in three acts. The title given to the comedy was "Worldliness." My valet liked it, seeing in it the means whereby he might get back to London; and we returned to London, my valet thinking of the happy evenings that awaited him in the Sun Music Hall at Knightsbridge, myself of the rehearsals at the Olympic, the Globe, or the Gaiety. It did not matter which; my comedy would suit any West End theatre.

Page 67
⟪ Is . . . going. ⟫ 1918.

It is always difficult to get past a stage-door keeper, and it is disappointing to find in him a rival dramatist, which I did at the Olympic. A copyist of plays, mine was, as well as a writer, and while waiting I learnt among other things that it would be well to have my play copied and the stage directions inscribed in red ink. These things he undertook to do for the play that I hoped Mr. Nevill would read; and he performed the same good offices for another play which my friend, Dick Mansell, would have produced if he had not just taken the St. James's for the production of Offenbach's "Bridge of Sighs."

We had good times behind the scenes of the St. James's, and it was not till the backers refused to supply any more money and the theatre had to be closed that I was seized with a longing for Paris, and returned there hurriedly, hardly able to bear with the hours that separated me from Marshall.

Page 71
⟪ This . . . It ⟫ 1889 E; slightly rev. 1904, 1917, 1918.

And as this young man always sought extremes, he went to Belleville, donned a blouse, ate garlic with his food, and settled down to live there as a workman. I had been to see him, and had found him building a wall. And with sorrow I related his state that evening to Julien in the Café Veron. He said, after a pause:—

"Since you profess so much friendship for him, why do you not do him a service that cannot be forgotten since the result will always continue? Why don't you save him from the life you describe? If you are not actually rich you are at least in easy circumstances, and can afford to give him a *pension* of three hundred francs a month. I will give him the use of my studio, which means, as you know, models and teaching; Marshall has plenty of talent, all he wants is a year's education: in a year or a year-and-a-half, certainly at the end of two years, he will begin to make money."

It is rather a shock to one who is at all concerned with his own genius to be asked to act as foster-mother to another's. Then three hundred francs meant a great deal, plainly it meant deprivation of those superfluities which are so intensely necessary to the delicate and refined. Julien watched me. This large crafty Southerner knew what was passing in me; he knew I was realizing all the manifold inconveniences—the duty of looking after Marshall's wants for two years, and to make the pill easier he said:—

"If three hundred francs a month are too heavy for your purse, you might take an apartment and ask Marshall to come and live with you. You told me the other day you were tired of hotel life. It would be an advantage to you to live with him. You want to do something yourself; and the fact of his being obliged to attend the studio (for I should advise you to have a strict agreement with him regarding the work he is to do) would be an extra inducement to you to work hard."

I always decide at once, reflection does not help me, and a moment after I said, "Very well, Julien, I will."

And next day I went with the news to Belleville. Marshall protested he had no real talent. I protested he had, and amid our different protests an agreement was drawn up and signed. He was to work in the studio eight hours a day; he was to draw until such time as M. Lefebvre set him to paint; and in proof of his industry he was to bring me at the end of each week a study from life and a composition, the subject of which the master gave at the beginning of each week; in return I was to take an apartment near the studio, give him an abode, food, *blanchissage*. As if to convince himself of his earnestness, he began to manifest prodigious energy, telling me three days after that he had found an apartment in Le Passage des Panoramas which would suit us perfectly. The news was not altogether pleasant, but the plunge had been taken. I paid my hotel bill, and sent my taciturn valet to happy evenings in the Sun Music Hall.

It

Page 80
☞FOOTNOTE ADDED 1904, 1917, 1918.

*Surely the phrase is ill-considered, hurried; "my convalescence" would express the author's meaning better.

Page 83
⁋[But . . . volumes.]⁋ 1917; slightly rev. 1918.

And the net result of Hugo's ambition is that nobody reads him except when the journalists quote him in the newspapers, which is more reasonable than appears at first sight, for an essential condition of a work of art is that it should be rare; another condition is that it should be brief. Of an entire poem, as has been said, it is seldom that we remember more than a stanza, and very often of the stanza only a single line remains in the memory:

> "Le clair de lune bleu qui baigne l'horizon"

is all that I remember of "La fête chez Thérèse." Villiers always used to contend that no poem should be extended beyond a single line:

> "O pasteur, Hespérus à l'occident s'allume."

The sweet, sad serenity of the evening air is contained in this verse. The star shines in the west, the lambs run to the ewes, and the shepherd leads the flock foldwards. Why add to the line?

I remember Villiers one morning, not long before Venus kindles in the west, telling a group that followed him from *café* to *café* listening to his stories that he had composed a drama on the subject of the Cenci, and that according to his poetic principle, he had compressed the entire drama into one line. "Beatrice," he said, throwing back his hair, "is not content with merely murdering her father; she has had him made into soup." The soup is served and is handed round to the guests at a great banquet given in honour of the assassination. It is at this point of the tragedy *que je place mon vers*:

> "Et les yeux du bouillon étaient ceux de son père."

Sometimes Villiers would add a morality to his single-line poems. Here is an example:

> "Pépin le bref est mort depuis onze cents ans."

Morality:

> "Quand on est mort c'est pour longtemps."

Page 92
⸿ mine . . . taste, ⸿ 1904, 1917, 1918.

Marshall's—strange debauches of colour and Turkish lamps—or mine,

Page 109
⸿ Dear, . . . Cromwell. ⸿ 1917; slightly rev. 1918.

Dear, sweet, Protestant England claims me. Every aspect of it raises me above myself, and there is perhaps no moment in my life more intense than when I stand and gaze admiring the red tiles of the farmhouse, the elms, the great hedgerows and all the rich fields adorned with spreading trees and smock frocks. My soul is cheered by the sight of a windmill or a smock, we find neither in the north; the north is Celtic and I am by ancestry a South Saxon. The country of my instinctive aspiration would be Sussex, the most Saxon of all. Its every aspect awakens antenatal sympathies in me. The villages clustered round the greens with spires of the churches pointing between the elms were never new to me. When I saw them for the first time they were familiar; and the church bells calling the folk to prayer, to sweet-smelling churches, without candles, without incense, drew my feet instinctively. I followed, and learnt to love God in Protestantism and to understand that when England ceases to be Protestant she will decline into the equivalent of the poor Celt who worships his priest and shoots his landlord. France never was Catholic, no nation is, and nowhere in France does the Catholic banner hang so limp as in the Nouvelles Athènes.

Page 130
⸿ for . . . work: ⸿ 1917, 1918.

and when I returned to London I could write English verse, but even ordinary newspaper prose was beyond my reach, and an attempt I made to write a novel drifted into failure.

Of my knowledge, or lack of knowledge, of the two languages I will give examples. Here is a poem that I translated aloud to Cabaner one night in the Nouvelle Athènes:

We are alone! Listen, a little while,
And hear the reason why your weary smile
And lute-toned speaking is so very sweet,

And how my love of you is more complete
Than any love of any lover. They
Have only been attracted by the grey
Delicious softness of your eyes, your slim
And delicate form, or some such other whim,
The simple pretexts of all lovers—I
For other reason. Listen whilst I try
To say. I joy to see the sunset slope
Beyond the weak hours' hopeless horoscope,
Leaving the heavens a melancholy calm
Of quiet colour chanted like a psalm,
In mildly modulated phrases; thus
Your life shall fade like a voluptuous
Vision beyond the sight, and you shall die
Like some soft evening's sad serenity . . .
I would possess your dying hours; indeed
My love is worthy of the gift, I plead
For them. Although I never loved as yet,
Methinks that I might love you; I would get
From out the knowledge that the time was brief
That tenderness, whose pity grows to grief,
And grief that sanctifies, a joy, a charm
Beyond all other loves, for now the arm
Of Death is stretched to you-ward, and he claims
You as his bride. Maybe my soul misnames
Its passion; love perhaps it is not, yet
To see you fading like a violet,
Or some sweet thought away, would be a strange
And costly pleasure, far beyond the range
Of formal man's emotion. Listen, I
Will choose a country spot where fields of rye
And wheat extend in rustling yellow plains,
Broken with wooded hills and leafy lanes,
To pass our honeymoon; a cottage where
The porch and windows are festooned with fair
Green wreaths of eglantine, and look upon
A shady garden where we'll walk alone
In the autumn sunny evenings; each will see
Our walks grow shorter, till the orange tree,
The garden's length, is far, and you will rest
From time to time, leaning upon my breast
Your languid lily face. Then later still
Unto the sofa by the window-sill
Your wasted body I shall carry, so
That you may drink the last left lingering glow
Of evening, when the air is filled with scent
Of blossoms; and my spirit shall be rent

The while with many griefs. Like some blue day
That grows more lovely as it fades away,
Gaining that calm serenity and height
Of colour wanted, as the solemn night
Steals forward you will sweetly fall asleep
For ever and for ever; I shall weep
A day and night large tears upon your face,
Laying you then beneath a rose-red place
Where I may muse and dedicate and dream
Volumes of poesy of you; and deem
It happiness to know that you are far
From any base desires as that fair star
Set in the evening magnitude of heaven.
Death takes but little, yea, your death has given
Me that deep peace, and that secure possession
Which man may never find in earthly passion.

The poem entitled "Une Nuit de Septembre" tells of a very unplatonic encounter in the forests of Fontainebleau and, perhaps, readers will be interested to hear that the lady still retains in face and figure many pleasant remembrances of her springtime, though, alas! her whilom lover has fallen into the sere and yellow leaf.

NUIT DE SEPTEMBRE

La nuit est pleine de silence,
Et dans une étrange lueur,
Et dans une douce indolence
La lune dort comme une fleur.

Parmi les rochers, dans le sable,
Sous les grands pins d'un calme amer
Surgit mon amour périssable,
Faim de tes yeux, soif de ta chair.

Je suis ton amant, et ta blonde
Gorge tremble sous mon baiser,
Et le feu de l'amour inonde
Nos deux coeurs sans les apaiser.

Rien ne peut durer, mais ta bouche
Est telle qu'un fruit fait de sang;
Tout passe, mais ta main me touche
Et je me donne en frémissant.

Tes yeux verts me regardent; j'aime
Le clair de lune de tes yeux,
Et je ne vois dans le ciel même
Que ton corps rare et radieux.

POUR UN TABLEAU DE LORD LEIGHTON

De quoi rêvent-elles? de fleurs,
D'ombres, d'étoiles ou de pleurs?
De quoi rêvent ces douces femmes?
De leurs amours ou de leurs âmes?

Pareilles aux lis abattus
Elles dorment les rêves tus
Dans la grande fenêtre ovale
Sous un cielegris comme un opale.

POUR UN TABLEAU DE RUBENS

"Dans sa gracieuse pâleur
Elle vit ainsi qu'une fleur,
Evoquant une fraîche odeur
Par la transparente couleur.

"Loin de l'émotion charnelle,
Rubens, oubliant son modèle,
Pressentit la vie éternelle
Qui s'incarne un moment en elle.

"Sa pensée est dans cette main,
Dans sa pose et dans son dessin
Et dans ses yeux pleins du chemin
Que traverse le coeur humain.

"Néanmoins pour toute âme en peine
Que son calme altier rasséréne,
Elle est l'image souveraine
De la vie éphémère et vaine."

VERS D'ALBUM [1923]

Je vois tes mains dans ma pensée
Jeunes mains fleurs de la rosée
Je vois ta main gauche posée
Comme par Ingres sur ton sein,
Et entre nous le beau dessin
Qu'il aurait fait d'après ta main.

Page 132
✿ 1917, 1918.

It would be easy for me to produce more poems in English and in French, for in my youth I believed myself to be a poet; my only doubt was whether my muse was French or English. But of what avail to print any more, since I have not written verse for many and many a year, and shall probably never write again in verse? But as I write these lines a poem of old time starts up in my memory, and it is one that there is more reason for printing here than any other. I'm thinking of the sonnet in which I dedicate "Luther," a five-act drama, to Swinburne.

> Je t'apporte mon drame, ô poète sublime,
> Ainsi qu'un écolier au maître sa leçon:
> Ce livre avec fierté porte comme écusson
> Le sceau qu'en nos esprits ta jeune gloire imprime.
>
> Accepte, tu verras la foi mêlée au crime
> Se souiller dans le sang sacré de la raison,
> Quand surgit, rédempteur du vieux peuple saxon,
> Luther à Wittenberg comme Christ à Solime.
>
> Jamais de la cité le mal entier ne fuit,
> Hélas! et son autel y fume dans la nuit;
> Mais notre âge a ceci de pareil à l'aurore,
>
> Que c'est un divin cri du chanteur éternel,
> Le tien, qui pour forcer le jour tardif d'éclore
> Déchire avec splendeur le voile épars du ciel.

Page 137
◖ But . . . tavern. ◗ 1918.

My days in Cecil Street are only a few years behind me, and already I have begun to regret them, or, to speak more exactly, to regret that chance misfortune did not plunge me deeper into what is known as low life, but which is really the only life. Cecil Street is remembered with a certain pride, for I went there to live on two pounds a week, determined to make my way in literature, for my Irish properties seemed at that time to be vanishing away, and to make one's bread at literature requires hard training, especially in my case, for I could not write printable English at that time—only a jargon that was neither French nor English. It was in that house in Cecil Street that I began "The Modern Lover," and wrote it out in copybooks from daylight till dark, and then went out to learn London, to assimilate, to become part of the vast incoherent mass which is London. To write about London I should have to begin by forgetting Paris, blotting out of my mind the Boulevards with their trees and the kiosque. Ah! the kiosque! Nothing is so evocative of Paris as the kiosque. The old women sitting before their trestles covered with newspapers; the men buying and turning into their *café* or sitting down in the chairs under the awning, an absinthe or vermouth in front of them.

These were the scenes that I saw in my mind's eyes when I walked out of grubby Cecil Street into the Strand, and turned eastward and mooched about in many various purlieus, wondering at the sordid public-house at the corner. It reminded me how far I was from the Nouvelle Athènes and the Boule Noire. It was the *café* that I missed, the brilliant life of the *café*, the casual life of the *café*, so different from the life of the bars into which I turned in search of a companion and the eating-houses where I fed between seven and eight on roast saddle of mutton, wheeled round the different pens and cut to the liking of the customer, with potatoes and vegetables. "Potatoes and vegetables" was the cry of the second waiter, and often I pondered the phrase. Why "potatoes" and vegetables? Are potatoes not vegetables? Strictly, I suppose they are tubers. These eating-houses were well enough from seven till eight; one met somebody connected with a newspaper or some shadowy rhymer willing to talk; but after nine o'clock London was a desolate place for me, and I walked thinking of the *cafés* that I had abandoned, and thinking, too, of the Mermaid Tavern in which the Elizabethan poets used to foregather very much as we did in Paris in the Nouvelle Athènes. But London has lost her taverns.

Page 145
⫷ I . . . librarian. ⫸ 1918.

It is strange that it should have come into anybody's head to think that our morality is dependent upon the books we read, and we begin to wonder how it is that Nature should have implanted so strange an idea into our minds rather than in the mind of some other race. But there it is, a perennial in the Anglo-Saxon mind, bursting into bloom at unexpected intervals, out of sheer lightheartedness, it would seem, for even the little children in the streets must know by this time that the morality of the world will always be the same, despite good and bad books. A strange belief it is, truly, that our morality depends upon the books we read, especially modern books, and harmful in more ways than one; for without it the three-volume system would secure a certain market to the writer for his first work and give him valuable leisure to consider and revise his subsequent works. But all the advan-

tages that literature might have derived from the circulating libraries
have been frittered away by a vain and vexatious censorship.

> Pages 147–48
> ⁋ But . . . literature. ⁋ OMITTED 1917, 1918.

> Page 149
> ⁋ It is . . . Holloway. ⁋ OMITTED 1917, 1918.

> Page 150
> ⁋ I . . . Therefore ⁋ 1917, 1918.

I was handicapped with dangerous ideas, and an impossible style, and

> Page 152
> ⁋ prefer . . . *littérature.*" ⁋ 1918.

are more interested in human portraiture than with searches made for
buried treasure according to scripts left behind by ancient mariners.
But for human portraiture models are necessary, and the drawing-
room presents few accents and angles, conformity to its prejudices
and conventions having worn all away. Ladies and gentlemen are as
round as the pebbles on the beach, presenting only smooth surfaces. Is
there really much to say about people who live in stately houses and
eat and drink their fill every day of the year? The lad, it is true, may
have a lover, but the pen finds scanty pasturage in the fact; and in
James's novels the lady only considers the question on the last page,
and the gentleman looks at her questioningly.

> Page 153
> ⁋ Plausible . . . him ⁋ 1918.

To carry the analysis one step further, we will answer the apology
that we conceive Mr. James would make to us were we to address him
in a question of this sort: "Why don't you turn your hand to a girl
who gets thirty shillings a week and thinks she would be very happy
if she could get thirty-five?" "The woman of leisure," he would
answer, "lives in a deeper intellectual mood than the work-girl whose
ambition is an extra five shillings a week." The interviewer in us would
like to ask Henry James why he never married; but it would be vain to
ask, so much does he write like a man to whom all action is repugnant.

He confesses himself on every page, as we all do. On every page James is a prude and Howells is

Page 153
⁊[Comedians"; . . . In]⁊ 1918.

Comedians," and after reading a few pages I fell to wondering how she had become possessed of the volume, and if it were true that she had enjoyed reading it; a sufficient matter for my wonderment surely, for myself, whom I supposed to be more literary than the landlady, was not able to come to any sort of terms with the book: or could it be that she had been told that George Meredith was "the thing" to admire by some lodger that had taken her fancy? Her admiration of the book I felt to be derivative, and this opinion was enforced by the discovery that she had not read any other book by George Meredith, and did not know that he was primarily a poet. She had never heard of "Love in a Valley" nor the "Nuptials of Attila," and I mentioned to her the lordly refrain—"Make the bed for Attila," forgetful for the moment that she sometimes made my bed.
      In

Pages 153–54
⁊[and . . . name]⁊ 1917; slightly rev. 1918.

and it is impossible for me to call to mind a book more like a cockatoo than "The Tragic Comedians"; it struts and screams just like one; but in "Rhoda Fleming" there is some wit. One, Antony by name,

Page 154
⁊[and . . . sand,]⁊ OMITTED 1917, 1918.

Page 156
⁊[quarter . . . falls.]⁊ 1917; slightly rev. 1918.

quarter, puts me on the trail of the book destined to achieve some intellectual advancement in me, and I read Mr. Hardy despite his name. It prejudiced me against him from the first; a name so trivial as Thomas Hardy cannot, I said, foreshadow a great talent; and "Far from the Madding Crowd" discovered the fact to me that Mr. Hardy was but one of George Eliot's miscarriages.

Page 158
⁋ possesses . . . interrupted. ⁋ 1918.

starts out with an idea, and it is a pity that he cannot mould his idea, shape it, breathe into it the breath of life; but he is better than Mr. Blackmore, who seems just to have happened once on a subject that interested people at the time; and if I speak of these writers, who certainly are inferior, it is because they are links in the chain whereby I returned from French into English literature, and having to speak of them, I relate my impressions.

Page 159
⁋ Troy. . . . decadent, ⁋ 1918.

Troy. Helen represents every man's desire, old or young, and it is this sense, shall I say, of the chord, that separates Homer from the fabricators of singular adventures. And it is this sense of harmony that separates us from circulating literature; our melody may lay itself open to criticism, but the chord is beautiful always. Even poor old Scott was not without some sense of—"Without some sense of what?" I asked myself, rousing suddenly from my meditation. Who was talking of Scott? I answer myself that Scott was succeeded by Lytton, and that a professor of literature would know enough about Landor to enable him to speak of stiff brocades, woven in Athens, somebody has written that, somebody must have written that, and I fall to dreaming of the great and beautiful men and women (exalted melodies) that rise out of Landor's pages—a writer as great as Shakespeare, surely? The last heir of a noble family. All that follows Landor is decadent—

Page 160
⁋ I . . . well-written; ⁋ 1918.

In this wise I used to talk in the Gaiety bar to the great amazement of its literati, always conscious that David Christie Murray, Byron Webber, and Richard Dowling were poor substitutes for Manet, Degas, Pissarro, Renoir, Cabaner, Villiers de l'Isle Adam, Catulle Mendès, and Duranty. But so long as men talked about art, I did not mind very much how they talked. That they were willing to listen was enough, and in pursuit of English literature I read what they wrote—"Joseph's Coat," by David Christie Murray; "In Luck's Way," by Byron Webber; and a Celtic romance, the name of which I have forgotten, by Richard Dowling.

These men used to arrive at the Gaiety bar about four o'clock, and at five the bar was in session, deference being paid to David Christie Murray, a clear-eyed, tall, blunt Northerner whose resonant voice bespoke his success with publishers. Byron Webber, the editor of a "weekly," a thick-set man, waddled into the bar with a black bag in his hand, and a red flush in the small portion of his face that was not covered with a black beard. His first question was, if Murray had concluded the arrangements with Chatto and Windus to write the serial for *Belgravia*. Murray answered that he had. Soon after Richard Dowling entered, a tall Irishman of flabby face and hands, without distinctive feature except, perhaps, weak eyes. His voice, too, was weak and pathetic from disappointment; for he had once imagined himself on the threshold of success, and now he spoke only of having been quill-driving all day, trying to earn food for the little family he had brought over from Waterford.

At half past five we were all sitting in the semicircular nooks under the cathedral windows, and at six, Tinsley, the publisher from Catherine Street, would come in, room being made for him instantly. He used to carry a bag containing fish for the family and a manuscript novel; and until seven whisky was drunk, and before dinner-time somebody was gleefully drunk, and a scowl began to appear on my face, for I was always annoyed by drunkenness. But there was nowhere else I could talk literature, and it was essential to drive the French language and French ideas out of my mind; till that was done a novel of English life could not be written. The Gaiety bar could do this, and I was impatient to be an Englishman again, and persevered day after day, month after month, till at the end of a couple of years I began to weary of the English language, an awkward, blunt instrument unfitted for delicate work it seemed to me to be in the works of David Christie Murray and Robert Buchanan. And one night in Cecil Street, I threw "The Seamy Side" across the room with a cry of despair. "All this is pure commerce," I groaned, and fell to thinking of Miss Braddon, remembering her with kindliness, for it was she who had put Shelley into my hand long ago, when I lived by the side of an Irish lake, and thought it would be a good thing to ride in the Liverpool Steeplechase. Ouida had inflamed me in my teens. At last I met Mrs. Lynn Linton, and liked her; but she was elderly, her style vehement and arid; and every night I went up to the Café Monico to buy a French paper which was publishing Goncourt's "La Fille Eliza," a story that enchanted me in my lonely lodging and awakened new dreams of the conquest of London. I read with disapprobation the "Story of an African Farm";

Pages 161–62
⁊ near . . . but ⁊ OMITTED 1918.

Page 162
⁊ That . . . Conway, ⁊ 1918.

She had the sense of rhythmical progression: but a woman cannot become a man, and it is not certain that, if pleasure be a condition of artistic performance, we do not get more from contemplating Elly than Maggie. Her golden head is sketched with a flowing water-colour brush on a background of austere French Protestants. We do not know whether the picture is true to nature; but we know that it is true to art; our objections do not begin till her marriage, which seems to us a jarring dissonance, the true end being the ruin of Elly and the remorse of her mother.

It was Margaret Veley who spoke to me first about "The Story of Elizabeth," when I was introduced to her in a Kensington drawing-room, a tall, shy woman, declining wittily, without regret, into middle age, and whom I preferred to the showy women scattered about the sofas and chairs on the look-out for a young man. In a few minutes she admitted to me that what I had heard was true; she had published a novel in the *Cornhill Magazine*. Such a success as that was the blue ribbon of literature in those days, and for it she became admirable in my eyes, and I took pleasure in her intelligence which I learnt in many visits. On her side she was beguiled by a certain alertness of mind, a curious absence of education, and it became her pleasure to correct my proofs, and with every correction she helped me out of the French into the English language.

All the world over there are women willing to sacrifice themselves, and Margaret Veley would have come into great literary honours, I am convinced, if she had not laid down her life for her sister, a woman stricken with consumption. One day I called to ask for some proofs, and received this note: "I am too ill to correct them; you know I would if I were able." And next day a soul passed out of life always associated in my memory with her beautiful novel "Damocles." Rachel Conway is to me none other than Margaret Veley herself,

Pages 162–63
⁋ The . . . doubt. ⁆ OMITTED 1918.

Page 163
⁋ The . . . suicide. ⁆ OMITTED 1917, 1918.

Page 164
⁋ What . . . what? ⁆ 1904, 1917, 1918.

Ask the same question about Milton, Fielding, Byron, Carlyle, Thackeray, Zola, Mr. Swinburne.

Page 167
⁋ Yes . . . blind. ⁆ OMITTED 1904, 1917, 1918.

Page 168
⁋ and . . . Moore; ⁆ OMITTED 1904, 1917, 1918.

Page 168
※ 1889 F.

un libraire anglais.

Page 172
※ A translation of Mallarmé's "Le Phénomène Futur." 1917, 1918.

III

The pale sky that lies above a world ending in decrepitude will perhaps pass away with the clouds: the tattered purple of the sunset is fading in a river sleeping on the horizon submerged in sunlight and in water. The trees are tired; and beneath their whitened leaves (whitened by the dust of time rather than by that of the roads) rises the canvas house of the Interpreter of Past Things: many a lamp awaits the twilight and lightens the faces of an unhappy crowd, conquered by the immortal malady and the sin of the centuries, of men standing by their wretched accomplices quick with the miserable fruit with which the world shall perish. In the unquiet silence of every eye supplicating yonder sun, which, beneath the water, sinks with the despair of a cry, listen to the simple patter of the showman: "No sign regales you of the spectacle within, for there is not now a painter capable of presenting any sad shadow of it. I bring alive (and preserved through the years by sovereign science) a woman of old time. Some folly, original and simple, an ecstasy of gold, I know not what she names it, her hair falls with the grace of rich stuffs about her face, and contrasts with the bloodlike nudity of her lips. In place of the vain gown, she has a body; and the eyes, though like rare stones, are not worth the look that leaps from the happy flash: the breasts, raised as if filled with an eternal milk, are pointed to the sky, and the smooth limbs still keep the salt of the primal sea." Remembering their poor wives, bald, morbid, and full of horror, the husbands press forward: and the wives, too, impelled by melancholy curiosity, wish to see.

When all have looked upon the noble creature, vestige of an epoch already accursed, some, indifferent, have not the power to comprehend, but others, whelmed in grief and their eyelids wet with tears of resignation, gaze at each other; whilst the poets of these times, feeling their dead eyes brighten, drag themselves to their lamps, their brains drunk for a moment with a vague glory, haunted with Rhythm, and forgetful that they live in an age that has outlived beauty.

Page 173
¶ I . . . produced. ▶ 1889 E, 1904, 1917, 1918.

"Carmen Sylva!" How easy it is to divine the aestheticism of anyone signing, "Carmen Sylva."

In youth the genius of Shelley astonished me; but now I find the stupidity of the ordinary person infinitely more surprising.

That I may die childless—that when my hour comes I may turn my face to the wall saying, I have not increased the great evil of human life—then, though I were a murderer, fornicator, thief, and liar, my sins shall melt even as a cloud. But he who dies with children about him, though his life were in all else an excellent deed, shall be held accursed by the truly wise, and the stain upon him shall endure for ever.

I realize that this is truth, the one truth, and the whole truth; and yet the vainest woman that ever looked in a glass never regretted her youth more than I, or felt the disgrace of middle-age more keenly. She has her portrait painted, I write these confessions; each hopes to save something of the past, and escape somehow the ravening waves of time and float into some haven of remembrance. St. Augustine's Confessions are the story of a God-tortured, mine of an art-tortured, soul. Which subject is the most living? The first! for man is stupid and still loves his conscience as a child loves a toy. Now the world plays with "Robert Elsmere." This book seems to me like a suite of spacious, well distributed, and well proportioned rooms. Looking round, I say, 'tis a pity these rooms are only in plaster of Paris.

Page 176
⟨[seventeenth]⟩ 1889 F, 1904, 1917, 1918. Twice changed to "eighteenth."

Page 178
⟨ 1889 F; slightly rev. 1889 E and again in 1904, 1917, and 1918.

CHAPTER FOURTEEN

Now I am full of eager impulses that mourn and howl by turns, striving for utterance like wind in turret chambers. I hate this infernal lodging. I feel like a fowl in a coop—that landlady, those children, Emma. . . . The actress will be coming upstairs presently; shall I ask her into my room? Better let things remain as they are.

Conscience

Why intrude a new vexation on her already vexed life?

I

Hallo, you startled me! Well, I am surprised. We have not talked together for a long time. Since when?

Conscience

I will spare your feelings. I merely thought I would remind you that you have passed the Rubicon—your thirtieth year.

I

It is terrible to think of. My youth gone!

Conscience

Then you are ashamed—you repent?

I

I am ashamed of nothing—I am a writer; 'tis my profession to be ashamed of nothing but to be ashamed.

Conscience

I had forgotten.

I

But I will chat with you when you please; even now, at this hour, about all things, about any of my sins.

Conscience

Since we lost sight of each other you have devoted your time to the gratification of your senses.

I

Pardon me, I have devoted quite as much of my time to art.

Conscience

You were glad, I remember, when your father died, because his death gave you unlimited facilities for moulding the partial self which the restraining influence of home had only permitted, into that complete and ideal George Moore which you had in mind. I think I quote you correctly.

I

You don't; but never mind. Proceed.

Conscience

Then, if you have no objection, we will examine how far you have turned your opportunities to account.

I

You will not deny that I have educated myself and made many friends.

Conscience

Friends! your nature is very adaptable—you interest yourself in their pursuits, and so deceive them into a false estimate of your work. Your education—speak not of it; it is but flimsy stuff.

I

There I join issue with you. Have I not drawn the intense ego out of the clouds of semi-consciousness, and realized it? And surely, the rescue and the individualization of the ego is the first step.

Conscience

To what end? You have nothing to teach, nothing to reveal. I have often thought of asking you this: since death is the only good, why do you not embrace death? Of all the world's good it is the cheapest, and the most easily obtained.

I

We must live since nature has willed it so. My poor conscience, are you still struggling in the fallacy of free will?

For at least a hundred thousand years man has rendered this planet abominable and ridiculous with what he is pleased to call his intelligence, without, however, having learned that his life is merely the breaking of the peace of unconsciousness, the drowsy uplifting of tired eyelids of somnolent nature. How glibly this loquacious ape chatters of his religion and his moral sense, always failing to see that both are but allurements and inveiglements! With religion he is induced to bear his misery, and his sexual appetite is preserved, ignorant, and vigorous, by means of morals. A scorpion, surrounded by a ring of fire, will sting itself to death, and man would turn upon life and deny it, if his reason were complete. Religion and morals are the poker and tongs with which nature intervenes and scatters the ring of reason.

Conscience (after a long pause)

I believe—forgive my ignorance, but I have seen so little of you this long while—that your boast is that no woman influenced, changed, or modified your views of life.

I

None; my mind is a blank on the subject. Stay! my mother said once, when I was a boy, "You must not believe them; all their smiles and pretty ways are only put on. Women like men only for what they can get out of them." And to these simple words I attribute all the suspicion of woman's truth which hung over my youth. For years it seemed to me impossible that women could love men. Women seemed to me so beautiful and desirable—men so ugly, almost revolting. Could they touch us without revulsion of feeling, could they really desire us? I was absorbed in the life of woman—the mystery of petticoats, so different from the staidness of trousers! the rolls of hair entwined with so much art, and suggesting so much colour and perfume, so different from the bare crop; the unnaturalness of the waist in stays! plentitude and slenderness of silk, so different from the stupidity of a black tail-coat; rose feet passing under the triple ruches of rose, so different from the broad foot of the male. My love for the life of women was a life within my life; and oh, how strangely secluded and veiled! A world of calm colour with phantoms moving, floating past and changing in dim light—an averted face with abundant hair, the gleam of a perfect bust or the poise of a neck turning slowly round, the gaze of deep translucid eyes. I loved women too much to give myself wholly to one.

Conscience

Yes, yes; but what real success have you had with women?

I

Damn it! you would not seek to draw me into long-winded stories about women—how it began, how it was broken off, how it began again? I'm not Casanova. I love women as I love champagne— I drink it and enjoy it; but an exact account of every bottle drunk would prove flat narrative.

Conscience

You have never consulted me about your champagne loves; but you have asked me if you have ever inspired a real affection, and I told you that we cannot inspire in others what does not exist in ourselves. You have never known a nice woman who would have married you?

I

Why should I undertake to keep a woman by me for the entire space of her life, watching her grow fat, grey, wrinkled, and foolish? Think of the annoyance of perpetually looking after any- one, especially a woman! Besides, marriage is antagonistic to my ideal. You say that no ideal illumines the pessimist's life, that if you ask him why he exists, he cannot answer, and that Schopen- hauer's arguments against suicide are not even plausible casuistry. True, on this point his reasoning is feeble and ineffective. But we may easily confute our sensual opponents. We must say that we do not commit suicide, although we admit it is a certain anodyne to the poison of life—an absolute erasure of the wrong inflicted on us by our parents—because we hope by noble example and precept to induce others to refrain from love. We are the saviours of souls. Other crimes are finite; love alone is infinite. We punish a man with death for killing his fellow; but a little reflection should make the dullest understand that the crime of bringing a being into the world exceeds by a thousand, a millionfold that of putting one out of it.

Men are to-day as thick as flies in a confectioner's shop; in fifty years there will be less to eat, but certainly some millions more mouths. I laugh, I rub my hands! I shall be dead before the red time comes. I laugh at the religionists who say that God provides for those He brings into the world. The French Revolution will compare with the revolution that is to come, that must come, that is inevitable, as a puddle on the road-side compares with the sea. Men will hang like pears on every lamp-post, in every great quarter of London there will be an electric guillotine that will decapitate the rich like hogs in Chicago. Christ, who with his white feet trod out the blood of the ancient world, and promised Universal Peace, shall go out in a cataclysm of blood. The neck of mankind shall be opened, and blood shall cover the face of the earth.

Conscience

Your philosophy is on a par with your painting and your poetry; but, then, I am a conscience, and a conscience is never philosophic —you go in for "The Philosophy of the Unconscious"?

I

No, no, 'tis but a silly vulgarisation. But Schopenhauer, oh, my Schopenhauer! Say, shall I go about preaching hatred of women? Were I to call them a short-legged race that was admitted into society only a hundred and fifty years ago?

Conscience

You cannot speak the truth even to me; no, not even at half past twelve at night.

I

Surely of all hours this is the one in which it is advisable to play you false?

Conscience

You are getting humorous.

I

I am getting sleepy. You are a tiresome old thing, a relic of the ancient world—I mean the mediæval world. You know that I now affect antiquity?

Conscience

You wander helplessly in the road of life until you stumble against a battery; nerved with the shock you are frantic, and rush along wildly until the current received is exhausted, and you lapse into disorganization.

I

If I am sensitive to and absorb the various potentialities of my age, am I not of necessity a power?

Conscience

To be the receptacle of and the medium through which unexplained forces work, is a very petty office to fulfil. Can you think of nothing higher? Can you feel nothing original in you, a something that is cognizant of the end?

I

You are surely not going to drop into talking to me of God?

Conscience

You will not deny that I at least exist? I am with you now, and intensely, far more than the dear friend with whom you love to walk in the quiet evening; the women you have held to your bosom in the perfumed darkness of the chamber—

I

Pray don't. "The perfumed darkness of the chamber" is very common. I was suckled on that kind of literature.

Conscience

You are rotten to the root. Nothing but a very severe attack of indigestion would bring you to your senses—or a long lingering illness.

I

'Pon my faith, you are growing melodramatic. Neither indigestion nor illness long drawn out can change me. I have torn you all to pieces long ago, and you have not now sufficient rags on your back to scare the rooks in seed-time.

Conscience

In destroying me you have destroyed yourself.

I

Edgar Poe, pure and simple. Don't pick holes in my originality until you have mended those in your own.

Conscience

I was Poe's inspiration; he is eternal, being of me. But your inspiration springs from the flesh, and is therefore ephemeral even as the flesh.

I

If you had read Schopenhauer you would know that the flesh is not ephemeral, but the eternal objectification of the will to live. Siva is represented, not only with the necklace of skulls, but with the lingam.

Conscience

You have failed in all you have attempted, and the figure you have raised on your father's tomb is merely a sensitive and sensuous art-cultured being who lives in a dirty lodging and plays in desperate desperation his last card. You are now writing a novel. The hero is a wretched creature, something like yourself. Do you think there is a public in England for that kind of thing?

I

Just the great Philistine that you always were! What do you mean by a "public"?

Conscience

I have not a word to say on that account, your one virtue is sobriety.

I

A wretched pun. . . . The mass of mankind run much after the fashion of the sheep of Panurge, but there are always a few that—

Conscience

A few that are like the Gadarene swine.

I

Ah . . . were I the precipice, were I the sea in which the pigs might drown!

Conscience

The same old desire of admiration, admiration in its original sense of wonderment (miratio); you are a true child of the century; you do not desire admiration, you would avoid it, fearing it might lessen that sense which only you care to stimulate—wonderment. And persecuted by the desire to astonish, you are now exhibiting yourself in the most hideous light you can devise. The man whose biography you are writing is no better than a pimp.

I

Then he is not like me; I have never been a pimp, and I don't think I would be if I could.

Conscience

The whole of your moral nature is reflected in Lewis Seymour, even to the "And I don't think I would be if I could." You would put me behind you if you could and return to the mending of the shameful little ballade, "La Ballad d'Alfred, Alfred aux Belles Dents," whose light o' love you enticed down here out of vanity, it being your vanity to destroy what remained in her of morality: it was her morality to give herself to no man but one except for money, and now she is really among the fallen. . . . What are you laughing at?

I

I am thinking of her trouble of conscience, of the qualms she must suffer, for she is a Fleming to whose bedside a priest would be called if she were dying; and the poor man, how would he shrive her, so strange would her point of view seem to him to be; so different from his other penitents.

Conscience

A shameful play of fancy. Let us be serious together; you surely can be serious, if only for a moment. Try to recall to your mind the disgraceful scene that occurred a few months ago in your bedroom, the landlady at the foot of the bed ordering the woman whose conscience affords you so much amusement out of the house. But no, it will be better to avoid recollections of that scene, forget it, and tell me if you do not think that you did Alfred an injustice by writing the ballade.

I

But he is represented as ruling the roost!

Conscience

The distribution of that shameful ballade in manuscript has caused great inconvenience to Anatole Pellissier, the painter, whose safest way home now is the longest way round. You have heard that he doesn't dare to enter his street before three in the morning lest he receive an ill blow.

I

And all because he is suspected of having written my little ballade.

Conscience

Your wretched little ballade, wretched verses, if they are verses; the opening lines of your second stanza zig-zags out of all possible prosody. Moreover, the ballade-maker who respects his art chooses a difficult rhyming word, and the choice of a word like "verre," to which a hundred rhymes might easily be found, is in itself a condemnation. Art is difficulty overcome.

I

Banville's poetic principle, I know it, but in the most famous ballade of all, the ballade that made the ballade itself famous, the rhyming is not more complex than mine.

> "La belle romaine
> Qui fut sa cousine germaine . . ."

"Ou sont ils vierge souveraine?" Why "ils"? Were "ils" and "elles" interchangeable in the fifteenth century? I can't see that "peine" is a more difficult word to rhyme to than "verre." My ballade goes very smoothly. Listen:

LA BALLADE D'ALFRED, ALFRED
AUX BELLES DENTS

Je suis Alfred, l'Alfred aux belles dents,
Un très grand macq'illustre dans le square.
J'ai du poignon et de beaux vêtements,
Fins escarpins, gants, bague à grosse pierre,
Car, sur le truc ma femme est la plus chère.
Toujours de l'or, trois guineas, au moins deux,
Pour le plaisir d'un petit ordinaire . . .
Il en faut bien des messieurs sérieux.

Je m'absente du billard par moments
Pour voir si la putain travaille. . . . Un verre

Bah! la tournée et plus d'emmerdements.
Copains, trinquons à la santé d'un père
Qui vient chez nous dans la nuit solitaire.
Il fait l'amour, il n'est pas de ces gueux
Qui casquent mal et sont si durs à plaire ...
Il en faut bien des messieurs sérieux.

Le maquereau seul parmi les amants
Plane au-dessus de tout amour vulgaire.
Il met la main sur les petits romans
Qui troublent l'âme et font manquer l'affaire.
Les temps sont durs: sans le miché que faire?
Et, nom de dieu! pourquoi se ficher d'eaux?
Je gueule au nez du roussin, ce faux frère:
Il en faut bien des messieurs sérieux.

ENVOI
Roi du trottoir je le suis, et très fière
Elle m'attend la voix pleine d'aveux.
Je prends la braise et je la fous par terre.
Il en faut bien des messieurs sérieux.

Conscience

Your ballade does not appear to me on second hearing any better than it did on the first. I cannot abide your ballade, so there's an end of it.

I

Now you're talking just like Gosse.

Conscience

One word more. You have failed in everything you have attempted, and you will continue to fail until you consider those moral principles—those rules of conduct which the race has built up, guided by an unerring instinct of self-preservation. Humanity defends herself against those who attempt to subvert her; and none, neither Napoleon nor the wretched scribbler such as you are, has escaped her vengeance.

I

You would have me pull down the black flag and turn myself into an honest merchantman, with children in the hold and a wife at the helm. You would remind me that grey hairs begin to show, that health falls into rags, that high spirits split like canvas, and that in the end the bright buccaneer drifts, an old derelict, tossed by the waves of ill fortune, and buffeted by the winds into those dismal bays and dangerous offings—housekeepers, nurses, and uncomfortable chambers. Such will be my fate; and since none may avert his fate, none can do better than to run pluckily the course which he must pursue.

Conscience

You might devise a moral ending; one that would conciliate all classes.

I

It is easy to see that you are a nineteenth-century conscience.

Conscience

I do not hope to find a Saint Augustine in you.

I

An idea; one of these days I will write my confessions! Again I tell you that nothing really matters to me but art. And, knowing this, you chatter of the unwisdom of my not concluding my novel with some foolish moral. . . . Nothing matters to me but art.

Conscience

Would you seduce the wretched servant girl if by so doing you could pluck out the mystery of her being and set it down on paper!

Page 179
❦ FOOTNOTE ADDED 1904, 1917, 1918.

*The use of the word sinful here seems liable to misinterpretation. The phrase should run: "Of a virtuous life, for remember that my virtues are your vices."

Page 179
🦋FOOTNOTE ADDED 1904, 1917, 1918.

*This should run: "Forgot your hypocrisy."

Page 180
❧ fifteen ❧ 1904, 1917, 1918.

ten

Page 180
🦋FOOTNOTE ADDED 1904, 1917, 1918.

*Vices, surely? note, p. 179.

Page 181
🦋FOOTNOTE ADDED 1904, 1917. 1918.

*Virtue?

Pages 183-84
❧ He . . . genius. ❧ OMITTED 1904, 1917, 1918.

Pages 187–88
❧ But . . . man. ❧ OMITTED 1904, 1917, 1918.

Page 188
❧ One . . . question. ❧ OMITTED 1904, 1917, 1918.

Page 188
❧ At . . . outline. ❧ OMITTED 1904, 1917, 1918.

Page 188
❧ I . . . dear ———, ❧ OMITTED 1904, 1917, 1918.

Page 189
❧ "Mon . . . jamais." ❧ OMITTED 1904, 1917, 1918.

Pages 189–90
❧ I . . . gentlemen. ❧ 1904, 1917; extensively rev. 1918.

No sooner had I begun to tell the story than it dawned upon me that it was impossible to tell it seriously; it was fundamentally an absurd story; and I lacked courage to tell Marshall that I looked upon the duel as a way to notoriety. The most courageous will shrink from admitting such a weakness, and, moreover, if it were admitted, Marshall might refuse to act for me; nor were my fears altogether groundless, for I had not related the whole story when Marshall interrupted me with the suggestion that he did not think the matter serious enough to necessitate a journey to Flanders. On seeing my face change expression, he added, to propitiate me, that if he saw any reluctance on the part of Lord ————'s seconds to apologize he would, of course, insist that reparation was due to me. He had no sooner spoken than I began to doubt the possibility of a bloody issue to my quarrel, and somewhat helplessly asked Marshall if he would care to go to the theatre. After the theatre we went home and æstheticized till the duel became the least important event and Marshall's new picture the greatest. At breakfast next day the duel seemed more tiresome than ever, but the gentlemen were coming to meet Marshall. He showed his usual tact in arranging my affair of honour; a letter was drawn up in which my friend withdrew the blow of his hand, I withdrew the blow of the bottle, etc.—really now I lack energy to explain it any further.

CRITICAL NOTES

CHAPTER ONE

1 Moore dramatizes a succession of "echo-auguries" which form the basic narrative pattern in *Confessions*. This use of repetition may owe something to Dujardin's use of leitmotifs in his interior monologues. Moore borrowed the phrase from De Quincey, and he uses it to designate a word which introduces him to a new enthusiasm. De Quincey defines "echo-augury" in a footnote, in words Moore echoes on pages *49, 52, 76, 94,* and *156* of *Confessions*, as "where a man, perplexed in judgment, and sighing for some determining counsel, suddenly heard from a stranger in some unlooked-for quarter words not meant for himself, but clamorously applying to the difficulty besetting him. . . . the mystical word always unsought for—*that* constituted its virtue and its divinity." (*Autobiography from 1785 to 1803,* 1 [London: A. C. Black, 1896]: 123.) Moore's emphasis throughout *Confessions* on "brain instincts" as the motivating force behind his aesthetic experiences reflects the strong influence Schopenhauer's concept of the "will" had on his thinking during the 1880s. (See Michael W. Brooks, "George Moore, Schopenhauer, and the Origins of *The Brook Kerith*," *English Literature in Transition* 12, no. 1 [1969]: 21–31.)

2 J. Spencer Northcote, the president of Oscott, the Jesuit boys' school in Birmingham which Moore attended between 1861 and 1866, wrote to Moore's father in September 1866, of his son's failure to learn. Like Moore, Northcote blamed failure on a lack of inspiration more than on an absence of ability: "My own belief is that if he were once seriously impressed with the vital importance of attention to these matters and he would apply his will to it heartily, things would soon mend." But he gloomily added, "If it really be that his abilities are on these points deficient, I am afraid these cannot be mended." (National Library of Ireland, MS. 4479, no. 45. The library will hereafter be referred to as NLI.)

3 In *Salve* (1912), Moore spiced up the story of his expulsion, with an uncertain amount of truth, by attributing it to his interest in a maidservant.

Wanting both to impress his fellow pupils and to enliven the dull days at Oscott, Moore says he one day gave a bouquet to one of the maidservants. He boasted of his gift and of a conversation he had had with her. A fellow student, overcome by vicarious guilt, confessed Moore's activities. Soon all the priests knew about it (according to Moore, who enjoyed impugning the security of the confessional), and out of fear Moore wrote the whole story to his father. He declared that if the maidservant were sent away, he would also leave and marry her. He could have been no more than fourteen at the time. His father, he says, came immediately to Oscott, talked with his son and Northcote, and agreed with the president that Moore would be better off out of school. At the end of the term, he left. In 1912, while writing *Salve*, Moore wrote to his brother, Colonel Maurice Moore, and asked him if he could remember whether or not he was left at school after this incident. (NLI, MS. 2647, no. 162, 18 June 1912.) According to Joseph Hone, Colonel Moore recalled no such scandal and reported that Moore was not expelled but rather removed from school when no special tutor could be found for him. Colonel Moore conceded that his brother may have shown special attention to a maidservant at chapel, but this was as far as the incident went. (Joseph Hone, *The Life of George Moore* [London: Victor Gollancz, 1936], p. 31.) Colonel Moore's version is probably the more accurate; Moore, unable to recall the actual outcome of the event, characteristically invented a dramatic one.

4 These experiences again proved useful when Moore wrote of horse racing in *Esther Waters* (1894). His father's horses were famous in Mayo, and their winnings had bolstered the dwindling finances of Moore Hall in 1861 and thus made it possible for Moore to attend Oscott. (Maurice Moore, *An Irish Gentleman: George Henry Moore*, with a preface by George Moore [London: T. Werner Laurie, 1913], p. 312.) Moore's father was elected to Parliament in 1868, and the following year the family moved to London.

5 The "great blond man" was James Browne, a cousin of Moore's and the model for Mr. Barton in *A Drama in Muslin* (1886). (Hone, *Life of George Moore*, p. 35.)

6 Moore's father died on 18 April 1870, only three days after he had returned to Mayo to deal with a tenant dispute. Moore suggested in the preface to his brother Maurice's life of their father that he had bravely committed suicide out of despair over the tenant-landlord conflict. Maurice Moore, a devout Catholic, was appalled at Moore's suggestion and added an *errata* slip to his book saying that his brother's version of their father's death was pure invention. Moore's assessment in *Confessions* of his inheritance is accurate: the "considerable property" equalled 12,481 acres and the income from the rents was £4,000 a year. (Hone, *Life of George Moore*, p. 40.)

7 Moore probably visited other studios and did not have one of his own at this time. He rented a studio in London in 1874, when he returned from Paris to seek a producer for his first play, *Worldliness* (see *Confessions*, p. 66). In *Vale* (1914), he says that he only attended other studios in 1872–73,

and this account is evidently more accurate. (*Vale* [London: William Heine-mann, 1933], p. 34. Unless otherwise indicated, references will be made to the Uniform Edition of Moore's works, published by William Heinemann, 1924–33.)

8 The melodramatic declaration of atheism which Moore added to *Confessions* is modeled on a scene Moore's brother Maurice recalled having witnessed at Moore Hall. (Hone, *Life of George Moore*, p. 30.)

9 William and Dick Maitland are the neighbours who introduced Moore to the life of the theatre. During this time, he was persuaded to back one of the Maitlands' productions, and only the fact that he was under age and could not be held responsible for his liabilities saved him from a financial loss. (Hone, *Life of George Moore*, pp. 41–42. See also *Vale*, pp. 43–45, and 147, where Moore claims Dick Maitland as the model for Dick Lennox in *A Mummer's Wife* [1884].)

CHAPTER TWO

1 The date on the writ of passage given Moore and his *Irish* valet (as *Confessions* admits after 1918), William Moloney, is 21 March 1873, less than a month after Moore's twenty-first birthday, 24 February. (NLI, MS. 2648, no. 1.)

2 In order to live nearer this studio, Moore and his valet moved to the Hotel de Russie sometime before the end of June 1873. His valet wrote from there to Joseph Applely, the butler at Moore Hall, and although Moore represents him in the later versions of *Confessions* as eager to return to the vulgar pleasures of Ireland, his letter suggests that the virtues of Paris were not wholly lost on him. His letter also offers a good picture of Moore during his initial exposure to Paris (it is quoted without correction):

30 June [1873]   Hotel de Russie
                                                  2, boulevard des Italiens
My dear Joseph,
... I begin to hate Paris I am broild to death both day and night and what I shall do for the next two mounths I dont know but in other respects it is the most beautiful place in the wourld, best brandy two franks a bottle and claret for a song peaches and grapes enough for two pence and *Women* for *asking* and after all like you I must say I like London the best but a good deal of it is because I cant speak french well I went to see the grand Prix run and of course I should put a couple of pounds on Mr Jimmy Merrys crack after winning the English Derby ...
  Mr George is as happy as a prince here, and not a foolish hare on his body but so good natured a person never lived He will be a great artist he can lick Jim Brown into saddlebags but he works very hard from 8 a c in the morning till 5 in the evening He is the devil to please when out of humours, Dear Joseph I hope both you and all your family are well as I hope to see you all next spring please God as we are sure to go this time at long last

It is a dam shame about the money they ought to be hung I remain my
Dear Joseph yours very sincerely

Wm Malony

(NLI, MS. 895, no. 836.)

3 "Marshall" was Lewis Welden Hawkins, a second-rate painter who was, as
Moore says, a native of Brussels. (See also *Vale* [London: William Heinemann, 1933], pp. 51–85.)

4 Moore mocks his youthful rhetoric in this passage in the chapter which he
added to the 1889 editions (see addition following Chapter 11).

5 "M. Duval" was Bernard Lopez, the playwright with whom Moore wrote
Martin Luther (1879). (See *Vale*, pp. 77–80.)

6 Moore's bibliographer Edwin Gilcher affirms that no copy of *Worldliness*
has ever been found and he suggests that the play was probably only copied
by hand and never published. Moore's only other comment on his first play
seems to be that made to I. A. Williams in 1921, when Williams was
assembling a bibliography of Moore's works. Moore wrote to Williams,
"Worldliness, a comedy that Lopez said disappointed him, the plot having
deflected; it should have been according to Lopez, Mr. Goldstick's plan to
marry his mistress to his friend Mr. —— alas! my memory fails me."
Williams noted that the author "believes, and hopes, that no copy of this,
his first published work, now exists." (I. A. Williams, *Bibliographies of
Modern Authors, No. 3. George Moore*, with a prefatory letter by George
Moore [London: Leslie Chaundy & Co., 1921] n.p.)

CHAPTER THREE

1 No evidence supports this assertion.

2 Moore remained in London much longer than he suggests by his brief
account of his visit here. He rented a studio in Cromwell Mews, near his
mother's house in Alfred Place, and he may have also attended classes at
Barthe's studio, where Whistler taught. (See *Vale* [London: William Heinemann, 1933], p. 34.) He found his own studio much too expensive. Late in
1874, he decided to return to Paris and he wrote his uncle, Joseph Blake, the
agent at Moore Hall, to assure him that he was reforming and abandoning
extravagance:

My dear Joseph
Mama is giving up the house that is one of the reasons I am going to Paris
another is that I can live cheaper there than in London because I shall not
require a private studio (which here costs 100£ a year) I shall limit myself
to 400£ a year at the most of course I do not go there for instruction There
is no such thing in painting but because it is more convenient as for spending the money there that I did last time or renting a rig of any kind [that]
is the most impossible of all imaginable things I have greatly changed I can
assure you.

However this is what I say I go to Paris between this and Christmas and shall not require more than 35£ per month inclusive of every mortal thing I shall not draw upon you for more in fact live strictly within that until I am entirely out of debt. Will you write to me at once. I shall have to pay my mother a 125£ and a 100£ pounds [sic] of my own personal debts some of which are long standing (two years) This is a lot of money and I plainly see my property cant stand it I must get out of debt and as London to me is much more expensive if I have a studio which I must have as much as I must have bread and butter in Paris I shall work in a public one which costs only forty francs a month. In London a studio is a 100£ a year and models cost from seven to ten shillings a day when I can live on ten shillings a day in Paris I wonder you dont see that I am right

Yours affect   George

P. S. I received the 30£ I owed my landlord 32£ Mama left me the other two so it is paid but I am absolutely with a half penny send me for god sake send me ten pounds I have lots of small things to pay for I have not had a quid in my pocket since a month

(NLI, MS. 4479, no. 52, undated. Moore's letters are uncorrected.)

3 Moore telescoped his memories from several Impressionist Exhibitions here, for there was no exhibition of Impressionist paintings being held at the time of his return to Paris. The first exhibition had been held in April 1874, when Moore was probably in London, and the second was in 1876, a year after his return to Paris. Furthermore, he describes *La Grande Jatte* as one of the paintings in the exhibit, but Seurat's large canvas was not displayed until 1886. (See Douglas Cooper, "George Moore and Modern Art," *Horizon* 11, no. 62 [February 1945]: 113–30. For Moore's later writings on the Impressionist painters see *Modern Painting* [1891] and *Reminiscences of the Impressionist Painters* [1906], which was revised and included in *Vale*.)

4 Moore here reflects his deep sympathy with Pater's impressionistic critical method. Pater wrote, "What is this song or picture, . . . to *me*? What effect does it really produce on me? Does it give me pleasure? and if so, what sort or degree of pleasure? How is my nature modified by its presence, and under its influence? The answers to these questions are the original facts with which the aesthetic critic has to do; . . . And he who experiences these impressions strongly, and drives directly at the discrimination and analysis of them, has no need to trouble himself with the abstract question what beauty is in itself, or what its exact relation to truth or experience. . . ." (Preface to *The Renaissance* [London: Macmillan & Co., 1912], p. viii.)

5 Moore is quoting himself in this anecdote by recalling with a touch of satire his own early adventures. He wrote to his mother from Paris, sometime in 1879:

I often wonder and wonder when we shall meet again. Am I ever to leave Paris? God knows! It seems so like my home now that I sometimes am startled when someone reminds me that I am a stranger. I go into the frenchest of french society now—houses where an Englishman never is heard of. I dine twice a week generally at the Princess de la Tremoille and at her most select dinners, dinners of eight ten and twelve. The other day I was very pleased for a lady told me the princess said that my manners were absolutely perfect. I was both pleased and astonished for it is astonishing it should be so; I can scarcely credit that the low society I have so much cultivated has not soiled me. Sometimes if I get away early I go to a low artists café, where with my two elbows on the beer stained [table] I scream the beastliest and slangiest french to groups of bohemians their is such an abime between the two that I often think "If the princess saw me now she never would believe me to be the same man who three hours before was talking across her dinner table." (NLI, MS. 4479, no. 14. Hone, *Life of George Moore*, var., pp. 77–79.)

6 Colonel Moore visited his brother in June or August of 1875, and later he remembered that Moore was generally away all day at painting studios; but, he said, "in the evenings I saw him in the hotel, and I remember that he talked mostly about Corot and Balzac. Hawkins too I remember; he was in low water, and was trying to make a living by painting on porcelain; . . . I did not get the impression that Hawkins was the scamp whom my brother afterwards described in his books." (Hone, *Life of George Moore*, p. 56.) Moore's own letters home during this time (November 1875 to April 1876) reflect a new diligence but make no reference to his agreement to support Hawkins. His account of the same agreement in *Vale* suggests that it did occur; Moore probably reasoned that his mother and uncle should remain ignorant of the fact that Moore Hall was supporting not one, but two aspiring artists.

CHAPTER FOUR

1 Moore omits here any reference to Miss Mary de Ross Rose, a young heiress whom he pursued to Boulogne-sur-mer, the "sweet seaside resort," during the summer of 1876. His letters to his mother and uncle indicate that he was contemplating a proposal of marriage but then changed his mind when he discovered her less wealthy than he had thought her to be.

2 Jean C. Noël has examined records of occupants at this address and has found no evidence that either Moore or Hawkins ever lived there. His address during this period was actually 61, rue Condorcet. (*George Moore: L'Homme et L'Oeuvre* [Paris: Didier, 1966], pp. 679–82.) Moore undoubtedly claimed Rue de la Tour des Dames as his address because the name of the street was as exotic as the apartment he describes there. Moore had already envisioned this fashionably decadent apartment when he wrote "Chez Moi" for *Pagan Poems* (1881).

> My white Angora cats are lying fast
> Asleep, close curled together, and my snake,
> My many-coloured Python, is awake,
> Crawling about after a two-month's fast.

The parrot screams from time to time my last
Love's name; the atmosphere doth softly ache
With burning perfume, lazily I rake
And sift the smouldering embers of the past.

The women I have loved arise, and pass
Before me like the sun rays in a glass,—
Alice and Lizzy, Iza and Juliette;

And some are blushing, some are pale as stone:
Heigho! The world spins in a circle yet . . .
My life has been a very pleasant one.

3 Victor Hugo, from "Booz Endormi," *La Légende des Siècles.*

4 Victor Hugo, from "La fête chez Thérèse," *Aurore,* in *Les Contemplations Autrefois.*

5 Homer, *Odyssey.*

6 Alfred de Musset, "Rolla."

7 Entire passage reads as follows: "Je n'ai jamais été cueillir sur le Golgotha les fleurs de la passion, et le fleuve profond qui coule du flanc du crucifié et fait une ceinture rouge au monde ne m'a pas baigné de ses flots." (Théophile Gautier, *Mademoiselle de Maupin* [Paris: Classiques Garnier, 1955], p. 190.)

8 Entire passage reads as follows: "Quelquefois j'ai d'autres songes,—ce sont de longues cavalcades de chevaux tout blancs, sans harnais et sans bride, montés par de beaux jeunes gens nus qui défilent sur une bande de couleur bleu foncé comme sur les frises du Parthénon . . . Mon ciel n'a pas de nuage, ou, s'il en a, ce sont des nuages solides et tailles au ciseau, faits les éclats de marbre tombés de la statue de Jupiter." (Gautier, *de Maupin,* p. 190.) Wanting here to represent his youthful excitement, Moore quotes from memory rather than from the text. He was afraid that Dujardin would correct his quotation and told him "I have my own way of expressing myself. In the April number, for instance, I try to remember a passage in Gautier; if it has mistakes in French correct them, but don't think it necessary to look up 'Mlle. de Maupin'." In 1917, Moore characteristically thought better of his earlier imprecision and revised the quotation to make it conform more closely, although still not exactly, to Gautier's passage. (John Eglinton, ed. and trans., *Letters from George Moore to Ed. Dujardin, 1886–1922* [New York: Crosby-Gaige, 1929], p. 29, 6 July 1888.)

9 Théophile Gautier, "Contralto," from *Emaux et Camées.*

10 Baudelaire, from "La Mort des Amants," *Les Fleurs du Mal.*

11 Victor Hugo, last four stanzas of "Le Grand Siècle," from *Les Chansons des Rues et des Bois.*

12 José-Maria de Hérédia, from "A Une Ville Morte," *Les Trophées.*

13 Moore's "explanation" here of Mallarmé's poem "Hommage (à Richard Wagner)" reveals how little he understood the subtleties of French symbolism. He was attracted by the spirit of symbolist poetry more than by the letter of their achievements. In *Avowals* and in "Mes Souvenirs sur Mallarmé" in *Le Figaro Supplement Littéraire*, no. 236, 13 October 1923, Moore speaks of his friendship with Mallarmé with a good deal more reverence. (See also Henri Mondor, *Vie de Mallarmé* [Paris: Gallimard, 1941] and Jean C. Noël, "George Moore et Mallarmé," *Revue de Littéraire Comparée* 32 [1958]: 363–76, for accounts of Moore's visits to Mallarmé's Rue de Rome apartment, which began in 1875 or 1876.)

14 Although Moore mocks the theory of correspondences here, he had experimented with the concept two years earlier in *A Drama in Muslin*. He described dresses at a dance as "white silk clear as the notes of violins playing in a minor key; white poplin falling into folds statuesque as the bass of a fugue by Bach." ([London: Vizetelly & Co., 1886], p. 162.)

15 While writing *Confessions*, Moore had asked Dujardin to send him a copy of Kahn's *Les Palais Nomades* (1887). Here he quotes a line from poem III and then all of "Intermède IX."

16 Paul Verlaine, from "Les Ingénus," *Fêtes Galantes*.

17 Paul Verlaine, "Parsifal."

18 Moore reflects here the French enthusiasm for Poe. "The Island of the Fay" is one of Poe's prose poems, and "Silence" one of his "Poems of Manhood." "Elionore" may be intended for "Lenore," another of the "Poems of Manhood." "Elionore" was changed to "Eleonore" after 1904, which brings it closer to Poe's title, and to the Lenore of "The Raven."

19 Sometime in 1878, Moore wrote from Paris to his mother, "My next book is three quarters finished Roses of Midnight." (NLI, MS. 4479, no. 11. Hone, *The Life of George Moore*, var., pp. 75–76.) And in the preface to *Martin Luther*, a series of letters between Moore and Bernard Lopez, Moore tells Lopez, "You haven't read my *Flowers of Passion* and I have not read you my 'Sappho,' 'Hermaphroditus,' and 'The Metamorphosis of the Vampire' (que j'ai en carton) which with many other *contes* of the same kind will be given to the world in defiance of Mrs. Grundy, in a handsomely bound square volume, entitled *Roses of Midnight*." (*Martin Luther: A Tragedy in Five Acts* [London: Remington & Co., 1879], p. 17.) "Sappho" and the "Hermaphrodite" did appear in *Pagan Poems*.
   Moore's first poems, *Flowers of Passion* (1878) and *Pagan Poems* (1881) were filled with echoes of Baudelaire, Gautier, and Swinburne. His themes were paganism, incest, death, Lesbianism, and hopeless love. The forced rhymes, archaic diction, and mechanical rhythms in the poems only served to complement the decadence of his themes. Some of his poems were translations, or partial translations, such as "Le Succube" from Mendès, "Song" from Gautier, and "The Balcony," partially from Baudelaire. The worst poems were those in which he attempted to recreate the world of

Baudelaire: in "Sonnet: A Corpse," a young man reverently kisses the detached head of his carrion lover.

When *Flowers of Passion* achieved some notoriety in the press, he proudly wrote to his uncle and offered him a copy. Two years later, when *Pagan Poems* elicited predictable abuse, Moore withdrew the volume but hoped to issue a censored version. He appealed to his friend William Michael Rossetti (brother of Dante Gabriel) for help in omitting the most offensive poems. Rossetti complied, but a revised edition was never published.

A few years later, Moore was anxious to disown the books of poetry. An unnamed American critic who wrote him in 1885 received a reply which prompted him to write: "Of course if you do not wish to be credited with the authorship of *Pagan Poems* and *Flowers of Passion* I shall respect your wishes in that regard." (NLI, MS. 2648, 6 January 1885.) It is not surprising that neither of these volumes is mentioned in *Confessions*.

CHAPTER FIVE

1 Moore echoes Balzac's story "La Femme de Trente Ans" in this chapter. He also reflects in a romanticized form some of his own experiences with young and older women. "I am playing my cards now to become the lover of the Marquiese d'Osmond," he wrote his mother in 1879, "she is very swell if not very young but I dont mind that (I mean the latter.) The first thing a young man who wants to get on in Paris must do is to get *under the wings* of some lady with a good name and in a high position that done with tact he can wriggle himself anywhere." (NLI, MS. 4479, no. 14, undated. Hone, *Life of George Moore*, var., p. 79.)

2 A. C. Swinburne, "Hymn to Proserpine."

CHAPTER SIX

1 These articles were probably "Le Roman Expérimental." (*Le Voltaire*, 16–20 October 1879.)

2 In his succinct account here of his marriage and divorce with naturalism, Moore omits any reference to his friendship with Zola. They were first introduced by Manet at the Assommoir Ball in May of 1879. Soon after he settled in London in 1881, Moore initiated a correspondence with Zola which was to remain fairly steady for the next seven years. Moore told Zola in ill-spelt, idiomatic French of the books he was writing. Zola suggested methods Moore might employ in his war against the circulating libraries. Throughout their correspondence, Moore addressed Zola as "*cher maître*," and during the early years of their friendship, he frequently declared his debt to Zola. He wrote, for instance, after *A Modern Lover* had achieved a modest success:

Que mon roman a eu de success peut vous interesser; car, comme je vous ai deja dit, je dois tout que j'ai a vous. (Bibliothèque Nationale, NAF 24522, no. 356, 17 September 1883. The library will hereafter be referred to as BN. Moore's letters are uncorrected.)

Even though Moore soon abandoned the methods of naturalism in his own novels, he maintained his allegiance to Zola. In August of 1887, while he was writing *Confessions*, the attack on Zola—the "Manifesto of the Five"—appeared in *Le Figaro*, 18 August. Moore immediately wrote to Zola and offered to write an article supporting *La Terre* (the novel specifically under attack) even though he had not yet read it.

Zola read *Confessions* as it appeared in *La Revue Indépendante* and Moore's denigration of naturalism surprised and angered him. Moore had been warned by Theodore Duret that Zola, among others, would be offended by his remarks. On 17 March 1888, Moore wrote Zola to defend himself in advance against Zola's probable annoyance at the forthcoming installment:

Quant a mon dernier livre que se publie en ce moment ci dans *la revue Independante* j'ai quelque chose a vous dire. Quand je parle personnelle-ment et j'en parle dans le prochain numero, je dis de vous ce que j'ai tou-jours dit, mais dans un chapitre intitule La Synthese de la Nouvelle Athenes j'enonce les paradoxes les plus polatres, alors il y a des choses disagréable pour tout le monde. Mais Duret ne veut pas, ou ne peut pas comprendre cela et chaque fois qu'il m'écrit et chaque fois qu'il me recontre, c'est toujours—"je ne comprends pas pourquoi vous avez cherché systematique-ment a être disagréable a Zola, Goncourt et Daudet." Je lui repond, mais lisez donc ce que je dis sur Zola sur une autre page de même livre. (BN, NAF 24522, no. 368.)

In "The Synthesis of the Nouvelle Athènes," Moore does not voice his own disillusionment with naturalism, as he does in the first reference to Zola, but rather echoes criticisms he has overheard in the café. In the same letter, he assures Zola that he means no offense, but is merely dramatizing the mood of that famous café:

Vous êtes mon ami, et croyez moi mon cher maitre que cela me serait tres penible de vous offenser d'aucune façon.

In May, Moore visited Zola at his home in Médan, accompanied by Zola's faithful disciple, Paul Alexis. Moore recreated this visit in "My Impressions of Zola." (*The English Illustrated Magazine* 11 [February 1894]: 476–89; pub. as "A Visit to Médan" in the 1926 edition of *Confessions*.) He relates in that essay how he sought to defend his remarks in *Confessions* and then assumes a pose of cavalier unconcern as he describes how his book broke his friendship with Zola. He affects the same manner in the 1904 preface to *Confessions*, where he recounts the episode again. In his essay and the later preface, Moore makes light of Zola's decision not to write a preface to the French translation of *A Mummer's Wife*, but in a letter written to Zola soon after this visit, he strikes a very different pose:

J'ai eu grand plaisir a ecrire cet article car vous m'avez fait bien comprendre l'erreur de prendre les sensations ephemeres pour les pensées, et ainsi de fausser le jugement. Du reste j'ai été bien puni, car cela, et avec raison, vous a empeché la preface pour la femme du cabotin mais plus que cela, sachant que je vous trouvais le plus grand esprit travaillent dans le district du roman depuis Balzac cela m'a profondement humilie de me voir dire des choses comme vous dites en français a coté. (BN, NAF 24522, no. 417, undated.)

The article he refers to is "M. Zola on the Side of the Angels." (*St. James Gazette* 12 [2 November 1888]: 3.) Moore praised Zola's latest novel *Le Rêve* extravagantly in his article and planned it to appear when Henry Vizetelly's trial began on 31 October 1888. Vizetelly was being tried for publishing Zola's novels; he was found guilty, fined, tried again in 1889, and sentenced to three months in jail, where he died.

Moore's contrition was sincere. He wrote to Dujardin and asked him to include some revisions in the book version of *Confessions*: "I mean to be fair to Zola and I have rewritten some phrases. Please cast your eye over them, for it would be terrible if my French were to appear 'mother-naked.' " (John Eglinton, ed. and trans., *Letters from George Moore to Ed. Dujardin, 1886–1922* [New York: Crosby-Gaige, 1929], pp. 30–31, 24 September 1888.) Only two revisions concerning Zola appeared in the 1889 French edition. The first modifies Moore's comment on Zola's theoretical writings, which in the original he called "the simple crude statements of a man of powerful mind, but singularly narrow vision" (p. 95). He added to this remark, "Les oeuvres seules résistent au temps; la critique passe; comme le vent, elle apporte le pollen; la fecondation fait, sa mission est accomplie." Thus he implies that time rather than inherent superficialities has rendered Zola's theories puerile. The other revision was in the passage in which he derides the language of *L'Assommoir* (p. 97). In the French text, by recasting his comment as a parenthetical qualification—"alors je n'avais lu ni Chateaubriand ni Flaubert"—he implied rather than declared that Zola's style was merely a faint echo of his peers. These concessions were small indeed and little altered the note of rebellion in this text. Moore's belief in his own explanation of these comments, and in the integrity of his text, finally overrode Zola's complaints; neither of these revisions appeared in any of the English editions. Nevertheless, he wrote to assure Zola that he had repaired the damage:

J'ai change les passages que nous avons lu ensemble. Ils ne representaient pas mas pensée quoi que ils ont chatouillés mon esprit quand je les ai ecrit; mais voilà mon cher maitre une facon d'etre que vous ne compriennez pas. J'ai vingt pensées contradictoires dans une journée, mais au fond ma pensee sur les choses essentielles rest la même. (BN, NAF 24522, no. 417.)

3 Shakespeare, Sonnet VIII.

4 Balzac, *Père Goriot.*

5 Balzac, *La Recherche de l'absolu.*

6 Balzac was one of the few writers, Pater was another, whom Moore did not renounce after having gleaned from him what he could. Balzac's influence on Moore's realistic novels was always sound; it helped turn Moore away from naturalism and its focus on the external qualities of character toward a realism concerned with psychological states. Baudelaire, Gautier, Zola and others bred transitory phases in his work which he would later denounce or revise away. His later autobiographies and critical writings contain many references to Balzac, and always he appears as a master worthy of continuing praise.

7 Balzac, "El Verdugo." Moore was probably attracted to this story because he had a rather romantic vision of himself as the last heir of a noble family. He retells the story in the first edition of *A Story-Teller's Holiday* ([New York: Privately printed, 1918], pp. 324–26) but omits it in the 1928 revision.

8 In *Avowals*, Moore remembers that Manet was the final link in the chain which led from Lopez to Villiers to Mallarmé. He visited Mallarmé often, he says; one evening, in praising Manet's illustrations for *L'Après-midi d'un faune*, Moore asserted that "Manet's drawings were the only modern drawings that had any character of their own" (p. 265). Mallarmé spoke to Manet of Moore and Manet invited him to come to his studio. Moore accepted the invitation, he says, and Manet proposed to paint Moore's portrait. Moore says nothing in *Confessions* and little elsewhere about Manet's portraits of him. Three are known to have survived: an oil painting of Moore sitting astraddle a chair in a garden with a flower-covered lattice behind him (dated c. 1878 and owned by Mr. and Mrs. Paul Mellon); an oil sketch of him with beard and derby, leaning on a café table (dated c. 1879); and a pastel portrait (dated c. 1879). The latter two are owned by the Metropolitan Museum of Art. (Etienne Moreau-Nélaton, *Manet Raconté par lui-même*, 2 [Paris: H. Laurens, 1926]: 52, 57.) In *Modern Painting*, Moore mentions one of these portraits:

Being a fresh-complexioned, fair-haired young man, the type most suitable to Manet's palette, he at once asked me to sit. His first intention was to paint me in a café; he had met me in a café, and he thought he could realise his impression of me in the first surrounding he had seen me in.
   The portrait did not come right; ultimately it was destroyed. ([London: Walter Scott, 1893], p. 31.)

Manet may have told Moore that the painting had been destroyed in order to quell his criticism. According to one of Manet's biographers, who quotes Manet on the subject, Moore was anything but a passive model:

He comes and bothers me, demanding a change here, some modification there. I shall change nothing in his portrait. Is it my fault if Moore looks like a squashed yolk of egg and if his face is awry? Indeed, this is true of all our faces, for the evil of our times is the search for symmetry. There is no symmetry in nature. One eye never matches the other; it is different.

(Henri Perruchot, *Manet,* trans. Humphrey Hare [Cleveland: World Publishing Co., 1962], p. 232.)

Manet was probably referring to the 1879 oil portrait of Moore. The vapid
face which stares out at the viewer incited some to term the painting
"Manet's drowned man." (Jacques-Emile Blanche, *Portraits of a Lifetime,*
ed. and trans. Walter Clement [London: J. M. Dent & Sons, 1937], p. 137.)
It is not among Manet's best works, and certainly would not have inspired
any praise from Moore.

9 Degas, too, drew a sketch of Moore, dated 1879. It is much less flattering
even than Manet's portraits, for it represents Moore as a tubular-shaped
body topped by a face with an empty gaze. If Moore knew of this sketch,
he chose never to mention it. (Ronald Pickavance, "A Newly Discovered
Drawing by Degas," *Burlington Magazine* 105, no. 723 [June 1963]: 276.)
According to Daniel Halévy, Degas testified to his early acquaintance with
Moore at the Nouvelle Athènes in a conversation in December 1890. Halévy
asked Degas if he had read Zola's *L'Oeuvre* (1886) and if he felt, as others
did, that Zola had based it on the period when Cézanne and Degas were
contemporaries. Degas replied that he had known Zola during a period
earlier than that in *L'Oeuvre.* "It was before that," he said, "with Manet
and Moore at the Nouvelle Athènes. We discussed things endlessly." (Daniel
Halévy, *My Friend Degas,* trans. Mina Curtiss [Middletown, Conn.: Wes-
leyan University Press, 1964], p. 41.)

10 Edmond Duranty, who edited the short-lived journal *Réalisme* in 1856,
wrote Stendhalian novels which never, as Moore says, received the public
recognition they deserved. Zola praised Duranty as the most original writer
he knew. Duranty was also an early champion of the Impressionists and
wrote *La Nouvelle Peinture* (1876), in which he placed Manet at the head
of the new movement. (Louise Edouard Tabary, *Duranty* [Paris: Etude
françaises, 1954].)

11 Moore's effusive praise of the musician Ernest Cabaner complements his
celebration of art as a sacred rite. Cabaner's selfless dedication to art has
its humorous side and anecdotes told about Cabaner suggest that he was
frequently lauded at the Nouvelle Athènes. Moore added a remark made
by Cabaner to the French version of *Confessions* and later repeated it in
Memoirs of My Dead Life: "Mon père était un homme dans le genre de
Napoléon 1er, mais plus fort, plus fort." Gustave Kahn, another frequenter
of the Nouvelle Athènes during the eighties, quotes this remark in a slightly
different form in his *Silhouettes Littéraires* (Paris, 1925). Unless Kahn borrowed from Moore, which seems unlikely, the repetition of the comment
suggests Moore's realist's facility for noticing and recording telling details.

CHAPTER SEVEN

1 Moore's enchantment with England dated particularly from 1886–87, when
he visited his friends the Bridgers in Sussex. It was there that he evidently
wrote much of *Confessions.* He described the Sussex countryside in a letter

to his mother which echoes his praise in *Confessions*: "I have spent [the] whole summer here—a real English village grouped round a green; a horse pond at one end and the long undulating line of the Downs at the other And the labourers cottages with quaint windows hung with roses and ivy, . . . how delightful,—what a vision of enchanted comfort!" (NLI, MS. 4479, no. 26.) In another letter written in December 1887, while he was writing *Confessions*, he told his mother of his new affinity for Protestantism: "I am very fond of my friends and have entirely adopted their life— have said in fact thy people shall be my people thy God shall be my God. I put on a high hat, take an umbrella and march to church every Sunday. I do not believe but I love protestantism. If it is not the faith of my brain it is the faith of my heart." (NLI, MS. 4479, no. 32.) Moore's dislike of Catholicism, although it dated from his youth, seems to have been particularly intense at this same time; he wrote to his brother Julian, sometime in 1886, "My hatred of Catholicism is limitless, it is the strongest fibre in my nature." (NLI, MS. 4479, no. 64.) He elaborates on his affinity for Protestantism and describes his final conversion to it in *Salve*.

2 Moore has extended the chronological boundaries of his narrative here, for when he was a frequent visitor to the Nouvelle Athènes (1878–79), Zola was at the peak of his career, and the reaction against him actually began with Huysmans' *A Rebours* (1884) and climaxed in 1887, with the younger naturalists' attack on *La Terre* in *Le Figaro*. In an article published in 1884, Moore reported Zola's prophecy that naturalism would soon relinquish its role as literary renegade and become an established and accepted mode of fiction. ("A Breakfast with Edmond de Goncourt," *St. James Gazette* 8 [13 May 1884]: 6–7.) Zola's optimism was naive, however, and Moore records in *Confessions* the kind of derisive remarks which were undoubtedly current in 1887.

3 Although Renoir, who had strong feelings on the dangers of mechanization, is scarcely mentioned in *Confessions*, Moore is probably quoting him here. (See *Vale*, [London: William Heinemann, 1933], p. 111, and also Jean Renoir, *Renoir, My Father*, trans. Randolph and Dorothy Weaver [London: Collins, 1962].)

4 The latter part of this remark is a reference to Edmond de Goncourt's novel *Les Frères Zemganno* (1879), which is a thinly disguised expression of his grief over the death of his brother Jules (d. 1870). Theodore Duret warned Moore that Goncourt, like Zola, would be infuriated by his comments. Duret's prediction proved true, for after reading this section of *Confessions* in *La Revue Indépendante*, Goncourt defensively noted in his *Journal* (8 May 1888): "Moore affirm que je ne suis pas artiste. . . . C'est trop bête au fond, moi, pas artiste! Alors qu'est-ce qui l'est donc, dans les ecrivains modernes?" (Edmond de Goncourt, *Journal* 15, ed. Robert Ricatte [Monaco: l'Academie Goncourt, 1956–58]: 110–11.)

CHAPTER EIGHT

1 Moore never names in *Confessions* the woman who wrote this letter, and

he has woven a mystery around her identity with comments made elsewhere which only he could fully appreciate or fathom. In *Memoirs of My
Dead Life*, she is referred to as a Polish woman, a Madame Albazi. Moore
tells how he took her to Manet's studio where the pastel portrait was
drawn and how, soon after that, he succeeded in becoming her lover. She
later went to the auction of his goods, he repeats, and bought the pastel.
However, the letter in *Confessions* is modelled closely after letters Moore
received from an American woman he knew in Paris sometime before
1883, Madame de Coëtlogon. (Hone, *Life of George Moore*, p. 55.) Several
of her letters have survived (dated 1883 to 1885), and although they shed
little light on the relationship, they do demonstrate how cleverly he
mimicked her verbose and charmingly affected manner. In one she characterizes Moore in a way which obviously amused and pleased him, for he
recreates it in his imitation of her style:

You will not find me changed at all, I think, perhaps a little naughtier and
more Parisienne, . . . I shall find you more changed I am sure. You will
have lost your coté Parisien, which was the nicest, if not the best part of
you, in your long sojourn in that dreadful British atmosphere. *Promise* me
you will never become an uncompromising John Bull.—as if you could—
It was all a mistake about you—you were born out of your sphere—you
were meant to have lived, loved, and suffered in Paris. And now you are
going to marry some square-backed, big footed British virgin and have
a dozen children après la manière de votre pays, and become a respectable
père de famille and think of us all here in Paris as pagans—it is all wrong,
it is not your vocation—but what is to be done about it! At any rate come
to Paris first, before you get impossible. (NLI, MS. 2648, no. 26, 28 November 1883.)

2 These lines are taken from a poem included in Moore's second volume of
poetry, *Pagan Poems*. In this poem, "The Portrait," the poet contemplates
a pastel portrait of his mistress, "a sketch unfinished / And signed by my
dear friend Edward Manet . . . It is a portrait of a Polish lady,— / I wonder
if she is now dead or living,— / I loved her once, but love is soon forgotten."

3 Jean C. Noël has uncovered the record of a sale held on 26 March 1881, at
61, rue Condorcet, where Moore was living before he returned to London.
The list of goods sold (especially the 200-volume library) suggests that this
may be the auction Moore refers to. (Jean C. Noël, *George Moore: L'Homme
et L'Oeuvre* [Paris: Didier, 1966], pp. 681–82.)

4 Moore's actual reply to his agent's bad news was less irruptive than the
violent outburst in *Confessions:* "The question of the tenants refusing to
pay rent is terrible! What does it mean—communism? If you don't get the
rents what is to be done? If I have never looked into my business at all
event I have never committed any follies. I never spent more than five
hundred a year and I was told when I came into the property I had ever
so much. Enfin I suppose you will do your best I will try to meet you in

Dublin if you like and have some understanding, about Christmas." (NLI, MS. 4479, no. 56, undated. Hone, *Life of George Moore*, var., p. 81.)

5 Moore echoes Swinburne's "Hymn to Proserpine" in this denunciation of the pale Galilean who ushered in Christianity, but he adds his own special note of vehemence. Moore's editor, Wigram, balked at the "blasphemies" in this section and deleted two long passages from it when it appeared in *Time*. Moore wrote to try to convince Wigram that he was not being blasphemous, but rather characterizing, through exaggeration, one aspect of modern society. He did agree to some deletions and wrote to Wigram:

My concessions are liberal and large and I hope they will satisfy your scruples. No one objects to anyone saying, "I don't believe", the only think [*sic*] that can be taken objection to is *abuse*. You will see that I have cut out mere statements. To take Christ as the socialist of Galilee, using socialist as I clearly do in the sense of God of pity, is not offensive; the rest is a bare statement of the fact that the modern potivist, [*sic*] the socialist, denies Christ, therefore that Christ is lost and whelmed in the final triumph of Christianity. This is not be orthodoxy but it is not blasphemy, and I take it that you conduct your business from as liberal a standpoint [as] Kegan or Paul or Chatto and Windus. Why should I not say that the new god, the god the potavists [*sic*] will create, will be dressed in broad cloth and wear a red necktie I cannot even conjecture—you struck out this passage. Besides this part of the confessions sounds worse than it is because it is not read in conjunction with the next chapter—There the first sentence shows that the paganism is merely a passionate outburst and must not be taken too seriously. However *I am sure* that as it now stands it does not pass beyond the most ordinary and usual limitations of modern speech —Tell the printer to print from what I send you, leaving out the passage marked in blue. (NLI, MS. 3888, no. 2, undated.)

CHAPTER NINE

1 Because *Confessions* is a concise and selective portrait rather than a complete history of his development as an artist, Moore has excluded here an account of his activities between the winter of 1879, when he left Paris, and the beginning of 1881, when he moved to the Strand lodging house. Moore's problems with the estate were not so easily disposed of as he suggests in *Confessions*. When he returned to London late in 1879, he worked, as he says, for a short time on the *Examiner*. Then sometime before August 1880, he left London and returned to Ireland, where he stayed with his mother, sister Nina, and two of his brothers, Maurice and Augustus, in a house his mother had rented in Dublin. (Hone, *Life of George Moore*, p. 83.) In the fall of 1880, he moved from Dublin to Moore Hall, where he stayed with his sister. Ireland plays a small role in *Confessions*, for during this period he sought to minimize its influence on his early life. Thus nothing is said here of his collecting rents on his estate, even though he most probably did so at

this time. (See Introduction for a discussion of *Parnell and His Island*, which reflects this period.)

2 This newspaper was the *Examiner*. Moore's editor, Heinrich Felbermann, later remembered that he had thought Moore "rather dear at two guineas a week." (Heinrich Felbermann, *The Memoirs of a Cosmopolitan* [London: Chapman & Hall, 1936], p. 113.)

3 The first appearance of these two poems and those added to subsequent editions is as follows:

"The Sweetness of the Past," *Spectator*, 11 December 1880, as "The Love of the Past"
"Nostalgia," *Spectator*, 15 October 1881, as "Looking Back"
"We are alone!" *Pagan Poems*, as "A une Poitrinaire"
"Nuit de Septembre," *Pagan Poems*, as a portion of a duodrama, "La Maitresse Maternelle"
"Pour un Tableau de Lord Leighton," *Pall Mall Gazette*, as "Les Dormeuses," circa February 1896.
"Pour un Tableau de Rubens," *Confessions*, 1917
"Vers d'Album," written for Lady Cunard in 1921 and sent to her as "Souvenir d'une Visite," on 14 December. (Rupert Hart-Davis, ed., *George Moore Letters to Lady Cunard* [London: Hart-Davis, 1957], p. 119.) Moore enclosed a copy of the poem, entitled "Vers d'Album," in a letter to Edouard Dujardin on 26 December 1921. (John Eglinton, ed. and trans., *Letters from George Moore to Ed. Dujardin, 1886–1922* [New York: Crosby-Gaige, 1929], p. 110.)
Sonnet dedicatory to Swinburne, *Martin Luther*

4 This lodging house was at 17 Cecil Street, the Strand. Moore shared rooms for a time with his brother Augustus, who was known as "Masher Moore" in London in the eighties. Moore says in *A Communication to My Friends* that he disapproved of his brother's carefree way of life. For whatever reason, Moore soon moved into rooms of his own.

5 The servant Emma, whom many critics see as a prototype of Esther Waters, also appears in Moore's early short story "Under the Fan" (*Tinsley's Magazine* 30 [February 1882]: 135–54) and in *A Mummer's Wife*. Moore's claim to a naturalist's objectivity in his description of Emma is as disingenuous as Zola's often was, for his sympathy with Emma is obvious. He uses her pathetic life as a stick to prod again the Victorian social reformers.

6 Racine, *Phèdre*.

7 Moore wrote an anonymous review of Swinburne's *Studies in Song* (*Spectator* 54, no. 2749 [5 March 1881]: 316–17). In it he quotes from "By the North Sea," which ends with the lines, "For the soul of thy son to inherit, / My mother, my sea." Moore was critical of Swinburne's "abstractions" and said he must return to nature if he hoped to write any more lasting verse. While Moore lamented the change Watts-Dunton and Putney had wrought

on Swinburne, he continued to admire and echo Swinburne's earlier poetry, as *Confessions* demonstrates. In July of 1887, Moore sent Swinburne a copy of *A Mere Accident* and wrote him as follows: "My taste in matters of art has undergone many changes but in my love of your work—prose and poetry—I have never wavered. Your attack on the school which you erroneously believe me to be a member of was in your best manner; the phrase: 'When I attacked the Philistine it was not with a chamber pot for a buckler and a dung fork for a spear,' amused me very much; indeed I had thought of replying in the same half serious half playful manner but a sense of deference, a feeling of loyalty to my admiration of you prevented my doing so." (British Museum, Ashley 1186, dated The Green, Southwick, Sussex, 5 July 1887.)

8 Moore invokes Schopenhauer here in a way which also suggests Wagner's theories of art. Wagner, himself deeply affected by Schopenhauer's writings, said, "In daily life the mere sight of an object leaves us cold and unconcerned, and only when we become aware of that object's bearings on our will does it call forth an emotion." (Richard Wagner, *Prose Works*, trans. William Ashton Ellis [New York: Broude Brothers, 1966], 5: 70.)

9 A. C. Swinburne, from "The Triumph of Time," *Poems and Ballads*.

10 Alfred de Vigny, "Le Cor," *Poèmes antiques et modernes*.

11 This same argument was used in a pamphlet published in London in 1888, entitled *Extracts Principally from English Classics: Showing That the Legal Suppression of M. Zola's Novels Would Logically Involve the Bowdlerizing of Some of the Greatest Works in English Literature*. The occasion of this pamphlet was Henry Vizetelly's arrest by the National Vigilance Association for publishing Zola's novels. The authorship of portions of the pamphlet has been assigned to Moore, but he denied it in Frank Fayant's copy of the pamphlet. (Frank Fayant Collection, Cornell University.)

12 The event which he melodramatically cites as having opened the villa's eyes is the Colin Campbell divorce case, an infamous trial held in 1886, which filled, as he says, the newspapers with detailed accounts of adultery. Moore also commemorated the event in a poem, "Farewell to 1886" (*The Bat*, 4 January 1887). Moore's optimism here was unfounded, for the divorce trial by no means toppled either the villa or the circulating libraries. Ironically, it spurred some journalists to demand that the less "respectable" papers who had not restrained their reports of the trial be subject to censorship. The *Spectator* commented, "We greatly fear matters will remain in their present disgraceful condition, and that the Campbell *cause célèbre* will have had no result except to vitiate still more the already vitiated atmosphere of society." Suppression of the unpleasant would remain the establishment rule. ("The End of the Campbell Case," *Spectator* 59, no. 3052 [25 December 1886]: 1746–47.)

CHAPTER TEN

1 The "leading journal" was evidently the *Spectator*. Robert Tener, in "The *Spectator* Records, 1874–1897" (*The Victorian Newsletter*, no. 17 [Spring 1960]: 33–36), identifies three unsigned articles by Moore which appeared there in 1881.

2 Throughout *Confessions* Moore emphasizes the purity of his interest in literature, and thus here he overstates his financial independence. His letters show that he was relying on the sale of his works for a good part of his income during the 1880s. (See also 1918 revision, p. 208.)

3 The works he claims to have written in 1881 can be only partially identified. He probably wrote a number of things which were unpublished and later lost. In 1882, he and his brother Augustus wrote the lyrics of the English libretto for the French opera *Les Cloches de Corneville*, for which they were paid thirty pounds. (An opera by Clairville and Gabet. Hone, *Life of George Moore*, p. 91.) In 1872 or 1873, he and Paul Alexis had translated into French W. S. Gilbert's play *Sweethearts* which, under the title *Le Sycamore*, was later produced in 1894. (Jean C. Noël, *George Moore: L'Homme et L'Oeuvre* [Paris: Didier, 1966], p. 221.) He also wrote the libretto for James Glover's play *The Fashionable Beauty*, which was produced in 1885. (Noël, *George Moore*, p. 76.) Moore told Zola in a letter written in 1882 that he was writing and publishing many short stories, but only one seems to have been published during this period—"Under the Fan." (See also critical note 19, chapter 4, for discussion of *Flowers of Passion*, *Martin Luther*, and *Pagan Poems*.)

Since he wanted to compress his narrative and emphasize his literary activities, he excluded two trips which he made away from London during this time. One was the trip to Paris and meeting with Zola, recounted in an article, "A Visit to M. Zola," which was published anonymously in the *St. James Gazette* on 26 May 1881. His other trip was a brief journey to Ireland which he made in October 1881. His agent, Tom Ruttledge, was having trouble collecting the rents. Moore stayed in Mayo as briefly as possible, for he was chary of any time lost to literature. "George insists," his brother Maurice wrote to their mother, with some annoyance, "on returning to London almost immediately; he says he must continue his writing." (NLI, MS. 10,566, 13 October 1881.)

4 Paul Verlaine, "Art Poètique."

> Car nous voulons la Nuance encor,
> Pas la Couleur, rien que la nuance!
>
> . . . .
>
> Et tout le reste est littérature.

5 Revision of 1918. Moore's comment that the lower levels of society are superior subjects for literature is repeated in *Avowals* and may derive from a direct encounter between James and Moore. He claims in *Avowals* that

he sent James *A Mummer's Wife* soon after its publication, in the hope that he could secure James's support in the controversy then raging over the book's moral quality. James, according to Moore, wrote two letters in reply: in the first, he criticized the length and style of Moore's novel; in the second, he replied to Moore's criticisms of *The Portrait of a Lady*, which Moore had made in answering James's first letter. Moore cites the second letter, in which James compared his novel to Moore's: "He said that the woman in *The Portrait of a Lady* represented a higher intellectual plane than Kate Ede, and proceeded to draw from the alleged fact the conclusion that she lived an intenser life than the workwoman" (p. 175). Intensity of felt life, the quality of character James sought always to express in his fiction, was too attenuated and effete for Moore's taste. E. M. Forster's criticism of James's characters, that "their clothes will not take off" (*Aspects of the Novel*), echoes Moore's derision of James's selective vision of reality. In later years, Moore, with the sort of invective which brought him many enemies, was fond of calling James a "eunuch."

6 Balzac, *Les Illusions Perdues*.

7 Thomas Hardy, *Far from the Madding Crowd* (1874).

8 Richard Blackmore, *Lorna Doone* (1869).

9 Margaret Veley (d. 1887) and Moore were good friends in the 1880s. It is characteristic of Moore to praise works by writers (especially female) who are his personal friends.

10 During the 1880s, Moore frequently visited Mabel Robinson and her sister Mary at their London home; it was there that he first met Henry James and Walter Pater. (See *Avowals*, pp. 173–207, and Mary Duclaux [née Robinson], "Souvenirs sur George Moore," *Revue de Paris*, no. 5 [1 March 1933]: 110–30.) Mme. Duclaux corroborates Moore's account in *Avowals* of his meeting with Pater at their home in 1885 but says nothing about James.

11 By 1916, Moore had totally revised his early displeasure with Stevenson's writings. (This is discussed by Rupert Hart-Davis in *George Moore Letters to Lady Cunard* [London: Hart-Davis, 1957], p. 95.) In the preface to *Lewis Seymour and Some Women* (the revision of *A Modern Lover*, published in 1917), he tells of reading Stevenson's *Travels with a Donkey* (1879) during the previous year and finding it "the most entrancing book in the English language" (p. viii). He now saw that Stevenson was an expert story-teller. He also expressed his new opinion in a letter to Sidney Colvin (whom he chides in the 1904 preface to *Confessions* for having wasted his time editing Stevenson's letters) on 8 March 1917: "I have to thank you for your edition of Stevenson's letters, which have given me the very greatest pleasure, revealing Stevenson to me even more perfectly than *Travels with a Donkey*, *An Inland Voyage*, *Men and Books*, etc." (Hart-Davis, *Letters to Lady Cunard*, p. 95.) No reference to Colvin is made in the 1917 preface to *Confessions*, but Moore did leave unchanged his critique of Stevenson in the text. He not only needed disparagement thematically at this point in

Confessions, but he also respected the fictional age of his book and did not replace an early opinion with a decidedly later one.

12 Moore uses artistic license in placing *Marius the Epicurean* at this point in his evolution, for he actually read Pater's book soon after its publication in the spring of 1885. He describes in *Avowals* the excitement he felt on reading Pater's book and adds there another reason for his enthusiasm: Marius' character and circumstances mirrored his own, and thus "at every page this story seemed to have been written for me" (p. 185). Even though Moore's friendship with Pater remained tentative and eventually dissolved, his admiration for *Marius the Epicurean* grew deeper each time he read it. Writing to Edmund Gosse on 13 August 1914, he said, "[In *Marius*, Pater has done] the one desirable thing—to write a work in all kinds of various meters and yet in one meter. He raises literature to the 'condition of music.' *Marius* is as beautiful in texture as Wagner's music or Manet's painting; it is like an old dream house built of old marble full of venerable memories and yet a thing of today." (NLI, MS. 2134.)

CHAPTER ELEVEN

1 The striking characteristic of this chapter is its tense. In contrast to the retrospection which dominates the majority of the narrative, Moore speaks here in the present tense. He offers an immediate response to his environment by recording the impressions and thoughts which are on the surface of his mind. As in Chapter 8, he again echoes Dujardin's interior monologue technique, which he had read in *Les Hantises* (1886) and *Les Lauriers sont coupés* (1887). Moore read the first work, a collection of thirteen stories with the epigraph "Seule vit notre âme," in February 1887, and he wrote to tell Dujardin how much it pleased him. In *Les Hantises*, Dujardin concentrates on the interior life of his characters; several stories are soliloquies spoken by restless, even deranged, sensitive men. Moore undoubtedly had this work, along with *Les Lauriers*, in mind when he created some of the soliloquy "thoughts" in this chapter. When Moore read *Les Lauriers* as it appeared in *La Revue Indépendante* (May–August 1887), he wrote to Dujardin to praise this book, too: "Your story is very good, uncommonly good: the daily life of the soul unveiled for the first time; a kind of symphony in full stops and commas. All I am afraid of is monotony. We shall see; in any case it is new." (John Eglinton, ed. and trans., *Letters from George Moore to Ed. Dujardin, 1886–1922* [New York: Crosby-Gaige, 1929], p. 20, 17 May 1887.) In 1897, he again wrote in praise of *Les Lauriers*: "You have discovered *the* form, the archetypal form, the most original in our time; but the psychology is a little 'naturalist.' That seems to you a contradiction in terms; but it is not, it is sound criticism." (*Letters to Dujardin*, p. 40, 22 July 1897.) After *Confessions*, Moore also experimented with the interior monologue technique in *Mike Fletcher* ([London: Ward & Downey, 1889], pp. 64–66). Mildred Lawson's revery in the opening pages of *Celibates* (London: Walter Scott, 1895) also owes something to Dujardin's stories. Moore's friendship with Dujardin led James Joyce to read *Les Lauriers* in

1903. In 1904, Joyce worked for a time on an Italian translation of "Mildred Lawson," but never completed it. He expanded the interior monologue method to stream of consciousness in *Ulysses* and claimed Dujardin as the originator of the technique. (Richard Ellmann, *James Joyce* [New York: Oxford University Press, 1959], pp. 131, 534.) In 1930, Joyce asked Moore to write a preface to an English translation of *Les Lauriers*. Moore told Joyce that he would rather not write it; in his old age (he was seventy-eight), he had reversed his opinion of Dujardin's originality. "I know nothing of the question which apparently agitates France, the discovery of the monologue interieure," he wrote to Joyce. "In England we don't believe that any discovery has been made. We think, rightly or wrongly, that the monologue interieure existed from time immemorial." (Richard Ellmann, ed., *Letters of James Joyce*, vol. 3 [New York: Viking Press, 1966], p. 197, 10 May 1930.) See also *Conversations in Ebury Street* (pp. 174–88), where Moore recounts how much he has learned from Dujardin: "Were I asked to tell in whose field I have harvested most profitably, I should answer: In Dujardin's." Moore's enthusiasm for Wagner, and later his interest in the higher criticism of Biblical myths, owed much to Dujardin.

2 Moore's use of his own name triggered abuse from several of his reviewers. "If Mr. Dayne had been educated," the reviewer for the *Athenaeum* wrote, "he would have learnt that one of the uses of education is to take the conceit out of a man, and he would have discovered that much of his originality was commonplace." ([31 March 1888], p. 402.) The reviewer went on to praise Dayne's candour, even though he deplored his vices. The reviewer for the *Academy*, William Sharp, who praised *Confessions* otherwise, regretted this "naive passage." In the 1904 and all following editions, Moore's name was removed.

3 Moore wrote an article on *A Rebours* ("A Curious Book," *St. James Gazette* 8 [2 September 1884]: 6–7) in which he praised it as an exotic book fit only for the "literary gourmet." In 1886, he wrote to Theodore Duret that he was rereading *A Rebours* with great pleasure. (Henry W. and Albert A. Berg Collection, The New York Public Library, Astor, Lenox and Tilden Foundations.) It was probably during his second reading that he more fully appreciated Huysmans' novel both as a literary achievement and as an innovative break with Zola and the naturalists. The book seems to have had a considerable influence on *Confessions*. (See Introduction, p. 4.)

4 Huysmans, *A Rebours* (Paris: Charpentier, 1899), literal and accurate translation from pages 265 and 264.

5 The two prose poems were originally published in an unsigned article, "Les Decadents," in *Court and Society Review* (19 January 1887). A third (see variorum note, page 215) first appeared in *The Savoy* (July 1896) as "The Future Phenomenon." The three are literal and generally accurate translations of Mallarmé's "Plainte d'Automne," "Frisson d'Hiver," and "Le Phénomène Futur" (poems also praised by Des Esseintes).

6 Huysmans, *A Rebours*, p. 263. The second phrase is a direct quotation, although Moore does not so indicate.

7 Addition of 1889. This added comment on the evil of having children, like the earlier addition on the death of his father, is expressly Schopenhauerian in theme and tone. His only direct comments on children during this period occur in his letters to his brother Julian and his mother. They all concern his sister Nina, who was prolific at childbearing. In one, he says "I hope Nina has brought no more children into this miserable world, for what she will do with them later I cannot think." (NLI, MS. 4479, no. 62, 3 January 1887.) Concern for her health was involved in his gloomy comment, but his Schopenhauerian distaste for the perpetuation of life also played some part in it.

8 Moore again quotes from Gustave Kahn's *Les Palais Nomades*: "Intermède XIV" and "Intermède XV."

9 Moore mentions Gautier's *Les Jeunes-France* earlier in *Confessions* and he may be echoing it here, for Gautier proclaims in a similar tone, "Au diable les verses, au diable la prose! je suis un viveur maintenant." ([Paris: Charpentier, n.d.], p. xviii.)

10 Added chapter. The added chapter (called, after Baudelaire, "Examen de Minuit" in 1889, but given no title in subsequent editions) was written while the French translation of *Confessions* was being prepared for publication in book form. "Have no misgivings," Moore wrote to Dujardin on 5 August 1888, "about the chapter I am going to add—just a dialogue between myself and my Conscience, who happens to drop in." (*Letters to Dujardin*, p. 29.) Moore wrote it in English and sent it to Dujardin, who translated it into French. When *Confessions* was published in England later in 1889, the new chapter was added to the book. Moore had made some revisions in the chapter before its second appearance. In several places, the French version was more outspoken than the English. Moore made comments on his sexual habits which were removed from the 1889 English version and replaced by passages which accentuated the Schopenhauerian tone of the chapter. Moore's reason for revising the English version may have been fear of the censor; or he may have decided to be less candid with his English audience. The two most extensively revised passages were as follows:

Jamais auparavant l'âme d'un homme n'avait été si embrouillée avec celle de la femme; et pour expliquer l'anormal de cette sympathie sexuelle, je ne puis qu'imaginer qu'avant ma naissance il y avait eu quelque hésitation de sexe. Pourtant j'étais un joyeux garçon, amoureux de l'aventure, et excellent sportsman; une fois un cheval entre les jambes ou un fusil dans les mains, je quittais toutes morbides imaginations, tous étranges désirs de jouer les femmes en travesti, de porter leurs bottines et leurs peignoirs. (P. 248, French. Included in the passage spoken by "I," p. 220.)

Pensez à l'ennui énorme de veiller toujours sur une personne, surtout sur une femme: et pour quelle raison! Expliqué ainsi, le mariage ne me parait pas raisonnable. Quelle promiscuité de corps et d'esprit! Je n'ai jamais passé une nuit avec une femme; de cela au moins je suis vierge. L'idée de ne jamais être seul, de perdre ce moi intime qui comme un oiseau farouche s'envole hors de vue pendant le jour, mais qui est avec vous—oh de quelle intensité—le matin, à l'heure de cette lucide paresse! perdre la camaraderie de son corps—car, comme votre esprit, votre corps est plus strictement et intensément vôtre au réveil et il semble que le sommeil vous ait rendu la possession des choses en allées . . . Perdre tout cela! (Pp. 251–52, French. Included in passage spoken by "I," pp. 221–22.)

Knowledge of this passage helps the reader to appreciate one of Moore's playful self-quotations. In "The Lovers of Orelay" (*Memoirs of My Dead Life*), Moore says, "I have never slept with any one in my life; *de cela au moins je suis vierge.*" His companion, Doris, remarks, "Now you are quoting from *Les Confessions d'un Jeune Anglais*" (p. 152). As Moore knew, only the French title here would do.

The chapter was slightly revised in subsequent editions. In 1918, Moore moved "La Ballade" from the poetry section (where he had placed it in 1917) to this chapter. "La Ballade" is a slightly revised version of a ballade Moore wrote in the mid-1880s and published anonymously (under the name "Pagan") in a four-page leaflet entitled "La Ballade de l'Amant de Coeur." In July of 1916, when Moore was considering adding his ballade to the 1917 edition of *Confessions*, he sent it to his friend Edmund Gosse and asked Gosse to punctuate it for him. Gosse evidently complied even though he thought the poem terrible. Moore quotes Gosse's amusing evaluation in another letter (1 August 1916): " 'I cannot bear your ballade but am devoted to you.' " (NLI, MS. 2134.) Gosse's dissent obviously placed no damper on Moore's enthusiasm. When Moore moved his ballade to this chapter in 1918, he decided to echo Gosse's comment on it. He told Gosse, obliquely, of his little joke in a letter dated 1 April 1917: "It isn't probable that you ever saw Confessions of a Young Man. [sic] You are mentioned twice—one mention is thirty-five years old and for that reason it seemed useless to change it in the later mention. I accept you as my conscience." (NLI, MS. 2134.)

CHAPTER TWELVE

1 Moore imitates Baudelaire's address to his readers: "Hypocrite lecteur,— mon semblable,—mon frère!" (From "Au Lecteur," *Les Fleurs du Mal*.)

2 The publisher (named in the 1918 *Confessions*) was William Tinsley, whose office was located directly above the Gaiety Bar.

3 The Irishman was a writer named Edmund Downey, who worked for Tinsley between 1879 and 1884 and edited *Tinsley's Magazine*. (See Edmund Downey, *Twenty Years Ago* [London: Hurst & Blackett, 1905].)

4 Moore never names this writer or his friend, but it is likely that the "long creature" was a writer named John Hill and the "little creature" a friend of his and Strand journalist, John Augustus O'Shea. ("Creature" was muted to "man" after 1904.) Downey describes John Hill in terms which mark him as a sure model for Moore's new enemy: "If any tiro came to London in the eighties with the intention of setting the Thames on fire that tiro was John Hill. He had the experience of two recognized Universities—Heidelberg and Oxford, and he had graduated from another university—the Quartier Latin . . . He was very tall—over six feet high . . . he had adopted a manner which was quasi-theatrical." (Downey, *Twenty Years Ago*, p. 88.)

5 Moore has telescoped two or three years at this juncture, for his ties with Tinsley were not severed until after Tinsley's publication of *A Modern Lover*. Tinsley published novels in the three-volume format and specialized in the type of fiction preferred by the circulating libraries. Since Moore wanted to write his second novel partially in opposition to the libraries and also to publish it in one volume, he took it to Henry Vizetelly, who agreed to help him in his campaign. He had met James Davis, the editor he describes here as the "Jew" with "bright witty glances" through his brother Augustus. Davis was editor of a weekly magazine called *The Bat*. The details of the event are not known, but according to *A Communication to My Friends*, Moore says he enlisted Davis's aid in extricating himself from his agreement with Tinsley. When he published *A Mummer's Wife*, he dedicated it to James Davis, "in payment of a literary debt." Moore joined the staff of *The Bat* sometime after April 1885 (not in 1881 or 1882, as he implies in *Confessions*), and he published a laudatory article on Zola's novel *L'Oeuvre* in November of that year ("M. Zola's New Book").

6 Moore explained his reason for including the duel episode to Mr. Wigram as follows: "I tried to write the last chapter but could not because I had not got it right, but now I have got it right (in my head) and I think it will be the best part of the book. The last chapter will be a long one; I shall tell the story of a duel Edwin Dayne was going to fight and the confession of his baseness—I suppose it is base to fight a duel for the sake of the advertisement—will be very fetching." (NLI, MS. 3888, no. 7, undated.)

7 The duel Edwin Dayne wants to provoke is very like a duel Moore nearly fought with Lord "Derry" Rossmore, an Irish landowner who was frequently present at Davis's house. In Lord Rossmore's remembrance of this near-duel, written in 1912, he refers to Moore euphemistically as "an Irishman whose name is well known as a writer." Lord Rossmore's account of the challenge corroborates Moore's. He also describes the visit of Lewis Hawkins ("Marshall") to him, which Moore only reports as having occurred, and characterizes him as an "offensive, dictatorial individual" who had come to demand an apology. When Rossmore refused to apologize, Hawkins, he says, declared, "Then I must ask for the names of your *témoins*. I have come over from Paris, and let us treat this affair in a Parisian manner." Eventually, an understanding was reached, and there was no duel. (Lord Derrick Rossmore, *Things I Can Tell* [London: Eveleigh Nash, 1912], pp. 126–27.)

SELECTED BIBLIOGRAPHY

BIOGRAPHY

Readers interested in Moore's biography may consult Joseph Hone's early and highly readable *The Life of George Moore* (London: Victor Gollancz, 1936) and, for a more detailed and fully researched study, Jean C. Noël's *George Moore: L'Homme et L'Oeuvre* (Paris: Didier, 1966).

BIBLIOGRAPHY

Edwin Gilcher's complete descriptive bibliography of Moore's works, *A Bibliography of George Moore* (Dekalb, Ill.: Northern Illinois University Press, 1970), places all Moore scholars in his debt.

CRITICISM

For an extensive bibliography of criticism about Moore see Helmut Gerber, ed., "Bibliography of George Moore Criticism," Parts I and II, *English Literature in Transition* 2, no. 2 (1959): 1–91, and supplement to vol. 3, no. 2 (1960): 34–46. Further additions in vol. 4, no. 2 (1961): 30–42. A useful selected and annotated bibliography by Jacob Korg is included in *Victorian Fiction: A Guide to Research*, ed. Lionel Stevenson (Cambridge, Mass.: Harvard University Press, 1964).

Entire books on Moore's work are not many. Among recent studies, Jean C. Noël's biography, listed above, also examines Moore's writings in some detail. Two useful collections of essays which cover various aspects of Moore's career are available: Douglas A. Hughes, ed., *Man of Wax: Critical Essays on George Moore* (New York: New York University Press, 1971) and Graham Owens, ed., *George Moore's Mind and Art* (Edinburgh: Oliver & Boyd, 1968). Malcolm Brown's study, *George Moore: A Reconsideration* (Seattle: University of Washington Press, 1955), is a lively introduction to Moore's career. Helmut Gerber's edition of Moore's letters to T. Fisher Unwin and Lena Milman, *George Moore in Transition* (Detroit: Wayne State University Press, 1968), is well annotated and provides an informative account of Moore's career between 1894 and 1910.

Readers interested in a complete variorum edition of *Confessions of a Young Man* may refer to Susan Dick, "*Confessions of a Young Man* by George Moore: A Variorum Edition" (Ph.D. diss., Northwestern University, 1967).

INDEX